An Artist's Muse

with warmest wishes

An Artist's Muse

Deborah E Wilson

Victorina Press
www.victorinapress.com

First published in Great Britain in 2019 by

Victorina Press
Wanfield Hall
Kingstone
Uttoxeter
Staffordshire, ST14 8QR
England

Typesetting and Layout: Jorge Vasquez

Cover design © Fiona Zechmeister

British Library Cataloguing in Publication Data

A catalogue record for this book is available from the

British Library.

ISBN: 978-1-9993696-2-0 (Paperback)

Typeset in 11pt Garamond

Printed and bound in Great Britain by 4edge ltd.

Dedicated to the undervalued.
People will endeavour to change you – it will be for nothing.
Eventually, you will live out your destiny.

"Life, although it may only be an accumulation of anguish, is dear to me, and I will defend it."
Mary Shelley, Frankenstein

PROLOGUE

Something was flourishing in London. It had arrived quietly, unnoticed for a long time, like the damp that permeates walls when they have been exposed to the elements for too long. It enjoyed the City; fed hungrily from its inhabitants, but never showed itself. An ancient and unfathomable force, its aim was to grow strong, to heighten its power. But it could not act alone. It needed humanity, frail and fallible though it was. And above all else, it needed talent.

Not even the innocents were without suspicion in this headache of a case. Not one of Inspector Conner's suspects had given him any reason to trust their testimonies: only his heavy-rooted gut instinct and wealth of experience allowed him to. Conner was a man who hated to be outsmarted, especially by criminals. Perhaps this criminal was testing Conner's supposedly unbreakable resolve. But accepting defeat was intolerable, and London's streets were filthy enough without allowing such a stain to spread. Conner, a retired inspector of Scotland Yard, had been privately employed to solve the case, and whilst its nature was appalling, to say the least, the inspector was more dismayed by his own ongoing failure to bring retribution. It appeared that he was acting in desperation, he thought, as he stood opposite the man who had hired him.

The room was part of his private office, bland inside, save for the illumination of one small gaslight, which hung from the ceiling, casting out a dusty yellow glow. Inspector Conner had taken his inquisitorial stance by the door. His arms were folded across his broad chest, his eyes like flint. Sitting a few feet away was his reluctant associate: a man named William Breslin. Unlike the inspector, Breslin had given up on pretence: his shoulders had slumped wearily over the polished wooden desk.

Even with Breslin in such a distinctly unthreatening state, Conner found himself avoiding the man's eyes. He wasn't the sort of man to tolerate pleading, questioning, desperate glances, and in his professional capacity, wouldn't be able to provide the reassurance Breslin needed. The current circumstances were distressing for Breslin, of course, but Conner hadn't got this far, he firmly believed, without hardening his heart.

In the faded glow of the gaslight, Breslin's pale skin and dark hair, stippled with premature grey, gave him the washed-out presence of a fading photograph. Aware that there were matters to be resolved, Conner wasted no more time in the barren silence. He brought a hand across his mouth, his thumb rasping against unruly grey whiskers as he considered the best course to take.

Breslin was distracted, his thoughts travelling to many places and times behind his eyes, but the inspector's restlessness finally caught his attention. The younger man gave a disorientated frown from behind metal rimmed spectacles.

'I don't expect the past month to have been anything less than torturous for you and your family, Mr Breslin, and this is a sincere regret. However, you entrusted me with the solving of this case, and it is therefore crucial that we continue to cover what you may consider to be well-trodden ground. To fulfil the terms of my employment, I must ask you once more to consent to questioning.'

The older man's firm voice reverberated against the office walls, and a glimmer of repressed irritation crossed Breslin's face for a fraction of a second. Conner knew that with men like Breslin, empathy was better than coldness, just as negotiation was better than force. Weak-willed men were incredibly volatile, and it was surprising how abruptly their trust could be lost if the wrong word was said. The inspector was walking on a thread's-width of ice, and he felt the chill biting at his ankles as his eyes met Breslin's for the first time. The room seemed to constrict until all he could see were the sharp pinpricks of Breslin's pupils. In an attempt to alleviate the tension, he spoke again, with forbearance.

'Galling as it may be to accept that your sister has been charged with murder, you must—'

'Clara is *not* a murderer,' Breslin interjected, his overwrought voice thin and raspy.

His knuckles were white as he gripped the table, and Conner felt the hairs on the back of his neck bristle. *Keep telling yourself that, my lad, and see how far it gets you*, he thought, letting his head fall back slightly and trying not to lose his temper.

Of all his suspects, Clara Breslin had been the

most cooperative. Realistically, the least likely murderess he had ever come across. But within one night of her being locked in a cell, other details had started to fall into place. Conner couldn't ignore his instincts, even as they jarred uncomfortably against his core of common sense – but until he had evidence to disprove her guilt, he would not speak a single word in her defence.

He saw the scandal was eating at her brother, polluting his mind. How could he possibly be brought to believe it? How could a woman of his own flesh and blood have committed such an act – and how would his business survive it? Any strength he had was failing at the thought of such a repulsive smear on his name. And Conner realised: if there was ever an appropriate time to extract the truth, it was now. Guilty or not, Clara Breslin was at the heart of the solution to this case.

'I implore you, Mr Conner ...'

The voice brought the inspector's wandering mind back to the tangible and he was taken aback – though not entirely surprised – to see tears streaking Breslin's face. He averted his gaze and cleared his throat in discomfort.

'Please, Howard—'

The use of his given name caught the inspector's attention, rankling him. He wasn't used to being addressed so personally by his clients.

'Mr Breslin,' he interrupted, raising a large hand in irritation, 'it is hardly professional, nor is it in my nature, to exert myself to alter Miss Breslin's fate – what with the case thus far being against her. She will hang, unless there comes to my attention some substantial evidence in her favour. The case has been almost exhausted, and frankly, so have I. If you can't provide me with any further information or aid, then I must conclude our meeting.'

Breslin rose to his feet, and the inspector braced himself. But the other man made no further move. There was a curious expression on his face, no longer fear or despair, and he was smiling at an indeterminable spot in the middle distance, his mind whirring behind his eyes. Any observer would have thought themselves in the presence of a lunatic, and Conner deemed that Breslin had finally buckled under the pressure.

'I do have a theory, Inspector.' The man spoke abruptly, his composure returning just as suddenly as it had left him, rendering him quite the epitome of seriousness. His voice was much clearer now, smoother, and his watery blue eyes snapped icily onto the inspector's. A businessman through and through – Conner could never mistake their trademark facade of professionalism. 'A theory, mind you: that is to say I have no certified facts to support it.' Sensing Conner's scepticism, the briefest of smiles flitted across his lips. 'But judging by the limping pace at which this case is dragging onward, I am sure that my conjecture will prove more a help than a hindrance.'

Conner would have reprimanded him for his sarcasm but, having detected just the slightest hint of anger in his voice, decided to hold back. After all, his involvement in this case could be subject to change should he enrage Breslin further.

The other man continued, 'I have had grave suspicions for a while, though I scarcely let myself believe…' At this, he paused self-consciously and altered his approach, his voice gaining a substantial gravity. 'I'm not a foolish man, Inspector. I don't jump to conclusions, and I certainly wouldn't even suggest such a thing had I not the most terrifying feeling that I might be right.'

Conner was watching him, head tilted with curiosity, but in that agile brain sparks were beginning to fire. Despite all rationality, the tone of Breslin's voice was agitating his usually concrete self-assurance. But there was something else as well.

Conner was aware, without thoroughly believing his senses, of another presence in the room. Was it a shadowed impression of a figure standing behind him, watching the conversation unfold? Or did it cling to the rafters, its back pressed to the wall, something like wings reaching out across the room and dulling the light? Or did it travel up, over their heads, slip out through the semi-open window sash and settle itself upon the window ledge? There was a weight to it, a looming, impending feeling that an unexpressed power was gaining momentum. He wondered if it meant that the case had far more importance than he could have ever initially predicted.

Unbeknownst to him, Breslin sensed it too.

'Even if there was an arrest, I can see no way of supporting my allegation. But that is what I hired *you* for. Before you condemn my sister to the noose, I must entreat you to do this final task.'

The inspector nodded grimly, the taste of metal in his mouth, his pistol suddenly heavier in its cradle. The seed of doubt had been planted, its tentative fronds now beginning to unfurl. Breslin was desperate to clear his sister's name – at what cost, the inspector wondered.

'I think it's about time you told me your theory, Mr Breslin.'

'ON THE DAY THAT THE BRESLINS' LIVES BEGAN TO
CHANGE, THE UNASSUMING FACADE OF BRESLIN'S
CURES AND REMEDIES WAS SHUTTERED AND
DRAWN...'

CHAPTER ONE

𝕿ime has no compassion. It takes its victims without warning, and often without reason. It leaves a profound mark on everything it touches. Even the most unremarkable moment can create a lasting impact.

The Breslins had never known true anguish; time had not yet imprinted its destructive mark. On the morning of their misfortune, there were no dark clouds to warn them. No thick smog came creeping around the street corners. Life was as it always was – and perhaps that was the ultimate deception. If you cannot anticipate your fate, how can you possibly hope to alter it?

On the day that their lives began to change, Breslin's Cures and Remedies was yet to open for business, the unassuming facade shuttered and drawn. Behind the shutters, its proprietor, a young man named William Breslin, had been preparing the place for opening for several hours.

The task of running the establishment did not fall to William alone. He also had the help of his younger sister, Clara. And though the running of this enterprise was a partnership, only one of the pair was engaged in preparing the place for opening. Clara was elsewhere preoccupied. She did not rise as eagerly as her brother, as a rule, for her interests lay in vastly different fields to his.

At the back of the shop, a rickety, almost severe staircase reached into the upper storey. Each aged step creaked with its own individual grievance, though the stomping of

1

William's highly polished boots answered them in kind. He would only ever ascend these stairs to rouse his inattentive sister, or to retire at the end of a long working day, hence his footsteps were not of the light, airy variety.

Clara's room overlooked the street below. Her door was always closed – from habit rather than necessity – and once opened, creaked as if it had not been used for centuries. As it so happened, this provided suitable punctuation for the sense of surprise any visitor would be prone to upon entering.

Clara's bedroom – should it even have deserved to be called so – was a highly peculiar room, distinguishable as such only by a tiny divan in one of the farthest corners. Each wall – and, it had to be said, much of the vacant floor space – was dedicated almost entirely to artwork and supplies. One could be forgiven for mistaking the room for an art gallery, were it not for the fact that art galleries tended to be a lot less disorderly. Reams of branded paper billowed out from the walls, leaves and leaves of them, far too many for the relatively small space, far too many to be aesthetically pleasing; it was a room inside a house of cards sagging under its own weight.

Art, and an interest in such, was an unnecessarily distracting pursuit for any young lady, but Clara had never adhered to any semblance of 'the typical woman'. Art was her one freedom; her one escape. And she clung to it, surrounded herself with it, submerged herself within it. Her room of paper sheltered her from a world that was not yet ready to accommodate her.

This particular morning was no exception to those preceding it, the tranquillity of the upper quarters being cruelly fractured by the scratching of implement against canvas. Clara was quite content to sit upon her bowed window seat, sketchbook and pencils to hand, clothed in the oldest and most worn garments she had, with her long auburn hair piled atop her head in the messiest fashion. This way, she could capture the movements, expressions and appearances of the people passing beneath her window, and the features of that insignificant pocket of the world that she found herself in the midst of. Whilst she endeavoured only to paint that which was beautiful or striking, such subject matter was difficult to come across in a place where one was particularly unhappy.

As she watched the passing crowds, she also found a sort of serenity in studying the many eccentricities of human life. This for her was not the material of true inspiration or enlightenment, but Clara felt at times that she could enjoy these simple observations enough to distract her from the inadequacy of her daily routine.

She whiled away the hours in the deepest hope that she might see just one extraordinary figure that would make her heart leap with wonder – one worthy of her intense study and meticulous absorption. The problem was that Clara could never be content with one such subject for long; she found that, after a time, even the beauty which had seemed so spectacular to her at first could fade. As fickle as the human mind is, Clara's subjects could only exist for a short amount of time there before they became distorted by her own doubt and uncertainty.

These subjects were also always kept at a distance. Her talents were kept a secret from those outside her intimate inner circle. Art could be a pastime, yes, but never a means of income. Women were not true artists, in the minds of many. Therefore, she had to be content with her detached study, and her unfulfilled ambitions.

Clara reclined serenely in the deep recess of the window, her eye still trained lazily on the street, but her eyelids felt heavy at the thought of the day's work ahead. Her sketchbook rested in the curve from the softness of her stomach to the bony arch of her knees, her pencil bobbing gently between relaxed knuckles. Already, she could hear William making preparations for the opening of the Apothecary – all the noisier in the hope that the sounds would rouse his sister into movement without him having to climb the stairs. But such attempts barely concerned her. She would occasionally humour his pretence that her aid was much needed, if only to make his day-to-day life a little less stressful. It was in honour of this small sacrifice that she decided to affix her apron and go downstairs. And she would have done so, just then, and with all due enthusiasm, had it not been for a sight that unexpectedly captured her attention.

The crowds in the street below had grown deceptively slowly in number and, as a result, Broad Street was quite the heaving mass of travelling bodies when Clara next glanced upon it. Its girth was so meagre that many of the travellers were being jostled against the sides of the ungainly buildings – a raging stampede in a narrow gorge. But the figure that Clara saw at that moment could not have possibly merged with any other around it – nor perhaps with any other figure in the whole of the City. His movements were not remarkable, but it was his outward appearance that made him far removed from his fellows.

His attire was remarkably eccentric: a white Shakespearean shirt teamed with scarlet-coloured breeches akin to those of the Regiment. These were tucked neatly inside polished knee-length boots. His hair was a deep, lustrous brown, curved about the planes of his jawbone, so dark that his tanned skin appeared almost pallid. But it was not these striking factors that were the most notable. The eyes which peered calmly from beneath dark lashes were unlike any that Clara had ever seen. Such a dazzling shade of the lightest green; they almost hummed in their vibrancy and gleamed like a cat's in the pale sunlight. An unearthly shade, one which it seemed no combination of oils would even come close to emulating. But there was something else.

A deep shudder rattled Clara's bones right to their core when she realised that, for the first time in three years, the bewitching eyes of a passing stranger were staring right into her own.

It was the briefest of visual exchanges, but in that split-second, a wealth of unnameable, indescribable sensations passed from the man into her. So dulled were her outward senses that her brother had to cross the breadth of her cluttered room and physically grip her by the arm to capture her full attention. Her eyes regained their focus, but she had to peer at the agitated face before her for a considerable length of time before her thoughts were realigned.

'Downstairs,' William said insistently, to jog the memory rather than to request.

'Bill ...' came her vague response as she shrugged herself from the arm-hold, furrowing her brow with the effort of keeping that one, startling image in her mind. Her eyes met his briefly and her mouth opened, the words pouring from her lips as if she were a ventriloquist's dummy, or an orator remembering some rehearsed spiel: '... and so it is that time of the morning again, and I am to head downstairs with much haste, for the day's custom will not wait on account of the daydreaming of an absent-minded young woman.' The words could have come from the mouth of William himself, and he remarked the subtle ways in which the inflections of her voice and the movement of her lips matched his own. Not mockery, but observant imitation.

'It is the truth, Clara. And it is also your obligation.'

'Then perhaps I am more fortunate than I had first supposed. For Heaven forbid I should be denied the pleasure of servitude: nay, instead I am *obliged* to a life of drudgery.' After fixing him with a marked glare, she left the room.

William could not fail to notice the sudden advancement in Clara's mood. Such assertiveness was uncommon for this quiet, contemplative young woman. This could only be an improvement, but if William assumed he would benefit from his sister's change in demeanour, he was desperately misguided. Clara's mood had altered significantly, only because the tedium of her situation was to be improved vastly by the contemplation of dark, angular features, rich, billowing fabrics, and those dizzying, lurid green eyes – eyes that were burnt into her mind like a firebrand, so that even the liberation of sleep would not deprive her of their clear, keen stare.

CHAPTER TWO

'**I** am in love!'

Such a statement should never be used too lightly. A proclamation of love, whilst fleeting in nature, carries weighty implications.

It could be seen as a moment of imprudence in which Ruth Davison chose to make her own declaration. The stage of choice was quite commonplace, though suitably idyllic: a slender path that coiled itself through Hyde Park. This was a place of unspoilt verdure in an otherwise urban wilderness; a honeytrap for high society, host to a sea of parasols and ornate livery. The pair had planned a typically fashionable outing, to include a promenade through said park, and afterwards a leisurely lunch at a nearby hotel.

Ruth's audience was far from captive: a rather disinterested Clara Breslin was soberly contemplating her own lethargic footsteps, with the air of a woman who had heard many such statements from this same pair of lips. Clearly, she would not be easily convinced. Her attempt at a sincere reply was feeble, but Ruth wouldn't have noticed in any case.

'I am overjoyed, if not entirely surprised. Your new-found radiance was enough to confirm it.'

'You are observant to note it,' Ruth replied, her smile brightening, 'but I must confess, I have been so elated that I am now drained to my weakest ebb.' The woman sighed and with the tremendous effort of one carrying a grave burden. However, the glistening of her slate-blue eyes betrayed her immense enjoyment. 'Now, you know as well as any that I do not fall for these foolish, fleeting infatuations of the heart. But you only have to see the way Albert cares for me to understand. He is the most exceptional man I have ever met.'

Clara knew well enough. If nurturing could be defined by the giving of expensive and luxurious gifts, of dazzling promises and sweet nothings, then Ruth was the most cherished woman in the whole of London.

'I am delighted to hear that. You deserve every happiness. And if he truly is as exceptional as you say, then you are indeed fortunate to have met him.'

Clara was trying incredibly hard to maintain a supportive demeanour as Ruth went on. It felt as if every fibre in her was wrenched as tightly as it could be in the strictest effort not to show her friend the true turmoil and anguish she was causing. Not because Clara was in any way bitter or envious of the match, but she knew that in this particular matter, her best friend was so utterly, perhaps dangerously, *wrong*.

Ruth Davison was an attractive young woman, petite in stature and light on her tiny feet. Her head shimmered with dusty-blonde tendrils, and her large eyes were the faded blue of the winter sky. Her every move was grace and refinement. She seemed to be the epitome of the fashionable, cultured woman.

She and Clara had grown up together. Clara could still see the same little girl who used to splash through brooks sprint through the Wiltshire fields when laughter lit up Ruth's winsome eyes.

But Ruth had always dreamt of a better life and had recently taken a small sum of money from her doting parents to travel to London. Naïve and unaccustomed to city life, she soon declared herself to be a natural urbanite, and that small token sum of money became many, many more imbursements as she became set on ingratiating herself with high society. There were always plenty of people who were more than willing to oblige a pretty, charming and unpretentious young girl with such a perfectly polished, engaging smile.

Perhaps Ruth was right. Perhaps it was truly Albert's intention to lavish her with gifts, astounding promises and theatrical declarations simply because she was the woman he believed to be the love of his life, and not because of the amount of dowry he was to expect from her wealthy parentage. Perhaps he would even finally be unable to find an excuse not to marry her. And perhaps Clara was just a little too cynical. Swallowing her anxieties, as ever, she looked up rather suddenly and gave her friend a warm, encouraging smile.

'And I am told that this budding love accompanies a lifestyle alteration – how are you finding your new living arrangements?'

Ruth had newly acquired a plush Kensington apartment – with all due thanks to Albert, of course. How could he possibly hope to court his new love if she was constantly flitting between city and country, unable to afford secure lodgings? Thankfully, the young lawyer's income was more than enough to support the extra expense.

Small talk was crucial. The longer Ruth was engaged in conversation about her favourite topic – Albert – the less time that Clara would have to listen. Adoration could become rather repetitive. And Clara wanted some time with her own thoughts: namely, the vision of a pair of startling, cat-green eyes she had seen that morning. It was imperative that she kept the impression of them in the forefront of her mind.

'Oh, it is certainly the best home I could have ever hoped for. But please, I fear that I will bore you to death with this frivolousness! This is a meeting of equals, and I feel I must honour and respect your need for variety, now that I have thoroughly dominated the conversation. We must change the subject before you begin to despair of me.'

It was no exaggeration that Clara had a strong mind when it came to matters of love. Eligible young men she had been acquainted with in the past had continuously led her to disappointment. Their conversation she had enjoyed, but that was all. And she could enjoy their conversation perfectly well without a compulsory promise of marriage. She had felt no overwhelming desire, as others had, to attach herself to anyone; it seemed such an odd thing to do when all she felt for them was a well-meaning friendship. Therefore, she eventually began to take the observer's perspective on all matters of love, learning to render herself invisible in the eyes of all but those closest to her.

She had witnessed many of her close friends' hearts being broken, taking a small pearl of wisdom from each of their grievances to store away in her own, unaltered heart. It had allowed her a kind of rationality that far surpassed her years, and yet, adversely, earned her that hard, cold cynicism which had prevented her from noticing the affections of any man since those first, fledgling years.

It came as no surprise that her parents eventually began to show concern at her lack of courtship. Mr and Mrs Breslin had seen fit to take Clara's future into their hands. Her brother William had already lived in the Capital for several years, making a name for himself as an apothecary. His knowledge of city life was enough to keep their daughter safe, and also to ensure that she would be introduced to many eligible suitors. Not only this, but he needed an assistant: someone who would perform menial duties that he no longer had the time or inclination for himself. Clara had proven herself to be hardworking and determined when it came to her private illustrations – her 'little sketches', as they were affectionately known – so who was to say that she couldn't apply such motivation to 'real' work?

That was how the concept arose that Clara would move in with William in the Apothecary. In return for her assistance, William would take her to various social events with his clients and contacts, in the hope that she would find a suitable husband. But years had passed, and now Clara was of an age at which people began to murmur: 'Twenty-three? And unmarried? Has she been living abroad?'

Whilst social expectations had no profound effect on her, Clara was beginning to despair at the impossibility of finding a love that would satisfy her. Were her requirements really all that unrealistic? She admired such qualities as integrity, humility and sincerity; as talent, wisdom and creativity – and felt that a potential husband should possess all of these – though not least a tenderness of spirit and an enthusiasm for extracting the maximum enjoyment from life. Attraction seemed to play a key role in the affairs of others – but she could not imagine feeling such; she had never been 'love-struck' and suspected such a phenomenon was entirely fabricated.

Perhaps she had become so intent on avoiding making the mistakes of others that she had completely immunised herself against the simplicity and enjoyment which made courtship such a joyful pastime. After all, that is the beauty of matters of the heart: they can occur completely independently of the rationality of the brain.

Perhaps as a direct result of this deficiency, Clara had also found herself quite incapable of showing any form of joy for Ruth. Ruth, knowing full well the predicament her friend was in and trying her utmost to remedy the situation, put her lack of enthusiasm down to her own misfortunes in love, and consequently had become even more zealous in her efforts to matchmake her friend with an eligible man.

Unbeknownst to the poor girl, this was the worst thing she could have done.

Clara was quite convinced that her friend had the worst possible judgement when it came to the opposite sex. The idea that Ruth could find the man Clara had come to believe did not exist was simply an insult to the fiery young woman. But the two friends were content enough to each obtain a false impression of the other. Their friendship remained intact whilst Ruth believed that Clara was simply yearning for love, when she was in fact feeling nothing of the sort and was completely repulsed by her friend's choice of partner. Similarly, it remained secure whilst Clara believed Ruth to be capable of eventually working out the truth about her future intended for herself, without any honest advice. In truth, the young beauty was so blinded by her love that she would not see any flaw in Albert's character, and that was her greatest shortcoming.

'I can only wish you every prosperity and happiness.' Clara's smile was sincere enough; her childhood affection for the other woman quite apparent. She wondered if this friendship could truly withstand anything or if the complex politics of love would be the one thing to ruin their bond.

'I shall not hear of it! That is to say, I cannot bear one more word to be said about me. We must now pay due attention to you, despite your predisposition to divert such attention from yourself. Do you fare any better at finding a suitor?'

Clara winced noticeably, shaking her head – and her finger – at the young woman beside her. 'No – no! Ruth! You said you would leave the subject lie! You cannot continue this love-talk by deflecting it onto me!'

Ruth laughed that light, airy, delicate laugh that was unmistakeably hers, and caused a pair of gentleman walking a few paces ahead to glance around admiringly. Clara, who went perpetually unnoticed – and preferred it this way – simply stared, awaiting her friend's inevitable rebellion. Perhaps it was to the blonde woman's credit that she saw in her friend that which so many others overlooked.

'I hoped you would allow me that one small indulgence. For I do hate to see you alone.'

'I'm not alone.' Clara knew that she was, but Ruth's exposure of it unsettled her in a way that was most unexpected.

'No, of course. You have me, and Bill, and you have your art and your theatre. I cannot deny that you live an intriguing life, Clara.' Clara in turn understood 'intriguing' as 'strange'. 'But you must, at some point, crave the love that has eluded you? Will you insist upon denying me the satisfaction of finally finding a young gentleman for you?'

'Yes. Because I do not wish for you – for *anyone* – to find a man for me. Men are not objects to be found, to be bartered over and eventually won. If I ever love, it will be by fate or by chance, and without consciously seeking it. I want my love to have been an act of destiny, not a result of toil, of competition and plotting. I want to find my soulmate.'

Ruth paused rather abruptly in her tracks, cocking her head like an inquisitive sparrow. She was not insulted by the outburst, for she knew that it came from a true suppression of strong feeling. She merely accepted Clara's words with a gentle, sympathetic bob of the head, seeing that her friend's own naïvety in a way that Clara never would. For Clara was too busy worrying herself over Ruth's inexperience in love to realise that, for all her observations of the heartaches of others, she had never experienced true love for herself. She failed to understand that, albeit tortuous, it is with hardship and trial that love becomes its strongest. There is no such thing as the perfect love.

But Clara Breslin was adamant that she would find hers. However, though she had considered what sort of qualities her 'soulmate' would have to please her, she had little considered what kind of sacrifices she would have to make to ensure that such a soulmate would be entirely hers and wish to spend the rest of his life with her. She was also yet to realise that love is all about compromise, and that she would have to compromise her steadfast viewpoints in order to show any sign of softness beneath the iron-clad facade she presented to the world, and truly expose her most vulnerable self to someone else.

Ruth gave a small sigh, and replied, 'You will find him some day, I'm sure. I just hope that he never proves to be a disappointment.'

Deborah E Wilson

CHAPTER THREE

The embodiment of one's love is a sight which evokes a feeling that many are incapable of describing. Ruth Davison was no exception. All she could be completely sure of was that the sight of her dear Albert provoked the deepest sensations of tenderness and devotion. She had just parted company with Clara after lunch and walked to meet Albert in Kensington. As she finally reached him, his height and presence caused a catch in her breath, as they always did. Feeling for a moment completely helpless, she stood rigid as a doll, trembling from her knees as he took her pale hand and planted a kiss upon it.

'Albert.' Her mouth formed the word, but the sound of her voice was barely audible. His smile was reassuringly confident. He always seemed to put her at ease, his every movement and nuance of speech communicating such a security within his own skin that she could not possibly doubt him – or herself – for a moment.

Ruth's behaviour was not unusual. The sight of Albert Barnes was enough to captivate most. Every slight suggestion of body language expressed a confidence that was quite unsurpassable. And he was indeed an impressive specimen of adulthood. Tall, regal in stature and with a steadfast frame that articulated a definite physical strength, he made no attempt to deflect any attention from his best outward attributes and took delight in receiving the attentions of admiring eyes. Ruth had fallen much the same way as many others; his dark blue eyes, thick dark-blond hair and elegant mustachios were only enhanced by the charm of his smile. And his taste in finery – fine tailoring, fine wine and even finer company – immediately enlightened her to the fact that he was precisely the sort of man she had hoped to make the acquaintance of. The short laugh he gave at that precise moment was the same that had stirred her all those months ago, when they had been nothing more to each other than a lawyer and a young country girl, having the fortune to be present at the same social event.

'My dear,' he replied simply. 'How was your rendezvous with Miss Breslin?'

He always seemed to refuse to call her 'Clara'. Ruth convinced herself it was due to a firm sense of propriety, and not her dearest's fondness for teasing. He did have quite a sense of humour, though not always with the kindest intent.

Poor Clara couldn't help it if she put across a rather prim demeanour and lacked the forte for conversation that Ruth herself found only natural. Despite a little disapproval, Ruth nevertheless smiled tenderly, the slight pursing of her rosebud lips the only sign of her true feelings.

'Most enjoyable, thank you,' she replied chirpily. 'We talked for such a long—'

'Oh yes, good,' Albert interrupted, a slight firmness in the creases at the corners of his mouth betraying an obvious lack of commitment to his previous question.

Ruth bit her tongue, so to speak, her eyes widening. She knew Albert's mind moved a little faster than most –

how else had he become such a successful lawyer? – so she forgave him for his discourtesy, watching as he smiled and reached into the inner pocket of his jacket. There was an unfathomable glint in his eyes as he changed the subject.

'Ruth, my darling, I have something for you.'

It was fortunate that Albert was not only the love of her life but also one of the wealthiest young lawyers in the area. Extremely fortunate.

'Albert,' she began, her tone reproachful and less full of gratitude than she had intended. 'You know I don't expect … I don't even ask …'

But as he presented her with a small box in deep purple velvet, she couldn't speak. Her slender fingers quivered as she reached to open it, her eyes locked upon his until the box snapped open and the glinting of multifaceted ornamentation caught her eye. His taste, as ever, was impeccable; an exquisite rose-coloured diamond necklace. More or less instantly, she snapped the box shut, her eyes still moist with surprised tears. Albert's silent triumph was quickly extinguished.

'I can't accept this.'

'Ruth!' He began to laugh again, but she cut him short.

'Don't mistake me: it is staggering, divine – above and beyond anything of its kind I have ever seen. But it is an inappropriate gift, my darling. I'm not yet your wife.'

Albert stared at her searchingly until Ruth began to feel quite on show. Finally, he managed to push out the words.

'I've just found you your own apartment. You weren't my wife then, either.'

Ruth was not disposed to argue. But in this case, she knew that Albert was distorting the truth. All due credit was owed to him for finding her such a gorgeous apartment, and for providing her with the means necessary to pay a monthly rent. But he had only put towards a sum of money that her parents had already given to her, and now the task of funding costly renovations also fell to her father's (thankfully considerable) bank balance.

'I'm aware of that. But surely you can understand my position on the matter? I can't continue to accept your kindness without the inevitable talk of those in our society! Most men don't bestow such generosity on women who they are not intended to.' She appeared thoughtful for a moment. 'You know, before today, Clara seemed to express a lack of approval of the apartment arrangement.'

'Really?' Albert's eyes hardened, and Ruth chose to ignore it.

'I'm afraid so. She tried her best to hide it, but I could see that she was sceptical. And she has no real consequence in society. Imagine the reactions of your friends at the law court. And your clients!'

She was beginning to grow troubled, her eyes pleading for a consensus. Albert glanced down at her with the affection of a parent for a child – he nearly patted her on her pretty little head – and responded with all the sympathy he could.

'Don't fret – *don't fret*, my darling.' He took both her hands in his. 'I know this worries you, but I haven't yet acquired the means to be a decent husband to you. I must secure my position in the higher ranks of my profession in order to delegate my duties to others. Only then will I have time and resources enough to make the best of our wedded life. Surely you can see the sense in that?'

Ruth nodded, though the sense of it wearied her. She did not want to see sense; she only saw the fact that time was slipping by like salt between her fingers.

'*I need you to trust me,*' he whispered, his head close to hers. His breath fluttered against her eyelids, and in her mind, she felt her feet slowly losing their grip on the earth. With immense effort, she opened her eyes and looked directly into his.

'I do. I always will.'

He kissed her gently on the forehead. Feeling enveloped in his warmth and compassion, Ruth felt her anxieties melt away. She knew, however, that it would only take a few moments without his company for the unrest to seep back in. She forced her will to accept that, eventually, Albert would honour his words. After all, he had no reason not to. Perhaps the wisdom that came with age also came hand in hand with an ease of mind that Ruth, thus far, was lacking – and Albert was merely being sensible in his insistence that the marriage be put off until the correct time.

Meanwhile, on the other side of the City, Clara had rounded the corner of Broad Street and was making her way back to the Apothecary. She hoped William would not begrudge her an extra hour's absence for lunch. She also hoped that her curtness towards him this morning had not soured relations between them both for the rest of the day. Much as their customers disguised it, she was sure that they could sense if a rift had occurred, albeit a minor one. And whilst her own contact with customers was minimal – much like her interest in the business – she didn't want William to suffer for her own preoccupations.

She looked through the window and eventually spied her brother behind the counter. Once he had served his customer, she briskly opened the door, the tinny rattling of a brass bell announcing her entrance. William glanced up from dispensing ingredients, met her eye, but made little or no sign that he had recognised her. The man he was serving made his exit, and Clara warily approached the counter, her feet like lead. She was already so tired from having to placate Ruth that she was really in no mood to pander to William.

'I'm back,' she muttered, for want of something frivolous to break the silence.

William looked up once more from his work, and Clara braced herself for what was sure to be a chastising of the most condescending degree. However, he surprised her (and probably himself) by greeting her with a small smile and a subdued, 'Hello.' He handed her an apron from underneath the countertop and pointed to a tray of empty jars to one side of him. 'Those need filling. Ms Watson questioned me just as I was lifting down a jar of vinegar – damned woman made me drop the entire thing.'

Clara chuckled softly; it was in fact the first time she

had even come close to laughing all day, and it did not escape her brother's notice. 'What did she ask you?'

William looked cagey before answering in the most sheepish tones, 'Oh, I'm sure you have an idea. Marriage seems to be the only thing that interests her!'

Now Clara did laugh, and it was a welcome sound in the small Apothecary. She knew full well William's aversion to marriage and envied him for the lesser pressure he received from their parents to find himself a match. Ms Watson, hypochondriac and relentless busybody that she was, took great delight in acquiring new and varied ailments, and finding someone to unload her gossip onto – if only for the fact that she had rather a soft spot for Mr Breslin, regardless of her age surpassing his by twenty years. Her unrelenting interest in his bachelordom was merely an attempt to acquire his favour. Even her request of vinegar was a ruse; any household in the country had such a commodity to hand, and as a cure for headaches could be handled by even a child. Unfortunately for her, William had not come close to proposing to a woman in the last ten years and was unlikely to change his ways.

'I can only empathise – for I too know many women with that singular interest.' The gravity of Clara's voice was the only indication of the true fatigue which that particular subject had caused her during the course of the day.

William groaned softly, placing the back of his hand to his forehead. 'Believe me, after that shock, it was I who needed the vinegar and brown paper. I've *still* got a headache …'

With an understanding smile that masked the

heaviness of her mind, Clara reasoned that a headache as the result of the tribulations of matters of the heart was the one thing that even her brother would be unable to cure. Her own, as proof, had tormented her relentlessly for years, and showed little sign of releasing her.

CHAPTER FOUR

nce Clara was back behind the counter, the afternoon showed no sign of renouncing its mournful drag. Much as it was a simple sort of living for a woman who had no designs for a prestigious career, time spent in the Apothecary only limped along more slowly for the fact that she longed for the end of each working day. The siblings had eased the tension between them by means of an unspoken truce; they kept conversation to a minimum whilst custom flowed thick and fast.

Each of them was immersed in their own respective duties. Clara worked rapidly and with the minimum amount of concentration, and yet made no mistakes. Essentially, she could work with such skill that she no longer even took note of her own actions. This was a small blessing, as the tedium of the work could be overlooked, leaving her mind free to be engaged with other thoughts.

Clearly, Miss Breslin's mind was not enraptured with thoughts of cures and remedies. It continued to be caught up with the mysterious gentleman she had laid eyes on earlier that morning.

Her brother had a remarkable talent for small talk. If he was not simply a purveyor of treatments, he was also a vendor of the finest repartee that side of the Thames. He could be understanding and empathetic; by turns serious and direct; and equally witty and charismatic, with charm in abundance. Perhaps it was his conversational dexterity that caused William's custom to arrive so readily and so obliging – perhaps, also, why the vast majority of his clients were female.

He made no secret of the fact that he was a wealthy young man, as yet unmarried, whose business was increasing in value by the day, if not the hour. And if any woman should choose to vie for his attention, he would commend her bravery with all due regard. Needless to say, he was onto too good a thing to succumb to any of these inducements, and whilst making it clear to each of these women that he was no way inclined to settle down yet, he never gave them an out-and-out reason to desist in pursuing him.

Aside from the unshakable Ms Watson, there were many more ladies closer to William in age who were keen to attract his interest. Such women never arrived with ailments more serious than sore throats or fingers punctured with sewing needles, and yet they often returned several times within one week. Clara found much amusement in observing the subtle changes in their hairstyles or the cut of their dresses as the days went by. And she was certainly sure that such details did not escape her brother's notice, as artistically disinclined as he was.

This week's principal culprit was a sickly individual named Miss Chesterton. She had such a poor constitution that she had had two bouts of cold, one sore throat and a twisted ankle in as many days; Clara wondered how she was able to get out of bed at all. She had an agile tongue, which allowed anyone to be fully aware of what was on her mind. Her hair fell into tight corkscrew curls of an almost anaemic blonde, which almost bled into her frighteningly pale skin.

Chaperoned by her maid, the woman left her reluctant escort outside whilst she employed the services of the 'wonderful' Mr Breslin. On such occasions, Clara allowed herself to be completely distracted. It was a daily exchange from which she drew great fascination – and perhaps a little amusement.

Miss Chesterton opened the door with a frail arm, the shop bell ringing just one, sorry note. She moved towards the counter where William was weighing out a variety of ingredients, pretending, as Clara suspected, not to notice her. Giving a feeble cough, she waited patiently until the apothecary saw fit to acknowledge her – at which point he swept his dark hair from his forehead with the air of a man much encumbered with a heavy workload.

'My apologies, Madam, I won't be a moment. I have orders piled up to the eaves, and barely the time to prepare them in.' He smiled vaguely for a while, with the young woman appearing increasingly annoyed with each passing second, until the penny finally dropped. 'Oh! Do forgive me, Miss Chesterton. Had I but realised it was you – how good it is to see you.' Clara noticed the minute change in the timbre of his voice; William clearly found these exchanges just as entertaining as she did.

The woman's face lit up instantly and a colour came to her cheeks that was most out of character for someone who was apparently so ailing.

'Mr Breslin,' she replied, matching his tone of enthusiasm. 'If only it wasn't for such a sombre reason that I find myself bound to pay you a visit.'

'A pity that your ill health is our only cause to meet

at all.'

The pallid young girl found some renewed vigour at the reply, almost clapping for joy where she stood. William, as a medical professional, may well have wondered if such movement was healthy for a woman who had just recovered from a badly sprained ankle. If he did, however, it was artfully concealed.

'How can I help you today, dear lady?'

'Such an amiable greeting is cure enough,' she replied with a blush. 'Though I am under much distress. I'm afraid I will require something of more lasting substance.'

'Whatever can be the matter?'

He reached across the counter and laid his hand upon her arm, after which the woman chirped in delighted surprise and her waiting maid outside thrust her nose closer to the window with a knot in her brow.

'Oh, Mr Breslin!' she wailed pitiably. 'I cannot possibly endure another hour without a cure for this rash on my neck!'

Clara had to duck behind the storeroom curtain, lest her derisory smirk give her away. Her brother appeared to exhibit a similar reaction, though he disguised it a little more effectively by arching his eyebrows in apparent shock and sympathy.

Any working-class housewife could have seen that Miss Chesterton's rash was nothing more than her skin's reaction to the heat of the day. It would disappear within the hour, if not within minutes, without any treatment whatsoever. William, however, did not betray such knowledge. The sight of Miss Chesterton's exposed neck was enough to keep his lips completely sealed on the matter.

'Ah, yes, I can see how that would cause you anguish – though I am pleased to inform you that it isn't a terribly severe problem.'

'Oh?' She seemed (understandably) disappointed.

'Such things are not uncommon amongst ladies such as yourself: with delicate constitutions.'

This cheered the lady somewhat, who did not object to 'fragile rose' comparisons from any quarter. 'Please, Mr Breslin, is there a cure? Or am I condemned to a wretched fate of discomfort and unsightliness?'

At this point, William paused thoughtfully, then gave a beguiling smile which meant he was distinctly in his stride, Clara knew.

'Luckily, my dear lady, I – unlike many of my fellow apothecaries – do provide an antidote for such a situation as yours. There is a salve that, if applied to the affected area once an hour, will clear the skin and restore it to its original … *radiance.*'

Miss Chesterton almost sighed into his arms for the relief of it all but instead sufficed to repeat his name many, many times with increasing liveliness and countless words of praise. Whilst her brother basked in the glory, Clara was given instruction to fetch said salve – which even she knew to be nothing more than a simple concoction of water and baking powder, beat into a featureless paste. Her brother used it as a base for other lotions, and although it would relieve the heat of the rash, it would not hasten its disappearance any more than if the skin were left to the elements. Nevertheless, if it meant the rattle of a few more coins in the till, William would of course promote its usefulness.

This was of no consequence to Clara, though she disapproved of the behaviour of these women and of her brother's transgressions.

Her true misgivings lay in her having to go to the store room. Not out of laziness or any kind of incompetence – her aversion stemmed from a childlike fear of what inhabits the vacant spaces beyond what the eye can see.

Anyone would be reluctant to enter such a place; years of neglect had caused the dust to reach choking levels, and the tiny barred windows let in minimal levels of light. As Clara passed through the curtain, pale shafts of sunlight illuminated patches of stale air which tremored at the intrusion. Briefly illuminated were tall stacks of shelves, much like the bookcases of a library, though these were filled with jars, phials, bottles and tins of every imaginable kind. The analogy of a library continued, as not only were the antidotes stacked to the ceiling, but also categorised (in terms of ailments), subcategorised (in terms of material), and labelled (in terms of its chemical or Latin name, and a translation in plain English for Clara). This system much reflected that of the shopfront – but whereas the cures stocked there were in single jars and presented clearly, the supplies in the back room were stockpiled as tightly as possible, sometimes precariously, ready to topple. The names of lesser-used cures were obscured by months of dust, and what seemed a simple request would often require almost an hour's searching.

Not averse to cleanliness, Clara still did not take it upon herself to improve conditions in the store room. This Library of Medication was William's domain. As long as everything was in its proper place, he was untroubled by the conditions of the room. His stock remained fresh and unaltered if the room was kept dark and air ventilation kept low. It did not matter that Clara found the place so disturbing.

In truth, despite the immoderate level of dust and considerable bleakness, there was little to fear. Her behaviour was irrational, the delusion of a mind too often escaping into the imaginary, but her thoughts rampaged in the hazy darkness.

Unnameable fears were waiting in the shadows for her as she crossed the room. Impossible for her to lose her way, but as light levels dipped, the place seemed less like a cache and more of a labyrinth.

Fortunately, the paste she sought out was easy to find, contained within a small stone jar in Section Six – Skin: Inflammations, Burns or Bruising, between its neighbours, ground *Aloe vera* and cider vinegar. Swiping the jar from a shelf at eye level, she clutched it to her chest and swiftly exited the room, the shadows reaching for her as she left.

She was relieved to finally re-emerge through the curtain. She could not help but focus on how rigidly the hairs on the back of her neck stood away from the skin, and how much warmer the shopfront seemed, despite its lack of a fireplace. Once rid of her delivery, she busied herself with studying the figures which passed the shop window and assailed her ears completely, her thoughts eventually drifting away from those of fear. She couldn't quite understand, however, why they then drifted towards the memory of an image – the clear image of an unknown face she had seen in the crowds that morning, still as vivid as if the man had been standing before her.

Her eyes searched the crowds intently for this particular face, though she could not see the sense in doing so, nor the reward should she actually see him again. She knew it to be a futile search, if not rather foolish.

After William had made a final wish for the improvement of Miss Chesterton's wellbeing, she left almost bounding down the street. Her sudden and bewildering vigour obviously baffled the poor maid, who could only scuttle in her wake. Perhaps she, like Clara, wondered how on earth the apothecary's cures worked before they had even had the chance to be applied.

Now that the siblings were without audience, the silence left in Miss Chesterton's wake left Clara unable to hold her tongue any longer. Irritated by her brother's conceit, Clara waited until the pale woman and her maid were out of sight before voicing her displeasure.

'You are a shameless blackguard, William Breslin!'

'Don't be such a hypocrite; you take as much enjoyment from my misleading those impressionable ladies as I do.'

'So you *do* admit you're misleading them, then. Men like you constantly restore my faith in spinsterhood.'

'It's not as if they'll be hurt by it! Little Chesterton there will probably come back for three more jars of that salve, and it will keep her content for months without doing so much as moisturising her skin. It's not my fault she comes to me with ailments that require absolutely no cure. Nothing will suffer apart from the heaviness of her purse.'

'That's not what I mean. And you know it.'

'Oh no, Clara, don't say another—'

'Misleading them where it is due is one matter. Misleading them where there are genuine feelings involved is quite another.'

'*Genuine feelings* … I never actually told any of them that their affections would be reciprocated! They aren't interested in me anyway, just the money. And as far as I'm concerned, it's their own damn fault if they think I'll be fooled by such pretence.'

'But you allow them to cultivate such an interest – to risk their public reputation in the knowledge that many other women are attempting the same approach. It is *such* a dangerous game to play, Bill. And, you know, I am not entirely sure that the business would fare any worse without it.'

William showed no patience. Clara knew full well how stubborn he could be. This was not the first time they'd had such a dispute, and her brother had long since pronounced himself immoveable on the subject. Nevertheless, Clara persisted.

'I'm cashing up,' was the only response she received, or was likely to receive, since William had little inclination to think of anything else.

She left him to it, being only too aware that once the till rang open at the end of the day, William accepted no interruptions. He catalogued each sale meticulously, so that he could ensure that he had the highest stocks of popular medication and always be ahead of trends. William's precision was unrivalled; he always managed to out-compete the other Apothecaries nearby. As a result, he was gradually accruing a serious fortune. For a man of thirty, this was no mean feat – and if anything could justify his treatment of the female patrons, in his own mind, the amount of currency in the till at the end of the day was sure to be it.

Once all calculations were documented to his satisfaction, he would put aside a portion of the day's earnings (a pittance, by comparison) as Clara's wage. It meant that she had money to spend as she pleased, on what she pleased. As her life held few small pleasures, this was either supplies for her art or tickets to the theatre. And because she had suffered through a rather wearisome day, she was not entirely in the mood to paint, so: the theatre it was.

'Wasting your time on that again? Well, I don't suppose I can prevent you. Though you know my opinion on the matter: you'd be much better off setting the money aside. Men are always impressed by a woman who can provide for herself.'

Clara didn't rise to the bait; nor did she show ingratitude by stating that her wages would hardly be enough to 'provide for herself'. She did, however, focus on an important oversight.

'And you, Bill? Are you going to set your day's earnings aside or spend them on an equally crucial resource?' His pause was uncomfortably long, so she continued.

'Investment in ale is only common sense, I'm sure.'

'Do I not deserve some solace after such a successful day's trade?' he asked, undoing the topmost button of his shirt and loosening his tie as a means of punctuating his argument.

It was not unusual for a working man to want to spend his evenings in one of the many nearby drinking establishments. For William, this was Squires': his local Gentlemen's Club. It was a world that was entirely alien to his sister, although she was quite aware that they did not meet purely for the partaking of ale, the heady scent of tobacco smoke and bet-making – nor in fact to lay eyes upon the sorts of women who only seemed to come alive after dark. It was the exposure to local word-of-mouth reports and the acquirement of important contacts that drew most of them there, and as a result the Clubs were responsible for a substantial portion of each business' wealthy and influential clientele. Clara could hardly blame her brother for endeavouring to gain such an advantage, but she rebuked him for his criticism of the way she spent her free time. She responded in her usual manner, though the fatigue of the day somewhat doused the fire in her.

'I would not deny you that opportunity. But the means by which either of us finds our solace is our own decision to make, I'm sure you'll agree.'

'Enjoy your play, Clara.' William sighed in reply, as a means of saying his goodbyes until the following morning, no doubt.

'Take care, Bill,' she called after him, trying to be less

severe. 'I don't like to think of you walking the City alone.'

With a nod of compliance, he withdrew upstairs, leaving Clara to bolt the doors and tidy the shopfront. The place seemed so austere without the buzz of custom, and exceptionally cold. Countless shelves of jars and phials, rigid wooden worktops worn with overuse, and the hollow darkness that only seemed to enhance the stuffiness of the air; the outlook inspired no fondness whatsoever. Clara felt no sense of obligation towards the place. She could not bring herself to regret either her frustration with her work or her conduct towards her brother. She tried her utmost to complete the tasks set for her and kept complaints down to the barest minimum. And to her, that was enough of a gesture.

Her errands completed, she left the clinical Apothecary and set off for the theatre, a handful of coins rattling gleefully in her pocket.

CHAPTER FIVE

The Theatre Royal, New Adelphi: an opulent peacock of a building standing proud on the Strand. During a half-century of life, this popular venue had not only changed its name, but its masonry. To date, the theatre had earned four different titles and a completely new construction – more than most of its wealthiest of patrons could boast of themselves. In its most recent incarnation, the theatre earned its 'Royal' prefix by way of its palatial facade. Its lofty columns and pointed roof paid homage to a kind of Grecian magnificence which wholly embraced pretention of all kinds. And so, the theatre-going classes flocked to appreciate such grandeur, hoping that their own status would be elevated simply by standing in its imposing shadow. For them, the night's entertainment played a secondary part, the title role being the benefit of being seen in one of the City's most sophisticated venues.

A pity that on this particular night the theatre appeared to have contracted a mysterious disease. A burgeoning swell was spilling from its open doors, despite obvious efforts to surge in the opposite direction. These blemishes began to spread into the streets, emitting offensive noise that tainted the building's noble exterior.

Only one explanation could be given: opening night.

As Clara neared her chosen destination, she dreaded becoming one of the throng of bodies. The New Adelphi was her favourite theatre, its troupe of actors as familiar to her as if she had known them all her life, but she could not abide the frenzy that accompanied the premiere of a new play. Sadly, such an event was an exhibition for the preening aristocracy. High decoration and outlandish expenditure caused more of a stir than the play itself, and the newspapers abandoned their reviews in favour of noting down the pioneering fashions that had been debuted. Clara couldn't help but feel that, as a result, the accompanying performance was always a little subdued; after all, who would be foolish enough to try to out-compete the bourgeois?

The night's performance was *Love's Labour's Lost*. Not an entirely original choice of production, but one of Shakespeare's lesser-known comedies, only recently having been recognised upon the London stages. Perhaps too highbrow and too ambiguous in its humour for much of the audience, it was the perfect choice of play for the upper classes; they were much less likely to be upstaged.

Clara looked over the spectacle with obvious disdain. She had seen these people before, finding nothing remarkable between them. Wrinkling her nose at their affectations, she felt no affinity towards them, despite the fact that once, in her earlier life, she would have been expected to join their order.

In the past, she had been introduced to wealthy families; her parents believed themselves to be influential in her Wiltshire birthplace and prided themselves with associating with the well-to-do. Needless to say, Clara hadn't relished this life of pretence and was glad to absent herself from it. In the City, she had been granted anonymity, choosing to avoid the entrapments of her former life and seek solitude.

When the siblings' lives were relocated to the Capital, her brother endeavoured to continue following the example set for him. But Clara preferred to belong to no distinct class, walking the streets unaccompanied as if she were of no means at all – even her plain habiliments did little to give her away.

She took an impish pleasure in imagining how the refined people of her parents' circle would look upon her, watching her light her own way home from the theatre with a candlewick in a brass lantern.

She knew her own mind and needed no guardian to judge or chastise her. She had become accustomed to serving others and she had become used to living modestly. She found it more of a comfort than a life of indulgence and constant leisure.

Once the lords and ladies had made their lavish entrance, the surplus crowds were merely livestock, and once corralled to an almost unseemly degree, Clara finally found herself within the grand foyer.

Being above the means of those who swarmed in front of the stage, and yet not of the prestige to be allowed a seat amidst the higher balconies, she was directed towards the mid-levels of seating. Not a single seat had been left unoccupied that night, and with the clamorous masses around her, Clara strived to focus her mind, reducing the sounds around her to a feeble hum of background noise so that she could absorb the play's every word, movement and expression uninterrupted.

The players assembled for the opening scene, and

Clara felt the familiar stirrings of excitement within her. Like most of the Bard's plays, she knew what was to unfold, remembering perfectly each character's identity and even of some of the more iconic lines. But this took nothing away from her enjoyment; in fact, every consecutive recital only increased her admiration. Regardless of whether she knew of a twist in the plot, she always awaited it with bated breath. And even if she was able to deliver the speeches of the actors under her breath, the emotions they invoked would strike her each time with no less intensity. A credit to the playwright's work, no doubt, but also an indication of the refuge she found by escaping into the lives of others.

This evening, however, she had wisely steeled herself for disappointment; as ever, the opening night performance was to be vastly overshadowed. The play's bittersweet conclusion was appropriate, matching her animosity towards the aristocracy. Their plush fabrics and expanses of feathers and lace were only a disguise for a distinct lack of decorum. What began as marvel and appreciation from the lower classes soon became humour and derision, and the whole evening took on an air of travesty which Clara simply could not stand. When the curtain had fallen on the actors' final bow, her sigh of relief must surely have been the greatest.

The rich, rowdy pageant left first, bundling noisily into waiting coaches. The disquiet of their footmen was mirrored by the nervy behaviour of the horses as each chaise departed, and more than one glass bottle flew with a crash from open windows. Clara did not envy their homeward journeys; nor did she covet those of the least fortunate, who walked huddled together in the gathering dusk, not an overcoat between them, endeavouring to keep warm. She too had to face the prospect of walking, but her wool cloak was thick and heavy, and her leather boots in decent repair as to protect her feet from the cold and the cobblestones. The streets were still humming with life, as the sun had only just begun its descent, and so she merged into the crowds with ease, tracing the path back to Broad Street without a pause.

She contemplated *Love's Labour's Lost* as she walked, eyes cast down to her feet and the soft shadows they threw out across the stones. Her candle-lantern hung from a hook at her hip, and its dull golden glow caused her brittle silhouette to sway erratically. Her head felt almost as heavy with its disappointment as the buildings that towered around her, sighing as their foundations shifted in the cooling air. As the dusk laid its heavy hands around her, she silently lamented the way the evening's performance had been so unfairly dismissed. She was sure that some of the actors had played below their usual standard to account for a distracted audience, and whilst she felt sympathy for a wasted evening's effort, she also wondered *why* the aristocracy were allowed such a hold over the rest of the theatre-going public. Surely, if these actors were true masters of their art, they would be able to account for such trials and grasp the audience's attention so voraciously that they would be unable to find any form of interruption.

It seemed as if no matter where she went or what form of comfort she sought, she was forever to be met with dissatisfaction. For the pretence of art, and not the pleasure of it, seemed to appease everyone around her. And it seemed that there were no actors passionate enough about their craft to enable their audience to see past such pretences.

It just would not do. She needed more.

> *If this austere insociable life*
> *Change not your offer made in heat of blood;*
> *If frosts and fasts, hard lodging and thin weeds*
> *Nip not the gaudy blossoms of your love,*
> *But that it bear this trial and last love;*
> *Then, at the expiration of the year,*
> *Come challenge me ...*

If *Love's Labour's Lost* were a vision of her own life, Clara would have conducted herself in the same manner as its heroine. A year was not an unreasonable wait to test the endurance of an undying love.

But it wasn't sufficient time to accustom oneself to a detached and objectionable way of life, either. From her own embittered experience, Clara knew that not even *three* years was enough. And her hopes for love were even more parsimonious.

She could not see how anyone would be willing to endure a way of life such as hers in order to secure the love of another.

Perhaps, more than ever, art had imitated life. It was unknown as to whether the hero of the play eventually passed his test, and Clara resigned herself to remaining equally in the dark as to her own future in love.

The swollen burnt-orange sun had only its crown visible above the horizon as Clara finally came into sight of the Apothecary. The tightly packed buildings were almost perspiring in the dull haze, a sheen of steam rising from their warm tiles, and their darkened frontages seemed to loom over her, windows staring vacantly.

Already, the evening's smog was gathering, hugging tightly at her ankles as she unlocked the front door. In moments, the mist would be waist high, and by midnight, even the stars in the sky would be indistinguishable. She stepped gratefully inside, setting down her lantern on the window ledge to light William's way in the dark. She knew before she had even closed the door behind her that he had not yet returned, even though the light of day would not last another hour. There was a chance he had entered into conversation with a wealthy shipping merchant, persuading them to provide discounted deliveries, in which case he would not return until the gaslights were beginning to dim, so that negotiations could be thoroughly meditated over.

She looked outside. The streets were mostly empty, and the only source of light bobbed on the end of a metal pike: a policeman was making his rounds, lighting the streetlamps as he passed by.

Climbing the precarious staircase in semi-darkness, Clara entered her room with the familiar injured creak of the old door, inhaling the scent of charcoal and oils with a smile. Swiftly, her pleasure to be home was engulfed by a wave of exhaustion. She dressed for bed eagerly. But rather than lying in bed, she moved to take her usual seat in the window recess, with her cotton nightshift tucked over her knees and hooked under her heels.

Thoroughly entranced, she knelt there, staring out into the blank, fathomless dusk, a small wad of paper and a sketching implement having leapt into her hands.

Nothing to inspire her that evening. The world was as a page daubed grey, not a single line or contour to give it the hint of dimension. She might as well have been staring into a void. But she had no desire to draw anything. Her artist's materials had worked their own way into her lap; she hadn't the remotest idea why she had picked them up.

The policeman passed by again with his lighted candle, possibly patrolling in case of riotous behaviour that often ensued as the alehouses began to close. Clara watched him blearily, shifting to rest the weight of her back against the side of the window seat, tilting her head backwards in her drowsiness so that her eyelids flickered half-shut. As her vision became distorted by her eyelashes, she watched the policeman take on a double form, his suspended flame splitting into two separate orbs of light. She smiled involuntarily. Fatigue pressed down over her like a material substance, and when all her muscles gave way to the limpness of sleep, her last waking thought was of how unusual it was for the moon to peer out from behind the clouds, rendering the smog temporarily transparent ...

It had to have been a dream. Such an image could not have been realised by a waking mind.

As her subconscious mind overtook her senses, the smog continued to clear before her, and Clara realised she had been mistaken. The policeman had not returned, nor was the source of light merely a candle hanging from a metal baton.

There were two points of incandescence, belonging to just the one person, illuminating the narrow alley below. Rather than being suspended in parallel to the moving figure, they appeared to be emanating *from* him. And although it was altogether too dark and hazy to be sure, Clara felt as though she recognised the lone walker from a long-forgotten past. His hair was dark as an oil slick, hanging in sharp points about his lower jaw and brushing his shirt collar. He wore no cloak to keep out the cold, his white cotton dress shirt open a little way down his chest, exposing olive skin that even the pale glow of the moon could not lighten. His steps were marked by highly polished black boots and his eyes were such a rich, lustrous green that they swallowed up the darkness and almost illuminated the path before him.

'*You.*'

Clara's lips soundlessly formed the word as she recognised the figure from that same morning, and the dream began to reach a shadowy conclusion. As the darkness drew in around her, and the moon was once more stifled by the dense mist, she was compelled to realise that the points of light in the street below were in fact the luminescence cast out by the man's own cat-like eyes, and at the moment that even the world of her dreams became enclosed in a dark veil, those shimmering green lamps had moved to focus directly upon her peaceful, smiling face.

'BUT SHE HAD NO DESIRE TO DRAW ANYTHING. HER
ARTIST'S MATERIALS HAD WORKED THEIR OWN WAY INTO
HER LAP...'

CHAPTER SIX

Clara awoke the next morning in the same position she had succumbed to sleep in. All her joints ached from having been cramped in the window recess for the night. The soft breath of dawn had only just begun to chase the greyness from the air.

Swinging her legs carefully from the ledge, she attempted to upright herself. Her back wouldn't straighten so she limped around the room for several minutes in a stooping posture, wincing with every step. Her pale eyes seemed sunken and dull in her vanity mirror, and although she couldn't remember having slept fitfully, she felt drawn, as if the weight of something important was hanging over her and she had yet to find its solution.

She looked over to the window to recall the cause of discomfort from the night before. Like sparks from a lit flint, a surge of memories showered her.

Her dream was broken with vivid clarity; those luminous eyes in the dark, shining like sunlight through a magnifying glass. It had felt, for a moment, as if she were being allowed access to a world in which she did not belong; another plane of thought. The strict laws of the physical world had been broken. Her recollection was so graphic that her chest tightened with excitement, and the rush of blood that followed began to overwhelm her. She reeled slightly where she stood, placing the back of her hand to her temple and finding it coated in a thin sheen of cold sweat. The paper-covered walls loomed in around her, her hazy vision causing each sheet to fray at the edges, colours and forms seeping into each other. The air suddenly became close, to the point of stifling. Staggering towards the window, Clara threw it open with a ragged intake of breath.

She glanced upwards, gaining a clear view of the morning sky. The sun was a watery smear across its blue-grey backdrop, yet its light caused an ache behind the hollows of her eyes. Placing her thumbs at either side of the bridge of her nose to clear her senses, Clara blinked repeatedly until she became accustomed to the light.

The slight rush of air had at least regulated her breathing and freed her mind of anxious thoughts. Maybe she had been suffering from the last vestiges of a night filled with vivid dreams, because as the morning materialised before her, she felt herself uplifted, invigorated. She looked with a renewed and unexpected affection over the street scene below; of small carts delivering baskets of bread and churns of milk, eager shop-hands sweeping dust from their doorways, and the usual hubbub of people making their way around the City. Hard to believe that the tranquil scene, predictable and dependable, could have produced such a disturbing vision as hers the night before. Her memory of the dream gradually lost its intensity.

The clang of the shop bell sounded below her, and she poked her head through the open window to see her brother stepping into the street. He had a broom in hand but apparently had no mind to use it, as his free hand was clasped to his forehead. He swayed slightly on the spot, the brush handle proving rather effective as a prop. Clara hadn't heard his return from the Club and had rather expected him to be in such a sorry state, once he had failed to wake her.

'Good morning, Bill,' she called from her vantage point.

After a lengthy pause, he replied in a barely discernible slur of sound, raising his head to meet her eye. The weak sunlight seemed to be as much an insult to his eyes as it had hers, and he shaded his face with a pale forearm as he spoke up to her, putting on an affected liveliness for the benefit of any clientele that may have been passing.

'Clara. It is nearly time for opening. Are you ready?'

'I'll be downstairs in a moment,' she replied, the warmth of laughter behind her words.

He acknowledged her with a nod, his reply little more than a grunt, before making a half-hearted attempt at sweeping the front step and stumbling back inside. She watched him with cool eyes, her smile hinting at a sort of amused tolerance, then leaned across to pull at the window latch.

She wouldn't have noticed, but she couldn't quite let her thoughts lie from the previous night. It was him again, she was sure of it. She was beginning to recognise him by the colour of his hair and the complexion of his skin alone. He stood apart from the rest; had no need to interact with anyone around him, nor any wish to. It was only when he had passed out of sight that Clara realised she had been rooted to the spot, willing him to look at her.

She eventually entered the shopfront to find the place empty – fortunately, because William had almost fallen asleep at the counter. His weight was propped up by one elbow, his spectacles sitting crooked on the end of his nose. One tuft of mahogany-coloured hair stood out at an abstract angle, as did one shirt cuff and one side of his shirt collar. It was not unusual for Clara to see him this way – but she knew that it could be equated to a positive outcome the night before. William was never one to drown his sorrows, but he would certainly toast his successes numerous times.

'I must owe you some form of thanks or congratulations – only for that reason would you be content to drink the day's earnings.'

As his eyes snapped open, William gave her a bleary smile. 'Business could not be better,' he answered, without a shred of dishonesty or conceit. 'You needn't worry – any earnings I drank last night will be back in the till with interest by the end of today.'

Clara knew he was right; anyone could see that the popularity of their business was escalating week upon week.

And yet she still felt dissatisfied – from a sense of loss, of missing something important – not from any particular irritation at William. Nevertheless, she continued to lecture him.

'You were late back.'

An attempt at neither apology nor explanation was made. What William did instead was make an offhand statement: 'I had an interesting conversation with a friend of yours.'

'Of mine?' Clara asked, before feeling a blush of shame creep across her cheeks. She had not meant to sound surprised and was embarrassed that she only had Ruth as a close friend.

'Well – at least he claimed to be an acquaintance. Young law-type? Alan something … Or was it Andrew?'

'Albert? Albert Barnes?'

William confirmed it was him before raising one puzzled eyebrow over his sister's reaction. Clara could not disguise her disdain and wondered how Albert had the audacity to name her a friend; they had only met a few times. She suspected that it was his superficiality that demanded he claim to befriend anyone, regardless of their connections, simply for the opportunity of social elevation.

'What did you speak about?'

'Nothing of any great consequence,' William replied ambiguously. 'He introduced me to some of his friends – other lawyers and so on. They seemed interested in my views on modern medicine.'

'I'm sure they were,' Clara replied, with no enthusiasm. She couldn't see why Albert had taken it upon himself to recommend clients to William and couldn't help but dread the day when he would seek repayment for the offer of goodwill. She was sure that, eventually, it would be her who would suffer for the alliance, and not her brother.

William had noticed her scepticism and, understandably, could see no reason for it. 'Once again: I meet with your disapproval?' came his rhetorical query, his eyes clear and inquisitive despite the lethargy of his mind.

And Clara felt sorry then – sorry for the fact that her constant displeasure was more often than not deflected onto William, despite his well-meaning intentions.

'Forgive me,' she said, unable to meet his eye. 'It isn't you I disapprove of, but *him*.'

'Bert? He seemed genuine enough.'

Clara shook her head, unsure if she would be able to articulate herself properly without giving way to suppressed irritation. 'There is something about his behaviour towards Ruth that gives me unease. It is almost as if he has too much to offer … too much to prove.' She risked a glance at her brother and was dismayed to see that he was smiling.

'I think you may be too hasty in your suspicions. Surely you can credit Ruth with a good sense of judgement? If she trusts him, you have no reason not to. Unless—'

'Unless what?'

'I can't really blame you for it,' was his only reply.

Clara could have cursed with the injustice of it. She knew what he was inferring, and it made her stomach churn.

'It is not jealousy,' she spat, and she knew that the subtle anger in her voice shocked him. 'It is true that I know nothing about the nature of their acquaintance, but never would I be resentful of Ruth's happiness.'

She could see in the blankness of his expression that he would not believe her, no matter how she protested.

'It doesn't matter.' She clipped him off sharply. 'If you and "Bert" are to become close friends, it is inevitable that you will cease to believe anything I say about him.' She left William with his doubts.

She couldn't help but feel that there may have been some truth to his words. She felt no envy over Ruth and Albert's relationship and did not yearn for any kind of love that was fraught with uncertainty. But she did wonder how love had evaded her for so long when it seemed to flourish despite the flaws of those who managed to attain it.

Customers soon began to arrive. As they came and went, Clara could not help but observe a number of unfamiliar faces. Word was certainly spreading, helped, no doubt, by William's profitable conversations the night before. These new clients were noticeably prosperous ones and took great care to introduce themselves to the proprietor.

With so many fledgling businesses competing to equip the nation's hypochondriacs with new and innovative remedies, any one establishment that was promoted by the 'right people' had the benefit of being in vogue – to be known to buy one's cures in such a place was almost preferable to being seen at the Adelphi on opening night.

Clara managed to set aside her hurt feelings in order to assure that the day's work ran smoothly, offering William advice where she could and ensuring she was attentive to every customer. Her brother's words stung like a recent flesh wound, and it took all the dignity she had to remain civil towards him.

She refused to say a word to her brother once the last customer had left. She did not wait around for him to count the day's profits, as she would wait until the next day to spend her wage in any case, hoping to purchase more art supplies.

She disappeared upstairs without speaking.

Cruelty was not a suit she wore often, nor did she take enjoyment from it. But neither was she offered any form of apology, and in the absence of such, she had no desire to continue any sort of pretence.

The evening passed with surprising speed, as Clara spent a few hours affixing her newest pieces of art to the already burdened walls. There was no particular method applied to the way she arranged the paintings and sketches, and as the years had passed, it became harder and harder to make a neat job of attaching them – in recent weeks, it had become more a case of finding a patch of blank space, and this alone could take several minutes. As wall space became more of a commodity, any art that Clara felt had lost its appeal would be removed from the wall to make space for a newer replacement, and these redundant pieces would be resigned to the floor. There were several ankle-high piles of such works already.

When her eyes began to ache in the waning candlelight, she finally resigned herself to bed. It seemed William had already retired; when she extinguished her candle, there was no light from the rest of the upper landing. No doubt he would present a more acceptable countenance tomorrow, once he had recovered from his overindulgence of the night before.

Clara decided she would put aside her emotional injury, for her own sake as well as his, and face the next day with that regulated self-will that she had cultivated so well across the years. It seemed she was forever finding new ways to impugn her brother, when in fact it had been he who had given her freedom. Freedom from the expectations of others, from a life of complacency. Never once had he expressed the same wish as her parents – to cast her off to the first eligible man that came into his acquaintance. He respected her right to choose and wanted nothing more from her than a willingness to work. She could not truthfully say that she had always held up her own side of the bargain.

My duty is to be your sister, and all this entails. It is certainly not to be your adversary. All I ask is that you try to understand me, where so many others cannot.

It sounded so comforting in her mind that she wrote it down on a small piece of paper, and, folding it in half, slid the note under William's bedroom door. Even the shrill creak of her own door seemed more muffled in the calm that followed, and Clara crossed her bedroom with a faint smile, passing the large window as she went.

'You.'

But she was not dreaming this time. This time, the thought was spoken aloud, strangely muffled by the paper-wadded walls.

It was only a silhouette; perhaps his shadow against the cobblestones or his imprinted image left upon the smog in his wake. But it was most certainly him, her Stranger – and this night, as the moon slid from behind its veil of cloud, she was fully awake.

Clara lay rigidly, trying to convince herself, as her

eyelids drooped and her breathing slowed, that she hadn't passed the window intentionally, hadn't been purposefully seeking him out.

CHAPTER SEVEN

*E*very day. At the same hour. She had not taken note, but she had even begun to suspect that it was the same minute. And he always walked in the same direction.

As the Stranger passed beneath her window, on the way to who knew where – once a morning, once a night – she hoped that the level of fascination she drew from his monotonous, almost absurdly predictable movements was justified. For much as he seemed to follow the same trajectory of anyone else in the Broad Street crowds, Clara could not see how something as superficial as his appearance alone would have attracted her to him. Perhaps she had a longing for novelty, of any kind.

During her working hours, she often found herself picturing *him* at the least probable moments. A worn-down patch of wood on the countertop surface would remind her of the dull olive sheen of his skin. A crow's feather, blown over the door threshold by a wayward breeze, reminded her of the oil-slick brown of his hair. A reflection of light in a glass jar would remind her of his eyes. *Those eyes.* Always, she was immobilised by the memory of *them*. The lingering sense of shock, from a dream long since past, regained sudden clarity at the thought.

She wondered how she would fare at sketching him. She began to contemplate the shades of paint she would use to render him in oils. These thoughts, of course, gradually led her to wonder how he would appear from less of a distance. She saw no feasible way of altering this. In her creative frustration, the limits of her view from the window seat seemed ever more restrictive, the leaded panes becoming prison bars.

The first time she decided to draw him, she had attempted to sketch the curve from the underside of his chin to the base of his neck. Small steps, and only the simplest details, were crucial here. No running before she could walk – not least where the speed of pencil on paper was concerned. She had seen him on a grey, overcast morning, and the shadows left by the clouds had set his bodily contours into sharp, dark relief. The lighting could not have been more perfect; she watched him pass below the window, occasionally letting her gaze dip back to the page where her hand was working under its own incentive. Watching the corner of the street long after he had gone, she felt her heart leaping excitedly in her chest, and was thankful that a wall of bone prevented it from escaping her completely. But all the favourable lighting in the world could not have cheered her when she eventually turned to look at the page. Her attempt was wholly unsuccessful; the form too vague, the lines suggesting bone and muscle not suitably defined.

Nobody else seemed to notice him. His habit of walking in large, bustling crowds meant that only those thrust aside to accommodate his extravagant movements actually paid any attention to him at all.

Clara noticed. Clara paid attention. Much as she wished to be able to reproduce all she could see of him on paper, she would not force such a detailed image onto her memory before she had the confidence to execute it. She focused on the expanse of forearm and wrist left bare below an embellished shirt cuff, sketching relentlessly, honing the lines and curves until the minutes that passed lost all significance. Eventually, the joints in her fingers numbed, her wrist stiffened, and her memory began to blur, so that she could no longer be sure that her likeness had ever been accurate.

Once more, failure. And her determination only redoubled.

He wasn't the ideal subject, nor was she finding it easy to draw him to her satisfaction, and so she did not push herself beyond her own abilities. But to see him, even for those brief snatches of time, left her light-headed and reeling in a way she couldn't quite explain. And afterwards, she could find limitless peace and comfort in mixing colours in a palette – *his colours*. Endless variations in shade and tone, which captured his physical being in the only way Clara knew. Even if her sketches and fragments of paintings never amounted to anything, she was, for once, relatively contented.

Once Clara's personal wellbeing improved, predictably, her professionalism suffered. She added to the sketches whenever a free moment arose – regardless of whether she should have been more usefully engaged at the time.

Her distracted behaviour was nothing new, albeit more frequent. It caused no severe problems with the running of the business. She left none of her daily errands undone.

Occasionally, a customer would notice a smear of paint on her cheek or see a scrap of paper pinned under a glass jar in front of her and inquire on the nature of the drawing, but under William's cautious eye she rarely gave more than the briefest of explanations. Often, she would feel obliged to lie, claim a smear of paint to be a spilled ingredient from the store room, a carelessly left piece of paper to be a child's sketch left behind.

Her brother's reaction to the change in her was subdued, as usual. The rapport between them had hardly improved, even since Clara had decided to give him the benefit of the doubt over his opinions about Ruth and Albert. They seemed to have returned to their usual truce: in which neither of them was expected to speak more than a few words to each other and were left to their own devices. It had nothing to do with resentment – they were able to avoid unpleasantness more easily if the number of words exchanged between them was kept to a minimum.

Almost a week after she had first seen *him*, the siblings were in the midst of one of these silences when an acquaintance of William's entered the shop. Like most of those within his social circle, this friend was quite wealthy and regularly frequented Squires' of an evening. He matched William in age, and even shared some of his physical attributes. But whilst both of them had the same rich dark hair and sandy-coloured complexion, William's eyes were a deep cobalt blue, whereas his friend's were a lively green. Clara took it upon herself to notice such things whilst the friend enquired after one of William's pioneering new cures. The man had his hair cropped a little longer than her brother's; it hung in soft points around the line of his jaw and sat in the hollows of his cheekbones rather smoothly. He turned to point out the ingredient he required, and Clara found her feet moving of their own accord … to stand directly beside the green-eyed man.

'Please, keep still,' she requested in a soft voice. Her head came to his shoulder, and she gazed up at him without meeting his eye.

'Excuse me?' he responded, his eyes darting to William in his uncertainty. William offered no explanation; his eyes were fixed intently on his sister.

'It won't take a moment: please do not move.'

She brought her head closer to his, raising her hand in front of her face. Her index finger was pointed out straight; she seemed to be tracing a line in the air between them.

William's friend was stricken to the spot. He wondered what manner of disease-ridden insect could have landed on his neck for a woman to have the courage to approach him where her brother dared not. As the hairs on his scalp prickled under her scrutiny, he tried his utmost to stop himself from yelling out – in fear, in embarrassment, he knew not what. All he could manage after a few seconds' silence was: 'Can – can I at least turn my head?' His neck was becoming rather sore.

Clara released a soft sound – something barely resembling a sigh – and nodded. As he began to turn his head away from her, however, she stopped him in his movements, reaching out with her pointing hand to hold his chin still between finger and thumb.

'There: that's perfect.' Her voice escaped her in a dreamy monotone, the corners of her mouth twitched upwards. She regarded his image for several moments, taking in every detail.

Something in the way he held himself, with his hair darkened near-black in the dim light, had captured Clara's imagination. As he had turned fractionally away from her, she watched as the afternoon sun highlighted his green eyes unusually, causing them to illuminate like points of phosphorescence. It wasn't the Stranger of her living and dreaming world – but she couldn't bear wasting the opportunity of seeing his likeness up close. It was just unfortunate that she had entirely forgotten propriety in the process.

'Clara – that's enough.'

William had finally spoken up, coming around the counter and seizing her by the elbow. Her grip on his bemused friend relented immediately, and she shrunk away from the two men, a dash of livid colour across each cheekbone.

'I'm sorry – please forgive me. I was not myself. I did not mean to … It wasn't my intention to …'

She couldn't finish a thought.

William quickly supplied his friend with the cure he had required, ensuring him that, no, there were no biting insects anywhere on his person, and that, yes, his sister was suffering from a mild fever, causing her to become disorientated, and had been approaching customers with strange requests all day – nothing to worry about: he would be sending her to bed with a remedy, and she would be right as rain in the morning.

Once the gentleman had left, William rounded on Clara. She had her back to him, busying herself with putting jars back in their places, but he could see from the rigidness of her shoulders that she was expecting a lecture from him.

'Clara.'

She didn't turn, but her hand paused over the unscrewed lid of a jar, and a muscle in the back of her neck convulsed slightly.

'Clara, what on *earth* were you—'

'I know. I behaved appallingly,' she replied, flicking a half-glance in William's direction before hanging her head over her chest, a few fingers pressed to her forehead. The next words from her mouth were barely distinguishable; William wondered if she was even talking to him at all. 'It wasn't *him*, I know that. But I had to see: I had to *try* and see …'

'Try and see what?' William asked, the sharp sting of exasperation entering his voice against his will. He wanted to be patient with her, but the accumulation of several days' unusual behaviour was beginning to leave him feeling completely alienated from his sister's world. 'You can't just … *lay your hands on anyone,* Clara. I don't spend my evenings trying to find new, influential clients for us for them to be scared off on their first visit by a woman with – with no comprehension of physical boundaries!'

'I can't explain it to you, Bill. You wouldn't understand.'

'But I *need* to understand. I need to understand a lot

of things, Clara. All these changes in behaviour … I cannot tolerate them. I will not stand idly by whilst you walk around this place covered in paint; whilst you leave your *little sketches* lying around for all and sundry to see. I've seen them with my own eyes, and I'm not entirely sure they are proper, Clara – is a man's shoulder muscle an appropriate drawing subject for a young woman? And now you begin to manhandle my customers!'

Clara had turned to face him. She was clutching one of said 'little sketches' in her hands, her grip so light that it barely dented the paper. Her gaze was steady, but her watery blue eyes had a mist in them, and her deep black pupils had lost their sheen. As William took a deep breath, swallowed his frustration, and asked her the question, he couldn't be sure she even saw him. 'What has got into you?'

Her pupils focused, unfocused, refocused. He thought she had been staring through him, past him – and he was right. But she wasn't ignoring him. Her mind was working meticulously. She was poring over thoughts, ideas, and even dreams, trying to come to terms with something she had not been able to comprehend. But now, there could be no doubt. The revelation frightened her and excited her beyond words. It would mean that her life would take a distinct turn for the first time in months – but she would have to keep her feet firmly secured in the real world, or else lose herself to her own imagination. William had no idea of the implications of his question, but she was sure that once she answered him, the dynamic between them would alter considerably. The alienation he felt at that moment would, in fact, be just the beginning.

She sighed deeply and held out the piece of paper to her brother.

From where he stood, he could see she had drawn a pair of eyes. The pupils were wide and unfathomably dark, even when drawn with a humble pencil. But it was the irises that struck him most, even from his distance. She had attempted to colour them with watercolours, and the shade chosen was a green that William could not remember having seen anywhere on God's earth. The eyes were luminescent. His first thoughts were of some kind of predatory animal: a cat, or a fox.

Clara's open palms moved a fraction, and the painting fell to the ground. William watched it fall, ready to urge her into answering his question – but as he looked back to her outstretched hands, he realised they were not yet empty. What he had thought was a single leaf of paper was in fact a small wad of pages. Clara tilted her hands toward the ground, her eyes still locked upon him, watching the realisation dawn in his face as he saw not one, not two, not even five, but tens, dozens of paintings begin to spill out and away from her body. They cascaded out over the floor, falling in a semi-circular tide around Clara as if she herself were a human waterfall.

And they were all the same.

Startling green eyes, staring with a piercing intensity that threatened to draw William into their dark core. Each time, the lurid green had altered slightly – barely noticeable variations in tone, shade, depth. Even William could see that this was a refining process: the means of reaching a single, satisfying end product. He looked into his sister's eyes as the last drawing fell; they were soft and soothing in comparison to the multitude of cat-green eyes which had fanned out in front of her.

'What has got into me? *Him,*' she replied, her hands sweeping out across the drawings by way of explanation.

William was shocked to see her body tremble slightly. Her vague smile made his muscles tense with unease.

'My muse,' she added, the words leaving her in a sharp release of breath. The admission was invigorating, and even as the words hung in the air between them, William could see her mind beginning to travel to new realms of thought, of possibility, leaving him and the Apothecary in a world that no longer held any immediate relevance to her.

Stranger had become *muse.* A momentous change, and in a world of causality: the first of many.

CHAPTER EIGHT

Clara didn't underestimate the significance of allowing the Stranger to take such a prominent role in her life.

Her confession had been the release of knowledge that had weighed her down, kept her tense with apprehension. She knew that the muse would invade any spare corner of her mind and that, in time, her brother would surely come to resent this. In admitting his existence, she freed herself from her own feelings of guilt.

She had to make preparations. Telling William was one important milestone, but there were many more tasks to be done, many weeks of demanding work ahead. Clara was preparing herself for an all-consuming obsession.

Her preoccupation may have been a worry to some. Her brother, on the other hand, wasn't unduly concerned. He had grown up with Clara and had witnessed her sinking into prolonged periods of reflection from a young age.

William could remember days from their childhood when Clara would take to the hills, sketchbook under her arm, skirts tucked into her boots, a determination in her expression that nothing could penetrate. She felt no fear of venturing out alone, at an age when most young girls were constantly under the watchful eye of a nanny. Their parents didn't object, as the countryside was a place of idyllic isolation and perfect safety to those who knew no better. Perhaps the sky was a tumultuous mass of dark clouds, perhaps the hedgerows had begun to sprout their spring blossom – whatever the motivation had been, Clara would spend hours in complete solitude, up in the hills that, to William, were only fit for grazing livestock.

Her family, and anyone in their acquaintance, despaired of the spirited girl. But they could not understand. They never knew what it was, to her, to run.

Running, until the world around her became a nameless blur, nothing but colours and tones and shades of light and dark. Pure freedom. The cold swell of air in her lungs, the horizon blurred, her eyes stinging as the sharp breeze hit them. Hills surrounding her in their rolling magnificence, bowing outwards like crashing waves; such an inevitability in their movements, suggesting that in centuries to come, they would eventually tumble and plunge into the rocks beneath, churning out the earth and dispersing the land even wider. The long grasses swayed violently as she passed, flailing in a wild movement that seemed to create a cushion of air around her childish body and ease her way onward. The tangy scent of wild blossoms, fields stained powder blue with cornflowers, and the songs of birds, filling her head with a curious light.

She would have run and run until the land stopped and the sea stretched out before her, except that she didn't know why she was running, where she was running to, or what she would have done had she ever run there. So, she simply ran, until her lungs heaved behind her ribs, until she was ready to sit down on the grass and pick up her sketching pencils.

As a child, Freedom was her muse. And that hadn't changed. Years had passed, and her new muse was nothing more than her latest means for escape. She knew this, and perhaps, within the confines of his cynicism, William knew it too.

Nature had been Clara's inspiration, her first true love, and the reason that a small corner of her heart allowed her to miss the Wiltshire countryside. As she had grown into adulthood, her inspiration had taken human form, and it was here that she came to accept her new way of life in London, filling the void left when those oppressive hills had faded away into nothingness in the steam from a train's furnace.

William dismissed her latest revelation and had no desire to discover who the muse was. He knew that this particular gentleman walked past the shop twice a day: once of a morning, and once of an evening. Never having seen the man himself, William took no fascination whatsoever from his recurring behaviour.

As William saw things, hundreds of men and women took the exact same journey as this stranger every day. He was sure that Clara would tire of him eventually. Eccentrics had flocked to London for centuries.

Time passed so easily for Clara when she was painting *him*. No longer did she struggle to draw an arm, a nose, a jaw; in fact, she could sketch his entire face and parts of his upper body and be more or less completely happy with the result. The fact that she hadn't yet been able to create a full painted portrait was no hindrance or concern to her – merely a goal yet to be accomplished. Her confidence and daring grew by the day, and she knew that once she decided to paint her final work, it would be the best piece she had ever created.

The sense of accomplishment, of moving towards a goal, was a thrill greater than any she had felt amongst the wind-beaten gorse bushes, running from life.

The eyes were still an issue. Beautiful and intoxicating though they were, she never seemed to manage to get a full glimpse of them. Their brightness was such that mere daylight did them no justice, and she had not been in his line of sight since the first day she saw him. The tone of them was something she had never come across before – not even her brother's Nature Journals showed any manner of creature with the same intense, acidic stare. But hour upon hour, day upon day, she came closer to achieving her favourable end result. And she didn't lose hope.

Fortunately, her muse showed no awareness of the intense examination he had inspired. Dependably, he continued to tread the same path.

At night, when the moon parted the clouds and smog for a brief instant, she would long for the visions of her dream to become reality – namely: for her muse's eyes to light up the imposing darkness, to illuminate Broad Street like beacons, to swathe it in green flames.

Understandably, Clara's thoughts began to turn to where. Where was he going every morning? And where did he return to every night? Questions that did not necessarily require an answer but she couldn't resist pondering over. Likewise, she was curious as to what manner of person her muse was. What was his profession? Where did he live? Did he have relatives, friends, loved ones? Knowing that she would never discover the answer to these questions helped to relieve her guilt – over delving into his life, over studying him so thoroughly without his knowledge. Her disappointment that she would never meet him in the flesh was lessened as her mind wandered over elaborate speculations.

The word 'infatuation' never once crossed her mind.

Business at the Apothecary continued to thrive, but Clara's work ethic fared as badly – if not worse – than ever. Her distractions remained solely in her own mind; those of the physical world held no further interest to her. She no longer obsessed over customers with similar features to her muse, as she had already stockpiled a vast collection of sketches bearing almost every minute detail of his appearance. On the odd occasion when she had looked upon the faces of the customers, she had frightened herself. Male or female, old or young, their features would be lost, and she would see only the face of the muse staring back at her. She had to remind herself that her imagination was a powerful tool, now in its element, stronger than ever.

She would usually refrain from conversation, finding no interest or solace of any kind in the words of others.

This proved problematic when Ruth Davison paid Clara a visit one afternoon.

On this particular day, the Apothecary was suffering from a rush of custom; both William and Clara were weighted down with orders, each occupying their own counter at opposing sides of the room. Many people standing at the back of the queue were craning their necks and straining their voices to be heard. Trips to the fearsome store room were inevitable as jars continued to empty, and this, mixed with the heat caused by an accumulation of bodies and the inconvenience, had dampened Clara's mood considerably. Any thoughts she tried to conjure of the muse were lost under a torrent of coughs, splutters and sneezes. Her apron was smeared and dirty, and her hair hung in sweat-dampened tendrils about her forehead.

When the shop bell rang out another arrival, Clara silently cursed. No one looked toward the door.

Soon, however, the sweetest of voices carried over the many heads in the room. The source of the voice could not be seen, although many men in the group were turning to cast an appreciative glance in its direction, and a polite sea of bodies was spreading to accommodate the newest addition. When Clara finally recognised the trilling note of the voice and lifted her head to hear it better, she could only see the top of a lavender-coloured bonnet bobbing across the room towards her. Eventually, the bonnet came to a stop in front of her, and she saw beneath it her oldest friend. It took her several moments to remember that she was supposed to smile at the recognition.

'Ruth!'

Thankfully, this was sufficient. Ruth's apple cheeks flushed brightly, and she leapt up to plant a kiss on her friend's cheek. Several murmurs of admiration arose from the crowd of customers, as if they had never seen such a soft-hearted display of affection as from this petite flower of a woman.

'Clara, my dear, I hope I haven't arrived at an unfortunate time. I had no idea you would be so frightfully busy! Perhaps I should return later, when I won't be depriving your valued customers of their remedies.'

Clara would've liked to say: 'Yes, Ruth, that is a splendid idea.' In fact, she would have preferred to say nothing at all, and let her silence communicate her agreement. But as it was, on hearing her words, many of the customers awaiting Clara's assistance had voiced their dismissal of such an idea, being instantly charmed by Ruth's courtesy. They would not allow her to be denied this reunion with her friend.

Ruth thanked them in her usual, delightful way and came around the counter to speak to Clara in excitedly hushed tones.

'Darling, you must forgive my intrusion. You know it is unlike me to visit you whilst you are working.' In truth, Ruth hardly ever visited at all. She would never say so, but Clara knew she found the idea of employment vulgar for a woman. She preferred not to think of her friend living this way. To Ruth, the world would be a better place if it consisted purely of parties and strolls in the park. 'I have something to ask you. And you mustn't say no: if you do, it will break my heart!' And at this, she laughed out into the room, pretending not to notice the adoring stares.

'Surely not.' Clara also laughed, but her own laughter rattled around her empty thoughts like hard stones in a glass jar. 'I would hope your heart would not be so easily broken.'

If her words patronised, she hadn't the propensity to notice.

Ruth cocked her head like a sparrow, mischief in her eyes and uncertainty in her smile.

'It certainly *would*,' she replied, unable to hide a tone of petulance in her voice. 'You don't know what it is I'm asking you, yet. Besides, I don't think you would say no even if you had the option – which, of course, you don't. You shall love it; it will cheer you immensely. So there!' She laughed again, but the laughter quickly subsided, replaced by a measuring look. It was as if she were waiting for something.

'If I am not to be given an option, then surely the premise of asking a question is an unnecessary one.' Heat was prickling beneath Clara's skin. She was in no humour to placate Ruth. She wanted fresh air. She wanted to lie down. No: she wanted to paint. And all civility escaped her.

In the face of such a rebuff, Ruth merely blinked. Then, she smiled. When accompanied with the devious narrowing of her eyes, it was clear that she had expected such an answer. It seemed to bring her a new rush of amusement rather than dampen her enthusiasm.

'*I knew it*,' she said simply and pointedly.

'What?' Clara asked, in a softer voice now. It was clear that nothing she could say could deter Ruth – and now she was slightly intrigued.

'You are not yourself, Clara Breslin,' she stated, as if putting forth a scientific theorem. 'I realised it from the moment I set eyes on you. Something is different ...' She leaned about to survey Clara from different angles, looking for clues.

'Yes. I am busy, and tired,' Clara droned in reply, feeling the onset of a headache.

'No – no, that's not it. Your mind is elsewhere – more so than usual.' Ruth raised her eyebrows light-heartedly. 'I do believe … there is a new gentleman in your life! You are entertaining thoughts of courtship, my dearest! Is it not so?' she asked, placing a hand on her hip and thrusting out her chin triumphantly.

Far from it; far from it, Clara thought, shaking her head with a weak smile. For that to be so would be a rare thing indeed – particularly when her thoughts were so thoroughly occupied by her muse that she hadn't had a full conversation with another living soul in weeks. She often lamented her deficiency in love – but of late, had found it much easier to cope.

She felt no affection when she thought of her muse, only reverence. Their bond was purely grounded in the physical, the material – more permanent than the fleeting hypocrisy of love. He was her art. He was strokes and colours on a page. He was more to her than love.

'Perhaps I am finding being attentive a little harder of late,' she admitted, holding her discovery a secret from Ruth for the while. 'But my thoughts are not so different than usual. You know me, Ruth: forever a slave to my art.'

Her friend brushed off this evasive answer with a small wave of her hand. She did not wish to hear of art and knew that her friend wasn't giving her the full truth.

'Well, Clara, you win. I will not press the matter. I'm sure you will enlighten your poor, unwitting friend in due course.' She sighed softly, giving Clara a stare that let her realise she was not off the hook just yet.

'Now, to the reason for my visit: Albert and I were wondering if you would like to come to the theatre with us tonight.'

'Oh, Ruth, I—' Clara hadn't the time to gather her thoughts. It was unexpected; Ruth often voiced her disinterest in all forms of the arts. It was a rare and generous sacrifice for her to make. And for Clara to be able to spend time with her one friend, enjoying a pastime that she loved, would have been quite refreshing – except for the fact that they were to be joined by a rather unwelcome addition.

'I *knew* you would be overjoyed!' Ruth cried, grasping Clara in a thrilled embrace. 'Albert has secured us tickets for one of the private boxes – he says that usually one would have to reserve such seats months in advance, but one of his clients changed his plans at the last minute and kindly allowed us to take his place. A private box!' she repeated, her voice a sort of tinny squeal.

'That is kind of him,' Clara replied, giving an uneasy smile. 'But are you quite sure I would be welcome? Perhaps Albert only meant for the two of you to enjoy the evening?'

'Don't be silly!' Ruth laughed. 'He wouldn't have taken them at all but that he knows how much you love going to the theatre. He knows that if you are happy, then I am happy. And that, of course, makes him the happiest man in Christendom.'

Clara knew she was obliged now – to Albert Barnes, of all people. The thought did not swell *her* heart. But at least

Ruth was happier for having delivered the news.

'In that case, I would be happy to accept.' She tried her best to match her friend in terms of enthusiasm.

'We will be watching a performance of *The String of Pearls* at the Drury Lane Theatre Royal,' Ruth said, appropriating the role of the Master of Ceremonies. 'Apparently they have the most magnificent chandelier …'

The String of Pearls was a particularly gruesome melodrama. Clara was rather unconvinced by the newspaper reports which had surfaced at the time of the first performances, claiming that the plot was based on the real crimes of a man named Sweeney Todd, who once had premises on Fleet Street.

She was also beginning to doubt Albert's generosity – his invitation to watch a play about slitting throats could not have been founded on the most admirable of intentions.

The wheels of the carriage clattered noisily against the cobblestones on the way from Broad Street to Drury Lane. Clara had made it quite clear earlier in the day that the transportation wasn't necessary, that she knew the way on foot. But Ruth had insisted; Albert was willing to spare no expense.

Now Clara felt as if she were an intruder: as if Ruth and Albert were a pair of swans drifting down a river, lifelong mates, and she was their lone cygnet, too old to be smothered with attention but too uncertain of the workings of the world to fly off on her own.

Cygnets are also, by comparison to their stunning, elegant parents, rather *grey*. To see Ruth and Albert, their conversation easy and fluid, their faces illuminated with the sparkling energy of their self-belief, Clara could not have thought herself plainer.

William hadn't taken well to her departure. However, he relented a little when he heard who was to be footing the bill for her night's entertainment. Already, Albert Barnes was gaining esteem, and Clara couldn't understand why. The man had connections, that was obvious – but so did every other lawyer in the City. It seemed to be just her damned luck that on having decided she disliked the man, he had not only become ingratiated with her best friend but her brother as well.

'Do you know of the play, Miss Breslin?' he asked.

The sound of his voice rankled her. Earlier attempts at conversation had not been inspiring: 'Evening, Miss Breslin – spot of rain …' and, 'Have you seen Ruth's necklace? Pink diamonds …' Even now she was tempted to limit her reply to a simple affirmative, but she knew from Ruth's wide-eyed expression that she was so hoping the two of them would get along.

'Indeed,' she replied, forcing her eyes to meet his. 'I didn't read the novel, but I hear that Pitt's adaptation contains much more bloodshed and bewailing.'

Albert chuckled softly, and Clara noticed a subtle shadow move across the deep blues of his eyes. He adjusted the lapels on his waistcoat and smoothed down his moustache with a spread of his forefinger and thumb.

'Apparently they are quite the tragic pair. Bit of a grisly end. But don't let it put you off marriage for life, will you, Miss Breslin?'

He laughed throatily, and Ruth's birdlike giggle followed. Clara heard the laughter leave her own throat shortly afterwards but felt its exit rasp her like sandpaper. She could have pretended not to hear him gently stress the word *Miss*. She could have pretended not to notice him lay his hand on Ruth's as he spoke, regarding Clara with the merest hint of superiority that would forever place her below his estimations. But it was her curse to notice every slight detail of the expressions, movements and postures of others. And whilst this gave her an ability to judge the characters of others in ways that many others could not, she knew for certain that her judgements of Albert would *never* inspire her artistically. To her, painting him would bring as much joy and fulfilment as painting one of Sweeney Todd's bloodied corpses.

As they were escorted from the carriage to their private box, Clara craned her neck to study the magnificent, cascading chandelier in the theatre foyer, seeing her red hair reflected in its crystal facets as she passed beneath it and watching the whole structure seemingly burst into flames. It was a stunning sight, as was the box itself. Fitted out in plush scarlet velvet and gold leaf, Clara felt rather out of place sitting on her mock-throne but noticed that Albert and Ruth seemed to take to it well – they even gave small, royalesque waves to some people calling to them from the lower aisles. She remembered her lowly wooden seating in the Adelphi and couldn't bring herself to feel contempt for it.

The play was a rich, dark, bloodthirsty spectacle. The music struck Clara's bones, and the actors were, as promised, absorbing. Fortunately, the chiming chords and anguished screams from the stage were so loud that conversation was rendered nigh impossible.

Despite the gruesome plot and morbid ending, Clara found it easy to immerse herself in the performance. Even a love story as turbulent and deranged as Todd and Lovett's held some fascination for her. The most dangerous minds could find their kindred spirit: was there *no* hope for her?

After the curtain call, Albert spotted one of his business associates in an adjoining box; making his apologies, he promptly left the two women alone, promising to return shortly. Clara looked over at Ruth with a gentle smile but saw that her friend was lost in her own thoughts, looking out across the auditorium at the now vacant stage. Clara had hardly expected to share views on the performance – the skill of the actors or of the staging and lighting – but nor had she expected this. Ruth's expression was clouded; she was obviously immersed in thought.

'I am sure it will be soon. He promised me: "one day". And I can't see how it should have to be much longer.' There was a wispy undercurrent to Ruth's words, like a long, drawn-out sigh.

Clara knew that at moments like these, encouragement was crucial – often less so than honesty. She placed her hand over Ruth's. Eventually, she replied, 'It is plain – for anyone to see – that Albert will do anything he can to please you and provide for you. If his proposal is overdue, do not suffer one more moment of disquiet – he loves you as surely as the sun is in the sky.'

'It is nightfall now, Clara,' Ruth observed. 'We have been courting for a *year* – *and* I have known him for longer besides. You cannot tell me that my worries are unfounded.'

Clara watched her pink diamond necklace shimmer in the reflection of the candlelight – the symbol of Albert's conceited opulence – and found that she held little optimism.

'Dearest Ruth. I am sure you will marry and live in complete happiness for many years.' Clara was only speaking out of hope, even if she believed there to be an uncertainty behind her words; an act of misplaced kindness.

Ruth smiled weakly and did not appear to doubt it herself.

'You must not place the burden of his delayed proposal on your own conscience. It lies with Albert alone. Surely, he will be able to appreciate your desire for reassurance? Talk to him – matters will right themselves. They always do in the end.' Again, Clara held onto the hope.

'You are right. I have tried to broach the subject on previous occasions, and he did explain that—' Here, Ruth paused, as if even she knew that what she was about to say would not hold water. 'It seems a little unreasonable, I know, but he did say that, in his profession, to take a wife at too early a stage in one's career can lose the respect of one's peers. "Too sentimentally-minded: not the correct constitution for one hoping to succeed amongst the cold objectivity of law," he said. I would certainly die of shame if Albert and I were to end up destitute – and it was all my *fault* …' She closed her eyes.

'But that's – that is just …' Clara was baffled by what she'd heard. Her brow furrowed as she turned the words over and over in her mind, trying to validate them. 'The cold objectivity of law' was one thing, but surely it belonged in the workplace alone? Could younger men not separate sentimentality at home from professionalism at work, unlike their more experienced contemporaries? It could hardly be so.

She couldn't think of a reply that would not betray her suspicion and sensed that Ruth was too emotional to say anything more. In the leaden silence that followed, Albert himself returned. He may have been aware of an atmosphere but paid no attention to it.

Ruth's expression remained pensive on the carriage ride home, but Clara's was clear as the cloudless night sky above.

When she arrived home, she would sit in her window seat and watch the muse walk by. And even though their eyes would not meet, she would feel an intense wave of some irrepressible emotion, just at the sight of him. For a split-second, she would be free.

CHAPTER NINE

𝕿he weather seemed unusually fresh. The sun, though no brighter than normal, illuminated Broad Street in an almost clinically clean glow. The windowpanes shone white with their reflections of it. Colours seemed purer, as though bleached, and every time Clara turned towards the vast shop windows she felt a fierce longing to fling open the door and run out into that brightness, those dazzling colours, and let them swallow her.

'Clara.'

She heard her brother's voice and responded without looking at him. She believed that staring at the floor would give her less incentive to think of flight into the street.

'Please will you take some Valerian root from the jar behind you?'

She turned as if under a trance and skimmed her fingertip across the shelf until she reached the 'V' section under Insomnia, Mental Over-Stimulation. In the small glass jar were half a dozen or so small furry brown buds. She picked one out, pinching it between her finger and thumb. To her, it resembled the small head of some goblin-like creature with its hair on end.

'Pestle and mortar,' he said matter-of-factly, which was her cue to find them.

Clara took a brief look at William's customer as she crouched down behind the worktop. She was a young woman of around her own age, around the same height and build, but with a terrible stoop to her back. Her eyes were swollen and bloodshot and she gripped the counter in front of her with one hand to hold herself upright. Clara would have believed her to be straight out of the workhouse, except that she could obviously afford the expense of William's cures. Clearly a woman in need of a sedative.

William ground the root bundle into a fine powder and poured it into a brown paper bag. He held it out to the young lady, who smiled weakly with relief.

'Heap a spoonful of this into hot water, Miss Hawksworth, and drink once of an evening, before bed. In a matter of days, you should find that your sleep improves vastly.'

'Thank you, Mr Breslin,' came her slow, heavy reply. Seeing Clara, she held up the bag to her. 'Thank you also, Miss. My master's brood have a relentless energy that far surpasses my own. I'm sure they would keep the Devil himself awake at night.'

'Imagine looking after children who are not your own, letting them keep you awake at all hours until they make you ill … I would have resigned months ago,' Clara half-whispered once the woman had left, watching the blank space on the threshold that she had occupied.

'It is her living – better that than to be on the street,' William replied simply, adding the coins to the till.

'I don't believe that even *you* would suffer to that extent for money,' she retorted, bemused at her brother's coldness. 'I could never endure such a sorry state of health for the sake of some overactive, spoilt children.'

'Then be glad you are not yet a mother!' William laughed.

Clara could have easily taken offence, but instead she replied, 'You are right, Bill. I am in no way fit for motherhood. I can't even find a husband.'

'Now, now, Clara, don't be melancholic. I was only speaking in jest.' William hated to think he was goading Clara in the same way that their parents did.

'Better that than to talk about my art, surely?' Clara countered, with a mischievous smile.

'Perhaps, perhaps.' William was smiling in a wistful way. 'But, you know, I don't find your art all *that* terribly irritating.'

'Well that *is* a first!' Clara laughed. 'Are you beginning to tolerate my fanatical behaviour?'

'I will always believe that art is a complete waste of thought and energy. But it brings you happiness. I cannot say I have seen you in better spirits than when you are sitting before a canvas.'

'You never watch me paint,' Clara said simply, though her smile was bright and affectionate. She rarely stopped to consider how fortunate she was, that William tolerated her total absorption in a pastime he detested. At the same time, it was hardly her fault that her talent lay in such a field, and that he had been destined for a different career.

'It may have been many years ago, but I used to watch you occasionally. I remember: at six years old you were *insistent* on catching butterflies in the garden to paint. You used to send me after them with Father's old fishing net. Do you remember?'

Clara laughed and stated that yes, she did. She also remembered that William used to keep some of the butterflies in jars and, when they died, would pin them to his desk and study their anatomy from one of his journals.

'I haven't been of great help to you recently. I thank you for your patience, Bill.' It wasn't an effort for her to say it, but she rarely demonstrated such gratitude.

'There's no need to thank me,' he replied, but there was added warmth in his voice that had not been there before. 'I have hardly noticed any more distraction on your part than I am usually accustomed to.' The tone of his voice changed slightly, and Clara felt the hairs on her arms prickle for no apparent reason. 'Besides, it is only to be expected … in circumstances such as these.'

'Circumstances …?' Clara questioned, tilting her head slightly. 'And what might those be?'

'Well,' William started, a wry smile creeping across his lips, 'I can hardly expect your mind to be on your work when your fortunes have begun to take a turn for the better.'

Clara meant to speak but could not find the words. She was puzzled. How could William know of her successes in painting if he had not watched her paint for years?

'I cannot imagine what you mean,' she said curtly, folding her arms across her chest.

'No need to be so evasive,' William continued, his smile broadening. Clara saw something of the conspirator in the way he approached her. 'You told me weeks ago, but I didn't believe you immediately. You said – do you recall? – "What has got into me? *Him*." I understand you perfectly now.'

Clara's expression was incredulous. She could not believe her brother capable of such thoughts. He was behaving like a gossiping schoolboy.

'He's not the same as all the others, is he? You've been painting him for days on end: that is normal. But I don't think I've ever seen you behave like this over a … what do you call them?'

'Muse,' she replied. Her tone was sullen.

'That's it. He's no normal "muse". You rush up to your room every night, waiting for him to walk past, don't you? And every morning: you told me he passes then, too.

'Is that why you haven't talked with me properly for days? You spend your working hours counting down the minutes until you see him again?'

'He walks past our shop *twice a day*. I can't help it if that makes him the perfect subject for study.'

'But surely – if he passes the shop so often, you *must* have been studying him for long enough to create a suitable painting? I can't see how you would need to watch him so often – unless …'

'You couldn't *possibly* know. It takes *weeks and weeks* to create a work of true art – but you wouldn't appreciate that. You don't *paint*, Bill. You *hate* art! Why should you even CARE?' Her anger boiled before she was even aware of its existence. Its sudden upsurge shocked her, and she was self-conscious in its wake. She hadn't realised that she could be so easily riled by such a trivial matter.

William's voice remained perfectly level. 'I didn't mean to offend, I just thought – you know, since you find him so inspiring – that perhaps you had planned to make the acquaintance—'

'It shouldn't interest you at all, unless you are beginning to agree with our parents and think that the sooner I set my eyes on a man – any man in the *street* – the better.'

'That is unfair, Clara,' William replied. 'You know it is of no consequence to me who you marry, or when, or *if*.' He half-turned away and began straightening some jars on shelves. 'I should never have spoken,' he muttered, glancing at her from the corner of his eye. 'I just want to see you settled here. And whether you like it or not – I *do* take an interest. I am your brother, after all.' He looked at her fully then, and gave a lopsided smile.

Clara sighed deeply and leant back against the counter, her fingertips slowly massaging her eyelids. 'I appreciate your consideration, I really do.' She thought for a moment, her eyes downcast. 'I can't say I have ever really displayed the same level of consideration for *you*, for this business. Perhaps, if we understood each other a little better, we would avoid these arguments altogether.' She looked over at William, giving a little shrug of her mouth.

'Yes – but how on earth would we find another way to amuse ourselves?' he replied, with a roguish grin.

The afternoon passed lazily, and it became apparent that there would be no more custom. The weather, whilst tempting Clara to distraction, was also perfect for any Londoners wishing to stroll outside. The air was so fresh that even the breeze that drifted gently in through the door of the Apothecary made Clara light-headed.

Perhaps it was having a similar effect on William. He made a decision that Clara could not have anticipated.

'We should close the shop early today,' he announced, slamming the till closed with a metallic clang after having just counted up the day's profits.

'We made so much money yesterday that I hardly see the need to stay open. And anyway – look at you. You've been staring longingly at that door for hours.' He raised his eyebrows at Clara, though not in reproach. 'Go on, go and walk outside – the fresh air will do wonders for that temper of yours,' he joked. 'I myself will pay a visit to the gentlemen at Squires', buy myself a mid-afternoon drink.'

'Hmm … I would hope there might be some cure for that impertinence of *yours* – but I fear that the drink will only make it worse.' She removed her apron and stepped forward to take a small handful of coins that William was holding out to her.

Clara watched William's figure slowly melt into the dense white light and felt a tremor of anticipation which spread through the entirety of her body. Finally, she would be able to feel the soft caress of the breeze, let the pure, vivid glow fill her lungs, and breathe colour. She rushed upstairs to collect her cloak, taking the rickety wooden steps two at a time.

The familiar creak of her bedroom door seemed to have a cheery crescendo this day, and the countless papers lining her walls glimmered with coloured shapes cast by reflections from the window, making even the uncoloured images dance and earn life. She spun lightly on the spot, taking in the new images of the muse that were nestled amongst her older pieces – pieces which had now paled in comparison – and felt a rush of delight at the sight of each one. She nodded at each in turn, as if greeting the muse himself, as if his very essence were embedded in pages. Then she took up a taupe-coloured cloak, which had been strewn in a crumpled heap across the end of her divan, and wound it about her shoulders. She took a deep breath and walked towards her window seat, treating herself to one last glimpse of that sun-drenched view before she would be able to enclose herself within its fibres …

'It – can't be …'

He blended so perfectly with the intense scene before her that she believed he had been painted onto it. *Her muse,* ablaze with colour, stood in the middle of the street. Not moving. His stance firmly set; his chin lifted slightly; his eyes – *those eyes* – half-closed, focused on the sky. Was he waiting for something? Watching? Listening?

His presence was much more striking to her, here and now, at this unusual hour. He was breaking the rules. He was not supposed to pass the window for several hours. Rather than be perturbed, the abruptness of his arrival thrilled Clara beyond all reasonable measure. She *had* to paint him. Of that, she was certain. She could not risk waiting and having him leave – having him break such a perfect stance.

She moved swiftly to the left of her window, and with an elaborate motion unfurled a large canvas propped upon an easel. It had been covered with a light cotton sheet to protect the fresh paint from sun-bleaching. But now, looking upon it, she realised that the present colours would not serve her purpose in any case. They were in no way bright enough to do justice to the living figure before her eyes. It was as if he embodied all shades, tones, lights, darks – with a lucidity that was not of the earth.

She hastily mixed a palette of basic oils: browns, fawns, muted pinks – and the colours of his clothes: deep scarlet trousers and a cream shirt. The green of the eyes, she had not the courage to attempt. Not yet. But she began to paint nonetheless, making improvements to a portrait she had begun to sketch only the night previous: her First Full Portrait of the Muse, a considerable milestone. She had begun to fill out the base colours to a reasonable standard – but today, the light was so dazzling that she could not fail to produce the perfect palette.

Paint smeared her arms, her clothes, her hair – but she was unconscious of it. The world around her ceased to exist but to contain the muse and the scratching of her paintbrush.

She looked up from the evolving image to take another glimpse of the man below – with each separate glance, her eyes drank him up and added a further layer of detail to the photographic image in her head.

But when she looked again, he had gone.

'*No – not now!*'

She dropped her paintbrush and dashed to the window, placing her palms on the window seat and leaning into the recess to scan the street for him. She saw that he had starting to move away, down the road. Making a strangled cry of annoyance, she pounded her fists against the wooden surface, despairing at a lost opportunity.

However, his departure was not a hasty one. He looked into each shop window he passed, perusing their contents, and stopped in his tracks to gaze at the sky, hands clasped behind his back, elbows angularly poised. Such a change to see him take a pace of leisure, no longer adrift on a tide of commotion ...

She wasn't sure what took a hold of her then.

Perhaps Ruth, in her own idealistic way, had been closer to the truth than Clara's pride would allow. Even her brother, inarticulate as he was, had begun to formulate the notion – one which Clara herself was not yet ready to comprehend.

Whatever the cause, Clara suddenly and overwhelmingly felt that she should find out where her muse was going.

She felt no fear – in breaching this most sacred of self-imposed rules, of bridging the invisible barrier that gave her muses their privacy and kept them free from identity.

Maybe there *was* some kind of weakness emerging on Clara's part; maybe because a warmth in her was beginning to wake to him, with the jagged uneasiness of an emotion long unused. If so, she felt it of little consequence. Any kind of sentiment she felt for this man would never lead her to sacrifice her art, to ignore his merit as a muse.

She wanted to follow him. And she did not have to explain anything to herself.

She bundled up her things hastily, not taking time to wash the paint from her arms or clothing.

She opened the shop door with a brash rattling of the bell, locked it behind her, and dashed off down the right-hand fork of the road. The muse was now barely a smeared grey blur in the distance, but she knew it was him, kept him in her sight, kept her pace regulated so that he would not hear her footsteps clattering the cobbles.

She did not realise, as she stepped out into the street: the bright, livid colours had engulfed her whole. And she hadn't felt a thing.

'HER MUSE, ABLAZE
WITH COLOUR, STOOD
IN THE MIDDLE OF THE
STREET. NOT MOVING.'

CHAPTER TEN

Clara was as weak and light-headed as a sufferer of vertigo. Her heart wouldn't stop knocking frenetically against her chest. A tight vice of apprehension seized her stomach. Clearly, the art of espionage was not one of her strengths.

Her worries were, of course, unfounded. If he saw her following, he would be unlikely to perceive anything untoward in her behaviour. For all of Clara's immediate relevance to him, she may as well have not existed.

But this reasoning did not ease her fretfulness.

Her apprehension only eased significantly once her focus had shifted to studying his movements. Her muse's demeanour had something peculiarly engaging about it. Perhaps it was the way his head sat so solidly atop his broad shoulders, in a way that suggested he was not carrying it at all, more that his body was some superfluous matter that floated beneath it; or perhaps it was the way that the shoulders, in their turn, rolled loosely with each swing of his body as it propelled forward. In fact, his entire body moved with an effortlessness that was almost eerie; it seemed that nothing would deter him from his chosen path, that the world around him resembled nought but shapes and shadows – obstacles to his sense of purpose to be negotiated or ignored.

Clara's steps became more deliberate, more considered. She was entering unknown territory. The her buildings on either side of her, whilst daunting before, were even more intimidating now that she didn't recognise them. Street signs lost all meaning and semblance of order because the places they denoted did not spark a single memory. Though her mind was ever-engaged in following her muse, she found that she was still able to take in notable landmarks from the changing scene around her – her subconscious taking precautions should she struggle to find her way back. Rationality was a constant whispering to her. Of the two sides of her brain – the creative and the logical – neither one gained precedence, and neither one would be disregarded. Her hunger for art was leading her into dangerous territory, and her intellect would not let her forget it.

She began to realise that, as her muse moved further and further away from the Apothecary, his pauses became less frequent and his movements became swifter. She found her own steps had become more hurried, but she dared not hasten too much. As a result, she allowed herself brief bursts of speed, followed by periods of brisk walking and moments when she halted altogether, mainly for the purpose of trying to establish her location. But this was proving all the more difficult, and harrowing. The streets were huddling closer together, the facades of the buildings growing darker, and the stale reek of age-old soot began to coagulate in her throat. Even her method of remembering landmarks was beginning to falter. Much as if someone had daubed a thick, oily wash over the surface of the world, everything around her began to merge together, to congeal into a monochromatic blur which she could not decipher even if she tried. The one variable was muse. He alone shone out against this mediocrity. He kept her anchored in her own reality, saved her from drowning in the obscurity of this unknown place.

She had her first severe attack of doubt when he slipped from the main trajectory of cobbled roads. With that haunting fluidity, he slipped into a narrow side alley. Basic instinct shot through her like fire through dried hay. This was not a safe place.

She knew all too well the City's unpleasant face, the alter ego that most pretended was an exaggeration. Only by personal experience or hearsay would one learn that after dark only a blade, a pistol or a well-calloused fist would stand between a lone traveller and any number of unspeakable evils. Even by day there was an unwritten code, declaring those places which were socially considered 'safe' and those which were considered otherwise. Clara was an independent soul, a confident city traveller – but even she was not reckless enough to enter a dark alley unaccompanied without some degree of forethought.

She waited at the entrance for several seconds, calculating the risks in her mind – they were certainly numerous, and were unlikely to diminish as the route unfolded. But her curiosity at that moment knew no bounds – rationality was not strong enough within her to quell the fire that ignited her imagination. She took a quick look around her, inhaled sharply, and plunged into the darkness after her muse.

She was rendered temporarily blind as she stepped into alley. She would readily have believed, in the all-consuming darkness, that the skies above her and the world around her had ceased to exist but for a postage stamp's worth of light coming from the far end of the passage which, in its frailty, provided little comfort. She relied on her fingertips to judge her distance from the walls on either side, each footfall inciting a panic, a fear of tumbling into the abyss. The hairs on her forearms stood upright. She realised that not a single breath of wind escaped down this narrow trail, and her breathing became shallower. She saw no looming shapes in the darkness, no hunched silhouettes waiting to reach out for her – but the sensation of a morbid intimacy, too stifling to bear, was on her, all around her, seeping into her skin. She believed she would stumble; she believed she would never find the daylight again …

Her muse had long since left the dark passageway. Once Clara's groundless fear had reached its summit and liberated her, she began to remember her objective. When she emerged at the other side, she was sure that catching him up again would require a deal of guesswork. A sickness that she may have lost her opportunity seized her … and the deep, instinctual terror of having lost her way and not knowing how she would return to safety and familiarity.

The bright sunlight that greeted her as she stepped forward sent a pulse of shock through her body, so that her anxieties became almost trivial. She had momentarily forgotten how dazzling the world was today. As if nature's colour palette had been intensified beyond the constraints of mere imagination … She stood quite still, in spite of her hurry, allowing the luminosity to bathe her skin.

Clara felt a renewed sense of purpose. She searched

the growing multitude of people for her muse, and after period of fraught uncertainty, saw his form becoming slowly engulfed by crowds. She darted swiftly after him, weaving through the masses of shunting bodies around her, letting nothing prove too big an obstacle to her and her cause.

It took a moment to realise that this was not just any street. As with any place of a distinctive character or illustrious reputation, Clara knew where she was without having ever visited this part of the City before. The scent in the air – or rather, the stench – was the first indication. Pungent enough to make the eyes water, it quickly soured her romanticism. London was hardly the most fragrant of cities, but here ... it was almost as if the sewer had never been invented. And it might as well not have, for all its efficiency in containing waste.

Covering her nose, Clara realised that the onslaught of unsanitary fumes and unsanitary substances was just the beginning. Buildings here were huddled up so closely that it was a wonder they had not done so of their own accord. Whilst there was enough space for walkers to stand two or three people abreast, the upper floors of the buildings sloped inwards, to the extent that sunlight from above was virtually blocked and people in upper rooms could climb into neighbours' bedrooms on the other side of the street if they so wished. Many of the shop premises had been boarded at the windows to prevent theft. In some cases, only the empty carcass of a building stood between its residents and the elements – besides the rags used for curtains.

Clara refused herself permission to look too closely

at the wretched citizens of this place. Whilst their plight was obvious and deserved her sympathy, she also knew that, being able to do nothing to help them, she should not be permitted to gawp at them like a tourist, to make their plight a point of fascination. To meet their eyes was to admit knowledge of her own powerlessness, and they had suffered too much to deserve such an insult. Besides, it did not take prolonged observation to take full measure of the lives these people endured. Many sat in the streets, wrapped in worn wool blankets, their heads drooped wearily onto their chests. They were not begging, and they were not without a home. Clara suspected they were simply waiting, spectators to the passage of time. Awaiting the time when money, food, shelter and work would no longer be of importance, be rendered meaningless. They were waiting for the blessed release of death.

The tiny network of alleyways spread into a vast, bustling hub, and she could not help but quicken her steps in the sheer relief of leaving behind the despair of quiet affliction and resigned destitution. Shoreditch High Street, by comparison, seemed a reassurance – though it was quite the opposite.

She had been instructed to never set foot in this part of the City; William had expressly warned her against it. During daylight hours, it could not be said to harbour the same dangers as became prolific after dark – but even now, glancing fearfully into the shadowed spaces in her peripheral vision, Clara could well imagine the extent to which evil had a free rein here. By comparison, the stale darkness of the

Apothecary store room seemed entirely insignificant.

Her muse had come to his journey's end. Clara came to a halt a few yards away from him and wrapped her arms about her waist, reassuring herself that her act of impulse would produce favourable results. She couldn't say what had compelled her, but perhaps she could discover what his profession was, who his acquaintances were, where he lived.

Unusual that no one had seemed to recognise him – even now, in familiar surroundings. She saw other men greet each other with small tips of the hat or by shaking hands. Her muse acknowledged no one. He stood, motionless as a statue, and let the world's frivolities transpire around him.

Then, remotely, came a low tolling: the tower bell of St. Leonard's. Clara had no time to count the tolls because as soon as the first peal had rung out, her muse began to move off again. She didn't have to exert herself to follow him; he had only taken half a dozen steps before she realised where he had been travelling to.

The building, like so much in this neglected place, was recognisable to Clara by reputation alone.

The Grecian Theatre. Not one of London's most renowned – but who could expect otherwise? Its productions of Shakespeare had not been favourably received. Clara had even heard of its actors being rained down on by various articles of rotting vegetation after a disastrous performance of *Hamlet*.

Seeing her muse head towards one of the side doors, to be greeted and slapped on the back by a similarly dressed man in full stage makeup, Clara began to have concerns for his personal safety. But she couldn't contain her exhilaration; the urgency to reach his destination on time, the extravagant dress, his exotic appearance – an actor. Of course! And in a matter of minutes, he would take the stage for the afternoon performance.

She had no choice. Though she ran the risk of shattering the illusion of perfection forever, Clara had to see him perform.

On approaching the theatre, she was reminded greatly of the facade of the Adelphi. Quite obviously, both of these properties shared a common homage to the temples and amphitheatres of Ancient Greece. But it was plain to see that the opulence and affluence of the Strand had not spread to this parish of Shoreditch. The mock-pillars were flaking, with roughly hewn wood protruding like a rash from beneath imitation gold leaf, and the roof was missing several of its slates.

Clara took in a breath and resigned herself to her impulsive decision.

Stepping cautiously inside the foyer, she nodded politely to the other patrons that she passed. Although there was nothing supercilious in her manner and her dress was plain, she was greeted with blank, almost uncomprehending stares. These people were clearly mystified to see even a person of Clara's modest background at their ramshackle backstreet theatre. As she approached the auditorium, some of the waiting theatre employees began to crowd around her, bowing and curtseying shyly, asking madam what her business might be at the Grecian today and whether she might be looking to support the place with some funds of her own? They were speaking of shutting the place down – did she know? – and without a theatre to provide them with work, there would be little opportunity left for them to earn the money needed to support their families …

'Let me take you to your seat, madam,' a tall gentleman – one of the ushers – offered, guiding her away from the amassing host with a careful hand to her arm.

Clara turned with a smile of gratitude towards her saviour as they walked but felt a need to decline his help. 'Oh, it's quite alright, I can find – and please, no "madam"s are necessary. My name is—'

'Best not pay too much attention to their pleading, madam,' the usher continued, as if he hadn't heard. 'They've only found out this week that their manager has hit some … financial troubles.'

Clara took the seat he had found for her and glanced up at him, hands fretting at her paint-mottled skirts. 'That is terrible news,' she said, sincerely. 'If there is anything I can do … I would hate to think that a theatre closed for good and I had done nothing to help—'

'As I said, madam, take no heed. Sit through our performance, if you can. You will see why the Grecian Theatre does not deserve help.' The usher gave a shallow bow and took his leave. There had not been a hint of derision in his voice.

This gave Clara cause for concern. If the theatre's own employees were not ashamed to speak so scathingly of its performances, what hope – if any – could she hold for the success of her muse as an actor?

There were no raised balconies or boxes in the Grecian, so Clara had been seated at the back of the auditorium with only a moderate view of the stage. She soon realised, however, why the usher had gone out of his way to seat her there. The throng of bodies that assembled near the front had no seats and jostled each other constantly for a comfortable amount of room to stand. Bottles were waved in the air, spilling their contents on unsuspecting heads, and the jeers of the crowd were likely to be heard beyond the outer theatre doors. Clara wondered how she would ever hear the actors speaking.

It was then that the curtain rose, and she realised that she didn't even know which play was to be performed.

An actor stepped out onto the boards. It wasn't her muse.

> Nay, but this dotage of our general's
> O'erflows the measure: those his goodly eyes,
> That o'er the files and musters of the war
> Have glow'd like plated Mars ...

Philo: the first to speak in *Antony and Cleopatra*. Clara felt a muddy churning in the pit of her stomach. A tragic tale of the heart's foolish endeavours: the premise of the play repelled her from the outset. Sitting through a performance would expose Clara's deepest insecurities. She held within her a constant fear of searching for love only to be ultimately disappointed – or worse, completely destroyed.

She knew what to expect from the narrative yet to unfold. Antony and Cleopatra were the Roman and the Egyptian, doomed by their fatal love. She seemed to know, even before he walked onstage, that her muse would be playing Antony.

'If it be love indeed, tell me how much,' the Egyptian queen purred melodically, pursing her deep red lips.

'There's beggary in the love that can be reckoned.'

The sound of the man's voice caused a deep convulsion to course through Clara's body.

Cleopatra's role could have been played a seamstress' mannequin for all that she actually mattered, and Clara barely noticed her. Though she was dressed gaudily in eye-catching faux gold and imitation ivory silk, she acted merely as a sounding board for the all-encompassing presence of Antony.

The voice matched the persona entirely: deep and rich, with a smooth Mediterranean accent. His stance was confident, poised – even the slight inclination of his chin suggested a man of high birth. And his eyes. That effervescent green, somewhat dulled by the weak gaslights, but just as entrancing from across the auditorium as the day she had first seen them, looked into them …

His costume was atrocious, but that couldn't be helped. It was little more than embellished sacking-material fashioned into a form of robe that draped over one shoulder and was tied at the waist with a belt. Clara narrowed her eyes to study the way he moved in it; despite the obvious discomfort of the garment, he wore it with ease. Clara could imagine that most would be fooled into believing that he was attired in the highest quality cloth.

He delivered his lines without difficulty. It was as if he had become the man, and that the two of them were indistinguishable. Clara began to forget who or what he had been to her before, willing only to concentrate fully on the persona he had stepped into.

She settled somewhat into her seat, reassured that she would be able to see the play to an end without distress. The worst shock was over. Her muse wasn't a part of the most prestigious theatre company in London, nor was he acting against the most talented in the craft. But the usher had played him down, that was clear.

In fact, the more Clara studied him, the more she found herself becoming entranced. It was a gentle dulling of the senses, at first. Her eyes felt a little heavy, her breathing slowed, and her posture began to lose its usual rigidity. Soon, however, her condition escalated, and she could not draw her eyes away from Antony; whenever he walked onstage she found herself captivated. All other movements, sounds, and scents around her became unimportant, unnoticeable. The auditorium around her became an insignificant blur of lights and colours, and all that existed was the stage, and Antony. She knew she was falling into a deep reverie but could do nothing to stop it. Even the beating of her heart seemed to create an unnecessary distraction, and Clara would have happily had it stop altogether in order that her concentration could be at its height.

The play reached its climactic scenes. Tears welled

in Clara's eyes and her chest was seized with a tremor of emotion.

Antony was dying. She couldn't bring herself to believe that her emotional investment would soon amount to nothing.

> The miserable change now at my end
> Lament nor sorrow at; but please your thoughts
> In feeding them with those my former fortunes
> Wherein I lived, the greatest prince o' the world …

The queen wept over him; Clara knew her sorrow to be worse. For she had stepped into Antony's world, more than this painted charlatan who claimed to be his only love. His final words had been so wrought with sorrow yet so desperately optimistic, even in the face of death. Clara had never encountered such a man and wondered why such heroes were destined only to exist in the minds of playwrights.

And that was how Clara found herself grounded once again in the living world: in the knowledge that her real experiences would continue to be a disappointment to her, whilst on an illuminated stage lay the key to all her dreams and deepest fears.

Cleopatra's death passed with much less feeling, on Clara's part. The conclusion of the play, which would once have been its greatest triumph to her, diminished into nothing in her mind.

She felt drained from her core, as if her blood had been transfused whilst her attention was fixed on the stage. Never could she remember having been affected in such a way by a performance. It was a sensation she couldn't feasibly explain.

Her muse hadn't returned to the stage, had not been present for the customary curtain call. Neither had the rest of the troupe. It took just a few moments for Clara to realise the reason for such impromptu behaviour.

This was the wrong audience. It was quite understandable; the setting in which they had been expected to engage with the performance was not the most awe-inspiring, and even Clara could not envisage enjoying a play had she had to stand for hours on end without refreshment. But she couldn't quite comprehend how anyone could witness the same brilliance she had and not be affected in the slightest degree.

People had risen to leave as soon as the curtain had fallen, bustling noisily around her to be the first to break out into the cool dusk. Clara's brow furrowed wistfully as she watched them pass, heard their jeering taunts and their cold dismissal of the marvel they had just witnessed. She couldn't understand how their opinions could differ so greatly to her own. But there it was.

Clara decided not to let these slurs taint the lasting impression of her own enriching experience. She narrowed her thoughts into focus around a small spark of pleasure: that of having seen her muse act upon the stage and having been further encouraged by it.

She stepped into the busy aisle, buoyant with the triumph of discovering unrecognised talent, and felt deep within her that her life was now to drastically alter for the better.

Reaching the double doors which opened onto the foyer, she recognised a familiar face: the usher who had shown her to her seat. He caught her eye and smiled – with what could only be described as an apologetic air – and this compelled Clara to approach him with a query.

'Excuse me, Mr ...'

'Thwaites. I hope you do not feel that your journey was a wasted one.' He had seemed to brace himself for a complaint, the pessimism evident in his tone.

'Not *at all*, Mr Thwaites – though I regret that I may be the alone in such an opinion.' She offered the man an understanding smile.

Thwaites raised one eyebrow, and his demeanour seemed to shift into the positive slightly. He conceded her opinion with a curt nod. 'Unfortunately for us, madam, you're right.' He shrugged slightly. 'And now you see why we find ourselves in financial difficulty. If only all our patrons were as enthusiastic as yourself ...' He trailed off, taking care not to be in breach of propriety, and averted his gaze from hers.

'It is such a shame. I already feel that this theatre will become close to my heart.

'I must know, Mr Thwaites: what is the name of the man who played the title part tonight? His performance astounded me, to say the least.'

Thwaites inclined his head slightly; his eyes narrowed

just a fraction. Clara could not detect the emotion he was masking with the tone of his voice as he answered, 'He is Matthias Tarasso, madam.'

CHAPTER ELEVEN

*T*he name drifted restlessly in the dark hollow of Clara's mind, long into the hours following its first utterance. It assaulted her unexpectedly, with no concern over the time of day or night, repeating itself in muted tones. Even when she was preoccupied with other things, she knew it was speaking to her: *Matthias Tarasso, Matthias Tarasso, Matthias ...*

When she couldn't stand its incessant whispering any longer, she began to say the name aloud. She played with the enunciation; let the sounds roll over her tongue, establishing a feel for the name. She felt that it linked the two of them on a more personal level, and this had an influence over the intimacy of her paintings. They were bound by some incomprehensible accident in time: a coinciding of two parallel lives. Of course, Matthias was still travelling along his own path, unaware of his vital importance to a woman he had never met.

Clara could not guess the man's ancestry, but it was obvious that the muse's name did not originate from British shores. The two simple words gave no other clue to his identity. But her stomach surged with a comfortable fondness and warmth whenever she was reminded of the moment she had learnt the name. It was as if she had achieved something pronounced, something that would contribute greatly towards some indiscernible end goal. She felt the same when remembering the afternoon she had first seen *him* perform.

Her journey back to the Apothecary after this first performance had not been an easy one. She had forgotten most of the memorable landmarks she had passed on the way to the theatre, and the vivid sunlight had begun to grow dull. She ought to have panicked, but her thoughts were light and free; there was nothing within her but a heady elation. The labyrinth of cobbled Shoreditch streets was a mere obstacle, easily overcome once she was safely within a hansom. Lulled by the rhythmic pulse of horses' hooves against stone, the drive back to Broad Street passed without further incident.

Upon arriving home, she had begun painting again immediately, with an inexhaustible zeal.

This artistic fervour continued for days on end. Her brother saw nothing of her for stretches of many hours. She would steal upstairs whenever there was a lull in custom in the shop and would re-emerge sometimes half a day later, skin, hair and clothes streaked with paint.

William said nothing – but he knew what had gripped her mind and saw no need to draw attention to it. If ever he ventured upstairs, he could hear the incessant scrit-scratching of her paintbrush, like the sound of a rat scrabbling about under the floorboards. He would steal a glance at her through the chink of daylight left by her open bedroom door and see her almost pressed against her easel, surrounded by a patchwork of discarded sheets of paper, pots of paint, frayed brushes and jars of colour-clouded water. Her every muscle would be tense with the effort of concentration, her focus so close that her nose almost touched the canvas.

After a few days of the same behaviour, he began

to lose curiosity and soon did not spare a thought for the obsessive processes of his sister's painting. For all he knew, her interest in the man had never extended beyond the boundary of her windowpanes.

In Clara's mind, everything seemed so much simpler now. She could render Matthias on canvas in any possible way she saw fit, now that she had seen him onstage.

Her brother was uninterested in her art but concerned for her welfare. She wasn't eating properly, barely sustaining herself with portions fit for a child. As long as her meals were small enough to hold in her hand and could be eaten without leaving her easel, she was content. This meant that she was acquiring a lean, almost gaunt look about her, and was beginning to complain about the lack of warmth in the shop, even when the sun streamed in through the windowpanes. Her wrist bones began to protrude outwards in shining lumps as her hand made its inevitable trail across the canvas.

He could also tell by her red-rimmed eyes that she was hardly sleeping; she had an infamously short temper in the mornings and suffered prolonged lapses in concentration. She would also wake in the middle of the night and pace the length and breadth of the building. He was often disturbed in his sleep by the sounds of the old floorboards creaking.

William wondered if all spirits were sleepwalkers in their former lives. The silhouette of his sister would have made a most compelling spectre, as she paced through the dull twilight.

Any evening Clara could spare was now spent within the dampening walls of the Grecian.

Matthias was always performing, whenever Clara had the opportunity to visit, and usually played a leading role. Clara could never find fault with his competence as an actor. He took to each role with aplomb, immersing himself in a character with such ease that it seemed he had spent his whole life practising for that part.

Each remarkable performance had a positive effect over her painting. Her first portrait of Matthias had been completed shortly after his performance as Antony. Each work seemed to be a slight improvement on the last until it seemed that most of her painting was done from instinct alone and only the finest details required her full concentration.

It was in the shop, in the anticipation of another one of Clara's infamous disappearances upstairs, that William finally decided to voice his concerns. He watched her from across the room, knowing the rush of customers that had just subsided hailed a prolonged period of quiet. As soon as the shop bell had rung out the last departure, he saw her face become soft and closed, a sense of calm radiating from her. He knew that she was planning to go to her room, and watched with a crooked smile as she smoothed her hands on her apron and moved them to the ties at the back …

'Clara,' he said softly, taking a half-step in her direction. His hand reached out as if to stop her – he placed it self-consciously on the countertop.

She stopped, her eyes moving to his face. 'Yes?' She was trying to remain calm, he could tell. She would only tolerate his conversation for so long before her irritation would begin to show.

'I …' His mind worked, searching for the ideal excuse. 'Did you check the stock levels for toothache cures?'

The slightest narrowing of her eyes. William wondered if she could sense his deception with the same increasing ease that he could read her emotions with.

Clara answered no and went to count the jars, her movements tentative. She paused as she passed William and he held onto a breath, hoping she would tell him all he wanted to know without him asking. It would save him some great difficulty.

She didn't. Her silence was as troubling as it was infuriating.

'There is plenty here: at least a dozen bottles of peppermint oil,' she replied. 'In fact, I seem to remember you replenishing these shelves only yesterday.'

'Yes? Well, my memory tends to slip during these busy periods,' he countered, with an uneasy burst of laughter.

'So it would seem. Perhaps it is fortunate that the place is quiet again, in that case.'

'Indeed.' He turned fully to look at her, sensing the correct moment had come. 'I suppose you will be taking your leave for several hours, now that an opportunity has presented itself?'

'I'd not yet thought of it, but yes, I suppose I shall.'

She gave a bright, almost over-indulgent smile and moved away from him, towards the stairs. 'That is, of course, if you do not object?'

'I do not,' he replied, though his tone was a little too heavy, betraying his thoughts to the contrary. 'However, I do feel the need to ask a question.'

Clara turned, another smile replacing the former. What was it? Triumph? Acceptance? Or a mask? 'And what might that be?'

'As it is quite obvious that you now mean to concern yourself with further painting, I would like to know who your subject is? Who is claiming such vast amounts of your time?'

'*Who?*' Clara's tone was all innocence, though her eyes glimmered darkly.

'*Of course ...*' William hesitated, forcing the irritation from his voice. 'Of course it is a "who". And I suspect who it is, much as I hoped you would have tired of that particular fixation, in your usual way.'

Clara's lips tightened and became pale. William knew he was close to the truth and was cautious of it.

She used her forefinger to trace small invisible circles on the countertop, consciously avoiding his eye. 'I wonder then: *why* are you wasting your energy in asking me, when it seems more than clear that you have outwitted your absent-minded sister once again?' Her tone was sharp and exasperated rather than petulant. Eventually, she felt calm enough to look at him again. 'Since you are already aware that I am going upstairs to continue my portrait of Matthias, I wonder why you have chosen to draw attention to it with your question, using my answer to form a spiteful attack on my most beloved pastime?'

Matthias. This one word took away the biting sting of her retort. William hadn't realised that she had discovered the man's name and it brought his concerns whirling to the forefront of his mind. A name implies familiarity, and Clara had never been familiar with her artistic subjects before. What more did she know about him?

He didn't dare raise any further questions, being aware of his sister's mood. Instead, he turned away from her and maintained a gentle patience in his tone of voice. 'Clara, please. Don't be sharp with me. I wasn't intending to "attack" you, and you can't chastise me too harshly for my curiosity. After all, it is true that your time spent painting should actually be your time spent here, behind these counters. I allow you your distractions without argument and can't see any harm in wishing to know about the subject of your artwork.'

He heard a muffled thud and knew that Clara had probably hit the countertop in her frustration. He didn't look in her direction, even when she spoke in constricted tones.

'I'm going upstairs.'

'No – Clara—'

'I'm *going upstairs*, Bill.' She whirled round on one foot to face him, her face set like fired clay. 'You *know* me. You know what I do. Who I am is your sister. And what I do, all I ever want to do with my average lot in life, is paint.' Her voice cracked slightly, betraying a coil of emotion long-time suppressed. 'Since you find the pursuit of beauty in art a complete waste of otherwise financially profitable time,

I can't see why you should take such pains to question me about it.'

'I take the pains because you are my family. Because, as you say yourself, you are my sister – my only sister – and I care about you.'

But Clara had already disappeared.

The questions would cease, but one feeling remained, fostered in William's uneasy heart. It was the slowly spreading smear of resentment, and its focus was a name, a name without a face. William was beginning to harbour dislike for Matthias, a man he had never met and never seen. Nevertheless, the emotion was surprisingly potent.

Once in her room, Clara was too angry to paint and wasted the next hour in frustrated silence, feeling that she had handled the argument badly. She could have done more to communicate the strength of her feeling towards Matthias. Instead, she had shied away and left William's insults unchallenged. She stared glumly out of her window from her usual position in the alcove, almost willing Matthias to walk by so that she could forget her feelings.

But he wouldn't come yet. She'd learnt that he would only travel down Broad Street in the evening, when theatres had closed for the day. She also knew that his morning walks in the opposite direction were taking him to the Grecian for daily rehearsals. If she peered hard enough, she could sometimes see him reciting lines under his breath. At least, that is what she assumed he was doing. Constant rehearsal would explain his flawless performances.

After a long while, Clara was jolted into alertness

by the clanging of the shop bell. Her thoughts of Matthias always seemed to draw her out of herself, to another place. Sometimes it was a place beyond the real, a completely new realm of existence, where the world was defined by her and no one else. It was a place of overwhelming freedom and tranquillity. She often felt nauseous with the disappointment of having to return, inevitably, to reality. She had not chosen to admit herself into such a regimented order and way of living, but she had to accept it, reluctantly, despite her longing for rebellion.

The shout rang in Clara's skull as she hurried downstairs: in the midst of her thoughts, she'd only just heard William calling her.

Brushing her way through the thick drapery and putting most of her emotional effort into a show of indifference, she was confronted with the sight of Ruth, smiling radiantly with pride. Her ivory-gloved hands were working enthusiastically as she spoke with William, the words coming effortlessly, her entire body bobbing like a garden sparrow with sheer delight. Unnoticed for the moment, Clara tried to prepare herself but found that she couldn't disguise her true emotions. Much as she could force pleasantry into her voice, she knew that her disappointed frown was set immovably.

'Ruth, what are you doing here?' The question was completely accusatory. Clara even found herself folding her arms.

Her friend's smile faded slightly, but her demeanour was infallibly bright. 'Clara, my dear, have I come at an inappropriate time? Do forgive me.'

Clara contemplated a polite response, but the words just wouldn't formulate themselves. To prolong the silence would undoubtedly be much worse than filling it. But before she had the chance to open her mouth, William spared her further discomfort by deciding to take his leave. He bowed stiffly to Ruth and dashed past her into the stockroom, his expression firm yet unreadable. Clara watched him exit the room. It was obvious that a new rift had formed between them: one with a name that she had a great affection for. But however uneasy their relationship seemed, Ruth hadn't noticed it. She was still looking at Clara with expectation.

'I'm afraid it is an unfortunate coincidence that you should happen by when I'm otherwise occupied.' Clara didn't offer any forgiveness, knowing that Ruth did not genuinely require it.

Ruth smiled – though it was a smile completely devoid of good humour. It seemed to Clara to be a smile of concealment.

'I wouldn't have come, if I'd known – but I wished to see you on a most urgent matter. There are no customers around; I assumed you'd spare the time from your duties, however briefly. Do you think me tactless, Clara?'

Clara knew what Ruth was insinuating – and the logic behind her words was undeniable. Why *would* she turn away a friend when the shop was empty and she'd been upstairs in her room when William called her?

Ruth certainly suspected dishonesty and hoped to discern the truth. But that was not acceptable to Clara.

She had been guarding the truth for too long now and wouldn't betray herself to Ruth, of *all people* – one of many who refused to take her aspirations seriously. She had only admitted everything to her brother under duress, and he was the closest thing to an ally she had ever known. Nor indeed would she expose herself to insult, having faced enough accusations to leave her completely dispirited already.

'Under the normal circumstances, you would be justified in your assumptions. But I must insist: I am busy. We have just taken delivery of a new shipment of goods; William has been at the docks all day bartering over price and I must assume the task of taking stock.' The lies came with remarkable ease. 'It really is the most unfortunate moment for a visit.'

Ruth frowned for a few moments and nodded in concession. 'I must say, he did seem a little … off.' In an uncharacteristic act of selflessness, she spoke stridently to her friend. 'You must certainly take charge here. Let the poor man have a few hours' rest. With any luck, he will be so grateful to you that he will allow you to close up early. Then' – she paused, hoping to invoke a sense of tension. Clara was unmoved – 'you will be able to meet with Albert and me, as I had hoped!'

'Oh Ruth, I really don't think—'

'You will love it – we are going to the theatre, and Albert has offered to buy us dinner. The perfect evening, I'm sure you'll agree. It really would be wonderful if you could join us, Clara darling.' Another thought took her as soon as the previous one had departed, and she spoke again in a conspiratorial tone. 'Between you and me, we are getting along so much better than the last time you met with us – his talk of marriage becomes more and more earnest with each passing day. He seems more determined than me, if you can believe that!'

Clara smiled obligingly – she couldn't share Ruth's optimism, but the hope that her friend would eventually earn the commitment of the man that she loved was entirely heartfelt.

'I am pleased to hear that. But it would seem good sense on my part, owing to these happy circumstances, for me to allow the both of you to spend the evening on your own. You should spend time together, with no one standing in the wings.'

'Clara, you do demean yourself! We wouldn't have asked you if you weren't considered a most welcome guest. Albert said that you could even bring someone along, if you so desired.' At the mention of the name, Clara had steeled herself for the inevitable unpleasantness associated with it. Ruth continued, and Clara tried not to grimace. 'I had the feeling that you might do so, owing to your – well, the recent trend in your behaviour.' She smiled mischievously.

As any caring friend would, Ruth was trying to play a role in securing Clara's future happiness in love. Clara wasn't willing to indulge the insinuation. She often withdrew from company, but always to paint. She hadn't given Ruth the slightest hint that she was involved in a new romance.

Was Ruth so sure that love was the only cure for an unfulfilled life?

The more Clara thought about what she had said, the more she felt hurt, outraged. A sense of pride overwhelmed her usual tolerance of Ruth's plotting as she reminded herself that *two* people had devised this particular idea.

Albert had decided to let her invite a gentleman on their evening's outing, knowing full well that, had Ruth's suspicions been unfounded, Clara would feel embarrassed and inadequate. She expected that from *him*. And she had known him long enough to endure his subtle gibes without succumbing to them.

She had known Ruth even longer, but she couldn't quite come to terms with her conniving. Had there indeed been a romance to speak of, Clara's reaction might have been different. But as it was, she was offended about being forced to reveal Matthias' identity – not only because she would be expected to regard him as a potential lover, and not the most remarkable individual she had set eyes upon, but also because she had no desire to share his existence with anyone. To do so with Ruth would degrade him. She wouldn't be able to comprehend the closeness that Clara felt towards him.

Clara knew what she would have to do. It was the beginning of a slow deterioration, but she didn't lament it.

'Ruth, I am unable to attend the theatre tonight. I am terribly busy and cannot foresee myself being able to endure it. I'm afraid that is my final word.'

Ruth didn't look disappointed. This, however, was due to her being too preoccupied with looking annoyed and suspicious.

'I wouldn't force you to *endure* anything, Clara, least

of all our company. Perhaps you will see fit to spare us some of your valuable time in the not-too-distant future. I shall pass on your best wishes to Albert. Good day to you.' She left in perceptible bad spirits.

Clara could almost hear the bubbling swell of thoughts within her brain – Ruth would not rest until she discovered the reason for the change in her. But Clara had no intention of revealing it. If keeping Matthias her own valuable secret meant that she would not be able to sustain her friendship with Ruth, Clara felt that this would be a reasonable sacrifice to make.

She released a sharp exhalation, without realising that she had been holding any breath, and turned towards the back of the shop to see William standing by the curtained partition, wiping his hands on a cloth. He was regarding her with an unusual expression. 'Shirking your work ... Shirking your friends ... If this tendency continues, I shall have to employ a new assistant.'

Clara said nothing. She wasn't expected to. But she accepted the truthfulness of his statement. He was running a business, after all.

She returned to her room without asking permission. Once there, her immediate urge was to drop onto her divan, all her vitality depleted. If she could have closed her eyes and melted into her bed linen, never to reappear, she may have considered it, in her current state of mind. Every element of her life – her delights and her aversions, her ambitions and her infuriations – amounted to a struggle, showing no sign of abating. She could see her life spread out before her like a landscape on canvas, and stare as she might, she couldn't contrive it into a pleasing image. She felt like rinsing out her brushes and black-washing the entire thing.

The way this struggle was escalating, she couldn't envisage herself having the strength to keep going. And yet, she had to. She had to prove to herself that her longing to paint Matthias wouldn't go to waste.

Clara sat up, peeling her dejected body from the bed with surprising ease, and tried to enliven her spirits by looking at her paintings. She was pleased with all of them, regardless of their merits, as each of them had materialised from the astounding luminosity of her muse.

She felt that every one of them was greatly important. All of them were needed, and somehow irrelevant without each other.

This was a thought that had occurred to her on many occasions, and one which had an unquestionable influence over the rearrangement of her bedroom. All other paintings were gone, stored away under her divan and in drawers and even, though it would have been unthinkable before, rolled up under floorboards. Now all that adorned her walls were paintings of Matthias – and they were great in number. They were beginning to form several layers, each piece slightly obscured by the painting in front of it and slightly obscuring the one behind, so that the room seemed to be wallpapered with a giant collage, and no one image was completely discernible. The floor, unfortunately, had become rather difficult to negotiate, being covered with piles of paintings of Matthias, which had begun to topple. In fact, her divan was now the only free space in the entire room. Clara had surrendered her habit of sitting in the window alcove, as this too had become a storage place for her ever-mounting portfolio. She knew the times that Matthias passed the Apothecary with clockwork precision now, and so the need to while away fruitless time waiting for him had been removed.

The window itself, once an invaluable vantage point, was almost completely obscured, leaving the room constantly smothered in an oppressive shade. Clara didn't feel hindered by the lack of light, nor did she particularly miss the view. She hardly seemed to care for anything, anymore. Matthias was constantly present in her thoughts. Her attention was thoroughly fixed. Contemplating defeat seemed impossible when she looked around her room and was reminded of just how much strength she had in her fortress of paintings. She wouldn't allow herself to give in – she would persevere and paint him as many times as needed until she found his true likeness.

The room hadn't been entered by anyone else for weeks. It wasn't unclean, but its neglect was rooted much deeper than that, having become little more than a storage space. It would only be a matter of time before Clara abandoned its upkeep altogether.

Clara didn't feel that she could judge whether her paintings were particularly accomplished or beautiful. She hadn't any notion of what the importance of this vast collection of paintings could be. One day, their purpose, her purpose in creating them, would be made clear. Until then, she was certain of one thing: that no one, whether family member, friend or complete stranger, would convince her that the profound awe in which she held her muse had been confused for a puerile romantic infatuation. Her lifelong search for love seemed secondary, if not completely immaterial, when compared to her current intent. Her link with Matthias was something powerful, something fundamentally necessary. If only Clara could fathom the exact reason *why*.

CHAPTER TWELVE

The paintings were one matter; Matthias was another. Thinking of him in two separate planes of existence had become vital, not only in allowing Clara to keep daily life and art separate from one another, but also in helping her to avoid overwhelming her mind.

The Matthias in her paintings was someone she shared a deeply personal connection with, someone whose aesthetic beauty had transformed Clara into an articulate artist. To inspire her artistically was to have access to the deepest core of her being, driving her relentlessly on from one day to the next, when everything else seemed to have a determination to draw her down. In essence, art was Clara; in her mind, it sustained her more than the circulation of her blood.

The other Matthias – arguably the only Matthias that truly existed – was almost a chemical opposite. Clara could identify him from twenty yards away, but she didn't know him: the living man, the actor, the eccentrically dressed loner who always travelled on foot. The personality he projected onstage changed night after night, under his many guises, to the detriment of his true nature. Clara had no idea if her muse was aloof, aggressive, resentful, haughty, poised, confident, tolerant, affable, lonely, frightened, or lost. But his skill at portraying the multiple facets of human identity was incontrovertible.

It was his capability as an actor that had been Clara's saviour – it renewed her interest in him time and again. Whenever she visited the Grecian, she was armed with a new perspective to infuse her painting with.

Often, Clara managed two or three visits to the Grecian in the same week. It didn't matter if she had seen the play before elsewhere, or even if she had seen multiple performances of the same Grecian production; Matthias was avidly watchable. As the passing weeks mounted, she believed his acting was improving – albeit imperceptibly to any other member of the audience. Most came to just one performance, finding the abysmal surroundings and the predominantly weak supporting cast enough to dissuade them from returning.

Everything around Clara might as well have dissolved into dust when her attention was focused on Matthias. The world outside the theatre became a semblance, and the world constructed upon the boards became real.

Many of the front-of-house employees had become familiar to Clara on last- and even first-name terms. They seemed revived by her unrelenting enthusiasm and *love* for the place. Disregarding Thwaites' constant protesting, she had insisted on paying double the usual ticket price, knowing that the theatre was in financial difficulty.

Despite Clara's infatuation with the theatre, she hadn't the courage to approach the acting troupe. Her warm rapport with the rest of the theatre staff could have vastly improved her chances of befriending the performers – a group of people whose profession she had always admired.

Nevertheless, she continued to sit in the back row, for two reasons. Firstly: so that she could be far removed from the disorderly group at the front of the auditorium. Secondly, and much *more* importantly: she would also avoid recognition by Matthias, who would surely begin to notice her after seeing her repeatedly in the audience week upon week. His suspicion was something that Clara wished to avoid at any cost. Much as she felt compelled her to make herself known to him, she was cautious – how could she be expected to stand in the same room as this man, meet his eye, converse with him, without betraying something of her secret fixation? It must have shown on her face every time he walked out onto the boards, which was why she knew that she couldn't let him see her.

Clara was completely and utterly devoted to the Grecian, because she was completely and utterly devoted to Matthias. She longed to meet him but was too afraid to do so.

That is, until one exceptional performance.

The play that changed everything was *The Taming of the Shrew*.

Clara had already seen Matthias act in a variety of Shakespearean adaptations. Unfortunately for the manager of the theatre, they were so badly received, despite his unflinching enthusiasm, that the billing could change as often as once a month, in which time a new play had to be produced in its entirety. The strain was beginning to show. Each new performance presented an increasingly exhausted-looking cast, ever-sparser set designs and pitifully incompetent advertising – its enticing value verging on futile.

In this case, it wasn't the whole play that inspired a change in Clara, as she was already familiar with the plot. Nor was it the role that Matthias was playing: Petruchio. He wasn't a character that Clara was particularly fond of; his opinions and actions – along with those of other characters – were misogynistic to an almost farcical degree. Clara had never fought for the fair treatment of women, but this was partly due to her good fortune of birth and circumstance. She was not ignorant of the suffering of others. Her own brother could be discourteous in the treatment of his female customers, and Clara often reprimanded him for it. She could never approve of Petruchio's behaviour towards Katherina.

Matthias playing Petruchio wouldn't hamper her regard for him, but she would never deign to accept the sort of detrimental principles the play was putting across – regardless of the playwright's genius in other aspects.

The curtain rolled open as it always did, revealing the usual underwhelming stage setting that the company always provided. The play began, and Clara prepared herself for another highly emotive experience, unprepared for the depth of the change that she would soon experience.

The play wasn't particularly notable until its closing scenes. Though she was loath to admit it, Clara wasn't taken with Matthias' performance until that point. He played Petruchio with his usual aptitude but didn't stir anything profound within her.

Perhaps Clara was becoming spoilt; in each of his

key roles, she had been impressed by his meticulous methods. He was almost a living mirror, reflecting a fractional part of each and every single audience member back at them. He did this in such a way that it seemed entirely unintentional, but Clara had almost equivalent aptitude for perceiving character, and admired him for his level of subtlety.

As the play reached its conclusion, Clara became uncomfortable. The ending was difficult to endure – regardless of the good-natured humour and wit present elsewhere in the plot. This time, Clara was more uneasy than usual, knowing that her muse would behave in a less than awe-inspiring manner as Katherina's new husband. He had moved her to degrees she had previously thought impossible, and she began to feel a clammy dread at the thought of being disillusioned.

'Katherina, I charge thee, tell these headstrong women / What duty they do owe their lords and husbands.' The smile on Petruchio's face was all at once self-assured, proud, and somehow childishly calculating.

Katherina moved to speak. Her movements were a little too rigid, her demeanour a little too self-conscious, her costume a little too reminiscent of the street seamstress for Clara to believe that this actress was fully immersed in her character, but she somehow found herself rapt with attention, eager to see how this particular Katherina would obey the request of *this particular Petruchio*. It seemed pivotally important that Clara listened to the speech in its entirety, appreciating it for every intonation, despite having heard it many times before.

Such duty as the subject owes the prince
Even such a women oweth to her husband;
And when she is froward, peevish, sullen, sour,
And not obedient to his honest will,
What is she but a foul contending rebel
And graceless traitor to her loving lord?

Something had changed within Clara: a vital shift in perspective, even as she was listening to the words tumbling from Katherina's mouth. Once she became aware of this strangeness within herself, it seemed doubly odd to her that it was the words of Katherina, and not those of her muse, that had realigned her thoughts.

Katherina wasn't a character that Clara aspired to emulate. She wasn't naïve enough to believe that strong-willed characters were infallible. Katherina, beginning the play as a woman with strident opinions about just what she was expecting from life, and love, must have believed herself to be irrefutable. But by its conclusion, her intentions had been decimated.

As never before, the play's concluding scenes had shocked Clara deeply. And it was only recent events, she believed, that could have caused this. She began to make parallels between herself and Katherina, in a way that would have seemed completely irrational to her a few weeks ago.

Clara imagined that the 'shrew', like herself, had discerned what she wanted from life, down to the minutest details. She contemplated whether Katherina had faced the scepticism of her peers and family, as Clara had; whether all of her efforts had proved futile, as Clara's had and were continuing to. But as the plot had unfolded, Katherina's fates had changed. And on reflection, Clara began to fear. Her future was yet to unfold, and unlike a play script, wasn't written out for her.

Katherina was married by the end of the play. But it wasn't the marriage she'd intended for herself. In finding a husband, her character had been altered beyond recognition (for better or worse, richer or poorer ...).

Clara had never, until this moment of revelation, thought of the implications of finding a husband. She had envisaged doing so, believing that she knew he would be all she had longed for. But she had never imagined beyond this point; never thought of the unfurling years shared with another, the trials and triumphs of married life.

What sacrifices of character would she have to make? Would she marry the wrong person, to spite those who doubted her, and find herself desolate, abandoned to a life of misery? Would she enter into a marriage of equals, unaware that slowly, over the years, compromise and complacency would lead her to forfeit so many of the things that she cherished when she was alone?

Would she have to give up her art?

That is when she realised that her muse *had* influenced this change in her, with his presence alone. The existence of Matthias Tarasso had provided her with all she would ever need. She could pour all of her affection and exertion into lifeless images of him, without expecting anything in return.

She could be married to his likeness, to the beauty of his face, without having to contemplate sharing her remaining years with him. In many ways, he was better than a husband. Living beings fade and die, and their memories rarely succeed them for a considerable length of time. Clara's paintings of Matthias could last forever. Her aspirations wouldn't be hampered by him; they would only flourish at the mere sight of him.

'Thank you, Katherina. My saviour,' Clara said softly. She didn't care if anyone heard her.

Waking from the mire of her thoughts just as the other audience members were preparing to leave, her eyes were assaulted by the glare of the gaslights, turned up to the fullest in order to encourage the prompt evacuation of seats. As usual, the curtain had fallen on the stage without so much as a word from the acting troupe, which seemed so much more amiss on this particular night than ever before. Just as well, then, that Clara had decided to use this opportunity, after her revelation, to finally introduce herself to the man that had given her life some purpose.

She would venture into the wings today, to speak to Matthias.

In a flash of deep russet, Clara was up and out of her seat, her hair glinting in the lamplight. She may just as well have been wielding a flaming banner above her head, proclaiming her intentions to the world. She was quite unaware of this visual marvel, however, as her focus was singular and strong.

She dashed through the foyer of the theatre,

hoping the pace of her footfalls would compensate for her overwhelming urge to flee. Thwaites may have called to her as she passed, but she wouldn't have heard him.

Thankfully, no one made an effort to stop her as she passed through the door to the actors' dressing rooms. She was working under the influence of fate and believed that any attempt to hinder her would be naturally destined to occur. So many of the recent twists and turns in her daily life wouldn't have happened at all, she believed, were it not for fortuitous coincidence. She wasn't prevented from her course, and so she knew she had to continue.

It was only when the battered door creaked to a close, and her eyes accustomed to the light in the dull, low-ceilinged corridor, that the gravity of the situation hit her.

This was an alien world. She had never been behind the scenes in a theatre before; in all truth, she had never desired to be. It was a place where artifice became all too apparent – even vulgar. Worse still, it was the place where actors shed their masks and gained the unsavoury label of 'normal'.

She didn't know which door led to Matthias' dressing room. Each door off the corridor seemed identical. She wondered whether Matthias would have his own room, or whether he would be sharing one room with several other actors. In the latter case, it would be impossible for her to request her audience with him – she would probably be assaulted with questions from the other members of the troupe and would be incapable of saying the words which had been revolving in her mind.

Even so, Clara would not be deterred from her course. She forced one leaden foot after another down the narrow passageway and listened intently for sounds of occupancy in each of the rooms she passed. The doors at first appeared unmarked, but on closer scrutiny were scored with various monikers: actors' names and running lists of characters played. The first few sets of etchings meant nothing to her, though she noted that the actors were indeed sharing dressing rooms and that they were segregated according to sex, as suited propriety.

She could hear muffled voices from each room she passed. She heard a degree of merriment that she wouldn't have thought the actors capable of, due to their constant lack of appreciation and occasional bouts of abuse. As she hastened down the corridor, she gained courage and risked the occasional glance into some of the open rooms, catching a glint of light from a dressing mirror or the brief flash of a costume being put into storage. Nearing the end of the passage, her heart began to take erratic leaps and she willed the juddering organ to steady itself, should the rest of her body – and mind – follow its example.

She decided that if she couldn't identify Matthias' dressing room, she would begin knocking on each door in turn until she found him. It would take the last vestige of courage she had, but she had carried this whim too far not to do so.

The end wall had a single glass sconce mounted on it, which cast out a lazy glow. As Clara neared the sconce, she began to see her warped reflection within it: her skin almost paper-white, her hair incandescent. If there was ever a time that she wished another countenance upon herself, it was now. Usually, she paid no attention to her looks, considering them irrelevant when it was her vocation to discover the beauty in others. But at this moment, when she knew that her appearance would be the first impression she would make upon Matthias, she regretted the slight uncouthness of it.

With a stagnant feeling in her stomach, she glanced impulsively to her right, towards a fractionally open door. She took a moment to examine it.

This door was somehow incongruous; it wasn't as scrawled-upon as its neighbours. As Clara leant in a little closer to study it, she realised that it hadn't been marked at all, nor did it seem in any way old and worn. Even in the dull light, she could see a faint stain of varnish upon its surface. Hanging upon the doorknob was a silk scarf of the richest dark red; it seemed casually thrown, except for the gentlest of knots which secured it in place. A premeditated sign of identity, Clara presumed, and her thoughts were automatically drawn to the one person in her knowledge who would be inclined towards that.

Her airway tightened, and she found herself unable to swallow. She was instantly convinced that this was Matthias' dressing room; the door was suitable for no one else. She felt a pressing need to reach out and brush her fingertips against the surface of the wood, as if its texture would give her more insight into the man. The scarf seemed a more promising source of information, but she felt unworthy to touch it, the silk being so pristine, the material hanging in a way which suggested extreme care.

Forcing herself to peer through the opening, she could see that most of the lamps in the dressing room had been extinguished. It was only then that she realised no sound of voices travelled through this doorway. Disappointment crushed her. The room was empty.

It seemed only logical. Matthias, being the most talented member of the troupe, must have been disillusioned by his lack of support – so why would he stay? Or perhaps he preferred to remain alone, which explained his being at the furthest end of the passageway.

But why was he so reticent about his achievements? Why were the names of his starring roles not listed proudly? Why—

Clara's curiosity was interrupted. She heard a door opening a little way down the corridor. A short, squat man in an unsightly wig left one of the rooms, laughter in his eyes. He waved and laughed to the party inside, turned in her direction and—

But Clara had already slipped through the polished door, stepping backwards in one fluid motion.

So that was it. Her decision made for her. No time for hesitancy. She released a swift sigh and turned to survey the room ...

The white-hot brightness of the light alarmed her physically before it did visually. She felt a tight spasm of shock beneath her ribs as she sucked in a whistle of air and the pain of the bright light focused in two deep needles behind her eyes. She squeezed her eyelids shut, red pools swimming before her. Tentatively, she opened them again, but the sudden assault had caused them to stream with tears and the room was completely indiscernible. She turned her face away from the glare and waited for the sparks to stop dancing in front of her pupils.

Once she had become accustomed to the dazzling brightness, she lifted her head again. But as her eyes regained their focus, the light in the room faded until it was almost as dim as when she first glanced through the door. It appeared she had been mistaken about the room being darkened at first, for each and every one of the gas lamps were flickering with a lively golden glow, illuminating the room exquisitely. In fact, it almost appeared that the figure sitting hunched at the side of the room was encircled in a sacred halo.

The figure at the side of the room.

Clara's bones threatened to tear themselves from her body at the sight of him. *Him.* It was undoubtedly Matthias Tarasso. She knew him well enough, on sight. He was seated before a bank of mirrors. Clara noticed many things now – such as the lack of bouquets and letters and gifts that would usually adorn such a room, the lack of theatre artwork and photographs, the lack of any mark of individuality in the room – before she saw the one, crucial thing that she should have seen before any other.

His eyes. In the reflection of the mirror, those unfathomable, impossible eyes were fixed wholly upon her.

She couldn't read them. And yet the image of them seemed imprinted upon her, as if they had been looking at her for all time. She felt like she wanted to weep, but her entire body was as immovable as rock under his gaze.

'Who are you?'

Clara noted that his rich, rolling accent was much stronger when he wasn't portraying a character. It was good for her to notice this. Small details kept her from acknowledging the true enormity of what was unfolding.

'I-I'm Miss Clara Breslin.' She cast her eyes down to her feet, ashamed of her ineptness. Her ability to speak at all was quite remarkable, as she couldn't feel her lips.

Matthias surveyed her still through the mirror. He didn't turn. He didn't move. Though she sensed a small change in him.

'What are you doing here, "Miss Clara Breslin"?'

Hearing her name from his mouth sent a chilling rush coursing up from behind her navel.

'I am here – to thank you.'

'To *thank* me. For what?' Matthias' lips curled slightly at the edges; he almost laughed. He gave her a strong, measured look, and after a brief pause added, 'What is it that you do for a living, Miss Breslin?'

Clara swallowed, quenching her dry mouth. The words came a little more swiftly, a little more fluidly, each time she spoke. 'I wish to thank you, Mr Tarasso, for your outstanding performances on the stage. For your unrelenting enthusiasm and determination. And to express my wish that you should continue. The London theatres would sorely miss you – whether they realise it or not.' It was a deep relief to have said the words, but after waiting so long to be expressed, they seemed to have lost their initial appeal, even before she had finished reciting them.

He gave no immediate response; the mark of a wry smile remained on his lips from the last words he had spoken, and his eyes were still searching. It was then that Clara remembered: he had asked another question. She was a little disappointed when she realised that he wouldn't speak again until she answered it. It hardly seemed to matter to her.

'I am an assistant at my brother's Apothecary.'

Clara gave a soft peal of nervous laughter in the wake of a continuing silence. In a moment, her heart sank as she realised that she hadn't instinctively replied 'an artist'. That irritated her in a way that caused the words to foster a place in the darker reaches of her heart.

This bitterness having settled itself for the time being, Clara found herself wondering: how had he established that she had to work for a living at all?

Then she remembered: minus her apron, she was in the all-duty cotton clothing that so many working women wore. Her excuse to herself was that she had been so eager to reach the Grecian in time for the day's performance that she hadn't wanted to waste precious minutes by changing. Truthfully, she had been working on her latest portrait, having given herself the rest of the day off work. She wouldn't have had the time to change, even if she'd wanted to. Also, she hadn't left the Apothecary that lunchtime with the intention of presenting herself in company. She was still slightly stained with paint.

Matthias still saw her reflection only, but his penetrating stare had softened slightly. He seemed amused by something; Clara couldn't guess what. She couldn't read his face. Only the slightest creases at the corners of his eyes betrayed something to her, emphasised by the ever-dimming light in the room.

'You enjoy coming to the theatre, Miss Breslin: am I correct? It can't be your first time here at the Grecian; you indicated that you have watched the company many times.' He didn't refer back to her words of thanks in any forthright way. Embarrassed, or maybe wary of praise, Clara supposed. 'Are you a follower of *all* the arts? Or just the dramatic?'

Now it was Clara who could not suppress a wry smile. Matthias, thus far, hadn't spoken to her without asking a question. It had to be suspicion – but she hoped that he might also be asking her these things because he was genuinely interested in her.

'Attending plays is one of the great joys of my life. I have been to most of the theatres in London. The Grecian appealed to me because ...' A sudden dread clawed at her heart. Because of *what*, Clara? Or rather, *who*?

It chilled her, how close she had come to revealing her secret. How close *he* had come to eliciting it.

She was reminded of the true peril of this situation. She had sworn never to acquaint herself with a muse. This was why.

And yet, to be in this room, to be close enough to him to see the laughter lines around his eyes, was an experience she wouldn't willingly sacrifice. That was why her resolve didn't break, and she dared to meet his eyes for a second time. They were unnaturally incandescent – even in near-darkness. She felt hooked into them, as if they would never release her.

Clara continued to speak.

'No, the theatre isn't my only interest. I enjoy art, also.' Concealing her occupation as an artist from him was now a comfort – no need to speak of her artistic influences. She could be merely an appreciator of art, so long as it kept her safe.

'Art.' Matthias' mouth worked slightly, as if he were chewing the word, moving it around his tongue and measuring it for taste and merit. It seemed to please him. He gave a short, swift nod. Finally, he turned to face her properly. As he did so, Clara was distracted by a slight flickering of the lamps banking the room. The gasworks in this part of the theatre appeared to be rather unpredictable.

Without the mirror surface to serve as a barrier between them, she felt completely under his scrutiny. Whilst the artist in her preferred to see his true countenance, she felt overwhelmed by intricate details. But why should she fear the real, the living, the breathing? *He* was the only thing that gave her art life.

My turn, she thought, with an intake of breath to ease her way. She took a step forward. 'I hope this isn't improper of me, Mr Tarasso, but I was wondering about your country of origin—'

His voice rang out to interrupt her again: rich and confident, but not at its full volume, as if he wasn't really speaking to her. 'An apothecary's assistant; a lover of the theatre; and of art. Tell me, Miss Breslin, what did you hope to achieve by coming here today?'

The two sentences he had spoken did not match. At least, Clara could see no logical connection between them. The question, too, was ambiguous. Where was he referring to as 'here' – the theatre, or just this particular room? She chose the latter, hoping that this would sate his curiosity.

'My purpose was to thank you – as I already have done. I felt I had to, because you never stay onstage after a performance to receive any thanks you may be given. It is something I am most unused to.'

'It is strange – do you not think, Miss Breslin – that you are the only member of our audience who has noted this? And more than that: to rectify the situation, you were willing to risk propriety by visiting the actors' dressing rooms?'

'Not all of them,' Clara responded, without thinking.

Matthias leaned back a little and narrowed his eyes. Clara's legs below the knee were completely devoid of feeling.

'Why did you choose the Grecian Theatre, Miss Breslin?' His tone of voice was slightly deeper, somewhat grave.

'I-I don't—'

'We are not a popular theatre. We never have been, even before I was employed here – or so I'm told. The manager speaks of closing us down, washing his hands of the whole business at the end of every week. But we manage to stay open. It is a marvel – or perhaps, a cruel twist of fate: she is prolonging our torture for as long as her conscience can bear it.' It didn't seem like torture; the man's smile was widening by the moment. 'Do you believe in fate, Miss Breslin?'

'I think that fate is a name that we give to coincidence when it falls in our favour.'

Clara didn't entirely believe this statement. She certainly believed that fate was the reason she had ever laid eyes on Matthias. Truthfully, she believed that fate and coincidence were two entirely separate and coexisting phenomena: one being deeply rooted in the creation of all things, and the other occurring undoubtedly in the present, a result of so many intricately woven lives existing on the same planes of time. However, she did believe that coincidence could be mistaken for fate, and vice versa, because of their similar natures and their similar propensities towards either fortune or cruelty.

'But this theatre doesn't stay open because of fate.'

'No? Then why do you believe it does?' His eagerness was unmistakeable this time. Matthias leaned forward in his seat, awaiting her answer.

'Because as much as your audiences may reproach you all, they cannot deny that the hours they spend within these walls are hours of pure escape, of forgetfulness from despair.'

Matthias pressed a pair of knuckles to his lips. He stayed silent for a while, watching Clara from the other side of the room. She began to perspire a little, the heat rising from beneath the surface of the skin instead of seeping into it. The glow from the gaslights contributed to the sensation of uncomfortable warmth; they maintained a new-found brightness, more akin to daylight than the dimness of a cellar-level room.

Clara tried her best to regulate her breathing. She was starting to feel agitated. She knew it was the intensity of his examination that was really causing her distress, not because she didn't wish to fall under his scrutiny but because her desire to impress him was so great. She would leave this room in worse standing than she would have if she'd never had the courage to meet him at all.

Her muse broke from his reverie imperceptibly. It was the melodic tones of his voice that alerted her to him again. She realised that she had been repeatedly clenching and unclenching her fists, to the extent that her fingers were beginning to stiffen.

'How do you like this room, Miss Breslin?' he asked, not taking his eyes from her to look around but making a vague gesture with his hand.

Clara didn't look around, either. She had taken it all in within seconds and had only to cast back her mind in order to answer him. She was used to the questions by now and no longer expected them to be logical.

'It is immaterial what I think, Mr Tarasso. The true indication of its worth is your own esteem of it – which I believe to be nil.' She anticipated his next question, adding, 'This is based solely on the fact that there are no marks of identity in the room, besides the scarf on the door. I don't disagree with this, however. You must believe that your career has the potential to end at any moment, and to decorate the room with personal effects would only – as you say –

"prolong your torture" at the thought of having to leave it.'

'Never denounce your own opinion as immaterial, Miss Breslin.' It appeared she had not anticipated the reply, after all. 'The person asking you for it will either require it because they believe it to be worth adopting themselves, or because they wish to disregard it as false. Either way, they have vested an interest, and for you to deny it is devaluing yourself, and your right to speak.'

Clara had always been headstrong and didn't take to this criticism, even though it contained worthy advice. 'I wasn't denouncing my opinion because I didn't wish to speak. Being in your acquaintance such a short time, I didn't want to be impertinent.'

Matthias smiled. 'Impertinence ... so your opinion would be a negative one? As I thought. A lover of art: you can't dissociate this from your opinion of everyday things – even something as detached from you as the dressing room of a Shoreditch actor.'

Clara couldn't help but smile in return; the expression felt alien upon her face. She hadn't smiled and felt the genuine emotion behind it for quite some time. 'Mr Tarasso, do you enjoy art?'

She knew he was thinking carefully.

'Why do you ask?'

'An inkling,' she replied, with an inflection of humour in her voice. 'Your clothes, firstly. I can't help but identify something artistic about them.' It was only when she was silent that she realised that once again, Matthias had managed to lead her into answering a question instead of

149

answering one himself.

'An art-lover – most impertinent – and observant.' He glared at her for a moment; she believed his sparkling green eyes would jump straight out at her. Then he rose from his chair and stopped in front of her after three smooth, confident strides. He held out his hand. 'My name is Matthias Tarasso – though you seem to have ascertained that yourself, impertinent as you are. It is a pleasure to make your acquaintance, Miss Breslin.'

Clara seemed to guide her hand through a hot mist to meet his. She worried that her palm would be beaded with perspiration, but when their hands touched, it was with an almost icy-cold contact. His grip was firm, resolute, and his eyes held hers for as long as propriety would allow. She could tell that he was still taking measure of her qualities, even in this briefest of exchanges.

Of course, she was doing just the same.

Had she passed some sort of test? Was the incessant questioning his means for deeming someone suitable to share his company? She couldn't be sure. She was impressed with her resolve: for having come so far.

'You are acquainted with Mr Thwaites, I believe?' Matthias asked, releasing her hand and gesturing to her to take a seat.

Clara gave him a quizzical look but obeyed his wishes and sat in a plush velvet chair opposite the one had had just occupied. He returned to his seat and sat facing her, his elbows resting on his knees.

'He has never mentioned you by name but speaks

to the troupe about a "benevolent lady" with whom he has had many pleasant conversations. This lady, I hear, has a continuing interest in this theatre, despite all the deprecating remarks that Thwaites has been able to concoct and anything she may have witnessed herself.'

Clara's flare of panic subsided almost instantly when Matthias showed no knowledge of her having asked Thwaites for his name.

'Thwaites' talents are wasted in the foyer; he has a *definite* flair for the dramatic ...' Matthias muttered, the inflection of his accent over the word 'dramatic' giving it a rolling flourish that made Clara's nose wrinkle in amusement.

'Mr Thwaites is too complimentary. I know that I shouldn't doubt his opinions on the theatre, but my own senses portray something altogether different than the impression he gives.'

Matthias inhaled sharply, paused, and turned his head before speaking. It seemed as if he wished to be a little more elaborate in his words but was reigning himself in. 'I don't wish to insult you, Miss Breslin, when I tell you that you are an unusual, but rather interesting, woman. How *did* you find this little backstreet theatre, and why the Devil did you decide to sit through *one* performance, let alone *several?* Why do you thank *me* – little more than a street-side actor who fell under fortune's arm – when it is *you* who deserve thanks – not only for your "benevolence" but also that your attendance may well be preserving this crumbling place? It is rather strange ...'

Clara was trying to ingest each individual question,

to have the slightest hope of being able to answer them all. But she resigned herself; she couldn't have answered them. Each one of his questions breached that unspeakable barrier which she had erected in her own mind, to shield him – and herself – from the shameful intensity of her interest in him as her muse.

She realised that Matthias was mired in his own thoughts, muttering under his breath – still trying to answer the questions he had put to her. Clara hoped he would agree that she had answered quite enough of them for one meeting. But she decided to reply, eventually, in the only way she could.

'As strange as I may be, I thank you for your compliments.' She spoke with sincerity, though she wasn't sure that Matthias had meant to compliment her. Quickly adopting the man's technique of asking a question when wishing to deflect attention, she continued, 'You describe yourself as a "street-side" actor, Mr Tarasso, though I find it hard to believe that you haven't been trained by one of the great masters: Bennett, perhaps, or even Kean, if he were alive. How did you learn your craft, and so remarkably?'

As ever, Matthias didn't seem taken aback by the question. Clara didn't think he was conceited; more that he had his thoughts trained on other things, things that far exceeded any notion of vanity. True to form, he didn't answer her and merely put across another query of his own.

'I haven't had the pleasure of seeing Mr Kean perform. Came to quite a regrettable end, or so I recall. I hear that he was a most exceptional man. Truly incomparable …' He nodded curtly to himself before training his eye carefully on Clara, awaiting her response. Unlike her, Matthias wasn't afraid of silence. Clara wished that she'd been more persistent in her desire for answers. But it was Matthias that she'd come here to meet. She would drink up anything he chose to tell her, like a thirsty root, whether she had asked it or not, because she'd known nothing about him for such a long time.

'Unfortunately, Kean was before my time. I have also heard of his magnificence. A shame, or perhaps providence, that some of his final moments upon the earth were spent on the stage. I am sure there are many actors who share the same passion for their craft who would begrudge the chimes of Death's toll for intruding on the final curtain.'

Matthias smiled. His thoughts on her opinions were unclear. She wondered if she'd used too much licence, considering that she wasn't in the acting profession. She wasn't adequately informed to pass judgement on the circumstances of Kean's death – or the depth of his 'passion'. But her muse's eyes had a strange new facet to them; not describable as warmth, though as near to that as eyes of a severe colouring could be.

'I couldn't say, Miss Breslin – that is, I can't speak for others, and can only validate my own opinions. Even speaking about myself, I would hesitate to give you a *conclusive* answer. I believe I am amongst the immeasurable proportion of mankind who hope their lives shall never end ...' His smile here was almost teasing. Clara couldn't decide what to think; she felt as if he were veiling something other than a sense of humour from her, though he had at last managed to give her an undeviating response. Clara felt as if she had been fighting against a beating tide of resistance so far, only to find that the waters were abating by themselves. She smiled softly, arranging her arms in front of herself for an addition of comfort.

'Well, I'm sure that, for those aspiring for immortality, forging a successful career on the stage is certainly one way of achieving it.'

'Unfortunately, I can't see the actors of the Grecian Theatre becoming part of a legacy that will survive the ages.' There was something in his smile; something self-deprecating and altogether charming. 'But it may be an aspiration. You are all kindness for attempting to alleviate my concern.'

Clara held on to a passive exterior. In acknowledgement of his approval, she inclined her head, giving a small smile that was tempered by self-consciousness.

'Many are placed at a higher advantage than others in life, but those who capitalise on the opportunities that are presented to them, irrespective of their circumstances, tend to meet their aspirations,' she said, and believed she was right.

Matthias made no verbal response, only leaned forward, his face set in an almost adamantine expression. Clara's chest constricted against her lungs, and she reduced in size under his scrutiny. He motioned her to stand with a smile and a small flick of his fingers, and Clara stood from her chair, watching as he rose simultaneously and crossed the small distance to her side of the room. She met him halfway, not ignorant of the ridiculousness of the gesture: as if she were about to receive a theatrical 'aside' from him.

Matthias spoke, and something in the warmth of

his voice seemed to dissipate into the room around them. Indeed, the gas lamps seemed to glow much more brightly, until it was all Clara could do not to shade her eyes from the perceived increase in glare.

'My exact origins are unknown to me, although I was raised in England and all of my memories are of this country. I have been told that I have Greek ancestry.

'I enjoy art immensely and visit galleries whenever I have the opportunity. Perhaps I do allow my appreciation for creativity to pervade my outer persona and the spaces I inhabit.

'I didn't learn my craft from anyone. Any success I have achieved – and I shall be the first to concede that it amounts to little – has been a result of my own perseverance. I shall also admit to you that the short years I have spent acting in the Grecian are my first bout of consistent work, of any kind.'

Clara couldn't react at first – but not for want of feeling. The assault of the information, impeccably considered in terms of both the questions she had asked and the order she had asked them in, was too much. She felt her own inertness and could do nothing to moderate it. Meanwhile, Matthias smiled, eyebrows slightly raised, as if he had predicted her reaction and she had delivered it faultlessly, and she felt herself dissolve into breathy, relieved laughter.

'Mr Tarasso, I really don't know what to say. You—' She laughed nervously, cupping her palm around her face to conceal her awkwardness. 'Your style of conversation is not something that I'm acquainted with!'

'I don't approach many things in the manner that would be expected of me, Miss Breslin. Reason doesn't apply its rules to me. But the same may be said for you, I can tell.' When Clara quirked her brow at him and prepared to retort, he simply stated, 'No chaperone,' and she was halted in the act.

He also said, 'Come, take a walk with me,' and for that she had no words whatsoever.

CHAPTER THIRTEEN

Clara wasn't aware of consenting to Matthias' request until the two of them were crossing London Bridge after walking for almost an hour.

Of course, she hadn't been unconscious of her actions. But it had been easier to *feign* unconsciousness; to pretend, on leaving the Grecian, that she was merely walking home with a newly made friend, one whom just so happened to be travelling in the same direction as her.

She'd wilfully guided him towards a different route when they were approaching Broad Street, in order to avoid the Apothecary. But she convinced herself that she would only be extending her homeward journey by twenty minutes or so, just to be polite to Matthias, who seemed to be enjoying her company. It was only when they had reached the bridge, and it became apparent to her that they were crossing the Thames, that her rationality finally returned from its absence. And *it returned* with a vengeance.

Matthias was entirely engrossed in their outing. The trajectory towards St James' Park had been set firmly in his mind, apparently before they'd even left the theatre. His stride was quick, though from excitement rather than haste – he had no need to return to the theatre until tomorrow and ample time at his disposal. He seemed to thrive in the outdoors, amongst crowds of people – though they parted around him in barely perceptible waves. His needle-sharp gaze dashed from face to face, almost as quickly as the words of conversation tumbled from his lips. He had told her many things in that hour's walk, mostly about his acting: his favourite roles (Hamlet, of course, and unusually, Richard II), and the traits that he most enjoyed discerning in others (he had, for example, appropriated twenty different laughs, each applicable to a different situation).

He was in the middle of explaining his fixation with London Bridge, saying that the foot traffic there was the most prolific in the City, when Clara stopped rigid. He was enjoying himself, and it took a few more solitary strides before he realised that she had stopped at all.

'Oh Lord. What am I doing?' Clara muttered furiously to herself. She glanced about her, panicking openly in a way that would have normally seemed foolish to her. In her peripheral vision were banks of faces and not one of them knew her; not one of them knew that she was, at this moment, expected to be in her quarters in Breslin's Cures and Remedies on Broad Street: painting, brooding, anything, so long as she was home and behaving herself. She was *not* expected to be on London Bridge, chaperoned by a man that she'd only been introduced to an hour ago (in fact, she'd introduced *herself* to *him*, and that wasn't entirely proper either). Often, it was better to be anonymous, and Clara relied upon it. But she drew no comfort from it now. She was surrounded by people, but Clara was alone, and even her muse was little better than a stranger.

Propriety had never been a primary concern of hers, and she knew that she'd sacrificed her own several years ago when she had decided to work for a living, flouting her social standing, because it was preferable to her, instead of taking a husband under false pretences. She hadn't met with overwhelming disapproval because she had few friends in London, and those fashionable people of her parents' acquaintance were so far removed from her now that she didn't care about their gossip. Even the scathing remarks from people like Albert were met with impassiveness.

But meeting Matthias on her own had been audacious, even for her. And walking unaccompanied with him for even the shortest length of time was much more offensive than travelling alone. She knew that she couldn't be the only young woman ever to rail against having a chaperone, but neither had she heard of a young woman's independence being celebrated. It wasn't without reason that society was watchful over young, unmarried women. Clara found it oppressing. But she knew that it was a societal expectation founded upon necessity. Matthias had charmed her, as she knew he would. In fact, he had charmed her before he had spoken a word to her. He could be anyone – *anyone* – to her now. And she had no means of protecting herself.

As if he'd followed the train of her thoughts, Matthias now spoke. He had come back a little way to meet her but kept a respectful distance, reading, no doubt, the obvious apprehension on her face.

'Miss Breslin.'

'Yes?'

'I don't believe that this matter is worth your anxiety.'

'Yes, but I – I'm sorry, I beg your pardon?' She hadn't

given any indication of her concerns.

'Do you always walk without a chaperone?'

Clara felt she should answer carefully. She didn't want him to think that she was entirely without decency. 'My brother is my chaperone, when we go out together. But he rarely accompanies me to the theatre, and he trusts me to conduct myself appropriately when I am alone.' She realised that her words implied that William would be exasperated at her for her conduct today. In all truthfulness, he would probably not even acknowledge that she had been absent for longer than expected. 'I travel on foot only when the distance is little. Otherwise, I am completely safe in a carriage.'

He nodded, smiling only slightly so as not to patronise her. 'I don't seek to criticise your actions, Miss Breslin. I can't comprehend what it must be like to be chastised for any independent behaviour. No doubt you fear that your decision to walk with me will have unpleasant implications. But I promise you that it will not. You are perceptive, but I know you would rather hear it from my own mouth than rely upon your instinct alone.'

Clara smiled with some effort, but her eyes betrayed her uneasiness. 'You are right; I don't doubt that I can trust you.'

'And yet you're worried that your own judgment may have deceived you?'

'It sounds a little absurd, when you say it – and I don't wish to offend you—'

'But your answer is "yes".'

'I have a compass for proper behaviour, Mr Tarasso,

as much as I may strike you as an unconventional person.'

'Quite right that you should. You have flouted convention enough for one day, perhaps. But I don't judge you in the way that many others would, Miss Breslin. You don't deserve that; your only crime, as I can see, is a compulsion to learn as much as you can about the world you are in and the people that are in it. If society hinders you in this, then that is society's own insufficiency.

'I would like you to accompany me to St James' and would be most grateful if you'd accept. It is aesthetically beautiful for the artistically inclined. Afterwards, I'll send you home, quite removed from any danger, in your own carriage.'

Clara found again that he only had to say a little to prove most persuasive. She was only susceptible to his suggestion because she wished so avidly to remain in his company.

'There isn't a lot demanding my presence elsewhere. And I find that I have many more things to ask you, Mr Tarasso.'

Matthias took great amusement from this; he tipped back his head and chuckled pleasantly. 'And perhaps I shall choose to answer you, Miss Breslin,' he teased, only beginning to walk again once she'd drawn level with him.

The walk to St James' Park was considerably easier once Clara had unburdened herself of her social conscience. They crossed Westminster Bridge absorbed in the same rich conversation which had proved a contented third companion throughout their travels across the City.

The afternoon had become a little paler by the time

they'd reached the lake's edge. The sun was a beaded droplet against a lace curtain of soft grey sky, framed on all sides by the reaching arms of trees which had become dark and sombre in the weak light. The water itself lay quite still, only feigning to glimmer with the sky's reflection cast upon it. Clara inhaled the air purposefully, deep into her lungs. The purity of it, whilst not entirely superior, was a definite improvement upon that around the Thames, which was tainted by the mildly unpleasant smell of the river water and the black fumes from steamboats.

'Do you wish to sit? We have walked a considerable distance.'

Clara looked around her, measuring the scene. There were many fashionable people arranged neatly by the water's edge, young ladies sheltering themselves needlessly with parasols whilst the men in their parties regaled them with humorous anecdotes. It seemed altogether too false and far too intimate a situation to find herself in with Matthias. And Clara didn't want to rest. She was relishing the afternoon's endeavour. It reminded her of the way she used to exhaust her youthful energy near her Wiltshire home.

'Let's walk a little more, take the path around the lake: I shall be returning home soon and will find all the rest there I could ever need.' She said this with more than a hint of resentment.

When they had walked a little further, Matthias intruded into their comfortable silence.

'You told me you had further questions. Whilst I feel that I've spoken about myself enough for one afternoon –

you did seem most insistent – it would be terribly impolite of you not to continue on as you'd intended.'

The top half of Clara's face wrinkled in a smile which didn't quite reach her mouth. 'Perhaps that's why I haven't hurried to ask them. I feared you might have exhausted all the interesting information about yourself.'

'Effrontery. Boldness beyond civil decency.' Matthias' smile reached his mouth and threatened to flourish much further.

Clara sighed swiftly through her nose. It was unavoidable: this question required an answer. But she had been hoping to delay asking Matthias *this* for as long as she could – for fear of what? Perhaps for fear that, in asking it, she might inadvertently reveal something of herself – and she couldn't afford to share too much.

'You've expressed to me that, in your profession, you have benefitted from few successes.' A short pause. Measuring her words before she spoke them. 'I, for one, feel that you have received far less praise than you deserve.' Yes, that was alright. A little more confidence now. 'I hope that you've been given some recognition for your skill?' And now the words were becoming difficult to control and so she finished in a rush, 'I can't be the only person you've come across that appreciates your talent.'

Matthias looked at her, not for the first time that day, as if she'd behaved in a way that he was thoroughly unused to. And it appeared that it pleased him greatly. Not because of any great vanity on his part, but because he couldn't imagine how there had come to be such a person in his life, who appeared to understand him whilst hardly knowing him at all.

'You are singular, Miss Breslin,' he said quietly. Almost gravely. 'And I say that not to be unnecessarily indulgent, but because the only other person who believes my acting displays any shred of "promise" is my *financially deficient* employer, who sees me as the best of a poor lot.' He shrugged his mouth in a self-effacing manner. 'His judgement hasn't proved rewarding for him, so I'm not complimented by his decision to keep me.'

Clara was astonished. Matthias was almost feverishly engrossed in his art; she knew that without any prolonged investigation into his character. But for him not to realise that his passion translated vividly into his every movement and intonation on the stage was incredible to her.

Matthias had noticed the change come over her face. 'Now you're supposing I am purposefully oblivious, attempting to garner praise.' He was nervous. Why was he nervous about this? 'But I surmise that I'm speaking with someone whose mind is comparable to my own. I feel the need to redress the mistaken impression that I have caused.

'It is a ceaseless frustration for me, knowing that there is a potential that I can reach and not having the means to attain it. I can't allow myself to be satisfied with the roles I'm playing, believing that acclaim will materialise, because it won't. I must keep striving; I must continue ever onward. And most appalling to me is that I'm not sure what my true potential is, even less how to achieve it. I console myself that it must be within my reach, because I'm searching for it persistently enough. But I know that I'm only on the first rung of the ladder towards genuine recognition. Worse still, I don't know how long I must continue in my current state of dissatisfaction.'

Clara ingested what he'd said without difficulty, though she was overwhelmed by the prolixity of his answer. It was clear that he hadn't shared these thoughts before. She stopped walking, showing him that he had her full attention, and attempted to encapsulate what she'd heard.

'You can't accept the praise that you've earnt thus far because you feel that you won't have earned acclaim in any form until you are satisfied with your own achievements.'

Matthias had stopped when she had, but his posture was tense, as if he didn't wish to elaborate further on the matter. When he heard her reply, however, his expression broke into an open-mouthed smile, and an exhalation that was part laughter, part sigh of relief eased the tension between them.

'You see? I was right. You are *singular*.'

Clara recognised how much she treasured such a belief on Matthias' part.

'I find it rather sad, Mr Tarasso. Do you not think that valuing your successes, as small as they may seem, could contribute towards personal fulfilment?'

Matthias was resigned, and less moved by her words than she'd hoped.

'It is how I have always been. I don't know how to behave otherwise. Perhaps I am naturally apathetic towards my own good fortune; or else I am fated to see myself as I should be and never as I am. The inconvenience of shortcomings is that one can never truly interpret one's own.'

Clara found herself more troubled, dissatisfied with Matthias' statements.

'I am in no position to advise you. We are still, for the most part, unaccustomed to each other. I can only say that, if you are intent on seizing perfection at all cost, it would help to remember that perfection is a deceitful term. It is aspirational and yet unreachable. Many who seek it grow tired of the process, only after having found that their lives have abandoned them in the process.'

Clara had conveniently forgotten how intensely she sought perfection in her painting. She was speaking to Matthias with the rationality of someone who sees their own faults in another person and, unknowingly, draws upon personal experience to advise them, entirely immune to irony.

Matthias said nothing. He was studying her again, unashamedly because he wasn't aware that she had finished speaking. Although he hadn't found her offensive, Clara didn't want him to dwell on what she'd said in case it dampened his spirits. She altered the course of the conversation – if only, selfishly, to learn more about him.

'However, strong ambition is a valuable trait. I don't doubt that it is the devotion to your art that compels you on, but are you ambitious in other ways? Is it something that has always been with you, from your earliest recollection?'

The actor was quickly inspired. He was somehow more youthful at the mere mention of his childhood. Clara didn't think he could be much older than she was, but now she was granted an image of him at her own age, or younger.

There was a rush of vibrancy in his expression.

'I was born into uncertainty, Miss Breslin. I wasn't raised by those who brought me into this world, and lived on the charity of others for many years. But such a beginning can instil something in a person. As a child I had many dreams that went unrealised for a long time. I used the limited resources at my disposal and eventually left what may be called my childhood home: an unhappy place, as I was not suited to it – or it to me. This departure came at some personal cost, and they were uneasy years. But I was able to build a career. I was free. I was the happiest I have ever been. I had never taken well to being constantly under a watchful eye – I needed to be left to choose my path.

'And here I am speaking of the past, Miss Breslin, and not entirely answering the question you asked. Although I suppose it may be said that a less ambitious man would still be under that watchful eye, letting his dreams be reserved for the twilight hours.

'I believe that artistic fulfilment is vital. It isn't easily attained, neither is it a kind pursuit, being selfish in many ways. I fear that I'm not always a pleasant man to know. But I have my fixation and must answer it. It doesn't let itself be ignored.' His words had taken a melancholic turn again, and Clara noticed that something like the shade under the trees had darkened his eyes. When he saw her looking, however, the shadow passed, and his face was as bright and open as ever. 'You see, I can acknowledge my faults. I paint a perfectly bleak picture of myself, when no doubt you expected the opposite – actors are expected to promote their virtues at any available opportunity, are they not?' His laughter seemed warm enough, and Clara couldn't detect any insincerity.

The mention of painting pictures made her think of herself and her favourite occupation. 'I can understand how many things may be forgotten, perhaps neglected, when your mind is engaged with your calling in life. Believe me; your honesty is most welcome. I share your perspective.'

Matthias seized upon this instantly. His narrowed eyes were keen. 'Oh? You do? Do you experience the same, in your brother's Apothecary?'

'Hmm?' She turned to stare, startled by his perceptiveness. Then she realised: he assumed she was referring to a fixation over her work *in* the Apothecary rather than outside of it. Her face softened, and she laughed. 'No, no!' She was quite emphatic. 'I mean that – I understand your way of thinking. I can't comprehend why so many can't appreciate true artistic talent. I believe the absorption you have described is *absolutely* necessary for success.'

'I see,' Matthias said, slowly. 'I don't think that many people would agree with us, Miss Breslin, in a society that labels irregular traits as pathological. But that is unimportant.' He demonstrated this with a wave of his hand. 'In any case, it is my aim to find out more about *you*, the next time we meet. The information you release about yourself, in however brief a manner, is more fascinating than anything I have said this afternoon.'

'The next time?' Clara jumped at the suggestion, trying to hide the quiver of excitement in her voice, 'Are you—'

'We shall discuss it later. You know where is best to find me, at any rate.' His smile was warm. 'It is about time that we parted ways.'

'Yes, it's time,' she agreed. She turned to look at Matthias, hoping her desperation at their parting would not be obvious. 'Mr Tarasso, thank you for speaking with me today. I hoped for a long time to be able to do so and didn't imagine that you would humour me for half as long.'

'Humour you? Not at all. I remember that it was I who asked you to accompany *me* on this outing. I should offer *you* the thanks.' This wasn't an honest answer, and Clara perceived that, yet again, he was showing his reluctance to acknowledge her praise and gratitude.

She made a soft hum in reply. 'I suppose that one of us must accept the courtesy – even if it happens to be mine – that you have misappropriated and adapted for your own use.' She smiled daringly.

Matthias laughed richly. 'Allow me to call your cab, Miss Breslin.'

She did so and was inside and rattling her way back to Broad Street in a matter of minutes.

The parting was far too brief. He had offered to accompany her, and she had declined. There had been a lack of words, spoken language seeming unsuitable and inarticulate. They had made do with 'goodbye', and even that seemed a mistake to her.

She was glad that he was prevented from seeing where she lived. Even the thought of letting him stand in front of the building troubled her, as if he could discover the dozens of paintings she had produced of him just by looking at the outside of her paper-covered window.

She began to worry as she moved along Fleet Street, the dome of St Paul's drifting dark above the rooftops before a sky that was gradually being drained of its colour. The illusion of the afternoon began to leave her, and she remembered in slow tidal drifts the normality of her life preceding – and no doubt succeeding – the time she had spent with her muse. She was an apothecary's assistant – and the apothecary himself was probably completely unaware of her absence. He would also be infuriated if he discovered where, and how, and with whom she had been passing the time. But returning to the daily life she despised wasn't her only concern. Having parted from Matthias, Clara reflected on the consequences of meeting him.

She couldn't count on meeting him again and wouldn't allow herself to dwell on the notion. But if they did, most worrying of all would be trying to keep Matthias ignorant about her real interest in him. He must not discover that.

It seemed that they shared much in common, but Clara didn't believe that her obsession with painting him would flatter him in any way. He had made it plain that he wouldn't accept praise from others – not ungratefully, but because he was a perfectionist and didn't want to become complacent and risk not reaching the status he felt he was destined for. If she were to show him her paintings, he would only retreat further away from her. She couldn't bear that. She couldn't let him shrink from her company, fading in her mind – and on her canvas.

He would never see her paintings. That was certain. She would destroy every last one rather than lose his presence in her life – which would lead incidentally to the same outcome.

Her cab clunked to a stop outside Breslin's Cures and Remedies. She glared tentatively at the closed door and shuttered windows, the whole street dulled by the darkness spreading from the eastern sky. The feeling of sickness began to build from the base of her throat at the thought of stepping inside.

If she hadn't had the refuge of her room, or the consolation of her paintings, she wouldn't be able to endure returning. Meeting Matthias had been calamitous for the woman she used to be. She was changed.

The shopfront was dark and still as Clara entered, and it appeared somehow dustier without the circulation of fresh air. She hurried through, bustling with her gloves and coat so as to distract herself from the strangely threatening feeling in the empty room.

It was only when she reached the partition curtain that she realised the room wasn't truly empty at all.

'Good evening.'

William stood behind his counter, rigid in his posture, clearly overcompensating for his suppressed irritation.

He didn't have to conceal it. She could hear the tremor of it in his voice. The cold gleam in his eyes was undistinguishable from that of the medicine bottles.

'Bill,' she gasped. 'Were you waiting for me?'

'Yes,' William replied tersely. 'I expect you would prefer it if I wasn't.' He was examining her clothing – noticing the paint stains, no doubt. 'In spite of your indifference towards telling me where you were – and, God help me, my own better judgement – I was worried about you. You've been gone a *long* time, Clara. It's your carelessness that concerns me. It could be one of my failings as a brother, but I hadn't realised that you'd become so ... *independent*. It's not a safe trait.'

'I know.' Clara swallowed the lump of nausea that had not subsided. She couldn't think of a way to excuse her actions.

William wasn't usually so attentive. She was grateful that he was still protective over her, but she didn't want to be reminded of how restrictive her life was.

William seemed to become calm in the silence that followed. Clara could see that his concern remained, but his words and tone of voice didn't match his outer demeanour.

'I won't question you. You're not a criminal before judge and jury. Besides, you will do as you please, regardless of any advice or warning that I may offer.' He scrubbed a hand across his face, the growing shadows etching themselves in the half-formed lines in his skin. 'Just—' He paused, deciding exactly what it was that he wished of her. 'Please, don't conceal so much from me that you can't reach me, when times become difficult.'

Clara understood. She had feared this threat all along – to hear him say it affected her more than she thought it might. Her heart shuddered painfully in her chest as she moved closer to him, extending her hand in an offer of companionship that he denied.

'Bill – Bill, *please* – you must understand. I don't mean to be secretive, but I do so many things on my heart's impulse that it is impossible to keep you informed.' She couldn't explain her hasty motives, and she didn't want to make false promises. Much as it pained her, she had to accept that she would continue to take such risks, even if it meant estranging her brother. *So be it,* said a tiny voice in her mind, and she tried to pretend that she hadn't heard it.

'You must be tired. We can discuss it later,' he suggested, but there was no conviction in his voice.

'Yes, I hope so.' She didn't want William thinking so ill of her. 'Goodnight.' Clara left William alone.

He stood as still as he had throughout their conversation. His eyes moved between different points around the room but lingered on nothing – saw nothing. He was thinking, piecing together, formulating an idea.

He had decided not to interfere and wouldn't ask Clara what had kept her away for so long. He should have done both, he knew. Apprehension and good judgement told him that he should get to the bottom of it all. But part of him was proud and didn't want to admit to being an inattentive sibling.

She wished to keep her painting, and the inspiration for it, a secret from him. Though he had accepted this, he resented it. But he knew that the blame for her long absences couldn't solely lie with Clara. One trifling thing she had said still disturbed him. And he had a fair idea of what – or whom

– she had been referring to.

She had admitted that in her 'impulsive' moments, she answered the plea of her *heart*.

CHAPTER FOURTEEN

It is usually assumed that the human character is dependable. Once a persona has been established, it is unlikely that these traits will ever be permanently contradicted. A case in point: the Breslins were a stubborn breed. William Breslin would never cease being an obstinate man – just as his sister wouldn't stop being a determined woman. Both were content in their stubbornness and both believed it yielded many advantages.

Refusing to ask Clara anything about her whereabouts was beneficial to William, as he believed it preserved his respectability. It was equally favourable for Clara, as Matthias was to ask her to meet him again. And that next meeting was only the start.

Each of their meetings involved Matthias indulging Clara with visits to her favourite venues across the City. Occasionally, he introduced Clara to his preferred venues, which had the same favourable outcome. Matthias' favourite places became counted amongst Clara's favourite places, which seemed natural to both of them.

They met and travelled together as they had done on the first occasion, but Clara no longer felt any concern or guilt. She had accustomed herself, perhaps a little too easily, to this unconventional arrangement. Matthias could be very persuasive.

The threat of recrimination had also been removed.

No one ever asked Clara to speak in defence of her behaviour. She and Matthias were relatively anonymous, and if they were recognised by anyone, it wasn't made known.

The biggest obstacle to this new arrangement was that Matthias and Clara still had their professional duties to attend to. Their clashing careers proved unfortunate. When Clara had finished working in the Apothecary, Matthias was beginning the preparations for his evening performance. The rare opportunities when *both* of them had free time, therefore, were appreciated all the more.

Their meetings were completely spontaneous. Even if Clara had wanted to keep her brother informed about her social engagements, it would've been impossible. But she had no intention of doing so.

The indisputable happiness that Clara was experiencing was fragile and fleeting, in her mind. She was terrified that she might sabotage it. As far as she knew, William was still ignorant about how, and with whom, she was occupying her spare time. It was also obvious that he had schooled himself not to intervene. Clara knew this to be true, bearing in mind the only serious threat that he had ever issued her with, several years ago.

When she had first been sent to live and work in the Apothecary, William had said that if he ever had 'a serious objection' to her conduct, he would tell their parents immediately. This had been enough for Clara to understand her boundaries, because they both knew that their parents would order her back to the family home without hesitation. Fortunately, William had never seen fit to execute this threat.

Clara knew that this might not be a permanent leniency and that there must be a threshold to the behaviour he would accept from her.

Perhaps he couldn't afford to lose the help in the shop. That would explain his reluctance to interfere in her affairs. As unreliable an assistant as Clara was, she was his only one, and business continued to thrive. For William, the strain of earning an improving reputation was beginning to show.

He had never visited Squires' so frequently or drunk so determinedly. Clara didn't ask for an explanation. She knew that William needed time away from the business, just like any other man in a demanding profession.

Clara wasn't in any position to judge the behaviour of others.

William found it necessary to tell her about the new contacts he had made after every visit to the Club, as if this excused any recklessness. He must've also thought he was educating her on how leisure time could be used profitably, instead of selfishly.

He would never understand how lucrative Clara's leisure time had become.

Between them, they set out to inform each other about all they knew and treasured. Matthias set foot every morning from a close-pressed, ramshackle dwelling in the most neglected part of Shoreditch, but it only mattered that he knew where to find many of the most exquisite and inspirational places in London.

Clara had discovered more about the City that was of personal value to her in a matter of weeks with Matthias than she had in all the years she had been living there previously.

She couldn't guess how Matthias profited – though he had seemed to enjoy the places she had shown him. He also requested her company more than ever, when he had the luxury of some unoccupied time.

Their most recent visit had been made to a new exhibition at the Egyptian Hall in Piccadilly that had been organised by the Institute of Painters in Water Colours. Matthias had been the one to suggest it. He knew of Clara's interests, but had no idea of the extent of her passions for the subject. Clara was almost sick with anticipation at the thought of simply being able to *enjoy* her passion in a public domain. It felt like the freedom she had long desired.

The exhibition had transformed what she thought to be a pipedream into something much more accessible. She had seen sophisticated brushwork and elegant subject matter. Matthias had told her that the exhibiting artists were renowned for the status they gave to things of beauty, and he had been right. But she had also discovered that some of the artworks had been produced by *women*. Women, who were making a *living* from their art.

'Do you favour watercolours, Miss Breslin?'

'Not necessarily. I also – *oh.*'

The question had caught her unprepared; she had been so rapt with the exhibits. She had forgotten herself momentarily. Luckily, she realised in time that he was referring to her taste in other artists and not her own preference in art materials.

'Oh?' Matthias' cat-eyes flashed.

'*Oh* – I adore this brushwork. Almost *tender*, don't you think?' She crept closer to the canvas in question, attempting to escape the cold prickle under her skin caused by his close scrutiny.

'I do. There is something remarkably gentle about this water-based medium that other substances seem incapable of matching.'

Matthias had told Clara he preferred watercolours over other art mediums; she hadn't used them often but could appreciate his opinion. Oils were more vivid and could capture texture as well as tone. But there seemed to be a *mood* to artworks rendered in watercolours: serenity. Matthias could be serene as much as he could be energised. She would certainly try to recreate him in this form, if she could.

Her mind worked as she stood silent, appearing to study the canvas in front of her. 'I can't understand why societies like this are *only* beginning to earn recognition. Did you say that watercolours are rarely exhibited at the Royal Academy?'

'Rarely, yes. And not to their credit. As though they do not deserve the eminence. Who could deny *this* beauty?'

Clara breathed out a sigh of laughter. She was not used to hearing others speak the way she thought.

Matthias continued. 'Amateur artists are also permitted here, which is an unusual honour.'

Clara felt her next breath fix in her throat. She swallowed the hard stone of her surprise somewhat painfully.

'That – is incredibly generous. I can't imagine the difficulty these artists have when trying to gain recognition. Having seen these exhibits, the space is unimaginable without them – and yet some would say that amateur art is unworthy of such fine surroundings.'

Naturally, she thought of herself alongside the group of talented people she saw here but couldn't believe that she would ever gain the right to display her pieces in a public space. She couldn't do so, at any rate, whilst she kept her paintings of Matthias a secret. Nor did she believe herself sufficiently talented.

'I can't understand, or tolerate, those who wouldn't give publicity to undiscovered talent.' He paused, looking around him before fixing his eye on a particular painting. 'The same might be said for those who sneer at female artists making a living.' He gestured at one of the women's exhibits for emphasis. 'They are tragically wrong, of course.'

Clara smiled and her insides basked in comforting warmth. He wasn't referring to her – how could he be? He had no idea about her paintings. But his support had a soothing effect all the same.

'They will regret their scorn, before the century is out.'

Matthias couldn't be certain – not within such a specific time scale. But Clara knew it wasn't a fanciful statement. Each new decade seemed to bring unprecedented changes and new schools of thought. It wasn't implausible to think that the end of the century would bring more, perhaps on a much grander scale. She could only hope so, for the sake of all female artists.

This didn't seem to be a mutually beneficial arrangement. Clara knew that, for the majority of the time, she was following wherever Matthias led. He was the one with the deeper knowledge, the greater experience. He had the open mind-set which led him to places that Clara would never have known existed. But she could contribute in lesser ways, such as introducing Matthias to her favourite theatre: the Adelphi.

The actor had an extensive knowledge of non-theatre venues, because he had rarely been at a liberty to visit other theatres when he wasn't performing. Clara had become attached to the Grecian, for the sole reason that it was the place where Matthias performed. She wasn't so blinded by her attachment to the muse to forget how desperately below standard the other actors there had seemed to be, and the sad deterioration of the building. The Adelphi, on the other hand, was the place where she had seen some of the best performances of her life, not to mention where she felt more at home than anywhere else in the City.

In a fanciful way, she believed that introducing Matthias to the Adelphi would show him his future. He couldn't continue to perform at the Grecian – not with his talent. He stood out like an ink blot on paper compared to the rest of his company; that didn't make for a permanent career.

He was destined for a renowned stage, and Clara wanted to be responsible for introducing him to that opportunity. She hoped that bringing him to a performance would give him the hunger to strive for it. She was also aware of how delightful it would be to sit with him in the audience for a play, rather than only ever seeing him taking the starring role in one.

They watched *The Merchant of Venice*. It seemed that Shakespeare was having his run of the stage in this, Victoria's, reign. Clara didn't have a theory as to why; Matthias believed it was because his words were so versatile that they could become anything for anyone.

This was a standout performance from the many, partly due to its exceptional casting. Clara devoured the scenes as she always did. For her, it was the subtle dances of movement, the small exchanges that carried the plot forward.

She hadn't troubled Matthias for conversation through the performance, preferring to be attentive to the events onstage. She had looked over fleetingly at him on occasion, but he had been wearing a contemplative, if not slightly concerned, look. At times he would mumble under his breath and shift restlessly in his seat; she wondered if he was picking up certain criticisms to share with her later. When she questioned him after the final curtain, he seemed apologetic.

'I'm not used to watching actors deliver lines and not replying to them! It is a disorienting experience. Such talent … confined to one space. It makes me feel – would it be over-the-top to say "suffocated"?'

Clara kept silent; she tried to understand but sensed

that Matthias couldn't define how he was feeling.

'This is an exceptional theatre,' he commented airily, not dwelling on the subject. 'I see why you favour it. Do you see me standing on these boards; is that your vision of my future?'

Clara's face reddened and she nodded swiftly without meeting his eye. But then she regarded him quizzically. 'You must believe it too, Mr Tarasso. Don't you?'

'I am only certain that my run at the Grecian can't last. It will be an empty husk of a building eventually, so that will be the end of it. Do I believe that serendipity will send me onto a path that is greater? Sometimes fantasies are dangerous. Often, not knowing what lies in store softens many a wound.'

Clara wasn't comfortable with what she was hearing. And she wasn't taken in by Matthias' self-deprecation. He couldn't be blind to his own talent.

'Perhaps I can be the certain one then, and later the fool who rues her words. But I am willing to take that risk. I believe that you will achieve the distinction you deserve.'

They continued to part in the same way. Clara wouldn't let Matthias accompany her home, though she would have been a little safer. Nor would she travel with him to Shoreditch, though he'd asked her several times over. He wished to entertain her in his home – partly, she believed, because he wanted her to see him in domestic surroundings for a change. He didn't disclose the true reason. But she carried on declining, as politely as she could. She didn't know why she was reluctant, but the thought of her brother's reaction was enough to dissuade her. He flared his nostrils at the mere mention of Shoreditch, let alone the home of her muse.

She could tell, on this day above all others, that Matthias was beginning to tire of her repeated refusal. He wasn't angry – he didn't appear to anger like most people did – but he seemed tired.

'Miss Breslin, you still can't escape your self-imposed limitations. You must go on acting as a conduit for the behaviour that society imposes on us all.'

Clara felt no need to control her temper. She agreed with him. But she was also resigned to things that he consciously railed against.

'Life is an illusion.' That loosely defined term 'society' fell under this maxim, as far as she was concerned.

Matthias shook his head. 'I don't think that life is an illusion. Such a viewpoint merely exposes humanity's inability to define this lonely existence.'

He was watching her think; when she became aware of him again, his gentle laughter was blowing away the trailing threads of her discomfort.

She was endeared to him more by every meeting – even after a conversation such as this, which was as close as the pair came to arguing. How was it possible that a muse could fill so many spaces of her life with his influence?

CHAPTER FIFTEEN

She ought to have known that her current good fortune couldn't last. Matthias couldn't spread like an ember through the tinder of her life and remain unknown to everyone but her.

Alone in her knowledge of him, she could at least protect him. She could guard the incarnation that she had created on canvas; and shield the man himself from the scrutiny of those in her circle. She knew that discovery would leave him vulnerable. Herself: more so.

It seemed inevitable that things would change. Clara had stemmed the propagation of these thoughts, fearful that if change did come, their present contentment would be lost.

The day didn't announce itself in any way. It was almost cruel, that it could have almost passed into memory as one of the more idyllic days of Clara's life.

Together, she and Matthias had visited an exhibition by the Society of Female Artists. She hadn't known that the society existed, but Matthias had enquired after it. The exhibition had given Clara cause to believe that her aspirations were within shorter reach than she hoped, even with the Society being as small and relatively unrecognised as it was. She realised that there were others being supported in similar ambitions, who were rapidly succeeding.

Perhaps she ought to have appreciated this time as singular, as never to reoccur. It was obvious that she could never recapture that first delight upon entering the exhibition space. However, Clara was naïve enough to believe that it would only be a matter of time before Matthias showed her something else, equal in value. In this City, how could the current trend not continue? How could they run out of attractions?

She didn't want to acknowledge that happiness such as hers was seldom, if ever, permanent.

They had exited onto paving stones stained dark by the setting sun, their steps hurried with exhilaration, voices merging as a harmony with the easy union of their conversation. Matthias told her that he had visited Prince Albert's Exhibition more than a decade earlier; he had been fortunate enough to see innovations unlikely to ever be surpassed. Clara had expressed her longing to have been there, although she had only a picture of its magnificence in her mind.

'It would be impossible to undervalue it: an amalgamation of elements from every imaginable point across the globe. It achieved something unique, unlikely to be seen again. Rarely can one be aware, as I have been, of witnessing a landmark in history being raised.'

She hoped to show that she understood; that she could comprehend the brilliance he described. In truth, she couldn't. She felt that Matthias was ahead of her in terms of his encounters and his knowledge, and her inexperience must have shown like a blemish on her clothing. She couldn't betray herself by vying with him in any way or trying to seem worldly-wise.

But it seemed unlikely that this was what Matthias expected of her. She believed he shared his life with her because it came naturally to do so. They fitted together seamlessly in the way of any symbiosis of nature, and whilst she benefitted from knowing him, it seemed that he also thrived on his contact with her.

Her only regret was that she could not tell him the true reason that they met: her almost parasitic desire to capture his physical likeness on paper. This knowledge was an aching, twisting knot in her stomach, and she felt it whenever she had almost forgotten herself – a reminder that she shouldn't be content in the muse's presence.

Their return route had taken them via the Strand, and in this busier district Clara noted the familiar entrance of the Drury Lane Theatre Royal. Never had she thought the sight of a theatre could make her feel anything other than nostalgia or anticipation. Unfortunately, her reaction to the Theatre Royal was eclipsed by memories of an evening spent with Ruth and Albert. *The String of Pearls*, too, had been tainted. The macabre spirit of the play had become a bitter portent of her blighted friendship.

Since their last conversation, Clara had not seen or heard from Ruth. Their exchange hadn't been offensive or aggressive. But it was assumed, on Ruth's part at least, that Clara should suggest a reunion, having hinted that a meeting with Ruth and Albert would be a waste of her time.

Clara was glad that she didn't have the burden of meeting with Ruth hanging over her. She knew her gossipy friend would look on her acquaintance with Matthias with a conspiring eye. Albert was even less likely to understand the bond between them – he who thought only in terms of the guilty and the innocent, the genuine and the false, thinking that there was nothing in-between. If her association with Matthias implied the loss of Ruth, Clara could accept this.

They passed the doors of the theatre just as a host emptied out onto the street, excitement and the unspent energy of three hours making their movements exaggerated and their voices loud. She felt the soft rush of the heavy doors swinging wide and felt the glow of the chandelier on her face as a phantom warmth as she passed.

Matthias had just begun to tell her about the history of a renowned actor who had worked in the establishment when he was cut off by a voice rising above the dissipating crowd behind them.

'Miss Breslin! I say, over there, Miss Breslin, I beg your pardon!'

The roof of her mouth ran dry and her bones became leaden as she heard the voice: an authoritative booming which still bounced with the sing-song lilt of a much younger man.

Albert Barnes. She had known from the first syllable and was resigned that this eminent young lawyer wasn't going to be ignored.

Turning, she fixed her face with the most natural smile she could afford, and clenched her fists secretly by her sides, in the frantic hope that Matthias would, by some miracle, remain unheeded.

Albert was carving a way towards them, barely needing to open his mouth to move anyone standing before him. Ruth followed a little way behind, her smile as fixed as Clara's, though more successfully, aided by the natural radiance of her features. She came to a halt beside the man she loved, keeping her proximity to him discretely, so that no one could be mistaken about their imminent engagement. Clara stood a way in front of Matthias, hoping to be able to shield him with her body and desperate thoughts.

'We ought to have expected you here,' Albert opened, his smile too wide to be complimentary. 'It has become a haunt of ours, but attending the theatre was always your proclivity, was it not?'

Clara smiled politely, refusing to verbalise an answer. Albert made the pursuit seem sullied by Clara's association with it. Or so she perceived.

'I haven't seen you both for quite a while. I hope I meet with you in good health?' She wondered if her voice sounded as mechanical to them as it did to her own ears.

'Indeed. Well perceived, on both accounts.' Ruth giggled pleasantly to mask the acerbity of her words. 'We have had the most delightful evening with friends. We have gossiped and laughed and made such a racket that I wouldn't be surprised if we are dashed across the newspapers tomorrow morning, cited as the most riotous group in London!' She twittered with ostentatious laughter; Albert did not. Clara supposed he didn't like the idea of making bad press.

He made no recognition that Ruth had spoken as he addressed Clara again. 'How is Bill?'

'He is quite well,' Clara replied, disliking the familiarity with which he referred to her brother. 'I don't think there are enough hours in the day for the amount of work he tries to force into them, but he is enjoying his success.'

'He is an industrious chap. Knowledgeable about his trade.' Albert appeared to think for a moment. 'I believe I last saw him at Squires', only a week ago. We seem to share the same weakness, as well as the same work ethic.' He laughed roguishly, a joke that could be appreciated by no one but himself. 'Although, it was difficult to get any sense out of him, as it was long past lamp-lighting hours.'

Ruth joined him in laughing at this; Clara loathed having to smile in agreement. Reputation was everything to her brother, and as a supposed acquaintance and man of (in his own words) similar morals, Albert should have remembered this.

Throughout the conversation, Ruth's eyes had darted between Clara and Matthias. Clara clung to the hope that she hadn't connected them together, but knew it was foolish.

'William's demands on your time must be more frequent than ever,' Ruth observed, her tone of voice light and innocent. 'Perhaps that's why we have seen so little of you lately?' Her eyes locked onto Matthias at this point, making it clear that she wanted him to speak, to make himself known. She must have realised that Clara would never be the one to introduce him, unless questioned outright – and Ruth was far too consummate a professional in these matters to show her hand so obviously.

'I'm afraid that may be a fault of mine,' Matthias admitted, stepping forward a little and out of Clara's protective shadow.

'I don't believe we've met, sir,' Ruth replied, all astonishment. 'At least, I don't believe Clara has mentioned you to us.'

'Matthias Tarasso,' he offered, dipping at the waist slightly in a bow, although the question hadn't been asked.

'Mr Tarasso,' Clara interjected, attempting to salvage what was left of the exchange, 'this is Mr Albert Barnes, the reputed lawyer, and Miss Ruth Davison, a childhood friend of mine.' She watched the three of them exchange the usual postures of pleasantry, awaiting her fate.

'Her oldest and dearest friend, Mr Tarasso,' Ruth corrected, smiling sweetly all the while, as if she were merely relaying the opinions of others. 'We grew up together, and since Clara moved to London I desired to maintain our bond by living in close proximity.'

'Mr Tarasso is an actor.' Clara felt weak; she knew she'd walked into a trap and had chosen to do so rather than face the worse consequence should she have fled.

'Goodness,' Ruth exclaimed, looking at Matthias with altered eyes. 'How interesting! Would we have seen you in any recent productions?'

'I don't recall seeing your name on any of the latest playbills,' Albert admitted, feigning to cast his mind back.

Clara was sick with dejection. She knew that everything had been ruined, and each further moment spent with these two was casting great tears through the ties that united Matthias and herself. He would never seek her company again. She would return to her room that night and stare at the canvases, knowing that her only way of completing them would be to resume her post in the window seat.

'My troupe isn't well known. Our theatre has fallen on sufferance and I don't believe we will recover. It isn't unexpected that you don't recognise me. As it stands, I'm sure I will soon be seeking alternative employment.'

Clara was both surprised and endeared by his lack of pretence.

'I'm sorry to hear that, sir,' Ruth replied, and there was something in her voice to show that his honesty had chiselled the facade from her, too. 'I'm sure that Clara will be affected by such news, as the theatre is one of her most wholehearted pursuits.'

'I can't speak for Miss Breslin, but I don't doubt that she has done what she can to support our theatre. If we are to close, it will be in spite of her best efforts.'

'I have enjoyed the productions I have seen at the Grecian. It's unfortunate that every theatre in London can't gain equal recognition; that those with the most prestigious guests are the ones that appear to prosper.' Clara wasn't sure whom she addressed here. Partly, she hoped to allay Matthias' concerns. Other establishments would fight for his employment, of that she was sure. At the same time, she knew that Albert and Ruth were judging her on the company she was keeping; she couldn't help but try to convince them that true friends weren't to be found in the most fashionable places, where superficiality reigned.

'Clara my dear, we must be on our way. Albert has an important trial in the morning. The Devonshire broker's case: I am sure you'll have heard of it.' If Ruth expected recognition from Clara and Matthias, she would be disappointed. 'Let's not part for such a long stretch of time again? You must join us for dinner within a fortnight, I insist.' She placed her hand on Clara's arm to suggest the most amicable reasons behind the request.

'Mr Tarasso, you would be more than welcome too,' Albert suggested.

'Oh yes, most certainly,' Ruth agreed, as if the notion hadn't occurred to her. 'You must tear Clara away from the theatre – I believe she forgets herself whilst she is there and is surprised to find that she has friends in the real world!'

'Working in the theatre myself, Miss Davison, I can only sympathise. I often find that I would rather spend an evening with *Titus Andronicus* than put the world to rights with any real friends. A pleasure to have met you both.'

He shook Albert's hand and bowed to Ruth whilst Clara stood by in bemused silence. His tone suggested nothing but politeness, but she knew he had risen to her defence. She still felt mortified about the unprecedented meeting, but her spirits were lifted. The worst had happened, and her new-found friendship had survived it.

As they parted, Clara assured Ruth and Albert that she would meet them again soon. She knew she couldn't avoid it; Ruth had been introduced to Matthias and knew something of his profession, but she wouldn't be satisfied with that. Clara had been far too evasive. She hadn't revealed how she and Matthias met, nor why they were spending so much time together. Albert would surely pass on the news of this meeting to her brother, who was unaware (or pretending to be) of Clara's association with her latest muse.

It was inevitable: Matthias would have to be introduced to William, sooner rather than later.

'Your friends are so charming. I can't understand why you didn't arrange this meeting sooner.' Matthias' face glowed with wry amusement as they continued along.

'It saddens me – but it would be foolish to hope that we could avoid them. London isn't so large a place, when it comes to that.' She smiled apologetically. 'You managed them admirably.'

'I hope I haven't damaged your reputation.' He spoke with all seriousness, which Clara hadn't expected. 'I wouldn't want to subject you to their gossip.'

'My reputation hasn't been intact for quite some time,' Clara admitted, with a light-heartedness that didn't quite reach her eyes. 'And to tell the truth: I have kept you to myself for far too long. No doubt you think I'm rather selfish, insisting on meeting you alone, limiting the company.'

'Miss Breslin, I am of a like mind. I don't believe in the pretence of a society that I don't want to entertain. Why create your own misery?'

'I've been told that's a derogatory attitude, which leads me to think that misery is just part of making yourself acceptable to others.'

'One day, Miss Breslin, you're going to realise that you shouldn't choose to believe everything that is said about you without question. We can't truly define *ourselves*. Why should we let others do it for us?'

Clara was struck by his candour. He spoke with

insight, as always, but his words brought into question everything she had ever been compelled to agree with. Could she ever teach herself to turn away from the derision of others? She wasn't sure she had the strength. Although, with Matthias by her side, she was starting to believe that she might be able to summon it.

'So rebellious, Mr Tarasso! I'm sure that Ruth and Albert will profit greatly from their decision to invite you to dinner.'

'I'll provide them with so much scandal that they won't need to go to a society ball for another year.'

They continued their walk, moving the conversation swiftly from the subject of Albert and Ruth to the date of the next important exhibition, and from that to the play that Matthias was currently rehearsing. Neither acknowledged the figurative smog which had fallen over them. How could either of them verbalise the grim subjects left unuttered?

For one: Matthias' future in his own profession – uncertain at best; at worst, non-existent.

For another: Clara's friendship with two people who, without question, regarded Matthias as a dubious character – worse still, a social nobody.

And finally: the decision that Clara had made to introduce Matthias to her brother, that same evening.

Deborah E Wilson

CHAPTER SIXTEEN

illiam moved to the front of the shop and held his lamp to a crack in the wooden shutter, earning himself a view of the empty street outside. The light was low, the sun almost disappeared, and the characteristic thick fog beginning to swim just above the level of the cobblestones. He listened out for the vibrating hum of carriage wheels or the soft patter of footsteps against stone. Clara had absconded across town again, and it was getting late.

His eyes accustomed themselves to the half-light and he peered into the shadows cast by the lofty buildings. For a while, he couldn't distinguish a thing from the hues of dusty grey. Eventually, however, discernible shapes began to appear from the darkness beyond.

The shapes stopped half a dozen yards from the shop. They were close enough that William could be sure they were human figures: a pair of them, one taller than the other and clearly male, and the other just as obviously female. William perceived that they were in the middle of a conversation. He couldn't be sure that the woman was Clara, but he was bound to wait for her return, and so he passed the time watching the pair talk to each other, straining to hear any distinct words or phrases.

Occasionally, the voices could be heard more loudly, but not enough for William to make sense of the conversation. As time passed, he became uncomfortably aware of the taller of the two. There was something about the masculine silhouette which prickled the surface of William's skin, unsettled his internal organs.

The light had dropped even further by the time the conversation had come to an end. Almost immediately, the shorter of the two figures moved towards the shop, and William saw the distinctive shade of red hair and knew her to be Clara, as he had half-suspected from the start.

He began to move to unlock the door, but not before the taller figure turned his head to look directly at him, and William would have been ready to swear that the man's eyes caught the lamplight in a burst of unnaturally bright green …

Rounding the corner which led them onto Broad Street, Clara brought Matthias to a stop with a warning in her voice.

'My brother's Apothecary is just beyond here.'

There was something searching in Matthias' expression. 'And your home.'

'Yes.'

He paused; she couldn't tell whether he guessed what was in her mind. 'I hadn't realised you lived here. I've walked here countless times. It is a regular route of mine.'

Clara felt a rush of guilt that almost unsteadied her. She avoided his eye.

'I've purposefully kept you away from here, I admit – for my brother's sake, rather than mine. But now I know that it was wrong of me to meet you whenever I wished and selfishly keep William unaware of it. He will open the door for me when I knock, and I ask you to stand beside me and be' – she exhaled a sigh – '*prepared* to meet him.'

She knew Matthias would be uncomfortable. She knew he would disagree with her sense of propriety.

But she didn't know him well enough.

'My goodness, Miss Breslin, of *course* I will.' He pursed his mouth and looked out beyond her, obviously thinking of something tactful to say. 'However, couldn't we postpone this until a more reasonable hour? I think it would improve my standing, a little.'

Clara smiled apologetically. 'It would. But it can't wait. It could be a fool's compulsion – and if I'm mistaken, I'm prepared to take full responsibility for my error.'

Typically, Matthias laughed. 'There are many words I have for you, Miss Breslin, but "fool" isn't one of them. This is about your friends from Drury Lane, isn't it?' He tilted his head. 'Does their good opinion really matter so much to you?'

Clara felt the anger rise in her throat but couldn't stop it. 'It has nothing to do with them.' Her voice was sharp. 'It is about the trust between my brother and me. He watches me leave this place day upon day but says nothing, doesn't pass on any guilt. I *do* feel guilty though, all the same. It is about *family*. Can't you empathise with that?'

Matthias shrunk a little as if hurt. Before Clara could speak, he corrected his posture.

'I understand familial loyalty. It doesn't explain your urgency.'

Clara had composed herself. 'I admit, I would much rather the two of you meet before my brother hears about our friendship from someone else.'

Matthias indulged himself with a small smile. 'I respect your wishes, and your family bond. However, I wish—' He caught himself, breathed heavily. 'I wish you could break the shackles of society and be free to live as you choose.'

Clara was no longer terse, but wistful, as she replied, 'It must be so easy for you. You don't have to live with the consequences of that choice.'

Matthias looked as if he had considered reaching out to her but resisted. Clara felt the impression of his touch nonetheless.

'Dear Miss Breslin. I was an outcast in this world, this *England*, from the moment I entered it. I don't belong, and people can sense that. By design I am a dissenter, not to be trusted.' He raked his fingers across his crown in exasperation but laughed all the same. 'Why else should I be accepted in the theatre?'

Clara admired his imperviousness to petty prejudice and told him this. However, she asked him to understand how difficult it was for her to be so unconcerned. As if it hadn't been his intention from the start, Matthias agreed to meet William immediately.

They began to move towards the Apothecary, and as they did, they heard the breaking of glass from within …

When he appeared behind the lifted latch, William was obviously perturbed.

'Bill, that sounded like a breakage – not a great deal of damage, I hope?' Clara's voice was light, but her stomach was rolling.

'An empty jar. I was distracted.' William's voice was devoid of emotion. Clara noted now that his arm rested on the door frame, barring entry. 'Are you going to introduce me to this gentleman, Clara?' His attention was on Matthias; there was wariness, rather than anger, in his look.

Clara felt a cold prickle crawl up her back. She turned to look at Matthias to see that his attention wasn't on her brother. Instead, his chin was raised, and his eyes rested on the upper window. As she spoke, his gaze quickly returned.

'That was my intention, yes. William, may I introduce Mr Matthias Tarasso. Mr Tarasso, here is my brother, Mr William Breslin.'

There was a stretch of time – perhaps the length of a single heartbeat – in which neither man spoke nor moved. Afterwards, simultaneously, two things happened—

'Mr Breslin.' Matthias bowed briefly—

'Who are you, Mr Tarasso?' William asked—

William's eyes followed Matthias' bow with a flick of suspicion as he spoke. When Matthias straightened again, Clara saw a flash of amusement touch his features. Internally, she begged him not to purposely point out the ambiguousness of her brother's question, as he would usually do.

'Sir, amidst a complexity of possible responses: I am an actor – supposing my occupation is the answer of most interest to you?'

'Of most interest to me is the reason that you are currently standing beside my sister. Had it been much later at night, I don't believe I would have engaged you in conversation at all. *Sir.*'

William's threat wasn't veiled. Taken aback by the curtness of the reply, Matthias appeared to show contrition. 'I'm standing here, like a villain on your threshold, at your sister's request. She wanted us to be acquainted.'

'That is obvious.' William looked towards his sister. 'Clara, explain yourself clearly. You might save Mr Tarasso a great deal of unpleasantness.'

Clara moved towards her brother, repeating a forceful mental command to the tears threatening her eyes.

'Mr Tarasso performs at one of the theatres I visit, Bill. It was inevitable that we would speak to each other. It transpires that we share many common interests. We are friends – but I was uneasy continuing our acquaintance without you knowing about it.'

William stared at his sister for two heartbeats, his pupils contracting slowly. 'I think our perceptions of what is "inevitable" differ somewhat.

'And I suppose the two ... *friends* have been sharing their common interests this evening? And other times besides?'

'Mr Breslin, I must offer you my apologies. It would've been proper for us to tell you about our acquaintance a long time ago. But I am forgetful in these matters, and the thought didn't occur to me naturally.'

'I don't know you well enough to presume to know your faults, Mr Tarasso, but I would say that this forgetfulness of yours must be severe indeed. Did you also forget to invite a chaperone along with you on your adventures with my sister?'

'After spending time in my company, Miss Breslin thought a chaperone was unnecessary. I must admit I encouraged the decision, because Miss Breslin has impeccable morals. If she needed a chaperone, I don't think you'd let her travel the City on her own. She knows her own mind and her own abilities exceedingly well.'

Clara wasn't prepared for such a generous endorsement, but she suspected that some of Matthias' answer had been cunning deceit. Regardless, she was glad he had spoken so admirably. Her brother had been so unkind that she wouldn't have been able to control her temper otherwise.

William had nothing more to say. Clara realised that Matthias' display of respect for her had improved his standing in her brother's mind. William began to smile (albeit lacking humour).

'Strong-mindedness is certainly one of Clara's most outstanding traits.' He seemed to be thinking carefully. 'As for the rest: before today, I would have agreed with you. I'm going to have to accept your word, aren't I?'

'That's entirely your choice.'

'I also have to accept *you*.'

Matthias stayed silent; a good decision, in Clara's opinion. William needed time to digest all he'd heard. The mere fact he had suggested accepting Matthias in his sister's life was consoling.

Matthias took a step backwards.

'I had better leave the two of you to a restful night's sleep; no doubt you will be rising early tomorrow.'

'Yes.' William sighed. 'This is certainly a business that requires an early start – though a restful night is something other entirely.'

Matthias smiled sympathetically. 'You must provide a great service to a great many people.' His attention gravitated towards the inside of the shop. 'I can't say my own profession is as beneficial, but it helps me become conversant in the art of … conversing.' He laughed softly.

Clara smiled at his remark; William, however, frowned as if he believed Matthias to be speaking another language entirely. 'I expect it would be most agreeable to spend my days in idle conversation. But I'm not at such a liberty.'

Clara couldn't prevent herself from speaking. 'You are exaggerating a little, Bill. It's clear that when you do have the time to speak to our customers, you do so most readily. But it is undeniable that our custom increases week upon week. Even my limited assistance doesn't reduce your workload.'

Somehow, the three of them had ended up inside the shop, with Matthias perusing the shelves. Clara wasn't sure how it happened. When she saw how easily Matthias found his way around the premises, an idea struck her. She couldn't understand why she hadn't had it much sooner.

'I have a suggestion.' She spoke tentatively. 'Bill, not

long ago you suggested to me, perhaps in a spirit of jest, that you may find yourself needing to employ a new assistant.' William opened his mouth to speak but Clara was resolved to continue. 'Mr Tarasso is under the unfortunate circumstance that his place of work is suffering financial difficulty. Couldn't you employ him as an extra pair of hands? Forgive me for speaking for you, Mr Tarasso.'

She continued – Matthias seemed completely at ease with the idea, whereas William had begun to turn a shade of grey.

'Bill – it would be hard to find an assistant with such a natural ease with words. As Mr Tarasso has already said, his other profession gives him perfect practice in the art of conversation.' Selfishly, Clara also held the hope in her heart that, with Matthias working in the place where she lived, she would not only have more time for painting, but also to study his appearance.

Matthias turned to survey the room, smiled and nodded to suggest he was thoroughly pleased with the notion. 'My audiences are flagging like overworked mules. The Grecian Theatre will soon drop its playbill to little more than two performances a week.

'I won't pretend that I've been anything other than a source of displeasure to you, Mr Breslin. But if I can entreat you – upon your sister's good word – I would work hard for you, relish occupying my free time and be most glad of the wages.'

William was kneading his forehead with the knuckles of one hand. 'You have no medical training. I know nothing of your employment history, except your talent for theatrics. Your reputation doesn't stand you in good stead, Mr Tarasso.'

'Indeed. Education has never been my friend. Nevertheless, it walks hand in hand with my success.'

William hummed out a short laugh. It was the best Clara had heard since he and Matthias had met.

'You will have a trial of one week. I'll see how you interact with my customers – many who, bear in mind, have bought their cures from me on a regular basis for many years. If you can manage the pace of the work, and avoid mistakes, then …' He lifted his open palms enigmatically.

Clara withheld the burst of feeling which accompanied William's decision. Instead, she whispered somewhat frantically, 'You will be glad of it. I'm sure you will.'

William's face creased reluctantly in a smile. 'He is certainly sure-handed with the stock.' As they spoke, Matthias was reading one of William's recipes and concocting a most respectable cough syrup.

'If you'll allow me, Mr Tarasso, I must close the premises.' William came up softly behind Matthias and appeared to be pleasantly surprised by the sum of five minutes' effort. 'You can start tomorrow, if your theatre can spare you.'

Matthias agreed to the arrangement and left William with the syrup he had made which, William had to admit later, was better than the syrups the medical students produced at his bi-annual conferences.

When the actor was out of sight, William

turned slowly towards his sister, who was too lost in self-congratulation to notice him.

'Does Mr Tarasso know he is your muse?'

The last word shattered her reverie and left her doused in ice-cold fear.

'How did you—'

'I recognised him. From your … drawings.' The last was said almost with a shudder, as William had seen how Clara's once innocent 'drawings' now lined her walls like five centuries' worth of old wall-hangings.

'No. He doesn't know. I have no desire to reveal it.' This was an unveiled warning.

'I don't envy you, having to conceal it,' William admitted. 'When he starts spending a lot of time under this roof, I can't imagine how you'll uphold the pretence.'

Deborah E Wilson

CHAPTER SEVENTEEN

By the end of the week, even the most faithful of William's customers thought that Mr Tarasso was the best thing to have happened to the business in years.

When asked the reason for this consensus of opinion, however, most people couldn't set it down to just one factor.

It wasn't just his liveliness, or his attentiveness and charm.

His sensitive response to people's ills and his respect for the materials of the trade weren't enough to recommend him either.

His knowledge of Shakespearean soliloquies was hardly relevant, but if he didn't regularly recite them to waiting customers, he wouldn't be thought of half as favourably.

Upon this single point they agreed: they could no longer imagine the place without him.

From William's point of view, these endorsements were pleasant enough, but gratuitous. For him, having someone else behind the counter was enough.

The custom passing through the door continued to swell, but with three separate brains and pairs of hands to share the work, the pressure was noticeably lightened. The days were also considerably shortened.

However, William couldn't be as openly complimentary about his new assistant. He was constantly concerned that Matthias might choose to act on Clara's attachment to him. Moreover, the way the man dressed was highly unsuitable for work. But he couldn't deny that his new assistant had a certain vitality and flair with conversation that could be considered attractive to the masses.

Clara didn't care about Matthias' reputation with the customers, or how his presence benefitted William as proprietor. Of course, it mattered to her, but it was insignificant when she thought about how wonderful it was to be continually in the company of her muse.

She constantly observed his features, to greater reward than she could ever have hoped when she'd watched him onstage.

It was also different now, because she could take the time to preserve these images in her mind. When they walked and spoke together, any prolonged period of silence would have roused his suspicion – he was most observant. Therefore, the weeks she had shared his company had hardly improved her art at all. Now, being almost always in sight of him and with more leisure than ever to paint him, she was developing day by day.

As far as anyone could observe Matthias' opinion of his new-found position, it was clear he relished the work; he thrived on the opportunity to apply a new skill; and he couldn't so much as open his mouth without expressing his gratitude towards his employer to anyone who would hear it.

And when Matthias' spoke, everyone within earshot wanted to listen.

Sickly Miss Chesterton, gossiping Ms Watson – in

fact, all of William's more devoted customers were pleased to have not one, but two young gentlemen to give their attention to.

Word soon spread that the handsome Mr Tarasso was also unattached, even if he didn't have the same potential and skill as Mr Breslin. It quickly became known that he wasn't only an apothecary's assistant, and that he aspired to a lengthy career in the theatre.

The regulars were delighted by Matthias' presence, but only admired William all the more for keeping such excellent company. They couldn't relinquish their devotion to such a consummate professional, not after his years spent providing the remedies they needed.

Fortunately, they discovered they'd been sensible in this decision. It soon became clear that Matthias was guarded when it came to expressing his affections, and people began to suspect that he held some secret regard towards the unmarried Miss Clara. When the young woman herself was questioned on the matter, however, she was resolutely unmoved on the subject and wouldn't consider it for a moment.

These same customers found they also couldn't discover from William where he had found Matthias to begin with.

It was unusual for an actor to become acquainted with a member of his audience (who wasn't in the business of sponsoring actors for their own financial profit), more so to find an actor who was in need of additional employment and just so happened to be proficient at apothecary work. All William would say was that Mr Tarasso had happened upon the place at the most opportune time.

The weeks passed, and there were more timely occasions to come.

'I require some of your Famous Purging Agent.'

'Forgive me, madam – would you repeat that, please?'

The lady, who was most certainly in need of a purging agent, judging by the yellowness of her complexion, spoke deliberately and with a slight tone of condescension. 'I require – some – of your Famous – Purging Agent – if you please.'

William shook his head. 'Once again I must ask your forgiveness. You see, at first I believed I had misheard you, and now I'm sure I've misunderstood you.' He rubbed his hands awkwardly, as he hated contradicting his customers. 'You see, we have many such agents which will perform the task you require. However, I know of none that would be regarded as "famous".'

The act (hardly a pleasant thing) of purging by the use of herbal remedies had become quite widespread throughout England. It was quick, effective and only mildly embarrassing and uncomfortable. One only needed to be laid in bed for a few days, by which time the cure would work most efficiently and rid the body of its unhealthy poisons. Expelling these poisons wasn't an elegant matter, and so most kept the details to the imaginations of those who asked about their recovery. The following period of lethargy was often cured by a few hearty meals, and rarely lasted beyond a month.

The lady wishing to try this popular remedy for herself was most insistent.

'That can't be the case. I have heard from over half a dozen of my acquaintances in Mayfair that Mr Breslin's Famous Purging Agent is the best to be found within a five-mile limit.'

William stared, uncomprehending. The words 'famous' and now 'Mayfair' had caused him the most bewilderment.

'It comes in a pale green bottle,' the woman sighed, with the utmost patience.

'Pardon my interruption,' came a voice from behind the stockroom curtain, 'but could this be the remedy you require?'

Matthias moved towards the counter, carrying a suitably pale green bottle. 'I've just finished bottling the latest batch. It *has* become a bit of a bestseller, Mr Breslin – this is the second batch I've prepared in the last four days.'

William looked at the bottle as though it may, at any minute, jump across the counter and bite him. 'This one?' he asked, suggesting that he didn't regard it as anything better than any of his other cures.

'Yes.' The lady was emphatic. 'That's it. That exact bottle is becoming renowned city-wide, Mr Breslin. I'm surprised that you are unaware of its popularity.'

A gentleman from across the room, who was discussing cures for insomnia with Clara, overheard the conversation. 'You know, most men of your profession have begun to "patent" their popular cures, Mr Breslin. Perhaps you should consider patenting this – what did you call it, madam?'

'Famous Purging Agent,' the lady confirmed, as if she were the one responsible for deciding the name.

William sent assessing looks between the pair of customers, apparently none too pleased at this sudden assault of opinion. 'That may be the choice of many in my profession, but I tend to mistrust a patented label. Having examined many of these "popular" cures, I have found that the majority of them are worryingly false in their descriptions.'

Very few of William's customers would disagree with his opinions; they only had to see the rapid success of his business to realise that he must be able to make considered choices.

The sallow lady left somewhat brightened in appearance, if only at the thought of using her much-recommended cure.

In her wake were a number of people who were curious to see this famous remedy for themselves. During the course of the afternoon, the whole batch of bottles was sold: for immediate use, for the use of those who were indisposed to travel, for medicine cupboards and for the medicine cupboards of relatives, masters and mistresses.

'I can't understand it,' William persisted, several hours after the notoriety of his mixture had been revealed to him. 'My sources haven't changed for several years; neither has my mode of manufacture. Perhaps my merchants receive their ingredients from better sources?' He glanced at Clara and Matthias and laughed at the wonderful absurdity of it all.

Once word of his Famous Purging Agent had spread, many of William's other wares became almost equally well-known by association. He couldn't attribute it to any further effort on his part. Eventually he became reconciled that well overdue recognition had finally been granted. His cures had always been superior to those of many other establishments, and all it took was a few choice words between the right sorts of people for the public at large to discover him.

It was more fortunate than ever that Matthias had been employed when he had, because William had become something of an overnight sensation. No one could know how long it would last, but whilst people travelled across town to visit the Apothecary to purchase some of the 'finest products in London', Matthias and Clara would be needed to help uphold the business. William spent the majority of his time attempting to satisfy people in perfectly sound health who wanted to hear tales of his rise to distinction. This might have irritated a more modest person, but William had always enjoyed flattery and a rapt audience.

Matthias was a respectful assistant, always aware of who was in authority and just how much he owed to him in gratitude. However, he also began to flourish.

Clara could have despaired at the constant bustle in the shop, and with it the thought of having to browse the stockroom more than a dozen times a day, but Matthias kindly spared her that ordeal. It was clear that he had built a swift and secure knowledge of where to find almost any material that he required. Even when he wasn't fetching stock, Clara would sometimes find him sitting in the stairway, amongst the shadows and dust, contemplating. It appeared that he'd become strangely fond of the room.

He'd proven himself to be perceptive in so many ways. Despite only having the meagre training that William could spare him, with the shop so busy, he seemed to understand the materials he was working with, and better still, the people requiring them.

He seemed to have recognised Ms Watson's hypochondria from the moment she stepped into the shop and behave accordingly, and, unusually, had revealed Miss Chesterton to be a talented singer; a preoccupation she had never revealed but was more than happy to demonstrate once he had observed a 'musical resonance' in her speaking voice.

Matthias was always mindful of his 'true vocation'. As an apothecary's assistant he was valuable, but no one who visited the shop could be in any doubt that his true domain was the stage.

He would sometimes engage customers in lively debates about current productions, and it was clear that he was using them to practise his articulation. In rare private moments, he liked to encourage Clara to philosophise her existence, in his usual way. Clara never grew any bolder, and she began to suspect that he provoked her merely to exercise his own mind. He must have known that she couldn't change so completely; he had seen how she worked and how she lived and who she was related to and there could be no room to misunderstand it.

Clara still travelled to watch the now infrequent productions at the Grecian. Matthias couldn't be at the Apothecary every day because of his modest two performances a week, but he would often intersperse a half-day in rehearsal with a half-day mixing and measuring.

Despite his change in routine and the dearth of acting employment, Clara still struggled to understand how the theatre could be failing with him as a key member of the troupe.

He was just as captivating, if not more so – and the extra work only seemed to be improving his demeanour upon stage. Perhaps the conversations he had with the patrons were stimulating his creativity; perhaps they helped his acting to be more spontaneous and genuine.

The audiences still underappreciated his talent. Clara often wondered why none of the customers from the Apothecary came to see William's charming new assistant in performance – could they really be so fickle that their admiration for Matthias was discarded at the shop exit?

Matthias didn't share her disappointment. On one occasion he thought to brand her, somewhat carelessly, a cynic. Clara instantly found herself defending the title:

'Cynic I may be. I don't pretend to be anything else. We are cynics because we are supposed to follow a particular set of values – but society, and those who feel no cynicism, provide no alternative. What if it is impossible to achieve what is deemed to be everyone's lot in life?'

'This isn't about insincere customers anymore, is it, Miss Breslin?'

'It's about *love*.' Clara expelled the word like a weight off her ribcage. She had never mentioned it to him before, and it felt like the world around her warped and buckled as she did so. 'If you don't find and create love, you aren't "normal". But no alternative is believed to be acceptable. And so what are we cynics left to do but criticise the nature of humanity, and even life itself?'

She hadn't meant to be so melancholic. She hadn't meant to talk about love to *him*. But, as ever, he'd found a way to trim back the thicket of sharp brambles she placed around herself and reveal her inner thoughts before she'd even had time to consider them.

'Even if cynics mistrust humanity and its doctrines, they can find something hopeful in other things besides them,' said Matthias in slow, delicate reply.

Clara made a noise of agreement. They were of a same mind, then. 'We *can* find something hopeful in humanity, on occasion. In case love forever eludes us – we seek other fulfilment.'

Clara knew he understood her then. For her, all that had happened before became suddenly all the clearer.

Running alongside William's rise to acclaim was Clara's studious improvement of her painting. More of her free time could be occupied with it now. She didn't have to sit in her room for hours on end, trying to remember expressions or postures she'd seen – Matthias was always near her, in plain sight, so close that she could have reached out to study the contours of his face with her fingertips, if she'd had the nerve.

She'd found it much easier to start her latest piece, having fresh images of Matthias in her mind which were strengthened with each passing day, rather than being allowed to fade with memory. Sometimes, she would even have the fortune to sketch him where he stood – but the sketching pad was secreted underneath the countertop and she could only risk adding to it whilst his attention was occupied by his duties.

One evening, she had been so absorbed in her work that she had stayed awake long into the night, performing the finishing touches by lamplight (which, she knew, wasn't conducive to creating accurate tones of colour).

Unexpectedly, this hurried completion didn't have adverse effects on the overall superiority of the painting. It showed Matthias sitting on a rooftop, looking like a statuette on the outer wall of a medieval building, in a position of ancient authority over the city streets. One leg dangled over the ledge, swinging freely in the open air; the other rested on the tiles and was bent at the knee. Upon this leg he rested his forearm. His eyes, rather than studying the busy scene below him, were fixed on an indistinct point high up near the summer sun, though he did not shade his sight, and he had a smile, almost of defiance, on his face. The rare green of his eyes shone in the sunlit haze she had created, their tone the most accurate she had been able to mix. It caught some of the true effect of Matthias' eyes, which was more than she could have hoped for. The richness of his skin, the delicate contrast in the textures of his clothes, were all captured in such a way to suggest that Clara had distilled a little of the soul of the man himself and somehow mixed it into her palette.

The following day had been the first emergence of Breslin's Famous Agent (still unpatented but shortened over time by those who didn't want the name to sound vulgar), and so she had no opportunity to discuss her proud achievement with her brother. The painting was laid to rest against the wall at the foot of her bed, and she woke every morning afterwards to smile at it.

Matthias remained ignorant of her activity. He showed no sign of William having told him, and Clara was careful to remove traces of paint from her clothes. But the absurdity of sneaking around like someone guilty of a crime often bored her.

She considered abandoning her reservations and telling him outright about her months' worth of effort spent on his likeness – now that she had reached a stage where she was *almost* content with her finished images (she couldn't remember having this with any other muse).

After all, he was a friend now, as well as a colleague. Surely the discovery of her paintings wouldn't lead him to remove himself from her life? That would inconvenience her brother, and he would lose out on wages. He might even become the victim of some unkind gossip over his sudden departure.

Surely, he wouldn't.

He might, of course, be unnerved by the extent to which she had endeavoured to create his portrait ... be concerned about her motives for befriending him ... be dubious about her true support of his talent ...

No. Clara wouldn't disclose anything. Only when she had the confidence to approach a gallery to exhibit her work would she be obliged to. Satisfied as she was with her latest piece, she couldn't foresee herself having that level of self-belief for some time yet, let alone the bravery needed to approach William with the idea. To distract herself for the time being, she began sketching out her next creation, which was to be Matthias on a golden stage surrounded by likenesses of himself in his different Shakespearean incarnations.

She painted without pause and with the utmost concentration for a number of days, hardly aware of life outside her room. Only when she needed reminding of a particular feature of Matthias' did she move downstairs. Once in the shop she became aware, as if waking from a particularly vivid dream, that there was another existence down here, and worse, that she had responsibilities to others. These responsibilities namely involved providing people with the Famous Agent, or assisting Matthias with bottling more of it, as orders hadn't lessened in frequency.

Clara couldn't imagine why so many people were in need of the remedy; perhaps it had become fashionable merely to have the bottle on one's shelf. The act of purging couldn't be considered stylish – however, being ill had always been à la mode for people who thought illness was a means of getting attention.

On her third day of absenteeism, Matthias paused in his attentions when Clara eventually came into view and fixed her with a wry smile. Clara stopped before she reached the bottom step and looked at him suspiciously.

'What is the matter?'

'Nothing.' Matthias returned to his preparation. Busying his hands with idle tasks, he added, calmly, 'For a moment I wondered if we were being burgled.'

Clara scoffed and pursed her mouth. 'I daresay a burglar would have more sense than to leave the place by its only staircase.' She tied her apron strings and stood opposite him, glancing at him occasionally over the box of bottles as she attempted to synchronise her efforts with his.

'Yes, forgive me, Miss Breslin. My reason had temporarily abandoned me.' He watched her from underneath impishly arched eyebrows. 'It is so rare for me to have company in the stockroom recently, that I—'

Clara cleared her throat pointedly in interruption. 'My apologies – I've been unwell.'

His eyes flicked over her momentarily. 'I am sorry to hear it – though I must happily observe that you bear no trace of it now.' He paused to cork a bottle. 'If I may say so: having seen you today, I can't say I've ever seen you in better health.' He didn't meet her eye, but the compliment glowed with no less warmth.

'Thank you.'

Seeing her expression, Matthias laughed. 'You needn't look so surprised!'

'Well, I'm sure you're exaggerating.' She smiled good-naturedly. 'Perhaps my self-imposed solitude has left me a little better-rested than usual.'

'If you say so, Miss Breslin, then I am in no position to argue.'

Clara said nothing more and it was her guilt that stopped her tongue. It was also partly embarrassment. But feeling the way she did about her success, she could almost be disposed to believe what Matthias had said about her.

William came through the curtain to ask Matthias to collect some stock for an order and was so preoccupied with the task that he only appeared to notice Clara once he had been given the ingredients he needed. His reaction to seeing her working bore almost an exact resemblance to Matthias' when he'd watched her coming down the stairs – though there wasn't the same good humour in it.

'Well, there you are. I'd almost begun to expect a note of resignation.'

'You know that would never happen – I live here, after all.'

'Ah, I see – you can't resign from your life.'

'No. I am resigned *to* it.'

William looked as if he had half a mind to leave the conversation but decided he couldn't concede in front of Matthias.

'Until death, I suppose,' Clara added. 'Of course, I haven't the experience to verify this.'

'Well, since you haven't had the inclination to quit your life,' William retorted, with dispassion, 'and you haven't been doing your share of the work, I suppose you must have been otherwise occupied.'

Clara was resolved not to panic. He wouldn't mention the paintings now. He couldn't! There wasn't any profit in it for him, and William never thought of anything but profit.

He moved over to Matthias, looking over his shoulder at the bottles he'd prepared. With a smile of satisfaction, he looked back at Clara. 'Perhaps reading? Or sewing? Did you ever remember to practise the piano?'

Clara felt the constrictions in her body loosen, but she didn't show any sign of relief or gratitude. He spoke to her like a cat torturing its prey before eating it, and yet if he didn't want to destroy her, why did he threaten her?

'Miss Breslin has been ill – she was just telling me,' Matthias said.

Clara wondered if he was aware that there was something he couldn't follow between her and her brother, something that had grown with them and had lasted too long to be unravelled. There was love in there somewhere, and she wondered if familial love was the motivation for many of William's cruelties. For neither the first nor the last time, she wondered if she disappointed him.

For the time being, the quarrel was forgotten, and William was distracted. He turned from Clara to Matthias and smiled. 'Then it is good that she works in an Apothecary. Come on, Tarasso – the customers will be three-deep at the counter by now.'

Matthias heaved the box of Famous Agent into his arms and followed William through the curtain.

Clara waited. She didn't like to walk in after them until she could be sure that she could move around unnoticed.

When Clara had managed to improve the flow of service sufficiently, she felt she'd done enough to allow her to return to her newest painting.

It was almost finished. Her hours spent working beside Matthias had allowed her to study the features she needed and add a few final brushstrokes.

As she climbed the stairs, she reflected on her afternoon – she'd been able to observe the way Matthias and William's working partnership had changed. They spoke to each other without forcedness: Matthias didn't have to be deferential to William, and he could make some decisions himself; William didn't feel that Matthias was an unknown character and left him to his own devices. They shared an equal amount of knowledge about the regular customers and had agreed on their approach to the new ones. Matthias had clearly studied the cures he was selling, and in return for this application, William allowed him control over the ingredients for the production of certain remedies. They were working well together, and the business benefitted from their accord.

Clara applied herself fully to the task of completing this second major piece. In a few brushstrokes it was done, but the few brushstrokes were the most crucial and each in itself required a significant period of thought. Her arm, her eyes, her mind ached as she took a step back from the canvas and potted her brush. But once again, she was thoroughly pleased with her latest depiction.

Matthias as she knew him, surrounded on either

side by the eight Shakespearean roles she had seen or heard of him play. He stood in the centre, in front of an implied audience and under warm theatre lights, but he didn't look like he relished the attention. He looked humbled to be so admired. The four figures on either side of him were identical in appearance and yet quite obviously copies. They were rigid like sculptures and held themselves in classical poses, their heads turned to look up at the spaces where the boxes would be situated. The original Matthias looked straight out of the painting, as if his gaze was directed beyond the audience, at a solitary spectator.

Clara placed the new painting next to the rooftop portrait that had preceded it. She had named the first *Muse Aloft* and decided that its successor should be named *Theatre of the Muse*. Whilst the two pieces were equal in value to Clara, she felt that this newest work had unique traits that distinguished it quite clearly from the first and made the pieces unsuited for direct comparison. When it came to identifying these traits, she found that she couldn't. She concluded that it wasn't the artist's duty to uncover them.

A few days later, she noticed that *Theatre of the Muse* had one conflicting detail. It would hardly detract from the piece at all but for the fact that in her own mind it didn't match the image she'd intended to create. The central figure of the painting, the true Matthias, had become slightly distorted, presumably through over-painting. His jaw line had been lit too severely by the theatre footlights, giving the face a vaguely gaunt, drawn appearance.

Though it caught Clara's attention, and had taken

its time to do so, this slight error didn't alter her opinion of the piece. Set alongside *Muse Aloft* in its own miniature gallery, it was still one of the best she had painted. In her haste to complete it, she had merely let her boundless energy overcome her usual meticulousness.

Deborah E Wilson

CHAPTER EIGHTEEN

She may have been able to enjoy an almost childlike vitality, but with a lack of sufficient rest, Clara began to find that her body was unable to match up to the pace of her mind.

Her uninterrupted study of her muse brought her a tranquil soul and a solid purpose, but it also meant that her life had become consumed by him, both physically and in thought.

She knew her mind would never tire of her muse, but whenever she thought of him, she found that she no longer knew how to do anything else. She thought nothing else deserved her attention.

She only ate when William brought her food. She only slept without having decided to do so. These brief intervals of sleep, therefore, were always interrupted as soon as she had realised her mistake. She didn't rest during the day, as this would have wasted valuable time for painting or sketching or studying her muse.

Her only recreation time also involved spending time with Matthias, as they still occasionally found time to walk around the City together, to visit galleries or theatres. She also continued to watch Matthias perform at the Grecian – but these opportunities, although valuable, were rarer still. He seemed to be distracted enough by his work at the Apothecary that the lack of performances didn't outwardly bother him.

At first, all she realised was that her body no longer seemed to respond to her commands. When it did, it did so sluggishly, almost peevishly. Her unanticipated periods of sleep were more frequent and longer lasting.

Later, she noticed the paintings.

At first, it seemed so cruel that she imagined it to be a trick of the light, or her overworked mind creating visions.

She noticed that the central Matthias figure in *Theatre of the Muse* was not the only one to have a flaw. Eventually, an incorrect detail with every one of the figures in the painting became known.

For one of them, she had painted an eyebrow so that it arched fretfully instead of serenely. For another, the curve of his lips became a wistful frown instead of a relaxed mouth. For some it was a detail of the costume, where the gold leaf of a crown or a sword appeared tarnished. She couldn't forgive these mistakes as easily as the first; her lack of attention to them began to resemble carelessness.

Soon she began to fear that all of her recent pieces held a fault of some kind, and the features she didn't approve of became intensified.

Her favourite piece, *Muse Aloft*, in its prime position, was turned away from her scrutiny to face the wall. She couldn't bear to find an error in that – but she began to believe that one must exist. The errors she did find in the others, whilst barely noticeable to an outside eye, were enough to ruin the impact of the image. The idea occurred to her to paint over the discrepancies or repaint each entire piece from the beginning. But the amount of work implied in such an undertaking was enough to overwhelm her already exhausted mind and body. She could only hope that her future works would be an improvement.

She tried to be optimistic about future paintings, but the disappointment of discovering that Matthias' beauty might be beyond her skill to paint affected her spirits badly.

She began to withdraw herself from any sort of conversation in the shop, barely tried to assist anyone, and thought only of intensifying her study of Matthias in the hope that the mistakes she had made would be rectified easily, once she had devoted the correct amount of time to it. But she no longer had the same endurance. Feeling as ill as she did, she only felt worse about her failings, and feeling worse about her failings, she caused her body more suffering in attempting to redress them.

After weeks of this, even her hours of sleep began to betray her ...

Before she enters the room she knows the woman has a sickness. Nothing tells her – although the corridor is dark and only lit by a scattering of tiny candle stubs. No smell of sickness has escaped from the room ahead, no attendant at the door forewarns her of the disorder she will see. But she knows that on the other side of the door, she will find a bedchamber and find the woman lying in bed and sick.

Her hand rests on the brass handle and she can't go in. She doesn't want to speak to the afflicted woman, can't bear to hear about her suffering. She doesn't want to see her, hair unbound and fanned across her pillow, body shrunken beneath the bedclothes, skin pallid and ghastly and shining with clammy cold sweat in the candlelight.

Nor can she leave. If she does, word will spread of her selfishness, of her hard-heartedness. If she could only convince them that it was neither of these things that stayed her movements: that it was – that it was …

Then she sees the red silk scarf hanging from the handle and no, she is wrong, this must be the wrong room, it cannot be his—

She is sitting in the audience at the theatre. She can't remember, and it isn't important, how she came to be there. The room is dim and the lamplight is low, and that must mean the evening performance is about to start. She can't see the faces of the people around her, but she can see their silhouettes in the periphery of her vision and feel their presence close by. The stage is entirely obscured; the curtain is drawn closed and hangs heavy and dark and almost like the still surface of a deep lake in the night.

She waits with the usual tense anticipation for the curtain to rise, to reveal the first tableau of the play. But as the moment draws nearer, she begins to feel that she mustn't be here to see whatever awaits her on the stage. She mustn't stay; there is something unnatural about this place and she soon comes to understand that the shadows and the obscurity and the outlying darkness around her pose some kind of threat. She has been lured here and if she doesn't leave she is in great danger of becoming a captive. But the vast expanse of the stage, still hidden, transfixes her; she is loath to leave before discovering which play is to be performed.

Can she risk awaiting the opening scene, in the knowledge that whatever danger awaits her may take its opportunity as soon as the play begins?

From the bottom of the pooling fabric of the curtain, a vague rustling, as if a breeze has agitated it. Or is it a minute twitching, as if a hand upon a rope is too eager to raise it? Impulsively, what little illusion of bravery she has departs from her. She rises to leave. The aisles are narrow and almost thoroughly obstructed and she can barely move past the people seated alongside her. She wonders why they do not make even an effort to ease her way. Polite entreaties do nothing; urgency only worsens her own state of mind. Time is forgotten and, somehow, she nears the end of the aisle, and coming free of it finally sees the face of a fellow member of the audience.

It is a sickbed face.

Clammy, cold, pale, with eyes that are glazed like an outward-facing window on a foggy day, and a crusted mouth. She feels both a childlike revulsion and an instinctual pity, but the panic that the semi-dark has induced in her causes her to abandon any predisposition towards empathy.

She feels her pace quicken as she travels down the central aisle towards her way out. Every face marking her way has the same ill, dishevelled look—

This must be the world as the birds see it.

She doesn't see herself flying, but by some means that escape logic, she is in the sky, seeing the streets from above as a living map. From this vantage point, London is a network of rat tunnels. She can't understand how she hasn't come to this realisation before.

She can see all of City life from up here. People are dots, with shadows fragile as cotton thread, who dash from place to place and become part of an indistinguishable swell as they join the heavier masses around Westminster and London Bridge.

Time may or may not be moving more rapidly than is natural;

on the other hand, she may merely have been watching the same scene for a long time and become immune to the passing hours. In one way or another, the sun has diminished before she has thought about its descent, and all too quickly it is late evening and all over the City, the lamps are being lit and London begins to shimmer.

It isn't the shimmer of the moon in the surface of a puddle, or the shimmer of daylight on glass. It is more the shimmer of candlelight upon the outside of a copper kettle.

With the sound of steam wheezing in a copper kettle on a range, her vision travels rapidly and comes to a narrow point upon a solitary figure that has somehow attracted her attention.

She knows it to be a man and she can see that he is running.

He is familiar to her, but she can't remember his name.

She watches, as if through a long-range telescope, as the man dashes towards a large four-storey house. His head darts quickly to look over both shoulders as he enters but the movement is hardly perceptible and already the door has closed behind him. She follows, materialising easily through the roof tiles and the dusty attic flooring so that she can survey the same gentleman from the ceiling of an upper bedchamber.

The room is in almost complete darkness, but for two stub candles mounted on the furthermost wall, looking out over silhouetted rooftops. Her eye is drawn by this so that the man, now hunched, and the figure in the bed are not remarked until a few moments later. By this time, it appears that she has already missed an important exchange, as the gentleman is weeping and the bedridden person he has just spoken to is now racked with coughing.

The man in the bed looks elderly but could be any age due to the degenerative power of his illness. His limbs could be bones propping up the bedclothes. His eyes are the shadowed sockets of a death mask and his skin shines ghastly pale in the weak candle glow. He whispers to the younger gentleman, who seems to know what will happen, for whispering is all he can do. The gentleman nods, opens a small pocket Bible which has been concealed within his coat and begins to read in hushed, reverent tones.

After a short exchange, the bedridden man is dead. She seems unable to avert her panic-stricken gaze as she watches the last breath of life leave him. She watches the bedcovers lifted over his face and is incapable of moving, breathing or weeping.

Before she can face the embarrassment of seeing the gentleman dissolve into tears again, she is inexplicably grounded, running down flights of stairs from the house and out into the street, where night has fallen and the familiar London smog has risen to smother all that would be visible.

The mist ascends rapidly, and Clara is alone.

Dreams are both an expression and an affliction of the brain, and Clara, being of a mind that could create works of art with boundless imagination, believed herself to have been more afflicted than most.

She had always dreamt in astounding ways, but her recent dreams disturbed her mind as it rested, so that when she woke again, her emotional state hardly varied from when she had first succumbed to sleep. She slept in a heightened state of agitation and fear and awoke exhausted. Hardly ideal conditions for someone set upon the most pivotal of undertakings. Her mind had its outlets but no refuge, her body much less than that.

'SHE IMAGINES DEATH... LEERING OVER THE BED, CLOAK FANNED OVER THE COVERLET LIKE AN OUTSTRETCHED WING.'

CHAPTER NINETEEN

'You must have noticed it.'

'I have – but it doesn't appear to be anything except … ordinary.'

'How would you know what is ordinary for her? Doesn't that require knowledge of her character as lifelong as mine?'

'I can't argue with you, Breslin. Still, having broached the matter with me, you might have warned me in the first place that I wouldn't be in any position to comment on it.'

William puffed the air out of his lungs in exasperation, pinched the bridge of his nose and looked at Matthias in a way that suggested his every word inflicted the pain of an insect bite.

Matthias looked back at him. It was clear he wouldn't venture any further remarks on the subject.

'I was beginning to hope for her again.' William was preparing for the day's opening but spoke over his shoulder. 'It would never be her choice to work for me here, I know that. But from her recent behaviour, I thought she might invest *something* of herself in the future of this place, for my sake.' His voice dropped a note. 'I realise that thanks are owed to you, in part.' And he walked through the partition curtain to avoid fully acknowledging his gratitude.

Of course, his thanks were owed to Matthias. If William had never extended the offer to work for him, he would have never kept up with the increase in custom. He would have had to hire further hands anyway, and in greater number, as Clara wouldn't have strayed near the shop half as often if not for the promise of being with her muse.

It was almost laughable, William thought – that of the two of them, the muse himself was ignorant of his status.

He still had some inexplicable reservations about his sister's attachment to the backstreet performer, but whilst Matthias was unaware of the depth of her feelings (at least superficially), he felt more at ease.

But now the balance had altered. The tenuous harmony that the three of them had been experiencing was now beginning to falter; Clara was no longer contributing to the running of the Apothecary in a meaningful way.

'A supposed illness is one thing; this is quite another,' William continued, re-entering the shop as if there hadn't been a pause in the conversation.

Matthias looked up from measuring herbs with a bemused but patient smile.

'You and I continue to work as hard as ever, Tarasso – she neglects *all* of her duties. This affects the whole business – the complaints, for one thing.'

The complaints, yes. People entered the shop in their dozens, within hourly intervals, but word had started to spread of an unpleasant nature.

Cures weren't producing their expected results – sometimes the opposite.

Customers would leave contented, and for a day or so their remedies would work exactly as advertised. But days would become a week and quite unexpectedly their benefits would sour. Prolonged exposure to an unfortunate number of Breslin's cures and remedies, now renowned throughout the City, began to exacerbate people's ills instead of diminishing them.

Only the Famous Agent seemed to have retained its efficacy, but its popularity began to wane nonetheless.

'She must be mixing the ingredients incorrectly because she's distracted.' William didn't have the heart to suggest to Matthias that *he* was the distraction. But his eyes accused the man without words and he knew that his sister would be unable to deny it.

Matthias sighed, bundled up a rag he had been using to clean with and threw it past William's head and through the opening in the stockroom curtain. 'I advise you to withhold any suspicions until your sister is here to answer for herself,' he said, curtly but respectfully. 'Once our cures are in their jars, there's no way of knowing which of us has mixed them, but I'm sure she will respond with honesty if she is confronted.'

'You are sure,' William repeated, with a little disdain in his voice. 'As her brother, I suppose it should be my natural inclination to be equally certain.'

Clara didn't appear that day, and couldn't be held accountable for her misdemeanours. William made the effort to coax her into working, but she replied (from behind closed door) that she'd slept badly and wasn't well enough for the day's work.

William and Matthias worked as best they could;

a successful partnership despite their uneasy bond, their conversation light and somewhat entertaining for the customers passing through. They knew to use their collective personalities to their advantage when speaking to indecisive new faces. William had the benefit of years of experience and knowledge of his craft, and Matthias could contribute with empathy and a well-judged timing for humour.

Few of the regular customers acknowledged that there should have been a female Breslin, and those who did rarely showed concern for her. Only long periods of waiting caused customers to ask William why he didn't have another assistant, to which he left Matthias to relay the apologies and excuses that caused him displeasure.

The late afternoon brought with it the cold and damp. Crowds crossing Broad Street diminished, retreating into waiting cabs and shrinking into doorways. The few that remained grimaced at the shrouded skies and hurried on, failing to spare even a glance into any shop windows they were passing.

Matthias had been watching the street for the past quarter of an hour, chin resting on the back of one hand as he used the other to measure out ingredients. William had long since abandoned his post, feeling no need to maintain his showman-like persona with no audience expected. Occasionally a sound from the stockroom reminded Matthias of where he was and to make sure he at least had the appearance of a man who was usefully occupied.

Nothing stirred his interest – until a movement caught his attention which had such purpose to it that he knew he must gather his wits.

Through a fine mist of rain crested the tip of a large grey umbrella. The body underneath was diminished by the vast span of the material shading it. It was the figure of a woman, clothed in grey to match the dreary weather, and her complexion almost drained of colour to match. She moved towards the shop with intent, but reaching the threshold, she paused and moved her head from side to side, searching the street. When she finally made her way inside, she hurried to close the door behind her. Matthias moved out from behind the counter in anticipation of a strained exchange.

Miss Hawksworth looked the same as she had several months before, when Clara had commented on her work ethic and dishevelled appearance.

Matthias hadn't witnessed this first exchange but had later seen the young lady over the course of the summer as she returned to renew her stock of ground Valerian root. For as long as Matthias had been working with the Breslins, he had known Miss Hawksworth to be a bright and talkative young woman in the best of health. The face that greeted him with wariness now was a poor reflection. He also noticed that she had begun to stoop when she walked so that upon reaching the counter, she had to place a hand out to steady herself. He tried to offer his arm to her along with his usual words of welcome, but she refused the help, as if she didn't want to admit to her current condition. She glared at him accusingly.

'Do you … require your usual prescription, Miss Hawksworth?'

'No.' The reply was brusque. 'I wouldn't have that stuff again – you could *pay* me, and I wouldn't.'

Matthias didn't enquire as to why.

'Then, perhaps an alternative—'

'Where is Mr Breslin?' The lady's eyes, surrounded by swollen flesh, were keen as a crow's – she peered towards the stockroom, attempting to edge past Matthias.

As if taking direction from the wings, William stepped through the curtain with confidence. Matthias could tell by the slight stiffness in his shoulders that he had heard their conversation and was cautious of the customer's potential for volatility.

'Miss Hawksworth.' His greeting was warm. 'Please tell me what is troubling you.'

She seemed surprised at first, as if she expected the apothecary to ignore her obvious ill health. She soon recovered her former coolness. 'You should recognise it, sir. This is your doing – I'm sorry to say it, but I would be a fool to pretend otherwise.'

William touched Matthias' arm to move him aside and surveyed Miss Hawksworth's appearance, looking into her eyes and examining her posture. Shortly, he stood up straight again and gestured to Matthias to pick up a notelet and pen.

'You have stomach aches. Your vision swims after overexertion, and you struggle to remain upright because your sense of balance is skewed.'

'Yes ...' Apparently, Miss Hawksworth wasn't expecting to have her symptoms diagnosed so succinctly.

William fixed a look to Matthias which could only be described as measuring. 'I can only apologise that a product from my premises has caused you such unrest. Please allow me to prescribe you an alternative remedy, which has no risk of adverse effects.'

'You admit it!'

'I would never deny a fault on my part. Though I must hasten to impress, my attention to dosage has never been remiss. If the fault lies with someone in my employ, you can be assured that no such mistake will occur again.'

No sooner had the words left his lips than the front door rattled open and slammed shut rather abruptly.

'Breslin!' An angry gentleman stood bristling behind Miss Hawksworth, the pinkness of anger in his face matched by the weary redness of his eyes. He charged forward and slammed a small glass jar onto the worktop.

'You said that this bloody concoction would help me sleep – it's done the complete opposite! Stomach aches were just the start of it – now I'm seeing twist-eyed and staggering like a bloody drunkard! Pardon my language, madam,' he added gruffly, finally seeing the young lady beside him.

'I share your sentiments, sir,' Miss Hawksworth replied, bemused. 'Won't happen again, Mr Breslin?' There seemed to be little leeway between laughing at the irony and angering further.

William was trying to suggest that the two inaccurate dosages must have been the result of a faulty set of scales when a third person entered the shop, only temporarily halted by the tense scene that confronted her. A middle-aged affluent woman, she covered her nose with a handkerchief as she drew level with the large gentleman. 'I see I'm not the only person to be expressing a criticism today. This Valerian root I've been prescribed is off, Mr Breslin – or mislabelled, or a complete swindle. It's done wretched things to my health! You must cease trade of this vile substance immediately, or you can expect your tills to empty within the fortnight! Word spreads quickly, Mr Breslin, and I have a voice which reaches further than most! What you have here is ruination, decanted for sale in a glass jar!'

'Please, Mrs Allen. I am in the process of explaining to these good people, who share your complaint, that—'

'If you have a useless assistant, Breslin,' the gentlemen huffed out, pointing a glare at Matthias, 'then you'd do well to discharge them and save yourself further embarrassment.'

'I can assure you, should that prove to be the case, I will not hesitate. However, I can't determine anything at such an early stage – I didn't know that the Valerian root was over-concentrated until a matter of moments ago, and the prescriptions themselves are all at least a week old. Short of engaging an outside party to investigate the matter for me, I don't know how I'll discover the cause of the error. But please – *please*, rest assured that I will respond with full diligence, and cures will no longer be dispensed without my having personally inspected them. Let it not be said that William Breslin is a careless apothecary.'

'Let it be said *no longer*,' Mrs Allen corrected him archly. With the mutual agreement that they would rather take their custom elsewhere for the present, the party of three left under no less tempestuous a cloud than that under which they'd arrived.

William leant back against the counter and made a sound somewhere between a dry retch and a groan of anguish. Matthias stared blankly at the floor, the only motion his breathing. Each knew what was on the other's mind, as they were both thinking about the same person.

It was the actor who first spoke, attempting to quell the elder Breslin's fury.

'Nothing will come of it. People are prone to use large statements in the ripeness of feeling. But three incidents – less than the thousands of successful cures you have prescribed over the course of your career – won't bear a permanent stain. It'll be forgotten by next week.'

It was the silence that frightened Matthias. William seemed shrunken, compressed and compacted within his anger. His expression was introverted, his features darkened like the gaping apertures of a skull.

Matthias thought he heard a distant twig snap in the fraction of a second that it took William to unfurl and launch his tremendous anger towards the staircase, taking off at a run.

'CLARA! WHAT HAVE YOU DONE?'

If Matthias had intended to follow, to mediate, his body and his face showed no sign of it. He wouldn't be able to intervene. Had he tried, he would only have succeeded in losing his position. Best not to come between two siblings, his reason told him.

Upstairs, William hammered on his sister's door with

both fists, his body tense with anger.

'Open the bloody door! You will stand accountable for this, God help me!'

From behind the panel of wood came a subdued reply. 'I won't do a thing until you calm down, you madman. You'll hurt yourself.'

'Hurt my—' William spluttered. He dropped his arms and stepped backwards, laughing with incredulity. 'It's all well and good to play caring and concerned now! When I'm ruined, will you express the same *concern*? Or was this your plot all along?'

'Stop being melodramatic. Has Matthias been giving you lessons?' Clara opened the door and faced up to her brother.

He failed not to flinch at the sight of her. She looked as if she'd not slept for at least one night. She hadn't changed out of her nightclothes or made any attempt to present herself respectably. Her face was rumpled like the pages of a discarded newspaper.

'Good God. What are you doing to yourself?' William's voice was quiet as a child's in awe.

'Nothing,' Clara replied honestly. She was doing nothing – nothing at all – until her paintings improved and she could see fit to face the day.

'You look wretched.'

'You had a problem?'

William remembered. 'Yes. You. You might have sent this place into the bailiff's books today. Three lots of powdered Valerian root, of at least *twice* the recommended concentration, given to customers in a matter of days. Customers accusing me as if I can't do my job, telling *me* how to regulate my staff! Do you know what Mrs Allen said? "I have a voice which reaches further than most!" If she tells her "circle" about this, I'll lose a quarter of my month's takings! You're a disaster! What have you to say?'

'You may as well dismiss me.'

'So, you admit full culpability?'

Clara closed her eyes and drew in a sharp breath. 'Would that stop you from behaving like a poor lunatic out of Bedlam? I don't know how it's happened, Bill. Has it occurred to you that it might have been any of the three of us that mistook the dose?'

'It has occurred to me that, of the three of us, you are the one who is absent-minded at her work.'

'In that case, dismiss me.'

'No. If I dismiss you, you go back to Trowbridge. You can explain yourself to *me* before you say anything to Father.'

'If you won't dismiss me, leave me alone. I have no answer to give that will satisfy you.'

'Very well. Shut yourself back in your hovel. Forget to eat and sleep – I find your current will to destroy yourself selfish in the extreme. But when your paint palette runs dry, remember that I will be paying you the wages to replenish it. Wages that you hardly deserve.'

Clara closed the door.

The corridor is only lit by a scattering of tiny candle stubs. Wax congeals around the rim of each candelabrum and has spattered darkly onto the carpet. The ceiling is low, the passage narrow. The walls are painted the colour of rich port wine.

Before she enters the room, she knows the woman is close to death. Everything is muted. Deathbed silence. All weeping has been done; prayers whispered and silently urged are over. Now, everyone waits.

Her hand rests on the brass door handle and she can't go in. She imagines Death waiting on the other side, leering over the bed, cloak fanned over the coverlet like an outstretched wing. She doesn't have the mettle to face up to mortality: the woman's eyes glassy and grey in the half-light, her last breath cracked on her lips.

Nor can she leave. How can she flout the end of a life? How can she pass this place again, see the black shroud hanging at the window, and know that she turned away—

She is standing in the centre of the stage. The room is dim and the lamplight shines from a sole spot, somewhere above her head. She can't see the faces of the audience but can see their listless black forms as they await her performance. She feels their presence like some crouched animal, estimating its kill.

She waits with the usual tense anticipation for the play to begin, for the first lines to be spoken. But this time the lines should be hers; this time she stands under the scrutiny of others. The room is silent, and nothing moves, as if this is a moment caught in time. A word, a movement from her might shatter it.

She knows that she can't go through with the performance. She mustn't stay; there is something unnatural about this place and she remembers that the shadows and the obscurity and the outlying darkness of the auditorium pose some threat to her. She won't risk witnessing the opening scene, knowing that danger awaits her.

Impulsively, she turns to leave. The wings are completely dark; she can't see the route which would lead her away. Moving even two feet leaves her lost and sightless. She has no option but to dismount from the stage into the audience itself. As she moves close to the edge, she realises what should be a short drop from the stage to the ground instead resembles a gulf. It would be a fall into complete and utter blackness. She looks around in distress and wonders why no one will assist her. Peering into the absolute gloom she tries to discern audience members — if she could only catch their eye, she could entreat them to help.

She sees now — no one will help. How can they?

Dead. Each and every one.

Slumped, propped into upright positions in their seats. Stiff and clumsy in their lack of posture. Eyes vacant and grey, like those of fish left to suffocate on the dockside. Mouths open and crusted, some twisted in final groans of pain.

Her stomach succumbs to tortured turns as she tries desperately to climb down from the stage and flee. Still it feels as if the audience is waiting, anticipating her first lines, or the unveiling of a tableau.

Why can she feel them watching—

The man is familiar to her and she can see that he is running. She would call his name, if she could.

Stop. You mustn't go there.

She watches, as if through a long-range telescope, as the man dashes towards a large four-storey house. He is inside barely in time for the doorman to allow him entry, and the door closes again almost as quickly. Before he has reached the upper floor, she is in the bedchamber awaiting his arrival.

The room is in almost complete darkness but for a gaslight swinging from a bracket in the ceiling. Her eye is drawn by this so that she doesn't immediately realise that the rusty squeak is the only sound in the room.

She casts her eye over the bed. The man is sitting upon it, speaking with Death. She can see that they are in conversation, for neither one breaks the other's gaze, but no movement is made and no sound of voice escapes either of them. Death is shrouded; there isn't a face to be seen. The arms of his cloak spread like a mother bird's wings, protective over the covered corpse beneath the bedclothes.

She wonders if they are bartering over the dead man, if the younger man desires to buy back his life, in some despicable way. Or perhaps Death speaks to the loved ones of every person who dies, before he takes them. She can't imagine what he could possibly have to say. Death is final. It can't be reversed.

She doesn't realise at first that they have moved to look at her. Death, the gentleman in mourning ... and the man in the bed. He is sitting up now. The bedclothes are still wrapped over his head so that she can't see his face, but she knows he is watching her. The three are motionless, chess pieces awaiting her move.

She tries to speak but her tongue is leaden. So are her feet. They must expect her to speak – to explain. She can't. It isn't her story to tell.

As if this lack of cooperation on her part concludes their meeting, she finds herself out on the street again, staring up at the house, rain pouring onto her face from the slate-grey skies above.

She feels as if someone ought to be standing behind her. But Clara is alone.

'It would help if you would sit for me. But I know that such a thing will never happen.'

Clara would never speak her thoughts to her muse, but in the solitude of her room, with the boundary of the staircase separating them, she felt that she could express them freely enough.

It was an unburdening of her inner frustrations. She couldn't say she felt anger towards Matthias – she didn't believe in deceiving herself. Her anger stemmed from her dissatisfaction with her recent work, her inability to express herself with her art as well as she could just a few months ago. Her feelings of uneasiness on the subject had only been compounded by her recent tendency to the most distressing nightmares – morbid visions which seemed to worsen as each night passed.

Shut away in her room, enforcing creativity (in itself a paradox), she believed she could correct this – if she isolated herself for long enough. Lack of distraction was a blessing, except when her brother would interrupt with words of scorn, but this was easily disregarded. Hunched over in the same spot by her canvas for hours on end, she noticed little.

Intermittently, in times of empty darkness and deep silence, her blood surged as she sat stiffly at the end of her bed, a swift heady lurching, as if she had received a shock. It provided her with a sudden nervous energy, which she gratefully applied to her work, but always with the feeling that something was happening around her which she had (perhaps ill-advisedly) chosen to ignore. In time, she knew the feeling to be a new-found, irrational fear of death which her night terrors had fostered, and she couldn't shut out the feeling that a black-cloaked figure waited in her periphery. For what, or whom, she didn't dare question.

CHAPTER TWENTY

*E*ach new day brought fresh fear. William was suspended by dread that each person stepping through the door could be another victim. He had been much more diligent with running the Apothecary, to the point of obsession, determined that mistakes wouldn't be repeated. But he'd no idea when the incorrect doses were dispensed, or whether the complaints he had received so far were the sum total. Some could be so incapacitated by illness that they were unable to leave their homes … He couldn't accept that his business might fail.

Matthias offered him condolence and support where he could. But now he was mistrusted by the proprietor and didn't dare speak as freely as he once did. He now only did as instructed and made no attempt to maintain the rapport they once shared. It wouldn't impress customers any longer. They didn't want impressive sales patter, or charm and flattery. They only wanted to know that the medicines being prescribed were safe and trustworthy. William could only sell half of the wares he used to now, and only with the utmost cajoling.

The two men were an uneasy workforce, and it was plain to see that if the business didn't revive its former reputation, it would be closed within the month.

Other Apothecaries, and the newer Chemist's shops, were thriving. The clientele that William had nurtured so carefully found it no inconvenience to take their custom elsewhere, finding the same cures at competitive prices and with peace of mind included in the bill.

Nearly a week after the first distraught customers had hounded William over his negligence, Matthias asked to speak to him in confidence.

'Good God, don't give me any more bad news – I can't bring myself to hear it.'

Matthias thought that William was like a glass pane about to shatter.

'I am truly sorry.' Matthias' dark eyes were brim-full of concern. 'You may believe I never really cared for this place – but you would be more wrong than you can know. Its decline – your pain – it hurts me as well.'

'Just say what you came here to say, Tarasso. It will mean nothing for now – it will be empty words. Tell me, and be done with it, for God's sake.'

'I have heard that some of our former customers are suffering from serious illnesses.'

William's eyes were screwed shut. He brought his hands close against his face as if he were praying. 'Will they die?' The idea felt weightless, as if he had been expecting this outcome all along.

'I am pleading with all my soul that they will not.' Matthias laid a tight grip on William's shoulder. They stood facing each other, hunched together like mourners on a winter day. 'Each case is different, just as different illnesses affect people of different ages. If a person has age in their favour, survival is better assured. If a person less well-favoured for recovery has an excellent physician, they may also defy mortality. In each case, there is hope, and we must, as fools do, grasp at that.'

'Your news is worse than I could have imagined.' William heard the empty, hollow voice leave his own throat and felt detached from his own words. 'I feel the deepest horror, that I am responsible for such suffering. That is – if you are sure that—'

'Yes, each invalid has taken an overdose of some prescribed substance in the days running up to the onset of their illness.'

'I am ruined.' William had the tone of voice of a man who finds he is shot and is astonished by the sight of the blood.

Clara appeared at the bottom of the stairs, a smear of green paint streaking one cheek. 'Who is dead?' she whispered, in a fraught tone.

Matthias turned swiftly at the sound of her voice. The blood had drained from Clara's face. 'No one. But there are at least five seriously ill people who have a connection with this place and can attribute their illness directly to a cure bought here.'

'And this is proven? There isn't another Apothecary that could have sold them the same substance?' Clara hadn't moved from the foot of the stairs; she didn't know which of the two men to approach.

'You forget, sister.' William had an ill-looking smile on his face. He shrugged himself out of Matthias' comforting grip and took a step towards Clara. 'Until a matter of weeks ago, we were set to be one of the most popular Apothecaries in London. Everyone bought their cures from us. I had a Famous Purging Agent, it was the talk of Mayfair!' He was laughing now – it was a sickly sound.

'Bill – please.' Clara did not know why she was pleading, but her brother's despair frightened her.

'What, Clara? What am I to do? What *am* I to do?'

Clara had recovered from her initial panic. Her premonition hadn't come true – yet. Though she knew it couldn't be far away. If her brother was to lose his livelihood, he ought to be sedated against the deep pain it would cause. There was time to put the situation right – and William's reputation could be slowly rebuilt, if he was protected from the repercussions.

For now, he had to relax his mind. Tearing himself ten ways over what might be to come was self-torture. If only she could be sure that the afflicted people would survive …

'This is what you must do,' she said firmly, tucking her paintbrush behind her ear. 'You must go to your Club. Matthias, you must go with him. Drink. Talk with your companions. Seek advice. Find someone who will fight for you in any legal row to follow. Tell people – anyone who will hear you – that you don't believe you are entirely culpable for these errors. That you were ill-advised by your suppliers, that your—'

'That my assistants are responsible?' William bit, his eyes narrow. 'Shall I incriminate *you*, dear sister? Or our actor friend here?'

'You must incriminate *no one*.' Clara's tone was

strident. 'Admit nothing, suspect nothing. That is the only way we can overcome this. If you begin to doubt, we are lost. Our solidarity is the only thing that can protect us. You must trust that we are in the right. If not, you are admitting defeat before the fight has even begun.'

'To Squires', then,' William said, unconvinced and overtly volatile but allowing himself to be guided out onto the street by Matthias. He called back to Clara, who had followed them through the curtain to the door, her knuckles white as she gripped the doorframe, though the two men couldn't see it. 'Pray for our safe return, Clara. Pray that we have a guardian angel tonight.'

Clara's stomach ached as she watched them walk away.

Matthias didn't look back. She wondered if he was angry with her.

She had never felt so tired.

William and Matthias returned when the chimes for midnight had long passed. They had done their best to gain the favour of the men at the Club, working in partnership as they once had, feeding off each other's remarks and matching each other like-for-like in expressions of emotion. They had met with a mixture of contempt and consideration. Those who sided with the people who had been wronged and lay close to death accused the men of the utmost negligence and added their disapproval of any serious business which relied on the assistance of a female employee. They suspected that, should any of these invalids die, Mr Breslin would no longer have a business worth speaking of, and that he'd better prepare to renounce his position, especially in anticipation of a legal enquiry – or at worse, an arrest.

However, there were others who believed that customers of an apothecary put themselves at risk by surrendering themselves household remedies rather than those recommended by medical science. Whether it was negligence on the apothecary's part or inaccurate understanding of dosage by the person taking the remedy, the blame ultimately lay with someone who sought to save money by refusing to be treated by a doctor. William met with a handful of supporters who expressed a willingness to look into his case and help him win out, no matter what the outcome. As a result, he left feeling that he had still, as Matthias termed it, a fool's hope. Perhaps there was nothing so bad in this world that it couldn't be overcome.

Except, perhaps, death itself.

Morning came swiftly. Matthias had arrived earlier than usual to relieve William from his duties. He stayed upstairs, sleeping off the alcohol consumed the previous night and the strain that assaulted his mind.

Clara was upstairs, too. She may have slept, in that new, strange way, peppered with night terrors and distressing visions. But she wasn't there to welcome the start of the day's custom, so Matthias manned the shop alone.

He didn't miss William's management – this had been erratic at best, of late. He barely trusted Matthias to do anything; the limit of his recent tasks seemed to be greeting customers, passing them cures prepared by William's own hand, taking their money and wishing them a pleasant day.

Clara's presence was never really needed – she was allowed even less freedom than Matthias: she was not to set foot anywhere near the stockroom, and was restricted to cleaning and occasionally providing customers with their orders, but only if they were checked over by William first.

Mr Breslin had taken on far too much, following the paranoia that his inept assistants were poisoning his customers.

The shop opened for business at the usual hour, but no customers came. The sight of the empty shop gave Matthias a sad heart. He propped the front door open, in the hope that this simple gesture might be enough to entice in reluctant clients. He polished the large medicine jars in the display window, in the hope that the bright glimmer might catch someone's eye. He swept the dust from the front step, in the hope that minute particles of dirt might be the one thing preventing a surge of custom.

Eventually, someone did come in.

The woman caught the doorframe with one hand as she reached it, to stop herself from reeling. She sobbed openly, mouth pulled down in a hollow grimace.

'Mr Breslin!' Matthias shouted, rushing forward to catch her before she collapsed.

William was by his side in less than a minute. Matthias suspected he might have been waiting in the wings all along, despite promising he would remain in bed.

The woman tried to speak. She kept upright, although it was clear she had no willpower to stand. She was the embodiment of utter devastation.

'Gone, gone …' she muttered, again and again, the word dry and broken on her lips.

'Please,' William implored, clutching the woman's sleeve in an ungainly manner, 'say the worst hasn't happened.'

The woman twisted her eyes horribly to look at him. They were empty eyes. 'But you …' she started, incredulous despite the lack of tone to her voice. 'It was you …'

'No!' William cried, frantic. 'Dear God, this can't be!'

'Murder,' the woman rasped, tears spilling from her eyes in great rivulets. 'Morphine. You killed her. My sister. Two days. That's all …'

An inarticulate noise barked from William's throat. He fell back against the counter, his legs shaking and struggling to support him.

'Mother had scarcely left Surrey …' The woman was rambling now, details that meant nothing to the two men, details that grounded her in reality, kept her from breaking. Her sister was dead, and her grief was so strong that she couldn't enact her fury against those responsible for her death.

'Morphine for the pain. She won't feel the pain now. She won't feel anything, anymore …'

William lurched behind the curtain so that he could

vomit. Matthias bundled up the poor bereaved woman in his arms and hailed a cab to take her home.

When he re-entered the shop, Matthias saw that William was sitting behind the counter, hunched over and blank-eyed. His own cheeks were damp with tears, and it was surprising that William's were dry. Perhaps he was beyond the relief of weeping.

'I'll lose everything. Perhaps I'll be hanged.' He didn't look at Matthias, who wasn't sure if he was being spoken to or not.

'You suspected this would be the outcome. You suspected a death. The visit to your Club was our protection against this. You know there are powerful men who are willing to take your side.'

'No. There *were* powerful men who claimed they would take my side, before they knew of a confirmed death. Wait and see, Tarasso. Wait for them to turn their backs on me now. Lofty promises are easy to express when there isn't any recrimination.'

'Perhaps you're right, but I don't think we should accept this outcome. As your sister said, it is only through our collective strength that we will be able to fight any accusations.'

William raised his head; now he stared at the opposite wall. Matthias didn't like the rigidness of his shoulders.

'My sister,' he repeated. 'She does well to offer her advice and clutch at straws. Were it not for her, I wouldn't have dreamt of a disaster such as this.'

'I appreciate that it must ease your mind to accept

that she is to blame. But it would cut her deeply. She may never show it, but your lack of trust in her would be a heavy wound to inflict.'

'Would that she could feel any pain – I don't think she feels at all. She is a cold and distant being, if you did but know it. If my livelihood – within it the imprint of my every breath and fibre and drop of sweat – were to fall in heaps around her feet, she wouldn't grieve for me. And you seem to disregard any notion that the blame might lie with her.' William twisted to look at Matthias, his stance aggressive and challenging. 'Do you doubt *yourself*, sir? Or by some vicious notion, do you accuse *me*?'

'How can any of us say for certain that we are innocent? You used the words yourself, Breslin, when you admitted that, just a matter of weeks ago, none of us could gather our thoughts because of the hundreds of feet crossing this threshold every day—'

'Scoundrel – you seek to besmirch my name,' William rasped, rising to his feet. He was still unsteady, his shoulders loose and his arms hanging limply by his sides.

'That isn't what I want,' Matthias retorted, with a tone of despair. He hated to see William in such distress. 'How could I? Where would be the sense in it?'

'You don't wish to incriminate my sister,' William reasoned, his voice now high-pitched with desperation. 'You don't admit to performing the deed yourself. Am I to believe that you think *no one* can be behind this act of murder, Tarasso?'

'The thought is naïve and beyond witless, I know.

But I can't bring myself to believe ill of those I am closest to in the world.'

William saw deepness in Matthias' expression that he didn't understand. He couldn't fathom the man's reasoning, couldn't shake the feeling that the blame was being placed on him, even if indirectly. Perhaps Matthias really was so far-seen in him and his sister that he couldn't imagine either of them capable of the deed. But that would leave Matthias with the smear of blame.

'If those you are closest to in the world are innocent, Tarasso, then you accept the guilt. Is that not so?'

'No. I do not accept it.' That deepness in his expression remained, stronger now in his determination. William felt that he should recognise what he was seeing, an emotion without a name.

'You would do well to leave, Tarasso.' William was eager for him to go and did little to hide the fact. 'I don't expect that you will be needed in the morning.'

Matthias turned to leave, offering no protestation. William followed him to the door and spoke tonelessly to his back as he headed down the street. 'Perhaps you'd do better to focus your energy on your next play. It might be the last you perform.'

Clara – lying stiffly in bed, her latest painting still drying on the easel – knew exactly what had happened that day, though she didn't speak to William or Matthias. She had overheard their argument and, shameful though it was, couldn't bring herself to leave her room in the wake of it. If she were honest with herself, she would accept that she was actually scared of facing her brother. She didn't dare speak to him, lacked the fortitude to defend herself.

But when she slept that night, she didn't dream at all.

CHAPTER TWENTY-ONE

eeding to rid himself urgently of any blame, to save his business, William turned to the law.

Know your enemy, and have them on your side, he thought.

He was sure that the illnesses, and the woman's death, weren't his fault. He had trained as an apprentice, and worked as an apothecary's errand boy before that, hearing the horror stories of misdiagnoses time and again. There were things that an apothecary simply learnt to avoid from the beginning: certain mixtures of ingredients and misuses of equipment. These were more than a code of conduct – more like unbreakable laws. There were already laws against murder, intended or accidental, and so the apothecary merely did all he could to ensure the legality of his actions. William was inherently fastidious, and always used optimal concentration when working. It was inconceivable that he could mistakenly poison a client.

So, the guilt fell on one of only two others who might feasibly be at fault.

His sister's unfavourable traits as an assistant were obvious to any who met her. William hadn't employed her because of her merits; he had been duty-bound by his parents and spurred on by his accounts. She had made her feelings about her situation plain from the beginning – but never to the customers, who only became aware of her reluctance when she drifted off mid-sentence into artistic reverie.

That was the essence of it – her inattentiveness; that could easily misguide her hand or fool her eye. She would never maliciously tamper with the cures – but she might unwittingly overlook a dangerous error.

The actor, Tarasso, had been another enforced choice. He was a man with no proper training, save the best guidance William could give him over a short induction period. He had no desire to be an apothecary, and so any interest shown in the business was superficial. He appeared to show a natural aptitude for dispensing and mixing ingredients, and William would admit now that he had been trusted to do so with hardly any professional qualification. However, the actor had only looked for additional employment with William after an introduction to his sister.

So, if it was discovered that Matthias had accidentally provided customers with toxic products, would William ultimately prove at fault? He could never trust the man again, but did feel, begrudgingly, that he had also been an enemy to himself.

William deliberated carefully, after the news of the lady's death. He didn't sleep that night, knowing that journalists would soon be at his door, followed by the police – he had to have a plan ready, to protect himself, before his arrest ruined him forever.

In the morning, when his thoughts and demeanour were calmed, he sought out a private detective. It was an unhappy query – one he ought to have deliberated over a little more – but it was either that or the police. They would probably arrive with a warrant for his arrest already signed.

When the deed was done, he felt he'd plunged himself into something that he would never be able to undo.

The man's name was Howard Conner.

William was directed his way by a member of his Club – it seemed you only contacted or met Inspector Conner via the friend of a friend who had once known someone who hired him to solve a case. It served the man well to be elusive – not least because he spent most of his time in anonymous pursuit of criminals.

William met Conner at his home in the early morning.

Speaking inarticulately in bursts of alternating panic and derision, he didn't endear himself to the inspector.

Conner kept him on the doorstep, blocking the doorway to prevent him going any further. He addressed his new employer carefully and coolly, refusing to discuss the case in any great detail until he could visit the shop himself.

William was instantly struck by Conner's all-encompassing presence; he would demand every eye in a room and hold their attention until – if not after – he had left it. His looks were measuring and unflinching. His posture was authoritative and in readiness at all times. He had the appearance of someone well-seasoned in his profession, though perhaps not abiding to every regulation of his 'Bobby' counterparts. He didn't advertise for clients in the presses; he didn't operate under Scotland Yard (despite insisting on the title of 'Inspector') – in fact, he believed he was more likely to make notable contributions to the London justice system working as a freelance detective and was determined to do so.

They climbed into a cab together, Conner taking

up the bulk of the seating, leaving William feeling slightly shrunken in one corner.

The inspector's profile and bristling hair were rather lupine, the apothecary noted. He felt uncomfortable in his presence, not only because the physical size of the inspector intimidated him, but also because he couldn't articulate anything, worried he'd meet with more disapproval.

In spite of this, he wanted to underline his perspective on the case – as it would now be called (not death, not tragedy, but something far more clinical) – before Conner saw the shop and … met his sister.

Conner spoke suddenly and brusquely, in such a way that only his lips appeared to move.

'I must say to you now: I know you have preconceived accusations. It won't do any good, but I know you won't be able to redirect your attention until there is a verdict. Allow me to disregard any assumptions until evidence corroborates them.'

This left William mute until they arrived at the Apothecary, when his first sound was a groan of despair.

Two policemen stood beside the gaping door. They were acting as sentries, preventing anyone from entering, whilst their colleagues scoured for evidence. They must have obtained the warrant last night, William thought numbly, mired too deeply in his own self-pity to reproach himself for his stupidity.

He immediately thought of saving his supplies, even though no one would be willing to buy them anymore. He wondered if the money needed to restock would be worth spending, now that his business was ruined.

He was eventually reminded of his sister. He couldn't imagine where Clara might be – she could have been in her room, he thought, with perhaps too light a humour. He could hardly imagine her rushing to defend his property, even if she heard intruders breaking down the door.

Conner made a small wordless grunt. 'Gone to task on the place already, eh, Breslin?' he observed. 'I'll soon have them on their way.' William couldn't be sure if he spoke in wry humour or not.

The policemen at the door hardly moved, except to glance through the windows at the inspection taking place inside or to answer the queries of anyone who showed interest as they were passing.

Conner was out of the cab and bounding up the street in an instant – the way a bull might bound, somewhat aggressively yet with purpose. At the rumble of his voice, the two constables exchanged pointed looks. They shook hands with the inspector, out of duty rather than politeness.

William paid the cab and hung back anxiously, petrified of being seen and apprehended. The policemen, however, were too deeply engrossed in conversation to notice him.

He didn't want to place himself too near, in case he was recognised, but he heard enough snatches of conversation to discern what was being said.

It seemed Conner was adamant that he should be trusted with a 'relaxed custody' of Mr Breslin; he accepted the apothecary as his employer, with the proviso that he would still turn him in for questioning and arrest if his guilt was proven.

William thought he would have appreciated being made aware of this earlier – but then, apprehension was ridiculous, as he knew himself to be innocent.

Eventually the policemen were made aware of William's presence. Under their piercing scrutiny, he felt a cold shock of irrational guilt. Sheer panic left him completely speechless, but he wasn't expected to speak in any case.

'With the greatest of respect, Mr Conner, whilst we agree to maintain our distance, it is our duty to remain on the fringes of this matter.'

'Our chief, you see, will expect regular reports—'

'You can collect 'em from me, lads – I keep detailed notes.' Conner was almost jocular, but still the most authoritative of the three. Seeing the men wanted to say more, but were keeping reverently silent, he added, 'Of course, you need to do your job. Mr Breslin has paid me to do mine, and I don't wish to undermine you – but I ask that you allot me the time I've requested.'

'We know we'll get rapid results from you, Inspector,' said the younger police constable – in the tone of someone addressing their childhood hero, William thought. Conner certainly wasn't a man to talk on level terms with.

Not for the first time, William wondered just whose services he'd enlisted.

If the two constables had seemed a little hostile at first, it must have been in anticipation of the sharp edge of Conner's tongue; now they knew they were working alongside him, their demeanour had changed.

Conner must be an intelligent man, William marvelled. A formidable man to have on-side.

Now they stood by to let Conner enter the Apothecary, and William felt a tug, something primal, like the apprehension of the imminent loss of a child. Everything he'd built and strived to maintain was now firmly beyond his control.

He trailed in Conner's wake and came to stop beside the two constables – a stranger at the entrance to his own shop.

He vaguely heard one of the men say that his stock containing morphine had been confiscated to run tests and that Inspector Conner, having placed himself in charge of the case, would receive the results. William didn't acknowledge that he'd understood; he shuffled numbly to Conner's side. The man was engrossed in his investigation already.

'Breslin – who lives upstairs?'

William hadn't remembered telling the inspector about the shop's living quarters – had he identified them so instantly?

'That's right, the sister,' Conner continued, not waiting for an answer, speaking to himself. 'No need for you now,' he addressed the three policemen inside the shop, almost in the same breath. 'Those chemicals you're going to be testing – I'd appreciate a swift verdict. Rest assured I'll be sharing my reports as and when I need to.'

To the men entrusted with scouring William's business for the smallest piece of evidence, this order – from a man who was hardly qualified to be their superior – must have been somewhat insulting. But William couldn't detect any ill feeling. He began to wonder if Inspector Conner had a habit of arriving at scenes of criminal investigation only to turn the police away and place himself in charge.

Rather quickly, Conner and the apothecary were alone. William: head in hands, propped against the counter; the inspector: searching the place diligently, a one-man force, needing no assistance or second opinion.

'The Greek fellow's bolted, of course,' he said eventually, as if he and William had never finished speaking.

'I don't know where he is,' William replied, 'although there are several obvious options.'

Conner rounded on him sharply, 'You will give me a list.'

'Of-of course.'

Now the inspector was handling and scrutinising the phials and jars that had been left unsystematically around the room in the aftermath of the half-conducted police investigation.

William watched with some scepticism; he hadn't expected Conner to know anything about his trade, but his expression as he studied the cures indicated that he understood what each should look like and would know if anything was amiss with any of them.

'No sign of these having been tampered with after manufacture. No seals broken, no discolouration or altering in state of any of these items. But a fatal dose dispensed all the same. Indicates the misdemeanour *must* have occurred

272

during initial preparation, in such a way as to have avoided detection. Mr Tarasso readily prepares cures of his own, after having shown what you describe as something of a "prodigious talent" in the field. As does your sister, although on a less regular basis, as she is "often preoccupied with other pursuits and is disinclined to apply herself to her work". And yourself, Mr Breslin: the proprietor, who I must assume apprenticed for the legal requirement of five years, and yet have confessed to being "over-tired, impressed-upon greatly by a great number of customers and lacking in sufficient time and opportunity to relax one's mind".'

William felt somewhat uncomfortable, being paraphrased by the detective. 'Obviously you—'

'Yes, obviously I must rule you out from the start – after all, why would you seek me out if you were the guilty party all along?' He didn't wait for William to answer. 'Of course, I can name a great number of occasions where that logic has proved counter-productive. Some criminals are disproportionately intelligent and have the ability to manipulate the law. Such a strategy has deceived lesser men, but I have the benefit of hindsight and personal experience.' He surveyed William's expression with a visible flicker of amusement. 'If it's all the same to you, Breslin, I won't withdraw anyone's name from the table just yet.'

William restrained his temper as best he could. 'I'd appreciate you taking some care to ensure my name – already sullied – should be cleared of suspicion as soon as possible. As much as I might like to be described as being "disproportionally intelligent", I'm certainly no criminal.'

Conner acquiesced – that is, he turned his back on William and continued his investigation of the premises, which was as much of a retreat as the apothecary could expect. Conner was no fool, after all. He needed this case – needed the notoriety of solving it, needed the challenge and the suspense of anticipating his adversary's next actions.

The next few years of his life would be the making of his career and he wanted them to be the ones that burnt the hottest and fiercest of all. He couldn't afford to lose William's confidence, fragile as it was.

William exercised the upper limits of his patience as he watched Conner work, desperate to occupy himself but unable to detach himself from the present moment.

He tried to transpose himself into the detective's thoughts – anything to take control of the devastation of his life. He wondered which objects, which past events that the building revealed, could point to a particular individual.

In his own mind, he'd already started to align his suspicions against one particular individual.

After their argument, he was sure that Matthias hadn't been open and honest. He definitely concealed aspects of himself most carefully, to the extent that William wondered if even Clara could say she truly knew him.

He was beginning to be a little more lenient towards Clara. Her apathy had, until recently, been the most enduring source of annoyance. But it seemed beyond contemplation that she could ruin his life and hers as nothing but an afterthought.

He felt almost sure that Matthias could be the only

one to cause the illnesses and death. Conner would surely meet the same conclusion in hardly any time at all.

Only quietly – no more than a whisper in a usually dormant part of him – dwelt the notion of what this outcome might mean to his sister.

Conner's scrutiny was thorough, searching parts of the shop that even William might have neglected to take into account.

He didn't venture upstairs, at this stage – to speak to, or even meet, Clara face-to-face. This seemed to show a lack of urgency, which rankled. William felt urgency like none he had ever experienced, furiously wanting to rescue himself from a disastrous fate.

He'd been offered the narrowest chance to salvage his future. It bothered him intensely that someone else was still in control, and that he was dependent on Conner for the faintest trace of hope. He was left with a mild sting of panic that Conner refused to eliminate him as a suspect. He couldn't even think of regaining his customers' trust until his name was cleared of suspicion.

He was considering suggesting to Conner that he should at least be introduced to Clara, when the inspector spoke.

'I ought to dispel your concern. From all I've seen so far, there isn't anything here to incriminate you. After all, it would take no more than a cursory glance in your direction to know that you are a fastidious professional. There may be aspects of your personal life still to uncover, but that will have to be a query for later.'

William was almost ready to thank Conner this small shred of positivity – but he realised that the inspector was implying he was going to investigate further on a separate visit. How long would it take to achieve a favourable result?

'You must appreciate my position. I can't make any assumptions about a particular individual at this stage. I foresee the list of possible suspects remaining unchanged until the end. Patience is a virtue which we all must exercise – for the moment, and for many to come.'

William wasn't comforted by this honesty. Feeling a long way from patience, he was struggling to control his anger. He couldn't understand how his own name wasn't already clear. 'I'm not a naturally tolerant man, Inspector. You find me at my worst. I'm really in no state to accommodate anyone else's wishes. If you'll forgive me, I'm quite obstinate about that.' He waited stiffly for Conner's reply.

The inspector assimilated the remark. Truth be told, he didn't want William to change his mind about employing him. Working privately was always a risk; it was only by reputation and experience that he could work alongside the London police force without causing offence. This was the sort of case he spent his uneventful days hoping for – the complex sort that needed unravelling. He couldn't afford, financially or fundamentally, to lose it. So, he conceded in the least painful way he could manage.

'I will attempt to do what you ask, Mr Breslin. Pursue leads that you suggest. Question those that you suspect. I can't ignore the natural suspicions that arise; but I appreciate that it is you who demanded this investigation, and so it is to you that I ultimately defer.'

William was, for the moment at least, placated. Inspector Conner was nothing if not a reasonable man – when it was required of him.

They parted company soon after. Conner mentioned that his next enquiries would be with Miss Breslin and Mr Tarasso, once he had spoken with the family of the deceased and those afflicted who were still living. He felt confident that he would discover the guilty party in a short time, though only with considerable diligence and forward thinking.

William could focus on nothing but his desperation for his life to return to normality. He didn't fear for his sister – because her innocence was plainly obvious. Nor did he feel any remorse for Matthias, who, in his opinion, was now a highly dangerous man.

In fact, he knew that Matthias ought to run and hide. Conner wouldn't spare any compassion.

CHAPTER TWENTY-TWO

Clara hadn't expected her brother to show such tenacity by hiring a private detective to prove his innocence. She had believed he would lock himself away, to drink away his misfortune and leave someone else to rescue his business for him. Clearly, she had underestimated his attachment to his profession. The shop was his livelihood, but she had thought he would be too irrational under pressure to be able to rise above an accusation of murder.

As it was, he had not only hired Inspector Conner, but also taken the time to help him with his investigation, giving him access to the Apothecary whenever he required, as well as suggesting possible lines of enquiry and assisting with collecting evidence. It became apparent to Clara just how much her brother was willing to do to clear his name for good.

However, she was still ignorant of the fact that her brother had lined up Matthias as the key suspect and had suggested to Conner that he should question Clara first, so that she couldn't – out of loyalty – tailor her responses in the actor's favour.

Conner visited the Apothecary the next day, after speaking with witnesses who had either used or observed the use of misdiagnosed cures. They hadn't provided any useful testimony, being unable to say who had dispensed their cures, as they had already been decanted at the time of purchase.

There wasn't any written or verbal indication of the person responsible either. Short of further evidence, Conner had decided that he would have to rely on a confession, or for the killer to make another error in judgement. Both required patience.

He had decided to comply with William and question Clara first – not that he agreed with the apothecary's logic. He hadn't detected any romantic attachment between Clara and Matthias, despite William's salacious stories of unchaperoned nights at the theatre and long walks by the Thames. Apparently, she fancied herself an artist – that sort was always embroiled in gossip over their relationships with the models who sat for them. But Connor doubted that a female artist would ever be so wild. She had her reputation to think of, whatever her diversions might be. But, if there was a romance to consider … Conner decided he wouldn't act divisively without finding the truth for himself.

The inspector arrived at what would normally be the Apothecary's opening time. Broad Street at this hour was a place he didn't want to be – he found himself caught in the small holes of its net, popular thoroughfare as it was. Fortunately, he had enough of a bite on him that he was rarely trapped for long.

William had suggested that Conner should visit at this time, to be more likely to find Clara firstly out of bed, and secondly at home. Conner doubted the interview would produce useful results; from what he'd heard about Clara, she spent most of her time contemplating anything other than the real world. But if she harboured any hidden resentment, or meant to conceal some aspects of Tarasso's personality, Conner would surely uncover it.

The shop bell had never sounded as distressed as it did when Conner burst through the door. The chime was enough to jangle anyone's nerves; for William, it was like being submerged in ice-cold water. He began to fear that the slightest mishap might push him beyond the realms of sanity. He wheeled around, ready to criticise the inspector for his carelessness, but Conner was already halfway up the stairs, striding purposefully towards Clara's room.

He didn't often observe propriety. Ladies weren't allowed to prepare for his arrival or rely on another member of the household to announce Conner's entrance before they greeted him. A killer wouldn't be polite, when they obliterated another person's existence. The thin web of society was nothing but an annoyance to be swatted away with the back of his hand.

He did at least pause to knock on the door to Clara's room before entering. Waiting in the dimly lit corridor, the inspector looked far too dangerous to be kept enclosed in cramped rooms.

The woman behind the door wasn't an unknown, but he hadn't had any contact with her. The description her brother had put forward was of a woman absorbed in her own affairs, workshy and petulant when adopting responsibility. But the inspector only had to look around the premises to see that there was no sign of a lack of respect for the business. Each shelf was painstakingly catalogued and stocked, and remained that way because of the joint effort of all three employees. If any one of them upset the system because of carelessness, the results would be instantly noticeable. Similarly, it was obvious that William kept a fastidious shopfront. Conner couldn't see a single speck of dust or stain of liquid. So, he surmised that the shop's other employees worked hard to uphold this standard of cleanliness. William was a hard taskmaster, a perfectionist, and those around him did their utmost, even if reluctantly, not to disappoint him.

But it couldn't be avoided that Clara had been forced to uproot her life to be here. Upheaval such as that couldn't occur without resentment. It was unclear whether she resented her family, or just her lot in life. She was a subversive character, but Conner couldn't imagine what might lead her to the sheer depravity of murder.

Eventually, the door unlatched with a click. It opened a fraction; enough for Clara to show she had the intention of speaking. Conner had already been warned that Clara had hardly been out of her room for days.

'Miss Breslin,' he said gruffly. The door opened a little wider.

'Inspector. My brother tells me I am your last point of research in this place.' The voice wasn't cold, but if this was an attempt at wry humour, there wasn't any trace of it.

'I don't work in order of priority, Miss Breslin.'

'You work by whichever order aids your investigation. I wouldn't presume to unpick your methods, Inspector Conner.'

'I'd prefer it if we found a place to sit down, Miss Breslin,' Conner urged, increasingly uncomfortable in the narrow corridor and wanting to proceed with questioning straight away.

There was a significant pause.

'I shall be downstairs in a moment.' The voice was stiff. With formality, it seemed. But Conner had vast experience in human emotion and knew it was actually nervousness.

Clara eventually clattered downstairs with a sprightliness the inspector hadn't expected. William had made himself scarce in the stockroom, and Conner hadn't objected – he didn't have to be experienced to realise that sentiments between the siblings were fragile.

She positioned herself behind the counter – a habit that Conner noticed instantly. She hadn't forgotten her role so entirely. Her palms brushed the countertop idly as she addressed him – idly, or in agitation, he wasn't sure.

'Ask me whatever you want. I won't hold back. My brother has given his version of events, no doubt, so I can only add to that. But I can assure you, I don't have any reason to withhold the truth.'

'Your brother is my employer, Miss Breslin. I work according to his wishes and demands. However, the conclusions I draw are entirely my own.

'I would like to start by asking you: are you happy here?'

Clara sucked in her cheeks almost imperceptibly, her line of sight moving somewhere above the inspector's right shoulder. He wondered why she deliberated an answer when her body language screamed the truth.

'No,' she said in honesty. 'This isn't my natural home. This isn't the destiny I planned for myself. But any dream of bliss is a falsehood. I'm not so juvenile to think I've been dealt a cruel hand. I can't rail against my allotted path. I do what little I can to give myself comfort in a rather cold, detached world. And I thank whatever powers may be that I have a home and a life of comfort and family close by. But happy? No. Content, surviving and seeking small ways to improve my situation, so I don't stagnate.'

'You sought out Matthias Tarasso, didn't you?'

The question wasn't unexpected, but its swift delivery unbalanced Clara, just for a moment.

'He's an actor you found in … Shoreditch?'

'The Grecian Theatre,' Clara admitted, a small tremble in her voice that the inspector took to be excitement at the memory. 'He is the most talented actor I've ever seen onstage.'

'That's a grand claim.' Conner couldn't withhold a smile. 'Better than Kean?'

'I couldn't possibly say. He is the most talented actor *I* have ever seen,' she stressed, becoming irritated quickly, Conner noted.

'Does he prevent you from stagnating?'

Clara didn't take kindly to having her words twisted back at her.

'He is a dear friend. He came to my brother's aid when he needed it. His talent inspires me, and I admire him greatly for it.'

'Miss Breslin, do you trust Mr Tarasso?'

A beat of thought. 'I haven't been given a reason not to.'

'That isn't a straightforward answer.'

'I object to the question.'

'You said you wouldn't hold back, Miss Breslin.'

'*Yes*,' she ground out, and Conner could almost feel the fierce heat from the pit of her stomach, 'I trust him.'

'Your brother isn't quite as sure about his assertion of trust.'

'I don't doubt that. Why should my brother trust any of us? He's almost been ruined. The guilt must lie with one of us, but does there have to be malicious intent? If it was done in error, then shouldn't it be dismissed as an unfortunate mistake?'

'Mistake or not, Miss Breslin, there is a fatality to address. By carelessness or intent, a guilty party must be found and held accountable. That's unavoidable.'

'I hope you find out the truth quickly then, so we can put the whole horrid mess to rest.'

'That is my intention.' Conner sensed he wouldn't get any further, that Clara had raised her barriers. He had broached an uncomfortable subject, and she wouldn't speak freely. But he had heard and seen all he needed. For now. 'We can conclude for today, Miss Breslin. Thank you for your time.'

'You'll visit him next?'

Conner surveyed her with hawk-like scrutiny. She betrayed nothing. 'I believe so. He is the only one of you I haven't spoken to yet.'

'Will you return here afterwards?'

Conner wasn't sure he understood the purpose of the question.

'I can't say. It wouldn't be beneficial for either of us if I predicted my movements at this stage.'

'So be it.' Clara was already at the foot of the stairs by the time she absently thought to add, 'Goodbye, Inspector.'

Conner didn't deem it necessary to speak to William at length, once Clara had returned to her room. After all, she'd hardly disclosed anything. Conner gave his word to return the next day and made his way back to his offices.

He'd previously sent his associates to search for Tarasso, who hadn't been seen for almost a week, since he and William had their disagreement and he'd been asked not to return. As far as Conner could ascertain, Clara hadn't seen Tarasso either, despite the pair being almost inseparable for months. He hoped there would be some report of the man's activities on his return.

For an hour or so, Conner sat alone, glaring at his mantle clock with thinly veiled impatience, until, fortunately, one of his men arrived with word of the actor.

'He rarely stays in one place – makes him damned hard to keep an eye on. He seems to travel all over the City on a daily basis – and even when he's close to home it's almost impossible not to lose him in that bloody Shoreditch labyrinth ...'

'Sensible men make themselves difficult to pin down. Guilty ones become adept at concealing themselves, leaving no trace. Did you observe anything *odd* about his behaviour?

The way Breslin paints him you'd think he was some sort of degenerate.'

'The oddness stems from his inability to stay in one place. That and the fact he isn't where you'd expect him to be at the time you'd expect him to be there. He doesn't seem to return to his home at sundown – unless we've managed to miss him every time …'

Conner reflected on this impassively.

'Next time you spot him, keep on his heels. Follow his movements for as long as you can. The moment you see, or hear, the merest hint of anything out of the ordinary, you must notify me at once. Breslin will be dissatisfied if all we can surmise is that Tarasso doesn't come home at the usual hour. We need to be able to say with certainty whether or not he is exhibiting the behaviour of a guilty man. Then we can go about proving it, one way or another.' After a moment's pause, he added, 'And if he's so adept at keeping out of bed after sundown, then that might be the best time to scour his lodgings. Offer his landlady money to deter her from telling Tarasso what you've been up to.' The detective smiled a doggish smile. 'Breslin is determined to trawl up some scandal, but I think it's going to be our job to do the donkey work.'

The smell of old paper was as comforting as a warm fire. It enveloped Clara like a shawl might, soothing her mind and relaxing her heart. But it was an inadequate substitute for the physical presence of her dearest friend. Especially knowing that every time she raised her eyes she would see his likeness on the wall: close at hand, but frustratingly intangible.

Clara was sure that the recent fatality was caused by the negligence of one of the three Apothecary employees. She knew she'd been careful with the more dangerous tasks, as these were the rare moments that she wouldn't let her mind wander. At first, she'd hoped that the customers were at fault when administering the cures at home. But Inspector Conner's investigations into the circumstances of the victims had disproven this. They had all taken the suggested dose of morphine on William's labels, and there were witnesses in all cases to confirm this. But if Clara wasn't to blame and neither were the victims themselves, then that left very few remaining suspects. How could she possibly begin to suggest who should have the greatest portion of guilt between her brother and her closest companion? She couldn't see any resolution to the matter – either would cause her the utmost grief. Not for the first time, she asked herself, *How have we left ourselves vulnerable to such punishment?*

It was at that moment she became vaguely aware of the sound of sobbing.

It was the high, trembling, disconsolate sound of a woman's sobbing. The sobbing of a heart torn to shreds.

Clara couldn't have ignored the sound if she'd tried. It permeated her thoughts, stirring empathy buried deep within her. Her own eyes felt hot, her throat tight – as if the grief of this unknown woman was a transmutable entity. Without another thought, Clara lifted herself from her divan and dragged herself to the window.

The rain was falling heavy. It pooled and swam in thick rivulets across any available surface, smearing the world into discernible blurs. The despair of the woman outside was so severe that it had dragged thick tears from the heavens themselves, blackening the sky so that it mourned too.

Clara wondered why a person might choose to walk out in the street to weep. Perhaps the rainfall helped to soothe distress and pain. She also wondered, seeing the figure standing in the middle of Broad Street, why the woman was alone – why didn't anyone try to comfort her?

She soon realised that the answers to both these queries were simple.

The woman was Ruth.

Ruth could see Clara at the window. Clara saw the blonde woman's paper-white face lift towards her, and where before the woman had been shrunken and pitiful in her sorrow, she now became tense and coiled, limbs moving in barely controlled aggression.

Ruth was blurred. Clara couldn't see her properly. Through the large droplets of rain crawling in slow tracks down her window, Clara saw Ruth's mouth move. She couldn't discern the words. She could see something in Ruth's eyes though, hard and dark.

In moments she was down the stairs and reaching for the door onto the street. She knew that the instant the door opened, her life would change. There was something focused about the events leading up to the action, as though she would remember all of her senses: touch, scent, sound …

The latch clicked. The bell rang a clear, solemn note. Dull light seeped across the floorboards.

Ruth was almost unrecognisable. Her pale hair hung in dismal tendrils around her neck and shoulders, greying where it was soaked through. Her clothes had been ruined by the downpour and hung clumsily from her small frame. Her back was hunched, as if she carried the weight of a physical burden across her shoulders.

When Clara stepped out to meet her, she spoke the words again. The rain muffled her voice, but it was no use anyway. She had finished sobbing, and now her throat was too hoarse to create more than a little sound.

When Clara didn't react, however, Ruth found her voice again. Cracked, rasping and shrill in frantic desolation, but she still screamed loud enough. It was a voice that would etch itself fiercely on Clara's memory, forever.

'HE'S ALREADY MARRIED!' she screamed, her voice cutting like barbs into skin. Clara's chest felt the deep tremors of those words. The scream came again, this time muffled, as if Ruth were submerged underwater. Clara watched her lips move but began to doubt if she was really hearing anything. Perhaps the rain had infiltrated her mind, as well as soaking her skin. Her skull began to feel heavy.

'It's raining,' she said, for want of any emotion other than deep regret, knowing all along that Albert couldn't be trusted but never having the courage to voice her doubts. 'Ruth, you must come inside.'

Ruth shook her head. That would be no use now. A roof over her head wouldn't mend her heart. Nothing would.

The world had nothing that could console her wildness of grief.

'His love is worthless now. I'm lost, Clara. I'm without the other half of my soul.' She was out of Clara's reach. 'I don't have a home, or a source of comfort. You see all that is left of me. It doesn't appear to be much at all, does it?' She laughed bitterly and wept equally so. Her whole body was contorted with the wrenching pain of those sobs.

But Clara was beginning to realise that she was unmoved by the declaration.

She couldn't console Ruth when matters close to her own heart were so fraught and uncertain.

She couldn't be Ruth's comforter when all along she had known that Ruth had placed her faith in the wrong person.

She cursed her friend's blindness, her need to be in love, regardless of the character of the person she trusted with her affections. She hadn't just given her heart to this man – she'd also given him her freedom and her future. And he'd accepted that willingly, knowing that if his dishonesty was discovered, Ruth would be left with nothing but her resentment.

Clara commiserated deeply with her friend's hardship. She would have to leave London, the city that she loved, with no alternative. The life she'd believed she was building for herself had proven to be pretence.

But Clara couldn't fully empathise. Ruth had boasted of her love to anyone, not caring about the effect these words might have on those who weren't quite as fortunate …

Ruth's announcement had realised Clara's concern over the jeopardies of falling in love. She remembered why she'd never let herself become infatuated; the memories were once again fresh to her, of all the similar episodes of heartbreak she had witnessed.

Ruth was no different to numerous women she'd met. She'd been deceived in love; she had sacrificed small yet important aspects of herself for another. And now those facets of herself were lost. All along, Clara believed, she had been cheating herself of being a whole entity, answerable to no one. Wasn't it better to be protected from emotional harm, content to be bravely alone?

She let Ruth go.

There were no words of support; no offers of help or lodgings.

Perhaps Ruth had finally realised that Clara had lost respect for her, that she had somehow predicted this all along – but had never expressed her misgivings. Ruth didn't ask for anything. She didn't suggest that Clara keep in contact.

Clara didn't think she could give Ruth anything she needed. Her friend had been lost to her for quite some time. Now Ruth was lost to herself. She would carry the imprint of his infidelity upon her, wherever she went, whatever she did, whoever she met. In the end, it could become a form of defence. Perhaps then, she would be the sort of person Clara could respect.

Clara had always known that death, dishonesty and devastation were never too far from the well-trodden paths of London.

Only now, however, did they seem to be converging around her.

'THE WORLD HAD NOTHING THAT COULD
CONSOLE HER WILDNESS OF GRIEF...'

CHAPTER TWENTY-THREE

'Where are we going?'

'I thought you might like to decide.'

'The Adelphi then.'

He'd stood facing the doorway like Ruth had. No knock, no announcing his presence. Clara hadn't been alerted by sobs – she hadn't been alerted at all. But with almost cursory movement she'd looked out of her bedroom window that evening and seen Matthias standing outside.

She couldn't tell, from her vantage point, how he looked; whether he was diminished by the Apothecary's ordeal, or whether he displayed any signs of neglecting himself, being dismissed from William's employment and not making any contact with Clara for several days.

In less than a minute she was at the door, opening it slowly so as not to agitate the bell beyond a dull clunk. William had left earlier – to visit Inspector Conner, she didn't doubt – but she still felt the need to be wary. Her brother wasn't a safe presence anymore; his actions were unexpected and impulsive. She felt that, like the private detective, everything William said or did concealed a purpose towards some end. And even when absent, he commanded a sort of agitation over her.

She was relieved when Matthias greeted her as he always had, without wariness, and suggested that they spend the evening together.

'What's on the billing tonight?'

'Something new, I think. I haven't paid as much attention to the playbills as I should have.' Clara focused incessantly on Matthias as they spoke, watching for some sign of turmoil. His outer demeanour, however, appeared unshakably calm. She knew that he meant to help her forget her worries by spending an evening as they used to, before the scandal. She was highly grateful for that. She knew he couldn't be unaffected, as his demeanour suggested, but she realised that if he was obscuring his real state of mind, it was out of consideration for her.

'Will your brother object to your absence?'

Clara couldn't fail to notice the slight stain of bitterness in the word 'brother'. She supposed it was their former kinship that Matthias missed, more than the employment. The two men had just begun to befriend each other, and now there was a poison between them. Clara wondered if it would eat through their bond completely, or if this matter would be resolved in time to heal it.

'He will be glad of it. He doesn't like to see me, to make conversation. All that is on his mind is … He doesn't even want me to work in the shop anymore. I offer help where I can, but I know he sees my presence only as an insult, with the place being so painfully empty.'

'He isn't acting under the governance of a clear and rational mind,' Matthias attempted to explain. 'The damage to his reputation, his livelihood, would weaken even the strongest man. All he sees, hears, feels now is pain, or is touched by pain. He is wounded by grief, which can surpass even physical harm.'

Clara's thoughts went to Ruth, who was also grieving, lamenting the loss of her reputation. She told Matthias about the woman's confession, knowing that he wouldn't condemn her cruelly, as others might.

'She's wrong when she says he doesn't love her.'

This immediate response surprised Clara. 'She believes his love existed, but that it wasn't the love of a whole heart. All the while, a part of it, however small, belonged to another woman.'

'The heart isn't readily willing to be divided. In love, it attaches itself to a particular individual, so strongly that it is often blind to any other. He loved his wife once. Now he loves Ruth – still loves her, until his heart seizes on a new intention. His marriage, as far as he is concerned, was part of another life, a separate existence – nothing to do with his relationship with Ruth – apart from it being a knowledge he had to disguise. It is to be expected that people conceal a part of themselves to make themselves appealing to a person they desire.'

Clara thought of her paintings, but knew it was different as she didn't *desire* Matthias. Admired him, relied upon him – yes. But she didn't wish to appeal to him. Their friendship had been a happy derivative of their meeting, nothing more.

'A person might conceal an unbecoming habit, or an embarrassing relative! Not a marriage!' She hoped the emotion in her words might mask the nervous leap in her voice.

'For love, a person might conceal the darkest of natures,' Matthias muttered. He watched the ground as he spoke, whilst Clara felt the cold prickle of a sudden breeze up her left side. She decided to be truthful.

'I shouldn't be so cold, but I'm disappointed in her. She shouldn't have trusted so unflinchingly; she should have questioned his intentions long ago.' She searched her feelings, and through a hard knot in her stomach, forced out the words, 'I wonder how things could have been different if we'd never been friends. She wouldn't have accepted my advice in either case. She would still be in the same sorry mess. But I might've been happier. I might've sought other friendships. Perhaps you might've thought a little better of me.' She was remembering their uncomfortable meeting outside the Theatre Royal.

'That isn't possible. I understand that your friendship with Ruth is part of your past, and you wouldn't be the same person if you'd never met her. You can't judge a person by their former friends, because you can't know what they've shared.'

Clara nodded, uncertain. She would never know who she might've been if she and Ruth had never been friends. She could only regret, and hope for fairer times ahead.

The billing at the Adelphi that evening was an encore showing of *The Streets of London*, an original script, adapted to address the inhabitants of the city in which it was being staged. It portended to be 'A horror of everyday existence!', 'A tragedy of greed, destitution and deception!', and Clara wasn't sure if it would benefit either her or Matthias to have such scenes enacted.

Nevertheless, she was away from the Apothecary with Matthias at her side, and even if the play didn't delight them, the darkened auditorium was a space for ordering her thoughts.

Watching the scenes of blackmail, poverty, ill-gotten gains, dishonesty, suicide, arson and incarceration, Clara took stock of all that had happened to her. At the height of her frustration, she'd told Matthias about her resentment against Ruth. Initially, she'd felt her burden lifted. Now, she wondered if she'd been too hard on her friend. After all, it wasn't Ruth's choice to be betrayed. She hadn't knowingly trusted an adulterous man. And even though she'd boasted of her love to Clara, foolishly, before deception had been revealed, was that really a punishable act? How could Clara pass judgement, when she'd never loved?

She thought that one day she might apologise to Ruth, tell her that she knew she'd let her friend down – but only because events in her own life had been so out of control. The two of them could reconcile their bond, having their misfortunes in common.

The play ended with a marriage. There couldn't have been a more ironic final scene. The majority of the audience would leave thinking wrongs had been righted, in some small way; but Clara and Matthias shared a look which made it obvious that they weren't comforted.

They left, hurrying against a fine drizzle of rain which peppered the chill air. Matthias hailed a cab and helped Clara gently inside. He shouted an instruction to the driver, which Clara didn't hear, and bundled himself quickly into the opposite seat.

'I think we could've had a more agreeable evening, don't you?' There was humour in the voice, but uncertainty in the eyes. Clara wondered why he looked so unsure; it had been her idea to visit the Adelphi, after all – her *fault*, if fault should be found with anyone. She told him this.

'At the heart of the matter: theatre is a means of escape,' Matthias suggested. 'It was a chance to distance ourselves from our current situation, but I suppose melodrama wasn't far enough removed from the conflict and pain we're already experiencing. By its creation alone, art closely imitates life – or it can, at least, speak to us knowingly, at our most vulnerable moments.'

'It may just be an unfortunate coincidence that our personal tragedy has been allowed to follow us across London,' Clara sighed. 'In striving to forget it, it has become stronger.'

'Terribly, terribly cruel.' Matthias spat his words in the direction of the carriage window, and Clara heard a suppressed anger in the voice which she couldn't remember hearing from him before. In an instant, he seemed to remember himself and looked back at Clara with a changed demeanour. 'But it can't rule us. It's something we must remove ourselves from – if only for one evening, until the new day dawns and our fears are fresh once again.' He paused now, and the anger that Clara had seen in him before seemed transformed into an outburst of exuberance. 'That is why I've asked the driver to take us to Shoreditch – even though you might feel obliged to refuse.'

Clara was alarmed – she hadn't thought Matthias could be capable of such deception. She certainly would have refused if she'd known of their destination before they departed, but now that the choice felt out of her power, she had time to contemplate the idea, to realise that she would at least escape the cheerlessness of the Apothecary for a few fleeting hours. Matthias had invited her to dine with him at his home many times before – but she hadn't wanted to risk it, in case she'd been seen by someone she knew. Now he'd almost tricked her into following him home, and although a part of her felt this wasn't entirely gentlemanly, she couldn't help but think that this visit was long past due.

'I find myself wanting to avoid home as much as possible, recently,' Clara said. 'It is an unwelcome reminder; a place of confinement. But you needn't have kept the truth from me. I thought that we were able to be honest with each other.'

'To speak truthfully, the idea hadn't occurred to me until the moment I shouted to the driver. I had every intention of taking you back to Broad Street, but – well, suffice it to say I acted impulsively – I didn't consider the implications for your reputation.'

'Reputation,' Clara derided. 'What a heavy shackle that word is.'

'Too often used as one – by those who wish to

restrain others, or themselves. But, as we both know, it can also be a destructive weapon – one that we could manipulate to our own ends or that could be used against us.'

'It might be difficult this evening, but let's try to talk about other things,' Clara said wearily, as the cab began to jostle to a stop.

'Gladly,' Matthias obliged, rising to open the door and help Clara onto the road.

The night was beginning, grey and damp. The rain, which had at first been swift and light, was now falling steadily, dulling the sky. Clara stepped out into the Shoreditch streets feeling that this was a place that would never be improved, or worsened, by the weather. Enclosed and oppressive. The rain stultified the senses, washing away the foul-smelling litter that gathered in the drainage channels.

'My home is just behind the main street. Do you mind a walk?'

Clara shook her head and kept close behind Matthias as he led her on, concentrating on following his movements rather than letting her attention stray over her surroundings. She'd passed this way often enough on her usual route to the Grecian but was always appalled by the poverty she encountered in this part of London. She still laboured to understand why Matthias had settled here; despite its proximity to the theatre, this wasn't a safe or hygienic place, and she didn't believe that Matthias lacked the means for a more hospitable dwelling. Perhaps he'd become strangely attached to the place – just as she had developed an attachment to her bedroom in the Apothecary, with its perfect window seat. She wondered if she should help him find alternative accommodation, whether he would let her or find it an insult to his pride.

Eventually, they emerged into a small brick-built yard criss-crossed with a large web of empty washing lines. The faces of the buildings were flat and impassive, empty of embellishment and blackened by soot. Their small windows were sunken and smeared with dust. The rooves were almost concave, drooping under an imaginary weight, the tiles overlapping like dry scales. As late in the day as it was, children were sitting by the low stone walls, shouting and laughing to each other good-naturedly despite the dismal weather, with no sign of being allowed inside. Women in grubby aprons knocked out dust from shabby linens and emptied tubs of grey water out into the street, their hands raw from all manner of laborious yet thankless tasks. None met Clara's eye as she looked. These could've been Matthias' neighbours for years, but none of them raised a glance or spoke a word of greeting. Clara presumed that being treated with anonymity was an advantage of living in the more prosperous parts of London, but it was now evident that even these communities kept themselves apart. That, or there was something about Matthias that set him apart from the otherwise friendly to-and-fros of this cramped little den.

She would never be so tactless as to ask Matthias why his neighbours didn't acknowledge him, so she resigned herself to not knowing. However, as they approached Matthias' rooms, she became aware of a reason why he might be ostracised.

'On the left here,' Matthias began to say, indicating a building that stood indistinct from the rest. 'I only occupy the upper two rooms, but my landlady provides a good meal when I require it. She won't cause any fuss; in the time I've known her she has never so much as—'

He stopped short. It seemed his landlady wasn't as discreet as he hoped – she had allowed a group of police officers to search the place. One of them stood talking with her in the doorway. A quick glance revealed the rest of their silhouettes in the upstairs window.

Immediately, Clara lost her nerve. They could not be seen. She couldn't bear the thought of Matthias being accosted and examined, seeing his possessions scrutinised, having to explain why he and Clara were alone together just before lamp-lighting. They'd endured enough; the evening's diversion had proved to be just the opposite, and now Matthias couldn't return to his own home without being apprehended? No, they wouldn't step willingly into Inspector Conner's mise en scène. She placed a halting hand on the actor's arm.

'We must leave.'

Matthias looked at her with distant eyes, his thoughts elsewhere. 'They will reach their own conclusions over what they find, whether I'm there or not. It might be best if I can't be manipulated by their calculating queries. But what else can we do?'

Clara's response was impulsive. 'You must stay with me. Even if they're gone within the hour, they could return – they might even try to interrupt you when you return home tomorrow, so it might be better for you to stay away until this same time tomorrow evening, in the hope that—'

'You're making this offer without reserve, Miss Breslin?' Matthias interrupted. His voice was quiet.

'Yes, without reserve, without a chance of changing my mind.'

'That is admirable. But this is the work of Inspector Conner. Therefore, your brother must somehow be aware of what is taking place. How can I stay with you at Broad Street when he'll be there as well?'

'He won't be,' Clara answered, the idea fitting into place more and more, as the obstacles fell aside. 'He'll be at the Club. He doesn't return before midnight on most nights. If you leave early in the morning, he'll never know you were there.'

Matthias was unreadable. His body was tense, as if he was fighting internally. He looked at Clara briefly, and when he did, she saw his usually vibrant eyes slightly darkened. There wasn't a smile in them; instead, a line of hardness in his brow. Had they come to a deciding path that would influence events to come?

'I don't want to meet any officers tonight. Let's go, Miss Breslin.'

The air seemed to prickle with nervous heat. Clara almost didn't recognise the Apothecary when they stepped inside – her mind had been altered so excessively by her decision that everything around her seemed transformed. She hurried through the shop, past the stock, not wanting to acknowledge anything that hinted at an ordinary existence. It had to be meaningless, just for tonight.

'You can have my room,' she explained, head half-lifted to speak over her shoulder as they ascended the stairs.

'You are very kind. But where will you sleep?'

'I doubt that William will take the time to notice if I set up a makeshift bed in the corner of the stockroom.'

Matthias faltered in his step. 'But – you can't—'

'Unfounded superstition.' Clara spoke disparagingly of her fear of the back room, with its unfathomable shadows and furtive sensation. 'A night's sleep in there will cure me of it.'

'It wouldn't be courteous of me to allow such a thing,' Matthias protested, as they neared Clara's bedroom.

'Nonsense. You're a guest. Whether welcomed by all parties or not.' Clara pushed the handle to enter the room whilst smiling in irony at Matthias.

Only when the door had creaked fully open did she realise her foolish hastiness; the utter calamity of her mistake.

Clara hadn't attempted a new painting for a considerable length of time, by her own standards. Since the news of the woman's death, she hadn't had the slightest inclination to pick up a paintbrush.

She'd also lost the desire to paint because her work, of late, hadn't been acceptable. Her most recent portraits had contained almost ludicrous mistakes – brought on, she suspected, by fragmented sleep. She'd produced occasional sketches, but these were discomforting – the pencil work too dark and heavy, Matthias' facial features appearing stone-like, almost lifeless.

But when her bedroom door swung wide and they were both greeted by the sight of over one hundred separate portraits of Matthias, lining the walls in layers, strewn across the floor, on the bed and stacked against easels, she couldn't believe that she'd become so careless.

She couldn't speak. She couldn't move but felt the beating of her heart behind her ribcage like a pestle pounding roughly against mortar.

Matthias walked through the doorway.

In the midst of the chaos, he seemed fantastical, unreal. A tangible manifestation of a myriad of static images, conjured to life.

At the end of an excruciating silence, he eventually spoke.

'So, here is the truth of you.'

'A mistake,' Clara rasped, her throat too tight. 'I can't – please – you mustn't—'

She stopped. He was looking at her. The absorption and intent behind his look alarmed and enthralled her.

'All along …' He seemed awestruck, looking at her as if with enlightenment.

'From the beginning,' she admitted, all pretence rendered useless. Her voice quavered – was it regret, or exhilaration? 'And before that.'

Matthias broke their eye contact and it felt like a physical cut.

He moved to look more closely at the paintings. With the lightest of reverent touches, his fingers crossed the canvases, studying.

Clara felt a strange pulling sensation from her abdomen as she watched him, almost maternal – wanting to protect her work from too much scrutiny and yet proud, so proud that he could finally see it, that he felt no anger towards her, or violation by her.

'I knew,' he muttered – and in a foolish, startled moment, Clara mistook his meaning, believing that he had discovered her secret long before. 'I always knew that there was something ... *exceptional* about you.'

A sudden rush of warmth spread right the way through Clara's body. Her delight was overwhelming, but she knew that she shouldn't believe it. This had to be some form of cruel fantasy. How could he think such things?

'I had never comprehended that you were so devoted to the arts. I still can't comprehend it. It is just ... astounding.'

His attention moved slowly, almost reverently, back to her now – and the look on his face was intensely intimidating to Clara, who was unused to any sort of recognition of her talents.

'You have no idea, Miss Breslin – how much I – the admiration I hold for anyone who pursues a talent as fervently as you have. For just a fragment of such a creative flair – what I would give for that ...'

Now she felt bold enough to speak. She couldn't remain silent on the subject.

'Mr Tarasso, forgive me, but that is ridiculous! You're

the most talented actor I've ever seen! Your ability to convey characters onstage is so true to life that I've found myself completely transported by your performances. How can you undersell your own ability? ... It is ludicrous.

'I'm no prodigy. I enjoy painting, and I've pledged to study you for several months. You ignite a compulsion in me to create art – to draft and hone my work until a semblance of accomplishment is created. But my talent is entirely derived from my emotional wellbeing – lately, I haven't produced anything; I've been overwrought, my nights disturbed.

'You have the ability to leave your everyday self behind a velvet curtain and emerge as someone entirely new. If that isn't true talent, I ...' She lost her thread of thought, wondering if she'd disclosed too much.

Matthias hadn't looked away from her once. His eyes were so intense in the half-light, so dark and rich – Clara almost couldn't bear to look at them.

'But you've acted your own part, haven't you? Concealing your incredible gift and denying your true vocation – to serve your brother and to keep up the pretence with me. I understand why you couldn't share this – you risked distancing yourself from me, and therefore the focus of your artwork. A fool might find this daunting, being the subject of someone's intense study. But it is the highest compliment. I'm truly *flattered* to have been your choice.

'If anything, I wish I'd known sooner. I wish I could've sat for you, watched you paint, been in this room when your remarkable works of art were created.'

There was something thrilling about seeing his

elation.

But Clara also found the demonstration of his feelings overpowering. She couldn't have imagined a more perfect reaction from her muse – but it was too perfect, too approving. After all, her study of him had been obsessive. Such a discovery would horrify any other person. Why was Matthias so pleased with the summation of her efforts?

'So, you aren't – you don't find this shocking in any way? I thought I'd have to apologise profusely; plead with you to salvage our friendship. But you are … *happy*?'

Matthias moved towards her. She felt a strange pulsing in the air; around him, the room began to grow dull. His eyes were startlingly distinct.

'Believe me, *Clara*, when I say that I have not been happier.'

The use of her first name – the only time he'd ever verbally acknowledged it – snatched her breath in a painful rush.

'Matthias,' she whispered – it could have been a reply, or an acceptance, or a warning, but she didn't move as he came ever closer.

Matthias had been her muse from the moment she had first seen him. His potential as a man had never been considered – it wasn't a thing that Clara had *ever* contemplated, of anyone. But as he stopped a matter of inches from her, their bodies completely aligned, she became aware of him in such a way that she balked – and yet … and yet …

In what other way could two souls find each other, know their deepest truths, and express the yearnings of their tentative hearts?

She realised that lifting her eyes to his would mean she consented to the transgression that he was too gracious to give voice to. Faltering, she couldn't bring herself to do it.

But in a moment of impulsive insight, her heart decided, its will stronger than anything else.

It was disorientating; they were finding their way in the dark. But at last – in consuming silence and resolve of mutual feeling – they found each other.

Deborah E Wilson

CHAPTER TWENTY-FOUR

$\mathcal{T}$he heavy cloud that had yielded rain the previous night now hung grey but dry under brighter skies above – giving the impression of being shrouded by a soft and feathery eiderdown.

Clara and Matthias watched the skies together, separate from the outer world. They were only conscious of each other; they only wanted to share tender silence and contentment.

Sharing the view from the comfort of Clara's window seat, they watched the gradual lightening of the morning before turning their attentions to the slow commencing of life in the streets below.

'It might be time for you to take down your paintings, Clara.'

Though the voice had been soft, she glanced up startled. Matthias was sitting opposite her, mirroring her tucked-knees position. Whenever she looked at him now, she would always be alerted to his eyes – their new darkened shade, set in lines of kindness and affection that soothed her.

'They are excessive; I know that.'

'Necessary, and not offensive,' he replied, reassuring her. 'I'm not suggesting it because of the volume of paintings. I simply meant that—'

'There's no need for me to study you so tirelessly.' Clara understood. Now that Matthias had uncovered her secret, she didn't need to observe him from afar. He would be there, for her to sketch and paint, whenever she required it. Muse and artist now had an affinity – stronger than Clara had ever envisaged.

Their attention was distracted by the street below, and Clara realised that she'd been watching the self-same scene when she'd seen Matthias for the first time.

'I didn't see you first at the Grecian,' she admitted, although she couldn't force herself to meet Matthias' eye. 'It was here. I saw you walk past the shop. And I felt that I had to know where you were walking to, hoping that I might speak to you, come to understand as much of you as I could to be able to paint you.'

Matthias didn't stir. She couldn't see his expression clearly so it was difficult to discern his reaction until he spoke.

'I've often wondered what made you approach me after the performance of *The Shrew*. You made your reasons clear to me, back then – but you never mentioned your art. I understand that now. Now I respect your courage all the more. You couldn't have known how I would respond, whether I would welcome your introduction or dismiss you.'

'I never contemplated that I might come to know you personally. It wasn't that which prompted me to speak to you. It was a need: greater than an admiring fan or a reverent artist. I felt it was supposed to happen – that my future hinged on that moment.'

That look from him again – one that brought the previous night to mind, so deeply dark and exquisite.

'We found ourselves swept along by that moment,

Clara. Didn't we?'

Broad Street grew steadily busier. Matthias pointed out an individual to Clara.

'Many of us have our hidden talents, of course. One would scarcely believe that the man over there – standing across the street from us, there – that he is a keen and knowledgeable astrologer.'

Clara looked at Matthias quizzically before turning her attention back to the man he had indicated. He wasn't distinct from anyone else in the street. His clothing was rather worn. His expression was bland, and he glanced at his pocket watch continuously – whether out of nervous agitation or a need to appear busy, Clara couldn't tell.

'Neither, I suppose, would that young lad there strike anyone as a talented pianist.'

Clara wrinkled her nose at him, furrowing her brow – was he trying to be humorous? Glancing over at the boy in question, she wasn't sure whether or not to criticise Matthias for his teasing – he hardly looked capable of cleaning a piano, let alone playing one. He didn't carry himself as a musician might: rather than moving lightly and gracefully, in control of his posture, the boy stepped flat-footed, shoulders hunched, shrinking what might have been an impressively tall stature for someone so young.

'And she—'

'*She?*' asked Clara, close to mocking.

'*Yes.* The best of all. She is practising to be a costumier. She can make replica gowns to match those at the most exclusive events. Better still, she makes them from fabrics half the price of the original, cutting them in such a way as to deceive people into believing they are of the finest quality.'

Clara saw the woman – who it had to be said, laughed attractively and sent charming looks out from beneath a pretty striped parasol. Elegant, yes. But a costumier? Clara couldn't see it being true. The woman was wearing a dress without any great impact – a plain white gown which had the usual buttons and frills but could've been stitched together by even the least competent dressmaker.

'Matthias, are you joking? I don't quite understand the observations you're making. Do you know these people? Are they acquaintances of yours? Or are you playing a guessing game?'

The actor smiled softly, shaking his head.

'It's a shame.'

'What?'

'That the girl over there will soon find herself detained, if she keeps picking pockets. She is an expert thief, that must be said – but she is too confident. That will be her downfall.'

Clara frowned now – what was he trying to do?

'How *do* you know these things?'

'It's a knack I have. I can sense when there is a true talent that someone might endeavour to hide.'

'Is this your way of telling me that you knew I painted all along?' Clara's lips began to twitch towards a smile.

'I may have had some inkling,' Matthias acquiesced, dipping his head with a smile of his own. 'Your constantly paint-stained apron was a clue.'

Clara reddened.

'But I meant every word when I said I didn't know the true extent of your ability. You are an extraordinarily talented artist.'

She looked away. Humility prevented her from accepting the compliment.

Matthias had always spoken highly of her – always praised her judgement, always supported her and respected her. Now that their relationship had altered, if she was totally honest in her feelings, she could admit that she'd suppressed her heart, for fear of sacrificing her work. However, the true merit of her paintings now seemed to lie in her admiration for her muse, as well as her deep affection for the man himself. She ought to have accepted her love from the beginning: used it to create works that were influenced by deep-seated feelings, rather than just recreating an acceptable likeness.

When she thought of her most successful pieces now, she wondered: were they an indication of how she truly felt towards Matthias, all along?

They began to take reams and reams of paper down from the walls – paper that was crisp from overexposure to sunlight, brown and curled at the edges. The task, which seemed easily manageable at first, steadily became more and more time-consuming. In half an hour, they had only managed to clear one wall.

The morning progressed, even without their attention to it. Clara suddenly realised, with a startled pause, that they hadn't heard a sound to indicate that anyone else in the building was awake.

'The shop – William – he hasn't opened up for the day, I'm sure of it,' she exclaimed, worried. 'With everything that's happened, I …' She knew she'd been careless, forgetting.

Matthias placed a reassuring hand on her upper arm. 'He might've decided not to open today.'

'But that is unlike him – even now, it helps him to keep to the established routine.' And in sudden alarm, 'Did he return home at all last night?'

Now Matthias also had a shadow of uncertainty over his features. 'If he definitely ordered the police search of my home last night, then …'

'We must find out where he is,' Clara decided, with a small tremor in her voice, reaching for Matthias' hand as she moved towards the door and down the stairs.

The shop bell rang as they descended.

Their hands were clasped, fingers carefully entwined, until they passed through the curtain. Then they fell apart, heavy and limp as corpses.

It was like a stage tableau.

William stood in his usual position behind the counter, as if waiting to serve an invisible customer. His face was devoid of emotion, but his knuckles were white where his hands gripped the countertop.

Sitting on a crude wooden stool, usually reserved for waiting clients, was Inspector Conner, his imposing frame hunched uncomfortably, his expression steely.

At either side of the doorway stood two police officers. They looked unconvinced about the whole set-up, their eyes darting uncomfortably to Conner, waiting for direction.

Matthias was the first to speak.

'Good morning, gentlemen.'

He rolled up the cuffs of his shirt and smoothed back his hair; the gestures, Clara thought, of a man about to begin a day's work. Perhaps he wasn't used to life without his apprenticeship.

'Good morning, Mr Tarasso.' The inspector sat up a little straighter, looking at Matthias with his nose upturned. 'I am Inspector Conner. Your employer hired me to investigate the tragedy that has occurred. I've been meaning to speak with you for the past two days, but you've been elusive. You must be able to imagine my surprise, finding you *here*? We've been expecting you to return to your lodgings all night. Or did you know about that?'

He'd intended to throw Matthias off-guard instantly; anyone could see that. But Clara watched her love with concern and concentration – he didn't falter.

'I won't apologise to you, Inspector – you can't be surprised by *that*.' He turned to William. 'I'm sorry I didn't come back sooner, Bill. I know we didn't part on anything vaguely resembling good terms, and now I'm here, unannounced, without consideration. I ask your forgiveness.'

Clara felt her stomach reel as her eyes slipped to her brother. He stood rigid. Not for the first time since the tragedy, she noticed how gaunt he'd become, how his eyes sat shadowed in deep hollows. His hand patted the countertop as he considered his reply, and not in a steady, calculating motion, but in a quick *patter-pat-pat* that made Clara's hair bristle.

'Where were you all night, Tarasso?' he asked, refusing to speak to him in an equally familiar tone. The flatness of his voice was unnerving.

'That doesn't matter, surely,' Clara interjected, hoping that the lawmen present wouldn't detect the anxiousness in her voice. 'Inspector Conner only wants to know why Matthias didn't return home – and the explanation is a simple one—'

'*Matthias*?' Conner interjected, like a dog on a scent. 'Are you on such familiar terms now, Miss Breslin?'

Clara felt her throat constricting uncomfortably. Her brother's eyes burned into the side of her face.

'Miss Breslin is right,' Matthias said lightly – but he couldn't correct the mistake. 'I have a habit of returning home in the early hours of the morning. I like to walk around the City – and find the twilight hours best for it, when the streets are at their most peaceful. Surely my landlady told you that?'

Conner smiled. It was a carnivorous smile; Clara didn't like it at all.

'Your landlady told us she hasn't seen much of you at all, recently. If only she'd known you were here …'

'Mr Tarasso isn't welcome here,' William snapped, and from the way Conner glared at him, Clara presumed he wasn't meant to be sharing his opinions at this stage. 'I find it completely *astounding* that he *is* here, after making it explicitly plain that he mistrusts both me *and* my business.'

'William, please—'

'You'll call me *Mr Breslin:* no *shred* of our former acquaintance remains, Mr Tarasso ...'

'You must understand – I would never hold any ill feeling against you, or your business. How could I? You provided me with a remarkable opportunity, one that I hardly deserved or was properly qualified for. I could never show such ingratitude.

'A tragedy has occurred – and in these circumstances, there has to be damage. But that damage surely isn't irreparable. The inspector has investigated and found no evidence. Isn't that enough? Can't we rally together, find the friendship that we once had and use it to rebuild your life's ambition?'

William whirled away like a man burnt. He moved to the window, clasping shaking hands behind his back.

'You seem to feel that the guilt lies with – *no one,* Tarasso?' Conner suggested, a hint of amusement in his voice. 'So, who do we punish? Who will accept liability for the woman's death? We can't call it an *act of God,* you know – it is, at best, an act of the utmost *negligence.* For Breslin to *begin* to restore what remains of his livelihood, we need to find the guilty party and punish them accordingly ...

'If we find evidence of *murder,* Tarasso – you know that it could mean far more than a broken friendship ...'

Matthias looked incredulous. Clara wondered if it was the first time she'd seen true humility in his eyes.

'I'm not ignoring the fatality, Inspector. But how can you presume murder lies at the heart of this matter, with nothing to support your claim?'

The silence that followed was as long and deep as that of an empty cathedral.

Clara watched Conner sink back, take stock of his chess pieces, remind himself of his intended game plan. Then the inspector spoke.

'You must understand, Tarasso: it's very odd that you've stayed away from your home all night, and that you're *here* this morning. Almost as if you have a reason to keep away – almost as if you're *hiding* here. That's what your actions lead me to believe. I'm being honest with you – you must know that your decisions leave an impression of *guilt* upon you.

'We need to have a conversation. You must answer my questions honestly. You mustn't evade justice any longer. And you must allow me – although I will do so whether you permit me or not – to decide which course of action is necessary, to decide with *whom* the blame lies.'

CHAPTER TWENTY-FIVE

Clara felt a clammy plug of nausea rise in her throat. Impotent and frightened, she could only watch the scene unfolding in front of her.

She had a startling feeling that in some way, Conner had already marked Matthias as the guilty party; that his questioning would only lure Matthias to incriminate himself, falsely. Any answer he might give could be construed as a lie. Her brother would only fuel Conner's suspicions; though no one had said the words, it was clear that the two men still wondered *why* Matthias was here at all – especially at this time of day. He couldn't justify that in an honest way without dishonouring Clara – and she knew he wouldn't lie.

Another truth was emerging: Clara was more loyal to her muse than ever before. She loved him. He was the reason she had excelled in her painting; he offered her an outlet from the waste of her daily life. If her brother was determined to force her hand, she couldn't be expected to side with him. Matthias hadn't stooped so low as to force her into rejecting her brother, but William would willingly have her throw Matthias to the lions.

Matthias had tried his utmost to heal their rift. But her brother was unmoved. In his time of need, he had decided to alienate those closest to him, instead of rallying alongside them.

Clara couldn't believe her muse was capable of

committing the atrocity he was close to being accused of, purposefully *or* accidentally. But she would have to be very foolish not to realise that for Conner, if the Breslins were both proved innocent, there wouldn't be another feasible possibility …

The realisation awoke deep panic in her, gnawing at her internally. Her mind boiled with disastrous eventualities. If Matthias was charged, it would be imprisonment, deprivation, degradation, devastation – and finally execution. She would cease to exist if Matthias' life ended. Perhaps her body would continue to function – that incredible phenomenon, the human body, able to withstand severe cruelties – but her mind wouldn't have any impetus, no reason to carry on in world which was devoid of her muse, her love.

Other people moved around her, ignorant of her suffering. The only one who seemed to remember that she was still in the room was Matthias, but he only communicated with his eyes. He was undoubtedly concerned for her, but he was also distracted. She knew he wouldn't fear for himself; he would only want to take the wisest action – and who could know what that was?

Matthias' wrists were bound whilst Conner laid a hand on his shoulder – not for reassurance, but control. Matthias was to be led to a place of interrogation – as if familiarity in his location might aid deceit. He would have the evidence against him presented – no doubt it would be strengthened by the fact that there was, as yet, no evidence against Clara or her brother which had any serious impact. After all, Conner had already questioned them both. Whether knowingly or not, Matthias had evaded the law and hadn't given any convincing denial of his guilt. No one would object to a guilty ruling, because no one cared about a little-known Shoreditch actor with no family or important connections.

No one, except Clara.

They could have been at the theatre still. Behind the scenes, a voice directing Conner to lead away the suspect, to give the audience a last look of reproach before doing so, to unsettle them, to inspire the shocking realisation '*It could've been me*'.

The leading man, his head bowed, sharing looks with no one. His frame hunched, shrunken, defeated. Once the curtain falls, they know that he will be this downcast, shadowed figure forever.

Clara's need to protect him was all-consuming, but she had no power to do so. She couldn't prevent the movements that unfolded like a melodrama before her. Once Matthias was convicted, there would be no mercy for him. She would lose him.

An animal ferocity surged in her belly. There was a rapid surge of blood to her limbs. Her mind sparked with frantic conniving. She would *not* lose him.

'*Wait.*'

The word had already been spoken when she became aware that she had placed herself between the police and the doorway; how she had done so, she couldn't explain. Her thoughts were focused on prevention.

'Reckless girl! Move yourself!' William spat curses from the other side of the room, but Clara couldn't see him.

Matthias and his captor were the only two people that existed in her field of vision.

Conner appeared to be bristling in all possible senses of the word; his eyes shone with anger. But it was Matthias' face that Clara longed to keep in her sights. She studied it intently – not with the interest of an artist but needing desperately to etch his features onto her memory, should it be the last time she could do so.

He returned her gaze, but his eyes were deep, full of meaning that she couldn't interpret. She didn't believe that he truly saw her. He seemed to be drowning in his own thoughts. He didn't reach out to her or plead with her. He met with her as only two souls can meet – surmounting physical presence.

She was reliant on him being unable to understand the depth of her love for him – how much she was willing to do, *for him.*

No one cared for Matthias, but her. Matthias had nothing to lose, no possessions to leave, no legacy to tarnish. *But neither did she.*

Clara did have one thing worth preserving. Happiness – that she would never have known if she'd never seen Matthias that first morning, from her window. Her love, and her paintings, were physical manifestations of that happiness, and she wouldn't part with either, knowing that Matthias returned her love and appreciated her art. Let the world know of her love, of her obsession, of her paintings – not out of vanity, but because her heart compelled her to do so. She would be silent no longer. Multitudes would know her secret.

'You're making a mistake.'

Conner assessed her in the manner of a sparrowhawk, sizing up a kill.

'Matthias didn't murder anyone.'

A small groan came from somewhere at the back of the room.

'It was me.'

The groan became an inarticulate shout of dismay. Conner seemed suspended by temporary indecision. Matthias' eyes flashed with intense brightness for the shortest moment, and locked fiercely onto Clara as if he hadn't seen her properly for days ...

'Miss Breslin, are you making a formal confession?' Conner sounded thoroughly dissatisfied with the idea.

'Yes.'

'You confess to the *murder*, the *calculated killing*, of one of your customers?' He presented her carefully and deliberately with the words, so that there could be no doubt.

'It was an act of desperation, Inspector. I added to the dose of morphine secretly, intending to cause severe illness, so that this business would be ruined and I would escape my misery forever. I didn't expect to be discovered – I was sure my crime would be untraceable. But Mr Tarasso mustn't be punished for a crime that is mine alone. I would gladly face execution if it means release from this incarceration some would call a life, when one isn't at liberty to live in the way one chooses – when all decisions are made by others, with no personal control.'

Her words would cut William deeply – betray his years of hospitality and companionship. They would lay a debt of guilt on his heart so heavy that he would never recover. But he had endangered Matthias' life, and done so knowing of Clara's bond with him. If that wasn't a deed worthy of guilt, she couldn't imagine any other.

Conner's judgement was so piercing now that she felt pinned down by it. He didn't take his eyes off her but spoke out to the room.

'I credited you with more intelligence, Miss Breslin. A mind capable of scheming to murder would surely have realised that the vessel containing the morphine would be easily analysed.

'The bottle hadn't merely been "added to" – it had been highly concentrated. The dose that Mr Breslin had instructed on the label had been more than *doubled*. Enough to cause severe asphyxiation, and most likely kill the poor woman more than once over.'

He tilted his head slightly as he continued to watch her – was that a *smile* on his face?

'Do you stand by your previous statement: that you were "*sure* that your crime would be untraceable"? It sounds to me like the act of a person *determined* to be caught …'

Clara searched her thoughts frantically for a response; she wouldn't retract her claim now that it had been made, but Conner was acting as if he suspected her dishonesty and wanted to shock her into changing her mind. She couldn't do it; she couldn't leave Matthias vulnerable to such malicious attack. He wouldn't survive. And she couldn't live with the knowledge that she'd done nothing to protect him.

Until now, the other two suspects in the room had

almost been forgotten. But in the stunned silence following Conner's challenge, both men found their voices.

'Clara, you must stop this! You can't believe that this lunacy is the truth!'

'Inspector, Miss Breslin is trying her utmost to shield me from harm. You know that her claim is flawed – don't accept this confession.'

William heard Matthias' pleas and was outraged beyond all restraint. 'A fine entreaty! Note that he doesn't hurry to implicate himself instead, Clara! In God's name, *why* are you forfeiting your integrity for his sake, when he would gladly let you die? He has no honour! He is a damned *coward!*'

Matthias was appalled by William's accusations. 'You know *nothing* of my regard for Clara. You are quick to condemn me, but neither have you put yourself in peril to save your own sister! If I am a coward, then *you* must be too. At least I will readily admit that I *am* a coward, I always have been! A spineless slave to my own shortcomings. But that doesn't make me guilty, and neither is your sister.'

'Yet again, Tarasso, you discount all other possibilities, leaving only the implication that *I* must be guilty of the crime. It won't do you any good; the inspector told me himself that he had disregarded my involvement in the woman's death from the start! I still can't comprehend your callousness; you persevere with this lie, to the extent that you would let my sister die for you rather than admit to your depravity!'

Conner didn't outwardly appear to have the slightest concern over William and Matthias' dispute. His voice was calm when he eventually decided to speak.

'Gentlemen, short of some kind of duel in the streets, this argument is unlikely to come to any satisfactory conclusion, and my time is valuable. Miss Breslin has made a confession: a weak one, but the only one I have received so far. When I have anatomised its flaws, I will return to arrest the one who is truly to blame.

'Now, if either of you are guilty, you need to search your innermost selves and decide whether you can live with letting this woman take the blame for your crime. In the intervening time, she will sleep in a cell – a likelihood which I'm sure she anticipated and fully accepts.' He looked at Clara in the coldest manner she had ever experienced, before he added, 'If she is found guilty, in absence of any evidence to the contrary and providing her confession is somehow validated, she will most certainly be hanged.'

Clara's hearing failed after the inspector spoke the last word; she was drawn out of the shop and didn't absorb what William and Matthias shouted, besides the insistence in their expressions. She was absently aware of both men having to be restrained before the officers' rough hands forced her to turn away. Not of her own free choice, she turned her back on her home, her life, her family and her love, all in one swift motion.

She didn't hear William swear to prove her innocence. She didn't see Matthias escape the arms detaining him and flee down one of the many narrow alleyways adjacent to Broad Street.

Several hours had passed. Clara had been left to 'think over her confession' whilst Conner arranged a thorough scouring of her room. She found it inconceivable that she should now be in an interrogation room. The place had a stale odour. The stone shone with damp. The ceiling was too low; in the absence of appropriate windows, it pressed down, dark and oppressive. Sitting opposite the inspector, on a matching damaged chair before an equally worn-out desk, Clara felt that she had been incarcerated already. It was difficult to imagine the outside of this building even now, because her mind was beginning to give way to irrational anxieties. But she wouldn't show Conner her fear. She wouldn't let him intimidate her. She would do what she needed to for love. Nothing could prevent that.

'Now, Miss Breslin, I assume that you've had enough time to think over your confession and will be able to add to or amend it, where necessary?'

'I don't need time, Inspector. My confession won't alter significantly. I've said all that I need to say at this present moment.'

The possibility of her death by execution seemed remote and unreal. She wasn't weakened by the thought of it, because she couldn't foresee a future for herself in which that would be the end.

She would have the right to a trial rather than being instantly hanged, which would save her, because in cases such as this, insanity could always be used as a plea.

That was it: she was out of her mind. Hysterical. Anyone who knew her would testify that she simply wasn't capable of such depravity. She would have to have lost her senses to even contemplate it.

Some might even go as far as to blame Matthias for corrupting her mind in some way, but that was acceptable. He wouldn't be punished for a murder he hadn't committed, and Clara could ease her conscience knowing that she'd stopped that.

'You appear composed, Miss Breslin.' This was observed with a note of concern. 'Most people, when confronted with a punishment for their crimes, regret their evildoing. You seem resigned – *unfeeling*, even.'

'If I feel anything, Inspector, I'll be sure not to disclose it to you. I shouldn't say or do anything more until my trial.'

'Perhaps you aren't well versed in the nature of trials, Miss Breslin. The practice of lawyers is to use all evidence presented *before* the trial, to support the case they make. For example, the prosecutor may choose to take into account your appalling lack of remorse for your crime when he puts forward a depiction of your character.'

'You don't know if I feel remorse or not. I haven't told you. And I've decided I don't want to tell you.'

'Again, I'm not sure you understand your situation. I could help you, if you'd let me. If you showed even a *shred* of regret, it would relieve my mind that you *want* to be forgiven, that you didn't intend to ruin several lives, besides ending the life of that poor woman whose airways closed excruciatingly whilst she was still conscious, causing her to die with the sensation that she was drowning in the open air.'

Clara forced herself not to flinch. 'The woman's death is unfortunate, of course. But I only did what I had to whilst at my usual work – what she chose to do with the cure, once she'd brought it home, was completely beyond my control.'

'So, because you couldn't see her dying, you were content to let it happen?'

'That isn't what I mean. As I've already said: I intended to cause severe illness, to prove my extreme negligence, so that my brother would relieve me of my duties. I didn't expect the woman to give herself enough of the morphine to kill herself. I suppose I knew it *could* be a potential risk, but I couldn't prevent that; I needed enough of a reason for me to cease working in the Apothecary.'

'This could be considered a risk in the utmost.'

'Then perhaps you begin to understand my desperation, Inspector.'

Conner knitted his thick eyebrows together. '*That*, Miss Breslin, is something I would *never* attempt to understand. *That* is the reason why I am sitting on *this* side of the table.'

Deborah E Wilson

CHAPTER TWENTY-SIX

'I think it's about time you told me your theory, Mr Breslin.'

William was adamant that his sister was innocent, and after a restless night, rushed to meet Conner at his earliest convenience. Conner couldn't draw any worthwhile conclusions from Clara's interrogation, besides her disturbing lack of repentance, and needed all the additional information he could gather. He was still uncertain about whether she was genuine or not. If she *was* actually innocent, there wasn't any need to repent. If she was guilty, her lack of remorse would surely indicate that she wasn't in her right mind. The dead woman had done nothing wrong – except deciding to purchase morphine for her pain and choosing to purchase it from Breslin's Cures and Remedies.

He knew, from his own wealth of experience in the field, that no one had ever been compelled to take innocent life without a dark agenda, unless they weren't of sound mind. Clara's purpose had been to remove herself from her situation, but she hadn't sought out a particular victim – neither (according to her) had she intended to kill. It had been chance, misfortune for the person who purchased the cure she'd tampered with. But her extreme desire to escape her employment had driven her beyond the realms of rational thought. Conner wondered if she'd debated taking her own life, rather than that of another. One noose hardly seemed so different from another, in that case – and a life might've been spared.

Breslin was a man destroyed. He no longer had the pride to hold up his head in company. He sat in the same interrogation room his sister had occupied – sat in the same chair, and yet he seemed to occupy half the space she had. Where she had been serene, resolute in her wickedness, he was diminished and frail, anxious, volatile and conflicted. Conner pitied him. He was clearly a man who had never contemplated that he might end up embroiled in a murder.

But he had his theory. He had his doubts, his suspicions. And Conner was willing to hear them all, whether it helped or not. His mind's eye flitted to an image of the woman lying in a nearby cell, and he wondered if she knew that her brother was fighting for her life, despite all she'd done to him.

'It has to be Tarasso. He's the only one. Clara's silly infatuation has led her to cover for him. That's the only explanation there can be. Keep investigating him, Inspector. I demand it. She might've been hiding incriminating evidence for him.'

'You know by now that I am not prone to exaggeration, Mr Breslin. Words such as "infatuated" rarely enter into my vocabulary. But I concede that a relationship exists between Tarasso and your sister that isn't exactly platonic. She is capable of being forthcoming and honest, but whenever I ask her about this man, she hides and evades. Her confession was a direct result of accusations against him; I have no doubt about that. However, we can't conclude that he is guilty until, as you suggest, some incriminating evidence against him is found. Otherwise, we are only presenting conjecture against an attestable confession.

'We should resume our search of your sister's sleeping quarters. I was refused entry on my last visit – but she isn't there now to block the door. And if, as you say, she would be able to hide things there for Tarasso, then it mustn't be overlooked.'

Here was a rare occasion that the inspector hesitated before speaking further.

'Of course, it is also possible that this was the last place Tarasso stayed the night, which increases its importance significantly. His own rooms are empty of anything useful.'

William swallowed his anger down thickly. Conner's comment was slander, but he couldn't fixate on that. He had to be reassured by the inspector's efforts to condemn Tarasso, despite having apprehended a suspect already. It gave Clara time that she might not have had otherwise; time, William hoped, to come to her senses and abandon her foolish martyrdom.

He decided to visit her before he returned to Broad Street. He doubted there would be much use in talking to her, when Conner had already warned him about her dubious mental state and cold, callous indifference towards the victim. In spite of this, he needed to see her. In an odd way, he was intrigued to see how she would react to seeing him at the station.

William approached Clara's cell, feeling his way along the almost lightless corridor. He'd watched her being apprehended, but even now he couldn't imagine seeing his sister in lodgings for criminals. Conner had obviously expected her to be struck with terror at the thought of spending a night here, but it hadn't had the desired effect. Rather than retract her confession so that she could walk free, Clara had withdrawn. It angered him deeply, to think that she couldn't see the insanity in sending herself to the gallows; that she held her life in such low esteem compared to another's.

The door was thick-set metal, with a latched opening at eye height. The bolt snagged rustily, screeching as William forced open the aperture.

It took a moment for his eyes to accustom themselves to the heavier darkness in the cell. On the far side, he could see the soft shape of Clara's form, laid stiffly on a wall-mounted bed, with her back to the door. She hadn't stirred at the sound; William wondered how often she was visited for her to become accustomed to it, and what thoughts occurred to her as she heard the latch open.

'Clara, I've come to talk to you.'

No reply.

'I have pleaded your innocence to Inspector Conner. Now, I need to know that I was right to do so.

'Will you *please* forget this foolish pride and admit your impetuous mistake?'

'If you implored him, as you say, then you must have betrayed Matthias by accusing him instead.' The words were delivered quickly, with staccato rhythm, but there was hardly any emotion in the voice. 'I should have known that you'd only come here to cause further misery.'

William instantly reacted to the enticement. 'Don't you understand that I only want to *help* you, not cause you pain?'

'It's not my pain I care about; it's that of an innocent man, who will be hounded.'

'You don't *know* that he's innocent, Clara. You're blinded by sentiment. I understand your reasons, and I haven't come here to talk you out of your attachment. I only ask you to use it to your advantage – blame this lapse in judgement on your feelings for him and save your own life, for goodness' sake!

'You care about his pain, but have you stopped to consider mine? Should I be expected to live with the devastation of losing my sister because she believed her life was a disposable commodity?'

Clara turned on the bed, with a force so harsh that the metal frame rattled.

'I'm mortified that you still claim that Matthias is capable of murder – there isn't a shred of evil in his soul.'

She stood facing the wall, still avoiding her brother's eye. In the darkness, she was ghoulish to him. 'At least I have the strength to stand by my convictions, and those I hold dear. It takes true courage to admit fault when it would be much easier to let someone else be accused in your stead. People who always find blame in others, believing that they are above reproach – they are victims of the ultimate vanity and delusion.'

William could've found himself goaded into rage again, but this time he held back.

'You won't change your decision, then.'

'I will accept punishment for the crime I committed.'

Nothing more could be said. The latch was closed and bolted, and his stomach lurched as he realised that this action was symbolic of what he now had to do to his sister.

He would've told her in gritty detail about Conner's investigation – about her room being searched, her paintings being studied by cold, disapproving eyes, her possessions being scoured and analysed. But it was clear that she wouldn't acknowledge anything he had to say, except to argue it.

She would know it all, soon enough.

The cold, crisp air filled his lungs, refreshed his mind, and made him feel that he should let his anger towards her subside, in the calm before the truth was uncovered.

It was still possible that he was wrong – in which case, she wouldn't live much longer, and would need his forgiveness all the more.

CHAPTER TWENTY-SEVEN

Alone in her cell again, Clara felt the seclusion of the dark more keenly now she'd spoken to her brother. It confirmed that they weren't acting as families should: united. He didn't want her to be persecuted for the crime, but even with her imminent execution, he wouldn't compromise his views in any way. He wouldn't let his experience of working with Matthias, and knowledge of his character, guide him to withdraw his suspicion. He wouldn't let Clara's testimonies convince him that Matthias was incapable of such an act. Even Clara's confession hadn't shocked him into reconsidering his accusations – if anything, to Clara's great disappointment, it had only spurred him on. He didn't see it as her own will, but as Matthias' manipulation. As if she were incapable of independent thought.

The cell wasn't a place of comfort. Clara didn't try to reassure herself with delusions. But it hadn't broken her resolve. Not yet.

Her brother's betrayal had weakened her more than a darkened room ever would, but even now she knew that nothing would alter her plans. She wouldn't leave Matthias open to persecution.

Not for the first time, she wondered if he would visit her. If he thought about her and the sacrifice she'd made. Or if he hadn't realised that she'd lied for him.

What if he believed her confession was the truth?

What if he believed she was a murderer? He could have decided never to set eyes on her again.

She would accept his dismissal, if it protected him from harm. She would endure anything for that.

What a strange phenomenon love was. That it could alter a mind so drastically; that it could cause such pain whilst being a thing of beauty and delight. Clara had always known it could be destructive, always known it could be deceptive. But finding her soul seized by it, she couldn't imagine life without it. It was as if a voracious, hungry part of her had woken and wouldn't rest until it had devoured all it could. In Matthias' absence, it grew more frantic.

The aperture in the door lurched open again. The appalling squeal of metal on metal made her stomach lurch every time, but she had trained herself to ignore it. No doubt Conner had seen her brother off and now felt like gloating to her about how her stubbornness would only cause her more suffering. She wouldn't respond; she had listened to his many attempts to threaten her and each had failed. He couldn't understand that she had no concern for her own life. She had met the pinnacle of her potential, or so she believed, and that was enough for her to die by.

'Clara?'

With a word, she was overcome.

'You.'

Her lips soundlessly formed the word as she recognised the voice she'd hoped she'd hear; the person she'd forfeited her life for.

'I couldn't let myself believe it until I could see you

here in front of me. Unthinkable, that anyone could trap you in this place, accuse you of a deplorable crime, without immediately denying your claims. I couldn't believe that you were arrested with almost no evidence, that they believed your testimony when there could be no truth in it ...'

Clara was relieved to hear that he hadn't believed her. It didn't help her plans, but it at least gave her hope; he wouldn't withdraw himself from her life, to disassociate himself from a killer.

'Matthias ...' She brought herself closer to the door, her fingertips hovering over its cold surface, as if some heat might radiate from him and reach her there. The light in the corridor was bad; she could only discern outlines in his face.

'You must abandon this madness, Clara. You'll be hanged for it, unless some evidence is found to disprove your claim.'

'They would hang you instead. Don't you realise that? Don't you realise I could *never* let that happen?'

'There are some turns of fate you can't alter, no matter what pains you take.'

Tears made hot, loose tracks down Clara's cheeks.

'That's what you may think, and in normal circumstances I would agree. But this is a wholly different situation. I must do what I can; otherwise I couldn't continue living, knowing that I stood by whilst you fell into danger. It is either my death and your life, or the end of both of us. You need to go on, Matthias. The world can't do to lose you.'

'Do you esteem yourself so low?' The words stuck in Matthias' throat as he forced them out. 'Do you think that someone of your talent could diminish from this world without even a whisper? When your paintings are discovered, Clara, you could be celebrated the world over!'

'This talk is no good. The deed has already been done, and if you try to change things, you'll undo everything I've sacrificed to help you.' Clara's shoulders sagged with the weight of her grief. 'You must talk about ordinary things.'

Matthias exhaled a sob of stunned laughter at her dismissiveness. 'Ordinary things – such as what? The fact that, in your absence, the world has continued as it always did? That, to my disgust, the sun still rises and sets, and mundane routines endure? It's all empty without you, Clara. Everything is a mockery. Other lives continue, whilst mine has stood still, in disbelief.'

'Have you seen Bill?'

'I haven't gone anywhere near your brother, or his shop. I couldn't – how would I look him in the eye? He is as cowardly as I am – he let his sister be incarcerated, just to save himself.

'I am *so sorry* that you are here, Clara. I can't bear it. I wish for the power to tear down this door, to bear you away and escape it all.

'How could I let things come to this?'

'It isn't you, Matthias: I decided it. I couldn't let them arrest you.'

'How could you care so little about your fate?' He was breathless, in humbled awe.

Clara's chest couldn't expand fully; the will to hold back her sobs was so strong that it caused her pain. 'I love you. I will die to protect you.'

If any words could create a disastrous chain of events, it was these. For the briefest of moments, time halted; the words diffused into the air and imprinted themselves on memory. Then the darkness loomed in, more imposing than ever, and Matthias opened the deepest chambers of his soul and poured out the poisonous bile from within.

'You mustn't protect me! You mustn't die for me! You mustn't be punished for the crime I allowed you to confess to, when all along, it was I that committed it!'

Clara began to feel that she didn't belong to her own body. She'd endured nightmares before, but she'd always woken from them. This *couldn't* be a waking truth.

'What are you saying? How could you have committed it? *Why* would you do such a hateful, unforgiveable thing?'

'You wouldn't understand if I told you. Only know that I want to end this now. I would never forgive myself if you died for me, Clara – not like the others. Believe that I love you, with as much of my heart as I can sufficiently give you, and that the only reason I waited so long to tell you about my crimes was that I hoped things would never degenerate this far.'

'You're *lying* – to save me, to implicate *yourself!* You mustn't do that, Matthias! Can't you see that it will mean death for us both? I don't believe you're capable of killing – I *know* you're not! Stop this! Accept that fate has conspired to rescue you from those who would seek to make you a victim!'

'You've only seen the side of me that I wanted you to see, Clara. I am a murderer; there is a part of me that has always been connected with tragedy.'

She continued to plead, to beat the walls with her fists, even when Conner, who had concealed himself to eavesdrop on the conversation, appeared with constables to detain Matthias without delay.

Her body no longer reacted to rational demands; only the frenzied needs of her brain were answered as she clawed at the arms that removed her from her cell, her voice hoarse with shouts of terror and dismay, whilst she watched Matthias become her replacement.

'A word-perfect confession, Mr Tarasso. I'm sure it will be enough to incriminate you. Luckily, one of my constables has also provided me with suitable evidence.

'They searched the Apothecary, Miss Breslin. They found *the book*.'

CHAPTER TWENTY-EIGHT

The room was dark. It reeked of festering damp. Rats chewed on unspeakable remains in the hollows of the stonework.

He could barely see the outline of the doorway, from his position at the far end of the cell. Everything else was shadow, things that were better off concealed.

It might be best if he were forgotten here. He definitely shouldn't be allowed out; others shouldn't be subjected to the sight of him. The memory of monstrous events would fade, and life would continue, much improved by his absence.

In his own mind, he didn't deserve the right to a trial. It would only delay the inevitable. Similarly, hanging would only be a means to an end, and why finish with a swift snap of a rope? Why not prolong his suffering, as he prolonged the suffering of all those he'd encountered?

He was alone. It gave him time to think, which wasn't necessarily beneficial. Dank, close, shadowy places such as this brought him back to his youth, when a night's rest came wherever it could be found. Where no one asked you where you were from, or spoke to you at all, if you found a place far enough from the hum of civilisation and didn't draw attention or ask any favours. Nights spent in fear of the dark, desperate for the morning, despite not knowing what the new day would bring. Wanting to be successful, but not having the means to become so, relying on fortunate incidents and what would become a strong talent, hoping to be recognised but moving only in the most restrictive of circles.

In some ways, he'd always known he would end up where he'd started: alone and hopeless. It wasn't as if he hadn't been warned, and warned for a long time.

His grief over Clara was too great to acknowledge. He made a stanch effort to suppress it, but it was gnawing at his mind, racking him with remorse. He felt poisoned by it, weakened and scalded. It was the dishonesty, the pretence, that he hated so intensely. She'd believed in a version of him that didn't exist, and never had. But he'd let her; he'd enjoyed it; she had made him forget the past.

Nevertheless, he'd hoped he would keep his secret from her for as long as he possibly could. He'd denied its existence in his own mind, so that he'd begun to personify his own lies. Perhaps he would never have told her if the woman's murder hadn't been discovered. But it couldn't be concealed. His past never could. It always seemed to evade his attempts to obscure it.

How could you let this happen again?

Why have you condemned again?

Haven't I endured enough?

Misery is all my life has known – don't I deserve the slightest happiness?

For the first time, I felt I'd done things right; that there might be hope ...'

At first, there was silence. Eventually, the darkness answered.

'It wasn't I that let it happen.

'You had to seek her out, just as you sought out all those others.

'She flourished from all you gave her, at first. But that sort of dependency could never last.

'Happiness isn't a permanent state of being. It is transient and false.

'The promise of happiness leads people of all kinds to commit the most foolish, the most avaricious and the most selfish misdemeanours.

'Tragedy is all that can, that must, follow. To remind us that all actions have their consequences; that all beginnings have their corresponding ends.

'You were born into this life, and you must accept its legacy.'

'It can't be a legacy that I am bound to relentlessly? There must be a way that I can escape the cold pull of tragedy?'

'You can't escape it.'

He waited for more, but this was the only response.

Despairing, he stared into the darkness, fearing that he was staring into a mirror of his inner self. Only shadow existed. There would never be an opportunity to let in the light.

'AT FIRST, THERE WAS SILENCE.

EVENTUALLY, THE DARKNESS ANSWERED.'

CHAPTER TWENTY-NINE

atthias had been right: life *had* continued as normal. Clara could see it now, moving past the windows of the carriage she shared with Inspector Conner as they travelled to Broad Street. The daylight threw a startling frivolity over it all. And yet, why shouldn't it? Why should normality be suspended to reflect their trauma?

Her heart had just begun to wake for love. Now, so quickly, it was broken. She'd never approved of that phrase, but feeling it for the first time, she understood. Emotional harm and betrayal manifesting as physical pain – not angry and intense, but pain that gnawed deeply, unmoveable, linked to the brain, so that every thought brought fresh waves of unspeakable sickness. Minutes passed agonisingly slowly; she doubted her ability to endure each one. What would entice her to go on living? What would urge her to fight? She knew there was only one end to all of this. And she didn't want to live to see it.

Conner didn't say a word. She hadn't expected comfort from him, or empathy. Though perhaps he pitied her. Maybe that kept him silent.

She could only dread the welcome she'd receive from her brother. She contemplated reasons why she wouldn't have to see him at all, but none were feasible, especially with the present company. She would have to face it all – with what little strength she had left.

The Apothecary was almost unrecognisable. Devoid of any pleasant memory that would have kept it a home in her mind, she could hardly believe it was the same place she'd left.

Conner silently escorted her from the carriage to the door. She wasn't aware of being unsteady on her feet until she realised he held her arm and it was only this keeping her upright.

The place looked blank and grey. In its darkest time, it seemed all the colour had been drained from it, all the life. The dust of neglect didn't hang over it yet; even now, William had enough willpower to keep it looking presentable.

She saw him, standing in his usual location behind the counter. It felt so absurd that he would welcome them in that way, as though he needed that comfort to be able to face them. Seeing her, he did at least appear humbled rather than boastful.

'Clara, I'm sorry. Sorry for any part that I've played in this whole despicable mess. I don't believe you knew what you were concealing when you handed yourself over to the police. Tarasso was clearly an expert liar. God knows he's fooled us all along this twisted path we've been led to take.'

'Don't say his name.' Clara forced herself to reply. 'It will be better for all of us if you don't.'

William clearly hadn't accounted for this response when rehearsing his speech; he was dumbfounded. He might have expected anger, hysteria of some kind, but not indifference. Clara was too overcome, too exhausted to exhibit any emotion. What she wanted most was to sleep.

Sleep, and forget.

'Inspector, perhaps you could show her the "book" that your men uncovered. It will help her to understand – to accept this turn of events, where our words won't achieve anything.'

Clara wondered why her brother was speaking as if she wasn't in the room.

'Yes, I'd like to see it,' she admitted, her voice surprisingly eager-sounding, even to her. 'I don't believe such a thing can be so incriminating. I'll uncover its insignificance, to prove Matthias' innocence.'

'*Innocence?*' William was still far from in control of his volatile temper. 'I'm sorry, Inspector, but have I misinterpreted the situation? I presumed my sister's return signalled Tarasso's arrest – am I mistaken?'

'You're not mistaken, Mr Breslin.' There was the quietest hint of a warning in Conner's reply.

'Then why on earth is the word "innocence" being used as if it is still a possibility?'

Clara rounded on her brother, her vision blurred with rage. '*As you well know, Bill, a confession can be made in full knowledge of that person's innocence, because they feel that there isn't another choice to be made.*' Her voice was hoarse from holding back her fury. Taking a breath, calming herself, she continued. 'A confession isn't an admission of guilt without evidence. Until I see this book, I won't believe it.'

Conner exhaled deeply. His presence in the room was a grounding influence on the others who occupied it.

'You can find it where it was left, Miss Breslin. The

room is still under supervision.'

'Where was it left?' Clara asked. The statement sounded so weighty.

'In your bedroom, Miss Breslin.' Conner said this with regret, in a way that made Clara feel cold.

She was led upstairs by the constable she hadn't realised was standing in the wings. The inspector and her brother chose to stay downstairs.

'He confessed to her, just as I thought he might. As soon as he entered the building, I suspected their places could be exchanged.' Conner wasn't looking at William. His eyes were trained carefully on a building on the opposite side of the street. If he had his back to Breslin, the man's responses might be slightly less guarded.

'In a way, she's helped the case, not hindered it.' There was astonishment in William's voice.

'He would've been arrested in any case. The book is enough of a confession, without the verbal testimony.'

William's mouth twisted, as if the thought of the book made him queasy.

'She doesn't believe it yet. The words came from his own mouth, and she doesn't accept it. Her blind faith is astounding.'

'He must've done all he could to conceal the truth. You heard her yourself. She didn't think he was capable of killing; she believed that the notion had never occurred to him. Of course, if we're only talking about a Shoreditch actor with a talent for mixing remedies, as she believes him to be, then his potential as a murderer seems remote. But knowing the other side ...' The older man shook his head in the weary way of one who has seen enough cruelty to become anaesthetised to it.

'So, you've locked him in a cell. What's your next move?' William seemed eager to put an end to it all – for good reason. There was a whisper of hope, where all had seemed lost.

'Of course, there has to be a trial. Not that it will do him any good. You know what this country does to murderers, Breslin.' There was some chastising in these words, as if Conner was thinking about Clara's welfare, after all. 'Perhaps, after that, you can rebuild your lives.'

The look on William's face suggested he was starting to believe that possibility.

'Have you read it?' Conner asked, purely to gauge William's reaction.

'It's the work of a madman. However, I don't think his insanity should protect him from the scaffold.'

'A madman, yes – or a murderer adopting an elaborate strategy to convince the world of his madness.'

Two police constables flanked Clara's bedroom door. She decided not to dwell on the strangeness of that.

It occurred to her, with the force of an object striking her at speed: the policemen had been in her room, so they had seen her paintings. Her only haven was no longer a place of privacy. She dreaded crossing the threshold more than she feared seeing 'the book'.

She pushed the door open. The room had been completely turned over; dozens of paintings had been torn down and thrown aside, her art supplies scattered across the floor, opened, emptied and left discarded, unusable. She hadn't expected the police to respect her possessions. Nevertheless, the sight of her treasured artwork left in crumpled piles and hanging limp from the walls provoked a strong sensation of loss.

The disorder upset her greatly. However, she became aware of just how neglected the place was. There were thick layers of dust everywhere, and stark patches where the covering had been disturbed. It hadn't bothered her before her absence. Now, even though her paintings were a link to Matthias, she began to feel a need to put things in order. A clearer space might promote a clearer mind, and she would need that to protest Matthias' innocence.

'At the head of the bed, Miss. On the pillow.'

She'd forgotten the others in the room. Looking where the constable directed, she saw that, indeed, a small book lay open on her pillow.

The book.

The name was worryingly ambiguous.

Others had hinted at its immense importance. It had incriminated Matthias. Seeing it left in such an intimate place, Clara realised that Matthias must have left it there purposefully, with the intention of her reading it. He couldn't have known that she would turn herself in to the police before she could see it.

In her absence, the book had provided enough evidence for Conner to arrest him. After Clara's arrest, Matthias couldn't return to the Apothecary. So, the book had stayed in Clara's room and, when he visited her and confessed his guilt, he may have already realised that it was only a matter of time before Conner discovered it.

Did this mean that Matthias anticipated his arrest? If so, he must've known that the book implicated him in the woman's death.

Clara felt a flash of panic. Innocent men don't react rashly, fearing their end. They have right in their favour. Was she foolish, to have faith in Matthias' innocence?

Looking more closely, she realised the book was a journal. It was open at the first entry. She lifted the book with trembling hands and began to read.

"THE BOOK."

THE NAME WAS WORRYINGLY
AMBIGUOUS."

CHAPTER THIRTY

First Entry: May, 18—

I find myself drawn to Broad Street by instinct. It isn't my usual route to the Grecian, but I now take it daily. The crowds are a constant drain on my vitality, but I must travel this way until I can discover what compels me.

I find the little Apothecary particularly intriguing. All places are accompanied by sensations, but this one almost calls to me as I pass, urging me to notice. Someone must reside there. I must meet them.

As ever, this insight is steeped in apprehension. I can't risk becoming attached to another person; their contact with me will cause misery. I have a parasitic effect on others – I leech the happiness from their lives, leaving devastation. Nevertheless, I am bound – this interaction is my life's blood – the force that maintains me, though I strive to avoid it …

Today, I looked into the upstairs window of that curious Apothecary. I saw a woman, watching everyone who passed. For a moment, our eyes met, and all that dwells inside me was conveyed to her.

I can't tell if she will be drawn to me, as others have been before. But I must walk along Broad Street again. I must pass the Apothecary, glance up into the window. To neglect this would almost stop my heart …

After today's rehearsal was over, I walked through the City.

Again, my steps led me to Broad Street. I know the way by heart — all the interconnecting lanes and alleyways. It was dark, but I could see the familiar outline of the building I was striving to find.

The upper window was in darkness, but I could see her silhouette. Was she watching, as I was?

Did she feel, as I did, that a waking dream had descended over us both?

Second Entry: May, 18—

I pass by the Apothecary even more often — but I don't always glance into the window my eyes are drawn to. I get the feeling of being watched, and I feel a distinct energy emanating from the place; the promise of something appealing.

My daily rehearsals are restrictive — I can only walk there once in the morning and again at night. But I know I shouldn't go near the place too often, so that I can prolong the connection as much as possible. Every time I pass, I give something of myself to this nameless woman. A positive influence, that improves with time. She might feel its effects: a growing sense of fulfilment, or happiness. The talents she possesses grow stronger, her confidence increases. One thing is certain: our bond can't be undone, once we meet.

It will all end in desolation, as it always does.

One day, she will decide to follow me. Tragedy has told me this will happen. I anticipate it eagerly but know that I should dread the day.

Third Entry: May, 18—

The time draws near. I am guided towards it — I know that today, I will succeed.

The colours are my design. The palette of the world was too dull. A lure was needed; a physical canvas of attraction. Everything intensified, mirroring the emotions waiting to surface.

My ultimate desire is that she will be tempted to follow me and want to meet me. I want to discover everything about her; understand what draws me to her …

I made my way to Broad Street at an unusual hour, hoping to capture her attention.

I took my time. It was important not only for her to notice me, but also to have time to really look. A hurried glance wouldn't be enough.

The more I conveyed to her, the more she would be compelled to meet me. The more we come to know each other, the more she will benefit from our connection – as will I.

It can't last – but in the early days, it is easy to forget, to enjoy the thrill.

Standing below her window was almost too deliberate, but I couldn't risk her not seeing me.

Waiting was a torment, but success was near. When I first saw her face, I felt something momentous. It told me she would survive longer than the others – but I can't be sure how long.

She saw me; I moved on, to inspire her to follow. A voice urged me on, promised me success.

It was infantile, playing cat and mouse with a person I'd never met. She didn't know this – she believed she was making an independent decision. My passing was unprecedented; she was acting on impulse, encouraged further by the dazzling colours outside.

Leading her to Shoreditch was a risk. Many refused to set foot near the place. But I knew she wouldn't be deterred. Once she'd begun, a change of heart was impossible. She believed she was lost. She believed I was an anchor to attach herself to. When she discovered where I was leading her …

Bringing her to the Grecian was the best choice I could've made. Entering the theatre seemed to enliven her spirits. The surroundings were unseemly, but the instant I set foot onstage, this would be unimportant to her. She would see only me, be captivated by my performance and find it like nothing she'd ever seen.

This isn't arrogance. This is magnetism. She is subject to forces she can't possibly comprehend. As am I.

My colleague Thwaites tells me she asked for my name. It will be an incantation on her lips.

Fourth Entry: June, 18—

She watches many performances. I feel stronger. I need her there; without her, I will fade.

She also thrives on our association. Whatever induces me to fixate on her grows stronger as time goes on.

That is always the way with that small few that possess true gifts amidst an unexceptional host of others. I am drawn to the gifted ones, until their abilities also profit me. What is left when my needs are sated? That shouldn't be mentioned.

Very soon, we'll meet. She doesn't know this. I have the advantage of foresight; therefore, I can plan the day – including the particular performance, when she decides to come to my dressing room. She won't like me at first. Then she will realise I'm all she could want for. I am, after all, her muse. And she is mine.

Fifth Entry: July, 18—

The Taming of the Shrew. *Petruchio is my part.*

He isn't a remarkable hero. He treats his heroine with contempt. There isn't anything to admire, and if redemption is to be found, it will be scarce.

But that is why I requested this play. Performing this part will surely decide her.

She can't be clouded by the words I speak, or by my actions. The words of Katherina will deter her from feeling anything other than an artistic regard towards me.

She will introduce herself to me, and our association will allow her to flourish ...

It is done.

I hadn't anticipated the effect that seeing her would have on me. She entered the room so silently it caught me off-guard. The shock of seeing her made fervour flare inside me that I didn't know I possessed.

I didn't mean to overwhelm her with the gas lamps. It was a potentially costly error; she might've left the room. Fortunately, I managed to bring myself under control.

It also gave me some time. She was so affected by the glare that she didn't see me at first. This meant I could consider how to approach the conversation. The first words that came to mind were those I'd contemplated most of all.

'Who are you?'

Her name is Clara Breslin. She spoke candidly, answering almost every question I posed to her, until I asked why she'd chosen my theatre. It was a little ambitious. I couldn't expect her to admit taking an interest in me just because I passed her window, which I know is true.

Her talent is difficult to decipher. She doesn't acknowledge her creativity, apart from appreciating art – which leads me to believe that she is an artist. The fact that she conceals this must be significant.

I thoroughly enjoyed her conversation. Her replies to my questions were carefully considered and quite insightful. She doesn't tailor her opinions to suit others; she forges her own path.

I needed to discover as much about her as I could, which meant I gave away little about myself.

I implied that Thwaites, our theatre employee, first told me about her. Rather this than reveal that I'd already seen her in the Apothecary; a small deception, better than admitting to seeking her out.

She complimented my acting, which reassured me. Not that my vanity needs indulging – but I knew that my performances had the desired effect. I wanted to inspire her, as she inspires me; feed her creativity, so that she might nourish mine.

But of course, She *had to interrupt us, abruptly, making the lights change erratically.* She *manifests herself in any way she can – and it was clear that* She *didn't want to be forgotten. I answered Clara's questions as quickly as possible and suggested that we should take a walk together – at least then* Her *influence wouldn't be so overwhelming …*

We walked and talked together with total ease – remarkable, for a pair who had never been formally introduced and barely knew each other.

Clara seemed to forget herself, become light-hearted. She walked beside me like an old friend, altered from a withdrawn person to one full of vitality. Her life could have been steered this way by external forces, but in truth, I had steered it. It made me believe that I'd actually improved her life by entering it. She used to act like she'd been caged; it gratified me to be the creator of her liberty.

I felt invigorated. Clara's exhilaration encouraged my own.

Regrettably, she couldn't be at ease for long. No one could be, under the strict rules our society applies. But I'm governed by different rules entirely; I convinced her that a short walk in the park wouldn't break any boundaries of propriety – not for the two of us, at least.

I couldn't tell her how her presence has been therapeutic for me. How she represents the ideal that spurs me onward; encourages me to improve by honest means.

I found myself talking of my childhood – but I was careful to overlook crucial details. It gave her some idea of where I have come from, who the years have shaped me into.

But not who She has shaped me into.

Not the years of being compelled to succeed – at all costs. I thrive on my accomplishments … but She ensures that I can't possibly fail.

Clara almost divulged her true talent to me, when talk turned to our careers. She mentioned total 'absorption', which I found extremely intriguing. What do you absorb your thoughts with, Clara?

I know she is concealing something spectacular about herself; that we are more alike than I first imagined. She is resolutely silent on the matter, but in time, it will become known.

I had to be content to say goodbye to her, but we arranged to meet again. I eagerly await my next opportunity to scrutinise her.

Sixth Entry: August, 18—

I can't rely on my conversation alone to inspire Clara, and so

I've been introducing her to venues around the City. Of course, I first had to convince Clara that we needn't be obedient to society's conventions.

Clara's happiness is inextricably linked to my own. I can't risk diminishing her creative impulses – they must intensify.

All humans grow tired; it's an indicator of mortality. But with Clara, I hope to prolong her thirst for creativity for as long as possible.

Our outings are unpredictable. We are forced to meet at the slightest warning, with the least preparation, due to our respective working schedules.

A sense of urgency, of seizing the precious little time we have, seems to persuade Clara that we shouldn't care about propriety.

Today we visited an exhibition of watercolours in Piccadilly. It was my choice; I hoped Clara would be captivated. I'm convinced her talent lies in creating art, in some form.

She did seem to study the paintings with great intensity. Her observations were technical, not purely emotional. She commented on the stylistic qualities of the art rather than the subject or the effect of the composition. It seems I've come closer to a discovery – I can only hope.

Wanting to encourage her further, I mentioned the number of female artists exhibiting, but suggested that it should be a much larger proportion. I told her it wouldn't always be this way; by the turn of the next century, female artists will have gained a lot more prominence.

She might've disregarded my conjecture. But there are sources near to me who see these matters with great clarity; who regard the future, present and past as intertwined, having seen more of time than most would dare suggest.

Seventh Entry: August, 18—

Clara decided to show me her preferred theatre. I rarely watch plays. Spending the majority of my time performing, it feels a little too much like relinquishing control – observing brings my own performances into doubt. But her creative mind ignites when she watches plays. I can't deny her that pleasure, or the favourable effect on me.

Her choice was the Adelphi. I've heard her mention it before, only ever in reverent tones. The night's performance was The Merchant of Venice, *and though it was artfully staged and competently acted, the accumulation of supreme talent in one room was almost unbearable to me. Any one of those actors could have been my next chosen, another artistic mind to scour for my own ends. But my attachment to Clara grows and grows – I can't foresee anyone tempting me to abandon her.*

The trouble is this: with those whose talent glows so brightly, they are often the most swiftly burnt-out. Clara is so quiet and unassuming that even now her flame is only beginning to kindle.

It was clear to me from the outset that Clara was trying to show me what my career could develop into. But I can't be so confident in my predictions.

My vocation is to foster the creative abilities in others, partly because this satisfies my own desires. But the result of my attentions can be disastrous. I can't be destined for any sort of glory.

In truth, I don't know why these powers have been afforded to me – they only cause grief. If only the circumstances of my birth hadn't dictated my path.

She still refuses my invitation to visit my home. I only ask her because it would prolong the time we have together. But she keeps propriety and won't disclose her thoughts.

I would never compel her. She is right to decline.

Eighth Entry: August, 18—

Due to my suspicions that Clara's talents must lie in art, I suggested a visit to the Society of Female Artists. I wanted her to realise that her work (assuming its existence) could display amongst this company.

I've never seen her so elated, have such a sense of belonging. I flourished because of her inspiration. The unnameable mysticism inside me was strengthened and fed ravenously on her happiness.

Unfortunately, our return journey took us past the Drury Lane theatre.

I felt, rather than saw, a slight change in Clara's mood. That was my warning.

Hearing a stranger call Clara's name was another. In the brief time we'd been friends, this had never happened before. In fact, Clara revelled in being unrecognised as she walked through the City. She'd never spoken of any acquaintances, besides her brother.

The gentleman who approached us wasn't a relation. Nor did he seem pleased to see her. The smile on his face was completely disingenuous.

Clara almost recoiled at the sight of him.

They exchanged uneasy greetings. Clara didn't show me any recognition, as if she'd prefer not to acquaint me with these people. But I didn't want to leave her when she seemed so distressed.

The man made such an entrance that I didn't see the young lady standing behind him. But the venom in her voice, which she tried to conceal, attracted as much attention as waving a brightly coloured flag.

The pair began an uncomfortable conversation with Clara. Eventually, it became obvious that I'd been noticed, and associated with her, although I hadn't been introduced or acknowledged. I felt obliged to address them openly, and was greeted coolly, as expected.

Albert and Ruth were ready to dismiss my profession. I wondered how a woman who claimed to be Clara's oldest and dearest friend could treat someone she'd befriended so contemptuously. I didn't try to restore my reputation in their eyes; for them, a judgment had been made, and I didn't care to alter it. My vanity doesn't need to be validated by strangers – if that were the case I certainly wouldn't be acting at the Grecian!

Clara, on the other hand, was ready to defend me. To the extent that when her so-called friends insulted her further, I decided to abandon my polite silence. They seemed to misunderstand her in every way possible.

We were invited to join them at a later date. I knew I'd been invited as an afterthought, or perhaps from curiosity – they'd certainly shown no liking towards me.

We didn't discuss the conversation at length, after they'd left, but it was clear that Clara wanted to put it out of her mind as swiftly as possible. She did, however, admit she'd been holding back from introducing me to them.

I don't want to entertain Clara's friends; they don't matter to me. They would only be a distraction and prevent Clara utilising the best of her spirit. She mentioned feeling obliged to mix with these people, despite not really liking them. Yet again, she referred to 'society' – as if a faceless 'they' could dictate her happiness. I wanted to tell her that no 'society' will ever know her better than she knows herself. She should consider her own needs, her own interests, because anything we choose to do will be met with derision by someone or another, no matter what …

We walked back to Clara's home together, for the first time.

Usually, she would let me walk part of the way but insist I made my own way towards Shoreditch, because accompanying her would be 'too far out of the way'. Tonight, however, her mind was occupied with uneasy thoughts and she didn't make any attempt to dissuade me from accompanying her, even when we stopped at the corner of Broad Street.

I had to feign a complete lack of awareness. I also had to suggest that I'd been walking there long before I knew her; that she'd had no bearing on my decision to take that route. She mustn't know that I intended it from the start. Perhaps, eventually, it won't matter. But for now, I must maintain the pretence. She mustn't be aware of the things I am concealing.

She told me she wanted me to meet her brother. Obviously, meeting the delightful Ruth and Albert had given her a taste for unpleasant introductions. I looked beyond her and could see the man standing at the window, waiting for his sister's return. Our eye contact created a force, as it always does. With Clara, I met her eye to transfer my desire to meet her. With her brother, I attempted to judge his reaction before I received it.

The coldness of his thoughts ran through me like a vein of ice.

I wanted Clara to postpone the meeting, but she wouldn't. She seemed almost angry when I said she shouldn't let my introduction to her friends affect her. She accused me of a lack of empathy.

As ever, our conversation turned to Clara's obedience towards society's expectations. She envies my comparative freedom. But I know a different oppression: being unfamiliar, being unwelcome, so that I can't settle anywhere. Being dangerous, so that I must constantly move on, leave no trace, fearing the past, the devastation I have caused.

I accepted her wishes so that the conversation wouldn't tend towards unbroachable subjects.

Glancing over to her brother again, this time I tried to temper his judgement with a little persuasion. With Clara, it had taken effect immediately, and with favourable result. In this case, my subject was highly resistant to my power. His mind resisted my control. I felt the rejection of my intrusion as a physical rather than mental push. As he also must have. There was a crash, the sound of heavy glass shattering.

We approached the shop. He appeared in the doorway, blocking our way. His mistrust was palpable. I prepared for the introduction ... but as if I'd been struck in the chest by a sudden blow, I felt the impact of a tremendous force, compelling my attention.

The source was the upstairs room, and I let myself stare at the window. The attraction was astounding; I wanted to race up the stairs, desperate to discover what drew me. Whatever it was, it was sure to be the place where Clara's talent flourished. I could sense her creativity like an unseen force; my mind drew nourishment from it, as a plant does from sunlight and damp earth.

'Mr Tarasso, here is my brother, Mr William Breslin.' Her words slid me into the present moment.

We spoke, two strangers, brought together by what level of corruption the brother could only guess. He spoke as anyone might, with complete disapproval. I could only state the truth: that Clara had engineered this late-night introduction, not I. She spoke about our friendship – which didn't help matters. It only spurred him to ask why I'd agreed to accompany her without a chaperone. To which, of course, I felt obliged to remind him that Clara had travelled that way long before she met me.

Surprisingly, this seemed to be a suitable reply; it appeased the brother momentarily. I could see that he didn't dare turn me away – he couldn't alienate his sister. He didn't like me, that was evident, but his

371

anxiety abated.

The time had come that I ought to have left. But my new-found sway over the elder Breslin had fired my confidence. I knew I had to engineer circumstances to allow me to spend more time in the Apothecary, to prolong my exposure to Clara's creativity. Fortunately, I didn't have to exert myself. The situation I needed almost presented itself. All it took was some subtle persuasion, as soon as William mentioned that he was exceptionally busy in his work.

All I had to do was place myself over the threshold of the shop – and nothing could prevent me from achieving my ambition.

Of course, Clara championed my cause. She made the suggestion of employing me as if the notion had come to her entirely by accident.

The energy emitted by Clara's creativity hummed in the air; I could draw on it to enhance my actions. Mixing a simple cure, for example. It needed no expertise, only being near to Clara. William was suitably impressed – and felt that his decision to hire me had been a brilliant one.

Neither of them could have guessed that I'd manufactured my abilities, altered their minds, clouded their perceptions. Which is just as well.

All is falling wonderfully into place. My strength will grow as Clara's abilities flourish. I can only hope that we can maintain this blissful creativity somehow. That the tragedy won't occur.

Ninth Entry: September, 18—

It has been easy to make myself indispensable to William's business. My link to Clara is now so strong that I can persuade anyone who crosses the threshold to fall under my charms. The customers all seem to agree that I've given the place a new spirit. That is completely intentional. They don't need to know that I'm an entirely unexceptional person, that there are indescribable forces which aid me. As long as they are deceived, I am safe.

William tolerates me, which is all I can expect from him. He doesn't trust me, nor does he understand his sister's attachment to me. But he doesn't question it openly and doesn't shun me, as I know he wishes he could. Again, he falls under the deception. He begins to believe, against his better judgement and all misgivings, that I may benefit his business.

Beyond all of this, far more importantly, Clara's talent is blossoming. Like a self-improving spiral, this also enhances my power, enables me to manipulate others to my own ends – ensuring that I remain in close proximity to Clara and continue the improvement of her creativity.

I would like to believe that this spiral will continue its upward trajectory. That improvement will beget further improvement, that all will exist in perfect happiness. But experience has taught me otherwise. I know that this is no spiral. It is a rapid ascent, and an even headier descent, uncontrollable and disastrous. Often fatal. Such is the nature of my affliction. It has been this way as long as I can remember, and as much as I hope that this time will be different, I know, by the rapidity of my success, that it can't be.

It has culminated in the triumph of Mr Breslin's Famous Purging Agent. An almost city-wide phenomenon in a matter of days, it has brought William unparalleled acclaim and boosted profits substantially. Of course, this has nothing to do with any special attributes of the cure and everything to do with the fact that it was I who prepared and bottled it. Everything I come into contact with now is infused with *my power, just as my successes are outward manifestations of the effect that Clara's talent has over me.*

Business couldn't be better; which justifies my presence as a new-found employee. William doesn't notice anything unusual; he is more than ready to believe his own publicity.

Clara isn't as enthused by the sudden influx of custom. She'd prefer the place to be empty – to suit her own ends. I try to make any opportunity I can for her to pursue her creativity. I often take up her duties as well as my own.

I also relieve her of having to speak to the customers. I enjoy it; it allows me to unearth all sorts of hidden aspects to their characters, small tributaries of sustenance, in the absence of Clara's great river of talent. All of these encounters allow my abilities to grow. Nowhere more so than in the theatre. Clara still visits regularly to watch my performances; she must see their rapid improvement. It is all part of the illusion: the grand trick. It isn't me improving – it's her. She advances beautifully; she is magnificent. And I bask in the warmth of her gifts, and it nourishes me. She recently admitted that she has never loved. I know that, for me, love is an impossibility – and yet, if something vaguely resembling love could ever exist, for beings such as us, perhaps it is this. A mutual understanding; a harmony beyond the comprehension of others.

She busies herself with her 'preoccupation' more than ever. Everyone has noted her absence, I most of all. To mention it, when she has been hoping to remain inconspicuous, would be tactless. I share her unutterable secret – although she hasn't disclosed it to me. I'm the only one who can empathise with her preoccupation, the only one who would encourage it rather than show disdain for it, as her brother so often does. But it's only right that I should encourage it – without her talents, I would be a shadow of myself.

Tenth Entry: September, 18—

A sense of panic has descended over me, which I can't dispel. I know that our descent has begun: Clara's and mine. Her body is bound by the constraints of mortality – she begins to tire.

Eleventh Entry: October, 18—

The cures have gone bad. At first, I hardly noticed it – it could've been coincidence. But the complaints are now numerous. They coincide perfectly with the dates I first noted that Clara was beginning to suffer.

I desperately wanted her to be stronger than the others, to withstand the drains on her energy. But these forces are merciless. They have their own priorities.

William blames me – as he should. I just hope he doesn't come to despise me, as so many have in the past. At present, he believes that I'm responsible for his sister's carelessness, in some way. That I could knowingly betray his trust is beyond comprehension – for now.

The Breslins' quarrels have been tempestuous to say the least. It must be a detriment to Clara's wellbeing – and therefore, a detriment to her abilities. With her deterioration, inevitably, follows mine. Follows tragedy.

Twelfth Entry: October, 18—

The after-effects of the cures worsen by the day. First, the customers grew ill; now, gravely so. There can be only one result – William suspects it, too. Even Clara, who has been shutting herself away most days, senses some danger.

She thought that William and I might be able to salvage the reputation of the Apothecary if we tried to talk around the members of his Club. Men from all professions frequent the place. Amongst them, she supposed, there would be someone to advise us, or champion William's cause.

Of course, we met with mixed response. Some seemed to welcome William's demise and expressed any possible criticism, yet some wanted to excuse these unfortunate events as a simple mishap. William felt he'd succeeded far more than he'd expected to. Even I was pleasantly surprised ...

This morning, I knew the worst would happen. If I'd had any hope of escaping, I would've fled, but I was too closely involved. I had to face up to the horror I'd created, and so I arrived at the shop much earlier than usual, before the Breslins themselves had woken.

The woman who brought the news at least gave us the mercy of being succinct. There could be no doubt that her sister was dead; no doubt that it was Breslin's morphine that killed her.

William instantly despaired. In his pain, he lashed out desperately, as if in death-throes. He wanted to blame everyone, including himself.

I did my utmost to defend each of us ... knowing full well that the blame lay with me. That everyone, anyone, I come into contact with might experience tragedy such as this.

But the blame doesn't lie entirely with me. I inherited it; I have no control over it. It's a part of me, infused into every drop of blood. It was my destiny, from the moment I was born. A prophecy I must fulfil, otherwise I cease to be.

William won't understand that. I can't expect him to. He has dismissed me. I don't expect we will ever speak to each other again.

It is all ruined. I can't help but regret it.

Thirteenth Entry: October, 18–

William has made arrangements to have me followed. It can only be him; he must've hired someone privately, as the men don't wear police uniforms.

For the past week, I've managed to elude them, thanks in part to my ability to enchant others. But even that can't last; my power fades, with all the rapidity that Clara's talents diminish.

It will all be over soon. I feel remorse that Clara will soon discover the truth. I had so hoped that our happiness would last.

I know they will search my home, and so I make a point of catching a few hours' sleep in the day and staying out at night. Eventually, this deception will also fail – before it does, I must make my final arrangements.

I will visit Clara for the last time tonight. We'll visit the theatre, honouring the more pleasant days we used to enjoy.

In the morning, I'll be arrested – and rightly so. But I can't let that happen without an opportunity to explain all – to the one whose good opinion I never honestly earnt but can't envisage living without.

Others will read this diary and think I must be insane. Perhaps they're right. I'll be incarcerated, in any case.

But you, Clara – you're the only one I want to implore. You must read this diary – which I've left purposely for your eyes – no one else's – and decide if you can believe my story.

None of this would've happened if it weren't for Her.

Melpomene. My mother.

She's part of my every action, every compulsion. She's with me constantly, a presence I can't hide from, or ignore. Her will drives me; her constant need to devour and devastate feeds my purpose.

She is Tragedy. *Her love for a mortal man produced me, and I was born with such terrible responsibility, to appease her. I'm only half-mortal. That is her 'gift'. But no gift ever came with so high a price.*

No one can understand the irrepressible desire of a Muse. She needs tragedy like you need air. She takes her sustenance from it, and so must I. Though it isn't tragedy that appeases me, as it does her. It is the talent of others.

You aren't the first, Clara. But I found you in the same way that I have found countless others before you — I sensed your talent, as a hound might be alerted to a scent. Knowing that you possessed remarkable ability, I decided to attach myself to you.

Being close to me, you could receive my mother's good favour.

As all Muses have done, in ancient days and throughout history, she possesses the ability to enhance people's talents. By meeting me, you unlocked the power of the immortals.

But she is the Muse of Tragedy. Any benevolence on her part can never last. She provokes the intense improvement of her victims, but only to suit her own ends. That way, their plummet into tragedy is all the more dramatic, and all the more wholesome for her.

That's why your creativity was vastly improved when you first met me. You might've believed it was something to do with me — my appearance, my personality, or a combination of these and other factors. I don't say this out of arrogance. In fact, it's been so long that She has dictated my actions that I suspect it is actually her who makes me look, act and speak in particular ways, to fit the person I'm luring into her clutches.

William also shared the benefits of my acquaintance. But you've both suffered by knowing me. William has lost his business.

You've lost your creative ambition. Perhaps, in the wake of all of this, you might never regain it. That is usually the way.

Now, Clara, you must search yourself. Do you believe that a woman is dead because an ancient, immortal being wished it? Or will you come to believe the accusations of the police: that I'm a calculating murderer who committed a vengeful act by tampering with William's supplies of morphine?

The morphine was concentrated – to create the tragedy from which we now suffer. It was Melpomene's doing – and she reaps the benefits whilst we face the devastation that follows. I am just a channel for her wickedness – how I wish it wasn't so. You know me, Clara – better than anyone. Would I choose to kill? Would I choose to destroy everything, when my heart belongs to you?

She won't let me love. That is her most unreasonable price. But if I were free to love, Clara, it would be you. Of course it would. You are entirely unique. I sought you out, as I have with others, many times before. But I've never regretted the action so much as I have for you. You understand me. You see a wonderful future for me, that no one before you has ever endeavoured to see. If only I wasn't governed by this dreadful bond. I believe we could've had a blissful life together. Perhaps the small amount of mortal blood I possess will help me escape my fate, shape my own destiny. But I fear that it will never be that way – I wish it could. I'm desperate not to lose you.

Regardless of the outcome: thank you, Clara. Thank you for having faith in me when I have neither earnt it nor believed anyone ever would.

Forever yours – whether or not I am free to be so,
Matthias

Deborah E Wilson

CHAPTER THIRTY-ONE

She let the book fall where she'd first found it.

Her first instinct was to believe – and it was her first instinct that she'd always followed. She believed Matthias had confessed the truth – believed it without question. Every element of his confession revealed details that validated so much about their bond. Not only that, but all those aspects of his personality – all those experiences which she'd known were beyond human … it all became reasonable, logical. She'd held him in awe, as a being beyond her comprehension, and now she knew this was true.

Nevertheless, he was a murderer. He'd admitted it, without remorse. He hadn't wished the dead woman alive again; only that his and Clara's happiness hadn't suffered as a result. He had matter-of-factly stated the circumstances of the killing, without a shred of horror at how easily it happened.

Perhaps he felt detached from the murder, as he hadn't been complicit in it – her death had been a by-product of someone else's plans and was out of his control.

He acted as a conduit for someone else's motives … so could the death really be his fault?

Knowing it would inevitably happen, should he have prevented it? Or would it have followed the nature of most misfortunes: if prevented in one way, an alternative route would be found? Would 'She' have sat in wait and attacked another innocent person if her plans had been thwarted?

That question would remain unanswered. Clara could only assess the events as Matthias had presented them.

The death had, seemingly, not been *his* decision. Not his calculated act. Therefore, it wasn't *his* crime.

Involving Clara, however, had been *entirely* calculated. He'd sought her out; it was perversely flattering but had a distinctly sinister edge to it.

She thought *she* was the pursuer: the artist seeking her muse. In reality, it was the complete reverse. *He'd* been the one to seek her out: the Muse's instrument, compelled to hunt down unsuspecting individuals and catch their attention, only to consume their lives.

Regardless of how their bond had changed over time, in those crucial initial exchanges, he had knowingly deceived her. He'd purposefully manipulated her to increase his power, and that was deeply hurtful.

She'd wanted him for her muse; she'd followed him, studied him and watched him from afar – which was, in its own way, deceitful. But her intentions hadn't been nearly as despicable as his. He'd known that his actions would culminate in … tragedy. All she'd wanted was to create works of beauty.

In spite of all of this, beyond the control of other-worldly influences, he'd fallen in love with her. It was because of this that he felt any remorse. Perhaps it was fortunate that he'd chosen her? In doing so, had he uncovered his own weakness and broken the cycle of despair and ruination by letting himself be caught?

Clara despised the circumstances of their meeting,

the sordid intentions that had brought them together, the devastation and death that had intertwined their fates. Even so, from the inevitable disaster, there was something salvageable, something scarcely redeemable … But was it worthwhile?

Before she'd read Matthias' journal, she'd believed their love was something life-enriching; something to fiercely defend, when everything else was lost. The rest of her life could be in tatters, maimed beyond recognition, but their love would endure.

Now, after having her every hope and belief betrayed and distorted, her pride was wounded. To say that her love remained unchanged would be a lie.

To believe her heart couldn't hold a place for Matthias anymore would also be a lie. His parting words had impressed emotions on her that she couldn't ignore.

She felt compelled to defend him, where no one else would. To find some circumstance in which admitting his motives would lessen his guilt. Knowing that others wouldn't believe his story only spurred her on, to prove its validity. She hadn't known him for long but had gained a truer picture of the man and his life than anyone else had. Even the truths he'd falsified to suit his own purpose were clearer to her than they were to the police; she'd witnessed many of them first-hand and had the benefit of her own senses to be able to validate or discount them.

Everyone would be waiting for her downstairs, she eventually realised. She couldn't stay suspended in this moment forever, with an eternity to decide what to do. She would have to let time blunder on, hoping that a wise decision would occur to her before Matthias' punishment was decided.

As she pushed herself dumbly through the stockroom curtain, the inspector and her brother raised their heads from intense, whispered conversation to look at her.

William at least had the decency to be sympathetic. 'Not an easy read,' was the understatement, as if he could comprehend even a fraction of her grief.

Clara didn't say anything. She sat down beside them, staring ahead.

'I hope you can appreciate, Miss Breslin, that as a piece of evidence, it may be tenuous at best.' Conner spoke slowly, carefully, but without condescending her with a compassionate tone. He only needed her to understand. 'All it gives us is a written confession of murder and a sample of the man's handwriting. But the smaller details ... it attempts to reproduce past events from his perspective, and we can't rely on any of that without accepting his bias – *unless* you can confirm anything he's written with your own testimony.'

'Surely the little details are inconsequential,' William said, sitting up a little straighter, his voice almost plaintive. 'He's told us how he did it – he doesn't even show remorse for what he's done.'

Conner glanced sideways at him, irritated. 'We need your sister's version of events, Mr Breslin. We need to make sure there aren't any minor loopholes which could mean the diary is discounted.' He paused, and a crooked, unamused smile appeared on his lips. 'Of course, if a plea of insanity is made, it will become evidence of an altogether different variety.'

'Unless the plea of insanity is overturned,' William rejoined, almost standing now, clearly agitated. 'You also suggested that the references to his mother might be a ruse to make us *believe* he isn't of sound mind, to garner sympathy, when in reality he's a ruthless killer.'

'You can't say either.' Clara didn't look at either of them. Her voice sounded strange to her ears. No trace of anger, in spite of everything. 'Matthias isn't insane. Nor is he a killer.'

The men exchanged glances. Neither questioned her reasoning. They'd expected her to be in shock and speak irrationally.

'Whatever you may believe, Miss Breslin, I must inform you: there's no chance Mr Tarasso will be proved innocent. The press is demanding justice – as are the local residents. There's no way we can argue against a verbal and written confession from a criminal – and if you're honest, you must admit that there's no sense in fighting for his innocence when the only other suspects are your brother, and yourself.'

'Let him go, Clara – he betrayed you.' William moved as if to come and comfort her, but he stopped, perhaps because she'd turned away to face the opposite wall. She dreaded relinquishing her emotions to him and was spared that heart-wrenching moment, at least.

Clara felt her anger boil inside her but couldn't express it. It was interspersed with her crushing disappointment. She knew there was nothing to be said. No one would hear her, no one wanted to help.

'Can I at least see him, before the trial?' She half-turned her head and shoulders to point her words vaguely in Conner's direction.

'As I have already said, Miss Breslin, the press is hungry for this one. They'll bother us blind until we set a date for the trial – and we intend to push things onward as swiftly as possible – by the next Assizes, preferably. It could all be over within a month or two.'

What that 'it' would mean, Clara was too horror-struck to consider. 'It would be ill-advised to grant Tarasso visitors before then; he'll only disclose things that he could come to regret. You might want to visit him on the day of the trial, to express any last sentiments …' Uncharacteristically, he tailed off. It was apparent that he disapproved. But perhaps he felt some sympathy. Clara sensed an almost paternal instinct to advise her. He was the champion of the afflicted, after all.

She was devastated that she couldn't visit him. But she'd anticipated the answer. Now that court proceedings were to be hastened along; now that the press was not only interested, but intent on a fair verdict; now that any revelations to come would have a direct impact on her family and her brother's business, she couldn't risk making foolish decisions.

'I certainly won't open for business until the trial is over.' William was matter-of-fact, ever the tradesman. 'After that, there might be a possibility that I can start afresh.'

'After Matthias is *dead*?' Clara's throat was sore with the effort of holding back tears.

William had nothing to say to that. He was capable

of feeling some regret – or so it appeared. 'I think you should go and stay with our parents for a while.' Clearly the idea had been formulating for some time. 'There isn't anything for you here. You need to get away and recuperate.'

'*That would ruin me,*' Clara whispered. She wondered if her brother comprehended that she could only withstand a certain amount of pain.

'I'm sorry,' he muttered, his voice wavering, 'I've already arranged it.'

'But how will I survive?' Clara was aware that her voice was pleading, fraught with helplessness, like a child's. 'I'll be cast away from *everything*, everyone I love!' She felt breathless, weightless: of less substance than a handful of dandelion seeds which could be scattered by the wind, if it blew strongly enough.

CHAPTER THIRTY-TWO

The cold autumnal wind had carried her to Wiltshire and dropped her gently to rest. Everything here was gentle, as if the ground beneath her, the sky above and everything in-between knew of her desolation and wanted to treat her kindly.

Without the sun, the colour had drained from the landscape. The pastures weren't richly green; the flora had long since wilted and died. At least the foliage had a romantic flush of auburn and red to it – to remind those who walked amongst it that nature's palette wasn't entirely dry.

Clara preferred it this way. She would've hated being presented with rich, beautiful tones, because she didn't have the artistic inclination to capture them. Mother Nature had subdued her brushstrokes; Clara felt that she might never touch a paintbrush again.

William stayed behind – to recover the remains of his business. He'd entrusted Clara's care to their parents. They knew as much as he did about the affair – Clara hadn't confirmed anything to either party, but she'd agreed to write to Inspector Conner with her own testimony of events. From the stilted and often purposefully abrupt conversations the Breslins had shared with their daughter, she came to understand that they had no desire to pry into the particulars of her association with a self-confessed murderer. They were relieved she'd not been 'corrupted by his influence', blessed reputation was still intact (so far as they knew) and were 'glad' to have her back home. Nothing else had been said. They'd barely seen Clara in the three years she'd lived in London, and so, in the spirit of continuity, they gave her as much time alone as possible. This suited Clara; she didn't want to share pleasantries with anyone and resented her parents for sending her away in the first place; she hadn't wanted to go, and it had brought her nothing but pain.

Within a week of being back, she heard that Ruth was in the area. She had also ended up lodging with her relatives – having been made homeless. Albert wouldn't pay rent on a Kensington apartment for a woman who no longer loved him. Her parents wouldn't support her living in the City, having come close to damaging her reputation forever. She was bound to be much more upset about the move than Clara was; her heart belonged in London, even if it no longer belonged to Albert.

After another day or so, Ruth tried to pay Clara a visit. The housekeeper asked her if she might care to receive Miss Davison, but was told no. 'Send her away, please. Tell her I'm not well enough to see anyone and won't be for the foreseeable future.'

She hoped Ruth wouldn't return. After all, what would they have to talk about?

Would Ruth want to find common ground with her, now that they'd both had their hearts betrayed? And would that serve as Ruth's apology for the endless declarations of loving bliss, which had only emphasised Clara's loneliness?

Or, now that Clara had been emotionally spoilt,

that her would she be expected to seek forgiveness, having treated Ruth so harshly when she had first heard of Albert's infidelity?

Clara didn't care for either prospect. Her friendship with Ruth had long since become soured; she didn't see any need to revive it.

Of course, it could've been neither of those. It could've simply been an opportunity for Ruth to undermine Clara, to exult in her misery, so that she could forget her own.

After what Matthias had done, she supposed she would always see the potential in someone to cause her harm, no matter how innocent their intentions.

Sitting alone by the window, watching the near-colourless landscape change as the hours passed, was her solace. There was no desire to socialise; no desire to paint. She stared at the outlook until her vision blurred.

Meanwhile, her thoughts always returned to Matthias. Could he avoid execution? Could he be forgiven for the crime he hadn't intended to commit? If only she'd been enough to persuade him to break the cycle, to stop being ruled by his mother's proclivities, before a life had been forfeit.

She couldn't know whose lives had been devastated before hers. There may have been other deaths, other loves. And if Melpomene had the power he suggested, she might always evade capture, evade justice. How could it be moral, that the son should bear the punishment for the mother's crimes? From the little she had read of her, Clara sensed that there was more to Melpomene than just an earthly presence; she was a malevolent force, capable of causing extreme peril.

In her darkest moments, she prayed desperately never to meet her; in times of clarity, she longed to find a way for the Muse and her son to change places.

These clearer moments rejuvenated her slightly so that she felt like leaving the house. She walked the rugged paths that, just a handful of years before, she would have pounded at a run, her lungs heaving with exertion, her body aching but her mind exuberant with the joy of open spaces. But now, her slow, dull steps were hollow. She didn't exult in nature – it had lost its gleam; a world that allowed beings like Melpomene to insinuate like a parasitic disease held no glamour for her anymore.

Nights were just as empty. She wasn't plagued with violently vivid nightmares – her sleep was devoid of memorable thoughts. Nonetheless, she woke every morning with a leaden stomach, her head reeling. Her appetite suffered more than ever – she often felt ill at the thought of eating. She felt exhausted, fraught with tension.

In a matter of weeks, the trial impended.

CHAPTER THIRTY-THREE

ecember brought the Assizes. At the Old Bailey, they came three times a year, such was the volume of heinous crimes. It was the first of the month: this date had been chosen for Matthias' trial.

Clara returned to Broad Street, summoned by Inspector Conner. The Apothecary was a ravaged mess, boarded to protect it from vandalism. The virtually bare shop was peppered all around with dead flies, the remaining few items gathering dust.

It was clear, apart from the cold welcome, that William didn't want her there – as if her presence at the trial would have any bearing on the verdict. He meant to testify against Matthias in court; this was hardly surprising. But knowing this, she could hardly bear to be near him.

Time passed indistinguishably in the days leading up to the trial. She was scarcely aware of being anywhere, of doing anything. Her will was focused on one thing. Everything else was superfluous.

'I hope that being away from here has restored you.'

Anyone taking more than a passing glance at her could see that it hadn't.

'Knowing our parents, it's unlikely they've given you any worthwhile advice.'

'I don't think they have the slightest concept of what has happened.'

Clara would have found amusement in this before, but not anymore. It reminded her of how alone she was; so far removed from people's understanding or pity.

'I must tell you, Bill: my opinions and my loyalties haven't altered. But I don't resent yours. What has transpired can't ever change, and what is yet to happen will do so, regardless of any grudges between us.'

He hadn't expected any grand revelations, quite obviously.

'We will travel to court together. But be prepared – we will be apart for the duration of the trial. I can't support the prosecution and stand by your side.'

Clara found that this final cruelty didn't surprise or hurt her. She knew she was alone in her support of Matthias – her brother's presence, or lack of, wasn't needed to confirm that.

'You said I would be allowed to see him, just once more.'

They stood in an anteroom of the Old Bailey, waiting for the trial to begin. The inspector looked at Clara with a measure of disbelief, as though he hadn't expected her to be here, to have such personal strength.

'You are. But only for a short time.'

Clara suppressed her anger; she'd become accustomed to that.

'You must realise, Inspector – this will be the last time we speak to each other.'

'Miss Breslin, the trial is imminent.' The inspector's tone was weary; he'd obviously had this conversation countless times. 'We can't let Mr Tarasso have any opportunity to disclose information that could alter his case.

'What is more, it will only upset you – to see him, to speak to him, knowing – as you already do – that nothing will alter the outcome.'

Clara raised her chin and squared her shoulders. 'This isn't about *my hurt*, Inspector. This is about a man who is condemned to hang and having one meagre opportunity to show him that in this world of hatred, there is one – just one – person who won't be pleading for his death.'

'I'll take you to him.'

The man languishing in a filthy cell was still the Matthias she knew. His eyes were sunken and grey-rimmed, his clothes were stained and stiff with over-wear, his posture was diminished, but she recognised something of his former self.

'You have suffered,' she stated, as a matter of fact. It was emblazoned on him, and the worst thought was that there was more to come.

'My only suffering is being separated from you when we have so little time left.' He managed a tender smile; one which tugged at her and made her throat constrict. 'I heard that you had returned home, to Wiltshire. Was it all that you remembered? Did it restore you?'

Clara let the tears spill. 'How can you ask me? There

is no home for me now. The entire world is changed.

'It was nothing of what I remembered. It was an empty place. Everything is empty.'

'Don't despair, my darling.' He longed to move towards her, but his arms were bound to the walls with chains. 'You have your freedom. More so now than you ever did.

'Let this be a beginning, not an ending. You must show your art to the world. Show them what I have seen. There are no ties binding you anywhere, now. You must let your talents flourish.'

Clara was appalled by his light-heartedness.

'You implied in your journal that I'd have no talent left to share.'

Matthias watched her with his unearthly green eyes – Clara knew he would never look at her like this again. She felt a need to commit the moment to memory; although it was indistinct from the first time she'd met his eye, all those months ago.

'I've asked *Her* for guidance.' He looked to an indiscriminate point over his right shoulder; Clara felt her skin prickle. 'She explained everything to me – in a way that made death seem like less of a hardship. Less of a cruel end.'

In that moment, Clara doubted her judgement of Matthias' character, and his sanity. It was the only time she'd done so. She extinguished the thought before it could embed itself.

'You must retract your guilty plea. Say that the woman must have overdosed on morphine by herself; that she knew you'd concentrated the dose and had asked for it to be done.'

Weeks of deliberation, and this was the best alternative she could produce. She knew it was a futile exercise – but feeling that she'd at least tried to help was better than doing nothing.

'It would only prolong the inevitable. I can't afford a lawyer to fight my corner with clever words. Any changes in my plea would be useless; the jury will think I'm clutching at far-fetched lies.'

'Matthias—' A hand reached to steady her arm as she stumbled forward towards the bars of the cell.

'I love you. Don't say anything during the trial, Clara. They will only denounce you if you do.'

Her body fell limp. She let herself be escorted away, her vision blinded.

She entered the courtroom alone. Sitting in the gallery, she placed herself apart from anyone she recognised amongst the spectators. Her brother being one, Ruth Davison another. William had at least the decency to meet her eye; Ruth did not.

Matthias was in the dock, his wrists restrained by iron cuffs. The judge, sitting opposite, busied himself by reading the indictment notes. The trial awaited the entrance of the prosecution lawyer. When he entered the room, Clara felt her stomach drop.

It was Albert Barnes.

'It's odd,' said Ruth, 'in all this time, I've never seen him in court. I could've visited, at any time. I suppose the whole thing seemed terribly morbid – and I didn't want to see him that way. But now, I suppose it doesn't matter at all.'

William looked at Ruth; at first, he presumed she was thinking aloud. But he realised she was waiting for his reply.

'I suggested Bert as a prosecution lawyer to Inspector Conner. He's a good friend, and I thought, because this case has attracted so much attention, it might be a boost for his career.

'I hope it won't be too upsetting for you, Miss Davison.'

Ruth swallowed deeply and gave a weak smile – in her usual way, as Clara might have said – hoping to gain as much sympathy for herself as possible, in spite of all that was going on.

'Oh, don't spare a thought for me, Mr Breslin. Think of your wretched sister, standing in defence of this man – this *murderer*.

'She is beyond help, isn't she?'

This was a delightful turn of events, as far as Ruth was concerned. She'd always resented Matthias: his ability to gain Clara's attention in ways she never had from her friend. But now he'd lost his power. He was one of the most hated men in London. So, she'd been right to mistrust him; right to interrogate him – in that way that had irritated Clara so much. Not to mention that Clara hadn't shown a shred of sympathy for Ruth's heartache: refusing to see her, even when their relationships had both taken a turn for the worse. They'd both been fairly punished, as far as Ruth was concerned. Or so Clara might have expected her to feel.

But Clara wasn't thinking about Ruth. She was waiting anxiously for the trial to begin, and cared about no one except Matthias. The arrival of Albert seemed to ignite the proceedings. A solemn hush blanketed the inhabitants of the room. The clerk rose to his feet and addressed them all.

'The case of Mr Matthias Tarasso: charged with wilful murder.'

Deborah E Wilson

CHAPTER THIRTY-FOUR

'**W**e begin by asking you to enter your plea, Mr Tarasso.' Matthias looked directly into the judge's face. He only seemed to have the strength to lift his head and speak.

'Guilty.'

The judge shifted forward in his chair and addressed Matthias in strict tones. 'You realise, Mr Tarasso, that entering such a plea dictates that your punishment, having been discussed by the grand jury before the day of this trial, can't be wavered. Do you accept this eventuality and stand by your plea?'

'Yes.' Matthias didn't let his head drop, but his shoulders trembled under the strain.

'I call on Mr Barnes to present the case.'

Clara recognised the formalities. Inspector Conner had at least had the decency to discuss this with her before the trial – preparing her for its plain brutality. He'd told her to expect the whole thing to last no more than ten minutes. The Assizes were so busy that a trial with a single defendant was a rarity. Often, several cases were tried at once, with the same jury making several verdicts.

Albert would present the case, making his prosecuting statements. He was allowed to call witnesses; and Matthias was permitted to cross-examine them, if he so wished. There wouldn't be defence witnesses. There'd been no time to arrange any – no time for Matthias to consider his case at all. That was how these things worked. Trials never swayed in favour of the defendant, making the prosecution's job as quick and efficient as possible.

Next, Matthias would state his case. If he was convicted of murder, he would be able to make a final address to the court, before being sent to his place of execution. Clara forced herself not to think of it.

Albert stood to make his address, behind the grand mahogany table where so many had done the same for almost one hundred years.

'Mr Tarasso, the prosecution states that you murdered Mrs Carter, who was a customer of your former employer, Mr William Breslin. You were able to do so by over-concentrating a morphine solution, creating a mixture which provided a fatal dose with just one administration. The victim died within hours of taking the morphine, of asphyxiation.

'The prosecution acknowledges the existence of a diary, which you claim to have written both before and during these events. In it, you confess to giving the victim this bottle of morphine, in full knowledge of the effect it would have.

'The reasons you give for doing so, however, are most peculiar.'

Clara felt her pulse quicken. It was humiliating to have Matthias' private thoughts aired in such a way. She wasn't sure whether she could bear to hear it all again.

'You claim to be acting under the direction – or command – of a mythical being. A "Muse", such as this court might have read about in the works of Homer or Virgil, able to exert her power over our physical world. You name this

402

being Melpomene – the Muse of Tragedy. She controls you utterly, or so you claim, and you wouldn't have killed a woman were it not for her.

'You write that she is also your mother.'

There were rumblings – and even some exclamations of disgust – from the spectators. Clara felt a twisting of her insides; her heart was filled with sympathy.

The judge interjected, speaking directly to Matthias.

'You claim, as Mr Barnes suggests, that your mother forced you to commit this act – and that she is some sort of immortal, bent on causing the tragedy that her name insinuates, with you as her human instrument. Is that correct?'

'It is.' Matthias still had the strength to appear defiant.

'You will have the opportunity to present your case, in due course. I must urge you, Mr Tarasso – and mind you, I have no obligation to do so – to consider your words carefully. You have incited much ill feeling in this court. People are contemptuous towards your version of events. If you feel any compulsion to change your position on this matter, follow it. Otherwise, you will be subjected to ridicule.'

Matthias didn't say anything. Perhaps by some bending of the light in the room, his eyes appeared to glow sharply – almost painfully.

'Mr Barnes, do you have any witness that you would like to call upon?'

Albert turned to face the gallery – under his scrutiny, Clara wanted to shrink down in her seat. Conner had warned her that she would be called as a witness – but she hadn't been able to gather her thoughts.

'The prosecution calls Mr William Breslin to the stand.'

William stood, swore his oath and faced Albert almost serenely. He had the air of a man who had right on his side, whose fate was about to be altered for the better. This was his stage; he could create for himself the best identity possible, inspire his customers to return to him more fervently than before – if only out of empathy, after hearing his version of events.

William repeated all that had occurred in the past months. Clara noted that he didn't speak a word of a lie – his oath was respected. Nor did Albert twist his questioning to suit an agenda – the case spoke for itself. It was extremely strong, with no trickery or persuasion needed. Clara felt her hopes slipping away, as if Matthias were a drowning man, their reaching hands struggling to maintain their grasp.

'And so, in summary, Mr Breslin: you believe that Mr Tarasso had immoral intentions in coming to work for you – whether he wanted to defy his mother or not, he knew what her ultimate goal would be and still administered cures, knowing the risks. He also had an "unhealthy" relationship with your sister, as you have suggested, and his obsession with her, along with her growing feelings of affection towards him, put you in the uncomfortable position of not feeling able to dismiss him, as this would upset Miss Breslin and sour your relationship.'

'That is correct.' William glanced at his sister and spoke again.

'Those who know us well will have seen that mine

and Clara's bond is not the strongest – we are distant towards each other, and lack understanding of each other's ambitions. But I wouldn't deny my sister's happiness out of selfishness; she only lives with me because our parents wanted her to move to London to improve her marriage prospects. I employed Mr Tarasso in this knowledge, and hoped ...'

'Your sister might have married him.' Albert exhaled deeply. 'No further questions, Your Honour.'

'Mr Tarasso, do you wish to question the witness?'

'I only wish for Mr Breslin to look me in the eye – knowing me, as a friend, as he once did – and tell me: do you believe that I am capable of deliberately deceiving you, either for my own amusement or some morbid desire?'

'And have you bewitch me with a look – as you claimed to do in that book of yours? No, Mr Tarasso, I will never meet your eye again.'

'Answer Mr Tarasso's question, Mr Breslin.' The judge ordered. He added, with a hint of dark humour, 'You are not required to make eye contact with the defendant.'

William was growing pale under the strain of keeping his composure. 'I can't know what lies your mind has created to help you live with your actions, Mr Tarasso.'

'I won't be living with them much longer, Bill – what good would it do me to lie? When my death sentence is already set?'

'*Enough*, Mr Tarasso. You may stand down, Mr Breslin.'

William stumbled back to his seat. Clara wasn't aware, until then, that her fingers had been gripping the bench so tightly that her fingertips and the insides of her knuckles felt bruised.

'Mr Barnes, your next witness?'

'I call upon Miss Clara Breslin, Your Honour.'

Clara drifted to the stand; she didn't feel her limbs move, or her feet treading the floorboards. Standing before Albert, she wondered if his questioning would reveal any trace of his bad feelings towards her – or if he would be totally professional, knowing that right was on his side.

'Miss Breslin, we have your written statement, which you sent to Inspector Conner last month during convalescence at your parents' home.

'In it, you testify to witnessing many events that Mr Tarasso mentions – specifically, your initial meeting, which you believed was your choice to orchestrate.

'According to Mr Tarasso, it was his engineering – aided, of course, by the Muse of Tragedy.' The courtroom muttered derisively. 'Do you believe this claim?'

Clara was physically affected by the keenness of the question. It left a hollow in her chest, like the after-effects of a mortal wound. But she felt oddly certain of her answer. There wasn't an internal debate, or a question of trust or truth.

'I believe that Matthias and I were destined to meet. Even now.' She refused to observe formalities, determined to refer to him by his first name. He was sitting just a few feet away from her, after all. His eyes were resolutely on her, almost unblinking.

'If I'd known Matthias wanted to influence me

towards his own ends, would I have refused to follow him to the theatre? I don't think I would've been able to miss the opportunity. He's the greatest stage actor I've ever seen.'

'He is also a *murderer*, Miss Breslin.' Albert looked down briefly, as if consulting his notes. However, he was steeling himself for a decisive manoeuvre.

'Do you love him?'

'Yes.' Clara spoke without hesitation, without fear. She didn't care what the spectators thought; only that she hadn't been able to tell Matthias that she loved him in return when they'd been separated. She loved him; better judgement and immoral acts weren't considered in conjunction with that.

'In these circumstances, we can't expect you to denounce the defendant. We must believe that he *does*, in fact, hold some power over you.'

Albert paused, for effect, to let the weight of these words register with the jury.

'But you didn't entirely answer my first question, Miss Breslin. Do you believe that Mr Tarasso acts under the control of an immortal being?'

Clara *did* stop to consider this. She'd never seen Melpomene – but could that completely disprove her existence? Would it make Matthias' death any easier to bear if she knew that he'd only caused such horror under someone else's power?

'You said it perfectly, Mr Barnes. My love for Mr Tarasso influences my judgement; I must believe what my heart tells me.'

For Clara, this was a satisfactory answer; even

retrospectively, she wouldn't have changed it. She didn't strongly support Matthias' claims, but neither did she come across as disloyal. She confirmed Albert's queries but didn't add weight to the prosecution as it stood.

'No further questions.'

Other witnesses were called. The trial seemed to take longer than originally suggested. Why so many were necessary, Clara couldn't imagine. Perhaps to give the press the 'performance' they'd been hoping for, give their readers something to discuss at length.

Matthias didn't question Clara. There wasn't any need – she wouldn't be able to help him. She was too biased; the jury knew that.

Albert went on to question the sister of the poisoned woman, and Inspector Conner for the particulars of Matthias' time in custody. Finally, everything had been said. Albert's prosecution was stronger than ever; Matthias' defence seemed all the more futile. But the formalities had to be observed.

'State your case, Mr Tarasso.'

Matthias looked as if he had nothing left to offer. He stood slowly. Clara saw he couldn't support his own weight and had to rest against the wooden rail surrounding him.

'I'm fully aware that, having already made my "guilty" plea, it is useless to fight to prove my innocence, or to beg for a reduced sentence.

'I simply wish to state that the crime I am guilty of committing – the murder of an innocent woman – was an act of complete desperation and wasn't decided freely or with a hard determination to kill. I want the jury to see the truth of these devastating circumstances and not rely on the easiest, most believable reasoning.

'I would never choose to jeopardise my happiness; would never choose to harm the people I consider myself closest to, when my life had been so devoid of genuine human connection and feeling before I knew them.

'I won't be rewarded for my sacrifice – so there is no incentive for this crime. I acted on the impulses and proclivities of someone else, with no escape from the force of their will ... except in death.'

The last word hung heavy, left a distinct imprint upon the courtroom.

'Mr Tarasso, we have heard your statement. We have also heard from the prosecution and key witnesses.

'To the jury, I put forward my own recommendation. As previously suggested, I hold Mr Tarasso's fantastical comments in contempt, and suggest that the jury disregard them when they contemplate their verdict. Examine only *concrete fact* when deciding whether Mr Tarasso is guilty of murder – *regardless* of any influence which the defendant suggests spurred him on to commit this depraved act.

'Murder is a capital offence, punishable by death. Mr Tarasso knew this when he murdered, as he openly admits, an *innocent* woman. He obviously perceives death as a release from torment – and yet his victim had no choice as to whether she desired such a terrible release.

'The court is adjourned – we return shortly.'

The jury were in no doubt of the power they held

as they were sent away to consider their verdict. The people in the gallery were invited to leave and return at their leisure whilst awaiting the announcement of the verdict. Most of them did. Clara remained.

She watched Matthias being led – or rather carried – to a holding cell. And she sat, absorbing the silence of the near-empty room, inhaling the scent of varnished wood and leather, and sensing a dreadful, impending disaster.

Within two hours, the jury had made their decision. The court was called back into session. Clara could hardly bring herself to look at Matthias as he was brought, once more, to stand in the dock. He seemed strangely resigned, almost calm.

'Mr Tarasso, the jury has discussed their verdict and come to a decision. I invite you now to make your final address to the court, before your sentence is passed.'

Matthias turned, his whole body facing Clara, and her alone. She knew this: she knew that he meant these words for her, that everyone else in the room had no significance to him.

'I'm sorry. I am *so* sorry for what I've done. Perhaps it could've all been avoided; perhaps I could've exerted independent thought and control and overcome the bonds which tie me to the power I both resent and fear.

'But if every excruciating moment of guilt and suffering was played over, continuously, forever, I would accept that, Clara. I would welcome it, if only to be able to see your face, to hear your voice, to look upon your paintings and see a talent beyond compare.

'From this tragedy, there is magnificence. It is you. It is the masterpieces you've created. They won't be tainted by my failure; they are a testament to *you*, and you alone.

'I hope you will forgive me, in time.'

Clara was ashamed to feel that a small part of her forgave him instantly. She was in love with him; she had to believe that he wasn't capable of intentional murder. She had to believe that the only reason he stood in this courtroom now was that, in some way, he wanted to be caught. He wanted to commit an act of tragedy so sensational that there would be no escaping justice – that he would lose his life, and finally be free of *Her*, forever.

The judge stood.

'Before passing sentence, it is customary, in cases such as these, to state the defendant's former crimes. Doing so is testament to the severity of the sentence, so the court will understand the weight of the jury's decision.

'Unfortunately, though we have many previous crimes which we *may* attribute to Mr Tarasso, it is impossible to verify that it was indeed he who committed them. Individuals severely affected by poisoning, with no witnesses to testify the substances being administered; other cases of disastrous fires and floods, where property was destroyed, and victims were either left destitute or without the most valuable items in their possession. All these events bear considerable similarities to this case, but with no validation of the guilty party. Mr Tarasso may have acted under other assumed names, or covered his traces more expertly – we can't be sure. We merely deem it necessary to enlighten the jury of their existence.

'It may be deemed crucial, Mr Tarasso, to try you under the assumption that you do, in fact, suffer from a form of insanity; that your defiant insistence of having acted under the bewitchment of Melpomene is actually proof of the instability of your mind.

'I have overruled this possibility. Presiding over this case and its conclusion, I instead propose that your claims of being descended from a mythical creature are only a ruse – to compel others to accept your insanity when you are, beneath it all, a killer who thrives on destruction.'

He paused. Clara clutched a hand to her lips, unable to bear the inevitability of the infamous words which were to follow.

'I hereby find you guilty of wilful murder.

The court doth order you to be taken from hence to the place from whence you came, and thence to the place of execution, and that you be hanged by the neck until you are dead, and that your body be afterward buried within the precincts of the prison in which you shall be confined after your conviction. And may the Lord have mercy upon your soul.'

Matthias looked at Clara, and only her, held her image in his sight, even as they led him stiffly back through the doors to his cell.

It was only once those doors were closed, once the heavy bolts had shunted into place, that Clara allowed her grief to envelop her like the buffeting winds of a violent storm, and the physical world slipped away, a blanket pulled from under her feet, leaving darkness, only darkness; an infinite void.

CHAPTER THIRTY-FIVE

Time passed beyond Clara's conception until the day of the execution.

She barely perceived anything. She hardly saw, or thought, or felt at all. Her mind possessed the will to ensure her survival, to allow her to attend the public hanging, to prove her continued loyalty to her muse. After that – she didn't know what she would do.

William was focused on looking after her. Clara couldn't ever remember him having been so attentive, so understanding.

'Bill, you don't need to maintain a bedside vigil. Think of your business …'

'I don't know what the future of this place will be – and for once, I don't care. Seeing you like this, Clara – I feel so *guilty* for causing you this misery.'

'I hope you can understand my motivation. How could I let such a crime, such a *murder*, go unpunished?'

There was a lot more he wanted to say – but he knew it would spare his sister's feelings better if he held back, saved his thoughts for his own private contemplation.

'Can't you go back to Wiltshire? I'm sure it would help you, to be removed from all of this.'

'No.' It was the only refusal Clara had any strength to make.

Her paintings were packed away now, confined to

darkness, along with all of her materials. She couldn't use them, couldn't stand to have them lying around – couldn't bring herself to look at her artwork. But she couldn't part with it, either; doing so would've only spited herself, after months of study and toil.

William had wanted to set fire to it all, burn away any trace of Matthias in their lives.

'But how will anyone remember him if we do that?'

William was of the opinion that he didn't deserve to be remembered, that his crimes had given him infamy enough. But he didn't disclose this to Clara.

Clara had also kept Matthias' journal. It was presented to her quietly after the trial, having been used as evidence for the case. She hadn't told her brother.

'I can't imagine that you will treasure it – but it seems only right that it should be you who decides what becomes of it,' Inspector Conner had said. Perhaps he was capable of compassion, after all.

He'd even attempted to visit on a personal rather than professional basis, to see how William was coping with the reopening of his business, and how Clara was coping with the imminent execution of the man she loved. William spoke to him briefly, to thank him for the results of his investigations and the trial, but Clara wouldn't come out of her room. She couldn't see how discussing her grief would alleviate it in any way, and she didn't feel any gratitude towards the inspector; no more than she felt towards her brother for hiring him. He would speak with unrestrained honesty, and whilst that might've helped under some circumstances, she couldn't bring herself to listen to it now.

Not long afterward, it was Ruth's turn, again, to call. Clara had her turned away. In a more rational frame of mind, she might have noted Ruth's generosity: returning despite being refused admission without a reason. But Clara couldn't see the good in it. Ruth hadn't spoken to her at the trial, when it would have been most welcome, when Clara had been completely alone, unsupported. She didn't want to rekindle the friendship; it would be pointless to try and restore anything of her life before the tragedy had occurred. She wasn't the same person; therefore, she couldn't expect to live the same life. Something like trying to recreate a photograph – no matter how much deliberation went into the attempt, some detail of the scene would always be different.

William worried that Clara would lose her sanity – imposing such solitude on herself would cause her mind to decay.

'I can assure you, Bill – once all this is over, I won't be any further burden to anyone.' She couldn't envisage her life after the hanging – how could anything 'bearable' remain?

'You aren't a burden *now* – I just wish you would try and speak to people, try to distract yourself. This endless contemplation will only destroy you.'

Clara couldn't bring herself to contradict him, but she knew: nothing could destroy what had already been irreparably damaged.

The day of the execution dawned as any other would. Clara had grown so used to being consumed with thoughts of it – so that there were scarcely moments where she thought of anything else – that it came upon her calmly, with an air of surety.

'Will you let me accompany you?' William knew the answer before he asked, but he hoped that some whim might alter his sister's plans.

Clara, of course, refused – but not for herself. She knew that her brother wouldn't have the courage, or the coldness of heart, to watch the man he had had convicted hang for his crime. 'I have the strength to endure this alone,' she insisted, feeling instantly guilty when she realised that Matthias would have to be so much stronger, endure so much more.

'Inspector Conner will be there,' William offered, by way of consolation. Conner would watch over Clara on her brother's behalf, without making himself obvious. It was his prerogative to keep his distance on most occasions, and William didn't want his sister to know that he'd enlisted someone else to look after her because he couldn't. She would've only refuse the help if she'd known, he presumed.

Outside Newgate Prison, the usual crowd had assembled to watch the murderers hang. For them, it was sport; it was entertainment. They'd paid for their seats, as one might pay for a theatre ticket. And Clara sat, just as she had in the Grecian, waiting for Matthias, as she had so many times before.

On this day, the gallows were his stage. There

would be applause, even cheers. How cruel, Clara thought with a leaden heart, that he'd never received such for his performances.

There was an eerie hush in the moments preceding the prisoner's arrival. Some of the crowd busied themselves reading pamphlets – supposedly bearing Matthias' 'dying words': his final speech. Clara wouldn't insult him by reading it, by believing the lies. She only wanted to see him – and yet doing so would only hasten the approach of his execution. It would be their final meeting – and they wouldn't be able to speak a word to each other.

A barred gate was opened, a shout given, addressed to no one in particular. Matthias was led towards the scaffold amidst jeers and taunts; no one tried to shield him from the waste matter being thrown or let him protect himself. His arms were bound behind his back, his head uncovered. By the time he'd come to stand beneath the noose, his clothes were covered in all manner of stains, and even tears where rocks had been thrown. Fresh bruises and scratches appeared on his skin; the shedding of blood seemed unnecessary.

'Standing before you is the murderer Matthias Tarasso, who used poison as his weapon under the nose of his trusting employer.

'Does the prisoner wish to say any final words?'

Clara hoped desperately that he wouldn't. *He mustn't give the crowd their cheap satisfaction.*

But he did speak – perhaps the lure of this one, final audience was too much to resist.

'This was always going to be my end. I chose it,

willingly, to be free of my curse. So that no more would suffer – so that tragedy will make its course in other ways, independent of me. But it will always find a way, will always exist.

'But there are ways to battle it. There are ways in which we make our own future and can defy those who would seek to do us harm.

'For every act of tragedy, there will be some small triumph, some redemption. Seek it out, fight for it, treasure it. That is what it means to be alive.'

A hood was placed over his head; afterwards, the noose.

The sound of a wooden door swinging open; a creak, a thud.

The rope straightened, tensed with a sharp crack.

Asphyxiation – a prolonged death lasting minutes, with blocked airways causing a slow but painful loss of consciousness. No morphine, this time. Nothing to ease the pain.

Clara witnessed the hanging with a strange impassivity – she would feel something, in time. In time, the memory would seize her in its fist and almost crush her with its strength. But not on this day. Matthias' final words were all she thought of as the crowds slowly dissipated around her, her hand protectively shielding the new life growing inside her.

Her sickness in Wiltshire had been the onset of pregnancy – she knew this now. And so, this was her triumph over adversity.

She'd always been dissatisfied with her life; had always found aspects of other people's lives objectionable, rather than sharing in their happiness – however fleeting. She always awaited the next setback, the next failure, the next disappointment. Always felt that contentment and fulfilment were just outside her grasp.

On this day, the most terrible thing imaginable had happened. Her muse was gone.

His legacy would remain – but rather than his feats upon the stage, it was a legacy of devastation and death.

She wouldn't let the grief feed parasitically upon her thoughts. She would devote herself to her unborn child, and appreciate this gift in times of misfortune.

Before Matthias' arrival, there had been other muses. She'd never let herself get close to them before – physically or emotionally. Never would she have believed herself capable of falling in love with one of them. But it had happened – she had let herself fall for a muse. And although it had damaged her – in some ways irreparably – it had also given her an opportunity to devote her love, her heart, to someone who would always be hers.

She was thankful for this child. She had a reason to hold on to Matthias' memory without regret, a reason to feel that she would not want to erase their meeting from history. From an act of evil had come the tiniest, most vulnerable, most fragile piece of *good*; a being, untainted.

'FROM AN ACT
OF EVIL,

HAD COME
THE TINIEST,

MOST
VULNERABLE,

MOST FRAGILE

PIECE OF *GOOD*...'

EPILOGUE

'Inspector!'

From behind a closed door, Conner briefly contemplated not answering the call; would they grow tired of waiting for him, if he simply refused to appear?

'You are needed urgently, sir!'

With a groan, and much shunting of furniture, he eventually emerged from his office. 'My business hours are eight o'clock in the morning till three in the afternoon,' he began, a speech he was used to making and constantly reinforcing. No one ever seemed to learn.

He stopped when he saw that the envoy was one of the wardens of Newgate Prison.

'What is it?'

The man worried his wool cap between his fingers. The colour had almost drained from his face. He seemed hesitant to share the message he had evidently been sent to deliver. Conner knew what it concerned before he even opened his mouth. But he couldn't have imagined the bizarre truth of it.

'It's Tarasso, sir – the body ... You'd better come and see for yourself, sir.'

'I see enough corpses, my lad – it'd need to be something exceptional to lure me to come and look at another.' As far as he was concerned, his interest in Matthias Tarasso had ended when he'd seen the man's body swinging from the scaffold.

'But that's just it, sir. There's no corpse to see.' The man looked greatly troubled by this admission – it certainly reflected very poorly upon his place of work. 'Newgate Gaol loses bodies' – not the best publicity to be had.

'No corpse? Are you telling me that the body-snatchers have resorted to committing their crimes *before* a body is even interred?' Conner would have been almost drawn to amusement if he hadn't been so bewildered by the declaration.

'We don't know how it happened, sir.'

'Then I suggest you tell me everything you *do* know.' Conner thrust forward the bulk of his chest, enfolding his arms around it.

The warden proceeded to tell him the manner of the disappearance of the body.

Men had taken down Matthias' corpse, laying it on a stretcher and covering it with a sheet in order to take it to the unmarked burial plot of the prison. For reasons which the warden was either ignorant of or reluctant to divulge to the inspector, in case they cast further embarrassment upon the gaol, the body was left unattended for an indeterminate period of time, during which no one working in the prison could confirm having seen anything unusual. However, when the time came for the corpse to be moved to its final resting place, the men found that the stretcher was empty, the sheet pulled back, as if Matthias himself had folded it and stepped out. As if he were simply getting out of bed.

Having seen the stretcher himself and questioned

the prison staff, Conner found the warden's account to be truthful. He immediately ordered a search to be undertaken, one which used up valuable police resources and time, and lasted several days. But no body was recovered. No one had seen a body being taken, and despite the most thorough of interrogations, no one from the gaol could feasibly explain why the corpse had been left unsupervised in the first place. Conner couldn't blame them; after all, one hardly expected to have to justify keeping a watchful eye over an inanimate, lifeless thing.

If the thing *was* lifeless.

Having no belief whatsoever in the supernatural, Conner didn't let his thoughts linger over the notion.

He expelled it from his mind, irksome as it was – an unexplained singularity, unworthy of his time.

And yet, from time to time, the empty stretcher would fade into his consciousness, like fine rain pattering against a window.

Deborah E Wilson

Acknowledgements

The book you are currently holding is a culmination of over ten years' work. The plot began to germinate even before that, other unfinished projects lending themselves, in various ways, to what was to become *An Artist's Muse*. Therefore, it may not be surprising that in its long journey to publication, the list of people to thank has grown considerably.

I would like to start by thanking my parents, who have always nurtured my creativity, and have continued to have faith in me becoming a published author along every step and setback. Thank you for being my proof-readers, advisors, editors and kindest supporters. The prologue definitely wouldn't be the same without you, Mum!

Thank you to all the family and friends who offered constructive advice, supported and encouraged me, read the book in its earliest stages and kindly gave me wonderful reviews.

Thank you to everyone at Victorina Press. The road to publication was every bit as littered with rejection as everyone said it would be! But I am so grateful for your faith in me. I'm proud to have an independent publisher with such an exciting outlook on literature. Thank you to the other publishing companies who graciously edited passages, critiqued the overall impact of the book and suggested ways for me to meet my goals.

Studying at Lincoln University was definitely a turning point in my life – having access to broad range of literature and being tutored by a remarkable team of lecturers, who continually fostered both my academic and creative writing, and long after my graduation, even offered support and advice with publication. Thank you for your guidance.

Thank you to the venues who supported me as a self-published author and allowed me to meet new readers (and even my publisher!).

Thank you to all of the Gothic authors who have gone before, who first spawned my fascination with monsters…

Of course, thank yous for the rest of my life to my husband-to-be, Onne, who was and will always be by my side, and never gets fed up of the persistent tapping of keys!

About the Author

Stories to haunt you...

Photograph © Danny Jones (DJ Imagery)

Deborah E Wilson was born in Worksop, Nottinghamshire. Her love of literature has been life-long but was truly ignited at The University of Lincoln, where she obtained First Class Honours in English. Her degree encouraged an interest in literature from a broad range of historical periods, including Victorian and Gothic Literature, and she also began to share her own writing in Creative Writing seminars. She moved on to a career in primary school teaching but has always been drawn back to literature and a desire to write it. Her hobbies include travelling back in time (or should that be into the future?) at Steampunk events.

An Artist's Muse, is her first novel, which introduces readers to a new breed of Victorian Gothic monster. The ink drawings are all done by Deborah E Wilson.

For updates, future publications and events visit:

Facebook: https://www.facebook.com/DEWauthorshaunt

Twitter: @DEWauthorshaunt

Author Website: https://deborahewilson.wixsite.com/authorshaunt

Some sources of Information...

Fyfe, G., *Art, Power and Modernity: English Art Institutions, 1750-1950*

Shakespeare, W., *Antony and Cleopatra*

Shakespeare, W., *Love's Labours Lost*

Shakespeare, W., *The Taming of the Shrew*

Deborah E Wilson